Madeleine Reiss was born in Athens  has worked as a stage mana communications specialist for var novels are *Someone To Watch Over M Goodbye* and *Live A Little*. *The Tak* historical novel.

https://www.madeleinereiss.com

Also by the Author

Someone to Watch Over Me
This Last Kiss
Before We Say Goodbye
Live A Little

THE TAKING OF IRENE HART

MADELEINE REISS

One More Chapter
a division of HarperCollins*Publishers*
1 London Bridge Street
London SE1 9GF
www.harpercollins.co.uk
HarperCollins*Publishers*
Macken House, 39/40 Mayor Street Upper,
Dublin 1, D01 C9W8, Ireland
This paperback edition 2025

1

First published in ebook by HarperCollins*Publishers* 2025
Copyright © Madeleine Reiss 2025
Madeleine Reiss asserts the moral right to
be identified as the author of this work

A catalogue record of this book
is available from the British Library

ISBN: 978-0-00-861423-2

This novel is entirely a work of fiction. The names, characters and incidents portrayed in it are the work of the author's imagination. Any resemblance to actual persons, living or dead, events or localities is fictionalised.

Printed and bound in the UK using 100% Renewable Electricity
by CPI Group (UK) Ltd
All rights reserved. No part of this publication may be
reproduced, stored in a retrieval system, or transmitted,
in any form or by any means, electronic, mechanical,
photocopying, recording or otherwise, without the prior
permission of the publishers.

For David, always.

Prologue

YAXTON, SOMERSET

May 1859

He wasn't supposed to be out at night, but the walls surrounding the house felt even more restrictive than they usually did. They clutched at him and squeezed him out of his narrow bed and into his thin leather boots and sent him down the steps, which creaked unless you walked sideways. He crept past the forbidden room, averting his gaze from the light that licked through the gap at the bottom, and moved silently across the tiled hall.

He was almost at the front door when he heard a noise – a kind of dragging, scraping sound coming from the floor above. He stopped with his breath trapped in his throat. He listened again. Three throbs from the clock on the wall, four thuds of his heart, and then the house quieted and settled back into its shadows. He stepped outside. The dogs were sleeping in a sated heap and didn't stir as he passed them. When he reached the gate, he was surprised to see that the bolts were already pulled back.

The lane was deep and dank. He walked with his head tilted upwards, the glittering sky falling around him as if he was moving through it. The clench in his chest eased, and he filled himself with the sweet greenness of the night. He couldn't see them, but he knew the hedges were full of nesting things. In the daytime, on a sanctioned excursion, he had seen a squirrel guarding two naked, seamed kittens. The goldfinches with their bright red heads, had been busy building their dangling woollen cups. He would never have anything to cleave to. He would never know the wrap and warmth of shared life, but its comfort was around him.

He thought at first it was a deer. They often crossed the lane from one field to the next, but some instinct caused him to step back, so that he was hidden by the trunk of a tree. A heavily cloaked figure was walking a few yards ahead. They were holding something in outstretched arms, as if what they held was precious, or perhaps fragile. He heard a wail, so insubstantial, it could have come from a hedgerow creature. A baby he thought, and by the look of it, just arrived. He had seen the dazed slump of the newborn and this one had the same shocked stillness. The person ahead of him – he thought it had human form, although he had often been lectured on the way the devil could disguise itself – looked behind, as though they thought they were being followed.

So great was his own terror of discovery, that Trench ventured no further, and turned back to the house. He had been taught that all truth and beauty was contained within the walls of the community. That what existed outside was beset with dirt and noise and sin. And yet, as the house closed itself around him once more, he felt the swell of something monstrous. He could not put a name to it, could not even really explain its source, but it was there, part of the darkness, part of the heavy, suffocating air.

Chapter 1

BRIDGWATER, SOMERSET

A month earlier – April 1859

'How is it possible that you can stay trapped in here for days on utter end and still carry on behaving as if you are happy?'

Ruby threw her balled-up shawl across the room towards her sister. It landed on Irene's lap, obscuring the book she had been attempting to read, despite Ruby's constant interruptions.

'I have breathed the air in this room hundreds of thousands of times. It smells of old fabric and stale cake and boredom.'

Irene smiled and folded up Ruby's shawl and placed it on the sofa next to her.

'You could at least throw it back! There is a certain point, Irene, when being patient and never getting angry stops being a *good* thing and starts being *annoying*.'

'Why don't you read aloud to me, or better still, go and sit by the window and tell me stories of who is passing,' Irene said, putting her book aside, and looking expectantly at her sister. Mired in sourness today, it did not help Ruby's mood to see that despite their incarceration, Irene's pale skin still shone with its usual lustre and her coppery hair glinted in the faint light. She thought that her sister's fiery tresses made her own dark curls look dull by comparison.

With exaggeratedly reluctant movements, Ruby moved over to the window and sat herself down on the cushioned ledge with a heavy sigh.

'Nothing... Nothing... Sky blueish. Infernal trees still there with not much on them. A seagull bothering some sparrows... Oh, hold on, some excitement... Lydia's husband just went by in his ridiculously tight coat. He walks as if he has got something up his trousers. How she can have married him is beyond all imagining. She says that at dinner he rolls his bread into tiny grey balls. She finds them afterwards all around his plate.'

Ruby gave a shudder and Irene laughed.

'There is no accounting for love,' she said, and Ruby noted the downward dip of her sister's head and the way she pulled at her fingers.

'Do you still think about him?' she asked, greatly daring, knowing that this was a subject likely to shut the conversation down.

'I do my best not to,' Irene answered. 'He is not worthy of my thoughts.'

Ruby was reminded of the iron that ran through Irene's veins. Although she was far more physically robust than her sister, Ruby thought of herself as lacking a proper core. She, who had so many words at her disposal, couldn't describe the exact nature of her shortcomings, only that her scattered thoughts and feelings seemed to pull her in all directions, so that she was never as certain as she would have liked to be about anything.

'I wonder where William is now. What he is doing,' Ruby said, unable to let the matter rest, even though she knew it was painful for Irene. Talking about him, saying his name out loud, made what had happened vivid to her again. She saw him walking up the path to the house for the very first time – his easy confidence, the way he held his golden head, as though he expected to be welcomed, his perfunctory one step back before the door was opened to him.

'I hope he is as happy as he deserves to be.' Irene pursed her lips in a way that indicated she had said all she wanted to on the subject.

Ruby felt herself suddenly close to tears, a fact she hid from her sister by turning once more to the window and her account of the neighbourhood. A young boy had pockets stuffed with the eggs he had stolen from a back-garden coop. A woman walking by with hasty steps and clumsily arranged hair, had just poisoned her husband. A young man with a turbulent brow and worn shoes was thinking of a woman who belonged to someone else. Cherubic twins in matching outfits, lagging hand in hand a few steps behind their nanny – they had just put earwigs in her drawers, and were waiting in suspense for the grand itch to begin.

'Do you know how much longer Mother is planning on keeping us inside?' Ruby finally said, when her powers of invention had ground to a halt. 'It has been over six months now and we have not been allowed to go anywhere except to see Cousin Anna, and then only on two occasions. You know your life is truly empty when a morning spent in the company of a woman tormented by the choice between white roses and pale pink lilies for her wedding bouquet, seems to be an exciting event.'

'I am not sure when we will be able to go out more,' Irene replied. 'Mother is still in mourning.'

'We all are, but that does not mean we shouldn't leave the house. It makes me feel better when I am moving. All the misery comes rushing at me when I am trapped on this wretched sofa with nothing to distract me.'

She thought of the moment when she had found her father in his study, sitting in his chair, staring at the ceiling, his hands open on his desk as if he had sent himself forth. She remembered the white glare of her surprise and then the pain that had left her mute for three whole days. Her eyes filled with tears again. She didn't know what was wrong with her today. Only that if she didn't get out soon, she would probably go mad.

'I am nineteen years old, and I have not even begun living!'

Irene tried not to smile at her sister's dramatic look of despair. Ruby never held anything back. Everything was felt keenly and given simultaneous expression, lending dull moments colour, making what joy there was, glitter.

She went over and sat down next to her sister and put an arm around her shoulders. Ruby felt an easing in the stretch and itch of her skin. It had always been like this – a kind of push and pull of comfort and irritation. Ruby thought, on balance, the comfort was greater. Irene's serenity had always calmed her down, and it had been Ruby that Irene had invariably wanted when she returned from one of her takings. Even as a child, Ruby would go into her younger sister's room and sit with her until it passed, and then rub her shuddering white chest with camphor. Love for Irene filled her as it always did – sharp and tender and edged with guilt.

'We will always have each other, won't we?' she asked.

'Until the end of the world,' Irene answered, putting her head on her sister's shoulder.

Chapter 2

BRIDGWATER

April

'The rain has stopped, it will do you good to get some air,' Ruby said, drawing the curtain and opening the window. The room smelt like a child's – a mixture of sweet talcum powder and sour skin. Her mother was lying curled up on her bed, her black silk dress, with its stiff border of crepe wound around her legs, her hair in a tangle of knots, her nails chewed down to the quick.

Ruby wished she could summon up more compassion. A daughter of the kind Ruby thought she should be, would surely feel solicitude and pity, rather than irritation at the sight of Hester lying squirming on the bed. The nature of her mother's grief was one that seemed not to include Ruby within its reach. Hester hoarded her sorrow, lingering over its heft, counting its facets, and piling up its weight, leaving Ruby no way to share the extent of the loss, or even to expend her own.

When Hester had been told about her husband's death she had smiled grotesquely, as though she thought herself the victim of a hoax, and then she had fallen to the ground. Ruby could still hear the crack of her knees as they had hit the floor.

'But I loved him,' Hester said, when she had at last stopped her keening cries, as if she couldn't believe that this hadn't been enough to keep him with her. As if someone had sneaked in and taken him away while she had been looking in the other direction.

After the first shock of her loss had passed, Hester seemed to decide on perpetual motion as the solution to her grief. She carried on running the house as though Arthur had just stepped out and was expected home at any moment. She and the housekeeper still planned the meals with his tastes firmly in mind. His side of their bed had the same three pillows, against which he had rested every night throughout their twenty-five years of marriage. She had taken over his daily task of winding up the clock in the hallway, mimicking the small puffing sound he had made as he rose from his chair, doing the same slide of the hand over the top of the wooden case where the crank was kept. Three rounds of thirteen, chanted out loud as she wound, just as he had done, like a charm that would bring him back.

All this activity ceased abruptly one day. She stopped, almost mid-step, as if she had suddenly forgotten where she was and where she was supposed to be going. Her sorrow froze and took on a terrible and implacable anger that was directed at her daughters, at the sight through the window of people walking down the street, at the very air around her. The clocked stopped, too, since she had forbidden anyone else to touch it.

'You might have seen this,' she had said accusingly to Irene one evening as she brushed aside her youngest daughter's attempts to get her to eat. 'You see stars and ghosts and goodness knows what else besides when you are having one of your turns, but you did not foretell your father's death did you?' she said, and had then taken to her bed with a petulant sorrow that Ruby found hard to bear.

'Leave me be. I am ill. Hot one minute, cold the next,' Hester said now, twisting painfully, as if her body hurt her.

'We could go into town and pick out dress fabric for Cousin Anna's wedding,' Ruby said, trying for a cajoling tone that did not come easily to her. She knew herself to be impatient, unwilling to go through the paces other people seemed to require.

'I cannot be expected to attend a wedding,' Hester said, with a promising flash of the indignation she had often manifested in the days when everything had still been in its rightful place. 'I will not be subjected to the happiness of others. It is too cruel.'

'Or we could find that ribbon seller you like so much. It is market day.'

'Everyone will be out and will see what I have become. I cannot bear their eyes on me.'

'You are the same as you always were, Mother.'

'I am no longer a wife. You girls have grown. I am an empty space.'

'You will always be our mother,' Ruby said, although she knew that where she was concerned the role had been taken on unwillingly. It was into Irene that Hester trickled her watery love, Ruby she seemed only to tolerate. Her father, on the other hand, had had a boundless capacity for affection. Its benevolent beam had been apparent to all who crossed his path but had been at its brightest and most unstinting when it came to his eldest daughter.

You are the child of my heart he had said to her, touching the side of her face in the way he used to – part mocking pat, part adoring stroke. *You are the most beautiful girl I have ever seen.* Being the focus of his attention had been like being in sudden, bright sunshine. But he had abandoned her and left her with her too-long face and too-wide mouth and a twice broken heart.

'Being a mother of women is not enough,' Hester said, gnawing at her fist and staring at Ruby with accusing eyes.

'Irene says it will make her sad if you do not come with us.'

'Does *she* want to go into town? All the same, I cannot go. I look terrible,' Hester said, but Ruby could hear the change in her tone. She was now only waiting to be persuaded.

'It will take no time at all to wash and put on your other dress. Shall I ask May to come up and attend to you?'

'Irene shares my sensibility. She knows how ill I am,' Hester said, although she was already pulling herself upright.

'If we meet anyone we know, I want you to do the talking, Irene,' Hester said as they crossed the iron bridge over the River Parrett. 'Ruby often says quite the wrong thing.' She was hunched and walked stiffly, expelling little complaining breaths at each step.

'Everyone will be pleased to see you out at last, after so long indoors,' Irene replied.

'At least no one can say I am not properly mourning my husband. I have seen others out much sooner, without a care in the world, as if they have simply been suffering from a common cold.'

'I know your heart is broken,' Irene said.

Black suited her sister, Ruby thought. It acted as a foil to her beauty, making her gleam more brightly and with more definition. She felt a familiar stab of envy and scratched fretfully at her chest. She hated the heavy, constricting fabric they were obliged to wear. Of course, unlike Irene, mourning dress did not enhance Ruby at all. It simply drained her features, which in her view needed the enlivenment of colour and shine to make them approach even an approximation of beauty.

The harbour was filled more tightly than when they had seen it last. Ships were anchored side by side with barely a width between them, and the noise of the men loading and unloading, dragging crates across the ground, clattering buckets, and shouting orders to each other, was louder than she had ever heard it. It seemed that in the time since their bereavement, the world had stacked up and launched itself with a swifter, more unheeding pace. Ruby heard the screech of knives against the hulls of the ships on the gridiron being scraped clean of their crusts of barnacles, and the crack of sails as they were pulled firm. She breathed in the soup of smoked fish and the acrid odour of burning fuel from the tile works, and the sulphurous scent of the river whose sluggish tides could not work fast enough to pull the waste deposited by the town's inhabitants out to sea, and so it lingered, frothing at the water's edges.

'I barely recognise Bridgwater these days,' Hester said, looking dimly out across the river as though she was looking for another place. 'I first met Arthur over there, where the glass works is now.' She indicated a place further down the bank. 'It was a patch of green then. And full of flowers. I was wearing a hat trimmed with lace and walking with Fran, who, bless her, was not the prettiest creature, although her arms were well shaped. He could not stop looking at me.'

The market, too, seemed busier than it had before. Perhaps it is simply that I have been indoors too long, Ruby thought, although she was sure there were stalls and people she did not recognise. She had a sense of being left behind, of there being things she did not know about and did not have a share in. At the ribbon stall, the variety of the colours on the stacked spools gave her a panicked feeling that she no longer knew what suited her. She hesitated over several shades of blue for so long that Hester started to make an impatient clicking sound with her tongue. In the end, she decided not to have any ribbon at all. What did it really matter? Who was there to care whether or not the sapphire-coloured satin or the teal velvet matched her hair and skin? Hester purchased a length of silky green that was wound with swift hands and placed in her basket.

'Irene can have it. It will suit her colouring. It is far too bright for me now.'

A crowd of people had congregated outside St Mary's Church and despite the lowness of her mood and the feeling that she should not, after all, have come out, Ruby's interest was piqued. Here perhaps was the beginning of a story.

'Shall we see what is happening?' she asked, pointing in the direction of the gathering. The people on the periphery were standing on the tips of their toes, straining to see over the heads of those in front of them.

'Maybe it is some kind of entertainment.'

'We still have to go to the dressmaker's,' Irene said. 'It shuts in an hour.'

'I really do not want to rub shoulders with goodness knows who, with goodness knows what kinds of infections,' Hester said. 'And besides, I am already getting tired.'

Ruby ignored her companions' protests and began working her way through the clustered women. Hester made a loud noise of annoyance but followed her into the crowd. Irene was not particularly curious about what was happening but wanted, as always, to be where Ruby was, and to see what she saw.

Afterwards, on more than one occasion, Ruby thought back to this moment. She wondered about what would have happened if she had not made the decision to investigate. If instead, she had simply walked on with her sister and her mother to the dressmaker and further deliberations over shades of blue. In life, even in what she saw as her own limited version of it, there was an infinite series of choices. It was impossible to see where a different decision would have led and perhaps, even though it had felt as if she had moved of her own volition, some other agency had been driving her. Maybe it had already been too late. If she had gone to the dressmaker's and then back to the house to have tea and lay fabric out on the dining table, what happened would perhaps still have happened, on another day or in another place.

The women made their way to the front. Beyond the noise and hustle of the town, here a strange quietness had descended. Everyone was gazing at a man who stood in their midst on a wooden box.

Ruby's first feeling was one of disappointment. She had hoped for dancing puppets or a troupe of wandering performers telling tales of untimely deaths, or even some musicians thumping out a tune on tin cans, but there was only this one man.

They had arrived midway through whatever he was saying and so what reached Ruby made no sense. She caught the words 'saints' and 'garden' and 'eternal life', and she understood, after a moment, that what he was peddling was some kind of religion. Her father had told her that at times of upheaval and change, which was apparently what they were living through now, there were those eager to offer an alternative. *There are many who are trying to sell an escape* he had said, leaning back in the living-room chair that still bore the dark mark left by his hair. *There will be people who, instead of embracing what is new, retreat to what they already know, or think that they know. It is because they want comfort.*

Ruby scrutinised the man she saw before her for signs he was a charlatan of the kind her father had spoken about. She guessed he was around forty years of age, tall and handsome with high cheekbones and a narrow, mobile face. He had a heat about him of a person trying to convince. She saw it in the way he held his arms out, as if waiting to deliver an embrace. She saw it in his fast-moving mouth, full of sentences that fell out of him as smoothly as silk. There was, she thought, something of the actor, although not quite of the kind she had been expecting in the centre of this crowd, in the way he stood astride his wooden box, as if it was a stage. The rain that had come and gone all day had dampened the shoulders and arms of his coat and flattened his black hair to his forehead. He looked slowly from face to face, taking his time, choosing who to fasten on, and the people in the crowd responded with an almost imperceptible tremor in reaction to his moving gaze, as if a breeze had blown over them.

She had determined that the entertainment was not of the kind she wanted and almost turned to push her way out, when his gaze fell on her and settled there. It felt as if he had been looking for her all along, and that in finding her, he had discovered what he most wanted. She faltered under the intensity of his dark eyes but found she could not look away. The distance between them seemed to narrow so that she imagined she could feel the burn of him against her skin. She saw the elegant line of his body, the slope of his shoulders, his long fingers. She felt a kind of longing, although for what she could not say then, and would not be able to explain later. It seemed an age before he unfastened his gaze, leaving her feeling as if she had lost something.

Irene felt the change in the quality of her sister's attention. Her sudden stillness was uncharacteristic in a person who seldom stopped moving, and she wondered at it. She saw a man at the mercy of great feeling. She wondered vaguely quite how he kept his balance on such a small crate. She heard the tone of his voice that changed at some point she could not quite define, from conversational, to suddenly sweet and soft, like honey across buttered bread.

'The world is changing,' he said. 'People no longer see what it is they truly need. There is too much noise and confusion. Too much striving for things that do not matter. There is a place I have created for you. A safe place where you can live and work with others who believe in my vision of eternal salvation.'

Irene felt the drizzling rain become a little heavier and scrutinised the colour of the sky. She was always careful not to get cold since a change in her body temperature sometimes triggered a taking. When she turned her gaze from the clouds, she saw that the man was looking at her. Despite the fact she had often been told she was beautiful, she did not feel herself to be. She thought that what ailed her was in some fashion visible and spoilt her, the way that roses sometimes developed sticky, unsightly clusters of small flies. As a consequence, she did not much like attention from strangers. It was the equality of the preacher's regard that struck her. This was not the sideways, sliding gaze of a man passing a woman, nor the assessing stare of one that had discovered her infirmity, nor even the grudging, pinched expression she had seen in the faces of other women, but rather the open curiosity of one person for another. She did not think that anyone had ever looked at her in quite the same way.

He talked for some moments more, then bowed, as if what he had delivered was a kind of performance, and stepped down from his box. A few of the women gathered around him, and the rest dispersed reluctantly, as though resentful of the obligations that took them elsewhere.

They had lingered far too long, and the dressmaker was shut by the time they reached it and so they turned to go home.

'Did you see how he looked at me?' Hester exclaimed.

She was walking fast. Her previous tiredness appeared to have gone and her hunched back had straightened. It was as if, Ruby thought, a hand had plucked her out and smoothed her down and set her back on the ground in a different, better place.

'He saw something in me. I am convinced of it! He saw into the very centre of me,' Hester continued, oblivious to the rain that was now falling fast and had turned the hair poking out of the front of her bonnet into the frizzy mass of curls she had always disliked.

'He certainly had a persuasiveness about him,' Irene murmured. 'And a very direct way of looking at one.'

Ruby kept her own counsel. She could not shake off the sensation of him. It clung to her, making her feel something that lay between elation and distress and yet, despite her distraction, she registered that he had looked at all three of them, and that all three had felt this glance as somehow especially bestowed.

Chapter 3

BRIDGWATER

'I cannot very well go by myself,' Hester said. 'You must come with me.'

'How do you know he is going to be in Bridgwater again today?' Ruby asked looking up from her book.

'I sent May to find out, and she asked someone who works for a Mrs Remington, who has been to hear him speak several times. May says he is going to be at St John's on Monmouth Street at midday. I have also found out that his name is Reverend Peters.'

'Can Irene not go with you?'

'She is feeling unwell and a carriage ride across town is not advisable. The last thing I would want is for her to have one of her episodes amongst such a large crowd.'

'Do you think he is going to draw a lot of attention?'

'Ruby, the man was positively engulfed, preaching outside on a rainy day! I imagine the church will be full to the rafters.'

'So, he is a preacher, then?'

'Well, I do not know how else to describe him. I have to say he is far more interesting than poor Father Landy, whose sermons always make me drift off, even though I pinch the side of my waist to try and keep awake. You felt Reverend Peters' power did you not?'

Ruby thought that the man certainly had some sort of strange influence, although she was reluctant to describe it as power. In the two days since she had seen him, she had begun to feel as if she might have imagined the intensity of his regard and its impact on her. She had been out of sorts that day, a bit bewildered by the way that Bridgwater seemed to have swelled in its dimensions so that she had been no longer quite sure of belonging. There was a part of her that was reluctant to expose herself to him again. She thought, in his fervour, he took away as much as he gave, and it unsettled her.

'But, Mother, what do you hope to gain from it?' Ruby said, getting up and sitting on the chair in the hallway to put her shoes on. She knew that she had no hope of a reprieve. She recognised the dogged look in her mother's face and was even a little glad of it. It had been so long since Hester had expressed any kind of intent.

'I do not know,' her mother said, taking a glance at herself in the mirror.

As Hester had predicted, the church was already almost full when they arrived, and she had to call upon her tenuous link with Mrs Remington to secure them somewhere to sit. Mrs Remington had a face like the back of a spoon and the manner of someone who carried all before her. She was clearly gratified that it was through her that Hester had heard about the event, and showed no hesitation in ousting a timid-looking woman and her almost transparent daughter from their positions on the front row so that Hester and Ruby could take their places.

Perhaps because this time he was on firm ground, but it was a more relaxed, even faintly swaggering man, who walked to the lectern. He was wearing a cape, chained at the neck over his dark suit, a garment that lent him the look of a medieval knight.

'I have decided that today, instead of talking to you, you are going to talk to me,' he announced, swinging the cloak back from his shoulders and placing one foot against the base of the lectern. As before, Ruby felt compelled to look at him. It seemed to her that he created a waiting hush around him, a kind of suspension of time similar to that experienced in the slow, unspooling moments before an accident.

'I welcome your questions.'

He looked enquiringly around him. It appeared at first that his audience was too awed to speak, but after a few moments of uneasy shifting in the pews, a woman in a ruffled white dress got to her feet and cleared her throat. She held on to the back of the seat in front of her, as if letting go would cause her to drift upwards. Ruby thought unkindly that if she did, she would look like a billowing cloud.

'Could you tell us, Reverend Peters, what life is like in your … community... It *is* a community is it not?'

The woman's face puckered anxiously in case she had used incorrect terminology.

'The Garden Kingdom is most certainly a community. It is set in extensive, beautifully landscaped grounds which contain a variety of buildings. Those who live there aspire to the title of saint. Sainthood is not automatically conferred. It has to be won through devotion and endeavour. We number several hundred and each of us brings what we can for the good of all.'

'And do all who live there have to work?' the woman continued, gaining enough confidence to let go of the seat, but still swaying slightly, as if she was being agitated by gusts of wind.

'Everyone has their special role to play. We work not for money but to earn salvation. There is none of the striving for status, nor the pressure to acquire that besets those on the wrong side of the wall, instead we serve each other.'

'It sounds like paradise,' the woman said, collapsing back into her seat.

'It is an earthly paradise that paves the way to eternal life,' Peters said, and looked around him again.

'It truly seems as if it would be the most wonderful place to be,' Mrs Remington said in a whisper to Hester. For her part, Ruby's mother had not moved since she had first sat down but had fixed the Reverend with an unwavering stare. She wants him to look at her again, Ruby thought. She wants him to see who she is because she needs to be reminded.

Suddenly, Hester was on her feet.

'Reverend Peters,' she said, her voice trembling a little. 'What can you offer in the community that I could not get elsewhere?'

This time Ruby was able to witness the way the man drew her mother in, without moving a muscle of his face, only turning, and fastening her, so that she appeared to lean towards him as though he was operating invisible strings.

'I saw you in the market square two days ago, did I not?' he said. Hester nodded mutely.

'I noticed you particularly. I was struck by your open, questioning look and by the way you held yourself, as if you know your worth.'

Hester made a noise, as though she had grazed herself against a wall, or put her finger in hot soup. Ruby found herself feeling unaccountably embarrassed by the sound, as if her mother had revealed more of herself than she should have. For the very first time in her life, she had an impulse to protect her.

'In answer to your pertinent question, about what will be offered to you in the community, I say that you will be given a life with meaning and purpose. It is a place where you will be seen for all that you are.'

Hester sat back down. The questions continued, and Peters answered them all in a calm and measured fashion, never raising his voice, even against a chaotic-looking man who had staggered in and stood at the back occasionally shouting out lines from the Bible. At the end of the allotted time, Hester insisted on going to meet Peters in person, she took hold of Ruby's arm and dragged her along. Ruby stared steadfastly at the floor, until directly addressed, and then raised her eyes to his face reluctantly.

'Ah, the young woman who is full of grief,' he remarked, and took her hand, and she felt the strength in him and a kind of tenderness that made her unsure about whether she wanted to leave her hand in his or pull it away.

On the way back, Hester was almost completely silent. She stared out of the window in a daze, her hands clutched in her lap.

'Are you all right, Mother?' Ruby finally asked as they approached home.

'I do not know,' Hester answered.

Chapter 4

BRIDGWATER

May

'Look, the clock is working! Mother must have started winding it again,' Irene said, as they came in the front door. They had been with Cousin Anna who had summoned them, along with some mutual friends, to discuss the most pressing issue of the day – the seating arrangements for her wedding. Ruby was happy for her cousin, whose sweet disposition and curving smile had caught the eye of a moderately handsome (if you looked beyond his slightly knock-kneed walk) and extremely wealthy man, but she wondered if the time would ever come when she would have her turn to love and be loved. The decisions about flowers and all the rest was not what she longed for, or even the day itself, but rather the sense that at last, she would be taking charge of what was to happen next. In the meantime, it was galling to have to expend so much energy expressing enthusiasm for table napkins.

'So, it is!' Ruby said, hanging her hat on the hook in the hall.

She and their father had once taken the clock to pieces and cleaned it, so that afterwards, the parts had gleamed like spread gold across his desk. Her heart felt sore now at the memory of the way they had stopped time for a whole day.

'Where is Mother?' Irene asked.

'I think we both know the answer to that.'

Ruby threw herself onto the sofa with her legs dangling off the end of it, a pose her mother had reminded her countless times was neither elegant nor seemly.

'We barely see her these days.'

Hester had been to hear Reverend Peters speak several times since the event at St John's Church. She had travelled to wherever he was appearing, even on one occasion, going as far as Bath, where she had been obliged to stay overnight and come back the next day. All of these trips had been in the company of Mrs Remington, who had taken charge of the arrangements with great diligence. Hester returned from these outings with new information that she shared with her daughters over the dinner table in a hushed voice.

'Reverend Peters says that all we could ever need is taken care of in the community,' she had said the evening before, running a finger round the edge of her wine glass, her food untouched on her plate.

'He is called The Beloved by those who live there, which I think is a fitting title. It conjures up his gentleness and his qualities as a leader. Did you know that there is a farm and all manner of greenhouses in the Garden Kingdom?'

'Mother is quite entranced,' Ruby said now. 'Do you think we should be worried by the extent of her regard for the preacher?'

'Meeting him seems to have restored her spirits and we should be glad,' Irene answered placidly. She took up her sewing – an embroidered shawl that she had been making as a birthday gift for Hester.

'I know the man is charismatic, we can both attest to that, but is it quite ... appropriate for Mother to be chasing him across the country?'

'What do you mean Ruby? There is nothing wrong, surely,

with being open to spiritual matters. After Father's death, Mother quite lost her way,' Irene said, leaning over and ringing the bell for the maid.

Ruby could not explain the reason for her unease. She thought of the way Hester had repeatedly stroked her throat and the bottom of her neck while she had been listening to the man. She had never seen her do such a thing before. She was a woman who had always stressed the importance of not revealing how one was feeling in public and of never fidgeting. Ruby's inability to sit still had been a constant bone of contention between them. The gesture had given her mother an uncertain, tremulous look, as if she was younger than she was.

Just at that moment, the front door opened and then banged shut with a certain degree of force and Hester appeared in the living room.

'Reverend Peters actually called me out at the meeting and asked to speak to me personally at the end!' she announced before she had even sat down.

Her face, which for months had worn an expression of bewildered grief, had, in recent days, been transformed with a new vivacity – a kind of hectic pleasure that alarmed Ruby much more than her mother's previous sadness had. Hester's black dress now looked less like an expression of mourning and more a conscious counterpoint to her blotched cheeks and gleaming eyes.

'Ring for May, Irene. I am quite parched with all the excitement.'

'I just have, Mother,' Irene answered, having moved her secret project under a cushion just in time for Hester's entrance, although in her mother's current frame of mind it seemed unlikely she would have seen it even if it had been left in full view. She did not even comment on the fact that Ruby was stretched out on the sofa with her stockings on display.

'And what did the Reverend talk to you about?' Ruby asked.

'Oh, so many things! It made my head spin. He explained that the saints do not live together, the men and women, I mean, even those that are married.'

'What is the point of being married then?' Ruby asked, sitting upright.

'The marriages in the Garden Kingdom are of a *spiritual* nature.'

'That makes no sense to me,' Ruby exclaimed, getting up and moving restlessly to the window. The trees had just sprung into green, giving the view a new softness. She saw her childhood friend, Nancy, walking by, arm in arm with her husband and she raised her hand in greeting but the two had their heads together and were talking intently and did not notice her. What must it be like to walk so close to another person, to be so wrapped up in each other that you did not see anything around you?

'That is because you do not take the time to understand, Ruby. Reverend Peters says that so many of the ills of the world are to do with the sins of the flesh. His purpose elevates those who live in the community above such passions.'

Irene, who had recently experienced something akin to the kind of feeling she thought her mother was describing, felt there was perhaps an advantage in being in such a place. She thought of the endless rooms in which she had been forced to sit, pretending to be what she was not, and of the pain she had felt when her true self had been revealed. There would surely be peace to be had in a community where her body, with its mysteries and frailties, was not judged in the usual way – as a commodity which might earn you what you wanted or might not.

'How is such a venture financed?' Ruby asked.

'Each community member brings what they can,' Hester answered, as May came in with the tea tray and set it down on the table.

'Yes, but how does that actually work?' Ruby persisted. 'Who pays for the accommodation and the food and everything else?'

'Reverend Peters says that true enlightenment cannot be

achieved when one is bogged down by mundane details,' Hester answered taking a long, irritating slurp of tea.

Chapter 5

BRIDGWATER POLICE STATION

'You can make some enquiries, talk to a few people, try to get the lie of the land, but do not spend too much time on it.'

PC Philip Hodge watched as his superior dipped a fat finger into the jar of honey on his desk and delivered a shining strand to his mouth and chin. Or, to be absolutely accurate, chins. Philip and his mother had given the chief constable the nickname 'Jowler' on account of his fulsome jaw and a certain sluggishness in his attitude to his job. He considered his most important task to be his daily monitoring of the local inns. 'It is essential work,' Jowler had said the other day, his lower face swaying. 'I see it as a service to the community to check on the accuracy of the measures and to curb unruly behaviour.'

'It is a matter of some concern, surely, that a baby should be left out in the open. It was a miracle the child survived,' Philip said, trying not to watch as Jowler licked his fingers with a wide, wet tongue.

'It will belong to some young girl of loose morals, shamed into secrecy. Sadly, there are rather more of those types of people around these days.'

The chief constable screwed his chubby face into an expression of disgust, his small eyes lingering on the jar of honey.

'The poor thing was found bundled into a hedge at the edge of the lane leading from Yaxton. No note. Nothing to identify the child. Just a scrap of blanket around its nakedness.'

The baby had been brought into the station the previous day in wooden box, as if she had been made ready for a funeral. Philip had assumed she was dead. Her skin had been a pearly blue, her head still narrowed by her passage to life, her tiny mouth sucked inwards, as if she had been caught in a moment of surprise. He had touched her gently on her chest and perhaps this had startled her into movement, because her curled fists, came up almost to his face, and she let out such a plaintive cry, it had entered his heart.

'Shocking, but unlikely to have anything to do with anyone who matters,' the chief constable said. 'We have to use our resources in the best possible way, and scurrying around the countryside, acting as if a major incident has occurred just because a baby has been abandoned, is not what we should be seen to be doing.'

Philip tried not to take offence at the description of his investigative workings. He loved the law. Not all the wearisome writing-things-down part of it, nor the vague contempt he was held in by many people for his lowly status, but the actual letter of it. The world could heave and buckle as it may, landscapes he had loved all his life could be broken up or hemmed in, but you could still rely on what was right and what was wrong. That didn't change. He knew he was unlikely to be elevated from his current position. He probably wouldn't even have a job when the long-awaited reorganisation of the Borough Force took place. It had been intimated by his superior that he might not be quite up to the grade.

'You don't have the required air of vigour, nor the capacity to make the right friends,' Jowler had said only a few days before, leaning back in his chair with a complacent sigh.

'I suggest you turn your attention to who might be lurking in the garden at Haughton. Mrs Preston has been in this morning, swearing blind she saw a man in a state of undress in her vegetable patch. I want you to go and have a good look round,' Jowler said now.

'You know yourself, sir, that Mrs Preston imagines all kinds of people in her garden,' Philip said wearily, dreading another lengthy interview with the voluble lady of the house, who he suspected made such complaints simply for the attention. She lived alone now that she had driven even the most patient of her children away on the wind of her endless words.

'Nevertheless, she is a person of standing, and we must act on her requests,' Jowler said, in a tone that indicated Philip was dismissed.

Although Philip reluctantly complied with his superior's instructions and endured a tour of Mrs Preston's garden, where he gamely squatted amongst the rows of onions and chard to examine the alleged footprints of the intruder he knew to be the marks left by a fox, he determined that he would not let the matter rest. Next time he was in the vicinity of Yaxton he would make a visit to the Star Inn. It could be that one of the late-night drinkers there had seen something from their vantage point over the lane. The baby deserved someone to at least try and find out who she belonged to.

Chapter 6

BRIDGWATER

June

'I would like you girls to come into the house. I have something I want to tell you.'

The sisters were sitting side by side on the grass, making daisy chains that were now so long they looped three times around their necks. They looked up at their mother who was standing at the door onto the garden. The sun was shining in such a way that Ruby could only see the dark shape of her. With her mother's features obscured, Ruby had the feeling that she was being addressed by a ghost.

'Can whatever you want to say, wait just a little longer, Mother?' Ruby asked, unwilling to leave the soft grass and the peace of splitting stalk and pulling through, which had a lovely comforting rhythm.

'It is hardly as if you are occupied with anything useful,' Hester answered. 'It is time you stopped such childish things and turned your mind to what is important.'

Her words, delivered as they were in tones of such solemnity, made Ruby feel a sudden chill, despite the warmth of the afternoon. As she stood up, her necklace broke, and she pulled what was left of the strands from her chest and let them fall to the ground.

In the drawing room, Hester sat down on what had been Arthur's chair. The one he had always preferred since it was nearest to the fire. Ruby had an image of her father's hands resting on his knees, the finger joints a little swollen, and the way she used to rub them with clove oil to ease the pain.

'You both know that for some months, ever since your dear father died, I have been struggling to make sense of things. I have been stuck, somehow, deep in myself. When I met Reverend Peters, I was set in motion.'

Ruby was obscurely repelled by the way her mother sat with her legs a little apart, as if she was readying herself for some kind of jump.

'I have talked with him at some length and find that what he offers, the life he offers, will do much to fill the empty space in my heart.'

She has fallen in love again, Ruby thought. She has fallen hard, and we will fall with her.

'What are you telling us, Mother?'

Ruby felt an almost overwhelming impulse to get out of the room and run and keep running. She got to her feet.

'Sit down, Ruby,' Hester said, and Ruby obeyed. Her legs felt suddenly weak, and her vision clouded as if there was something dark gathering at the edges of the room.

'Are you all right, Ruby?' Irene asked, inserting her hand into her sister's.

'Reverend Peters has extended a very generous invitation. One I hardly dared hope for. He has said that all of us, all three of us, are welcome to come and live with him at the community,' Hester said.

Her eyes were wide and incredulous. She stared at them, passing her gaze from one to the other, as if she expected them to express the same glad astonishment.

The Taking of Irene Hart

'And what did you tell him, Mother?' Irene asked, her voice soft, as if she was talking to a creature that needed soothing.

'I told him that there was nothing I would like more.'

There was a silence so profound that it had a noise all of its own – a kind of humming sound.

'What do you mean...?' Ruby managed. The words seemed hard to formulate.

'I have told him that we shall be moving into the community ten days from now.'

'I shall be doing no such thing!' Ruby exclaimed and she felt the pressure of Irene's hand increase. 'You can throw in your lot with a street preacher you barely know, but I am staying here.'

'He is *not* a street preacher. You cannot stay here Ruby.'

'Why not?'

Ruby felt such a murderous rage she thought she might strike her mother. She was horrified by the way Hester sat smiling, as if she had given them some kind of gift.

'In order to secure our places in the community I have signed everything over to him. Each person has to bring what each can afford.'

'What exactly have you signed over?' Irene asked.

'The house and its contents, the carriage, the money we have put by ... I have given it all to Reverend Peters. He says we will need for nothing in our new life. Everything will be provided for us.'

Ruby stood up, knocking her teacup to the ground. Irene looked at the dark stain spreading on the pink carpet. She could not seem to take her eyes from it.

'You cannot ... you cannot do this without asking us.'

Ruby was deeply flushed. She stood over her mother with her fists clenched.

'Why did you not ask us if this was what *we* wanted?' she asked. She sat back down with her head in her hands. 'This is our sacrifice, too, not just yours. Has every penny of our money gone?'

'You and Irene will not inherit your share for another year. The Beloved says that my money alone will ensure our places there.'

'Is there any chance that you might withdraw your offer, just for a short time until we can fully consider the implications, Mother?' Irene asked.

'My mind is made up. There is no going back on it.'

'Father would not have wanted this for us. I know he wouldn't,' Ruby said. She hated the fact that her face was wet with tears. 'How will I ever be married now?'

She stood up again and kicked the fallen teacup at the wall. It broke into three sharp pieces.

'I am not aware you have any prospects in that direction, Ruby.'

'But surely, there will be someone…'

'I hate to say it, Ruby, but your wildness and lack of discipline is such that you have not exactly endeared yourself to anyone in our circle. You are getting left behind. Nancy is exactly your age and has been married for a year.'

'I am only nineteen! And if there is not, after all, anyone I want, then I will do something else … something useful … be a nurse, perhaps, or … or … travel. Father spoke of many wonderful places.'

Ruby had no real sense of what being useful might actually involve, or where she might travel to, but she thought doing anything else would be better than being locked away amongst people she did not know.

Hester gave a sigh and shook her head.

'Your father was a wonderful man, but I fear he put unsuitable ideas into your head. I am doing what is right by myself and by you girls,' she said. Her voice had no doubt in it. 'We will become saints and we will be safe. There is no longer any need to be married in the conventional way. We will be brides of Christ.'

'You have lost your mind, Mother. I refuse to come. I will go and live with Nancy. I am sure she will have me,' Ruby said.

'What about Irene? Have you given your sister any thought at all? I think it unlikely that Nancy will be willing to accommodate both of you, not with Irene's indisposition.'

Irene felt a great wave of desolation. The prospect of going to live in some out-of-the-way place was not as terrible to her as the thought of being separated from Ruby. The former she could just about bear since she felt she did not properly belong anywhere, but the latter made her feel as if she might die. She did her best to look at her sister calmly, without revealing what she was feeling. Being in such a place would be terrible for Ruby and if she had the chance to stay in Bridgwater, she should take it. She too got to her feet and put her arms around her sister's shaking shoulders.

'Go now and talk to Nancy,' Irene whispered in Ruby's ear and smoothed her hair back.

So Ruby went and snatched her shawl from the banister and ran the three streets to Nancy's house. She stumbled twice and almost fell and arrived gasping. Seeing her from the window, her friend came quickly to the door.

'Whatever is the matter?' she asked, her round face and small eyes troubled. Between sobbing breaths Ruby told her what their mother had decided.

'We are to live somewhere I have never even seen – a place called Yaxton, amongst people who think themselves saved.'

'What a strange and sudden decision! Whatever has come over your mother? Has she no thought of how you might live? What *you* might want and need for your future?' Nancy exclaimed. 'You know you are welcome to stay with me, Ruby.'

'But I shall be nothing but a burden to you. Mother has given away everything.'

'I do not care about that at all. Henry keeps saying how rich we are. He owns three factories now, which make horrible piles of iron. We can spend his fortune on pretty shoes and cakes. Henry is indulgent but is away a lot, and even when at home, spends rather longer than I would like with his boats on the lake. He says it is an antidote to the great demands of his work, but I fail to see how pushing toys around a puddle with a stick is a proper way to fill your spare time. If you live with us, it will be like having a sister. *Say* you will.'

At Nancy's words, made so sincerely and with such affection, Ruby felt an enormous relief that she would at least be able to live an approximate version of the life she had always known. It would mean that for a while, until she came into her own inheritance, she would be beholden to Nancy and her husband, but at least she would still be able to see the same people, attend the same parties, look out at the same views. She would have the chance to find love, to take what was hers and make the most of it. It would never be, could never be, a life fashioned under her own terms, but there would be space in it to move as she had always expected to be allowed to move.

Over a silent supper, at which only Hester managed to eat anything, Irene smiled at Ruby, and in her face was everything she most admired and cherished about her sister and also what she found the most infuriating. Ruby could see the fortitude with which Irene was facing their present predicament. She could see her pain at the prospect of being abandoned, which she was doing her very best to disguise. Above all, she saw the way that Irene's own impulses and hopes had been set to one side so readily. She was so heartbreakingly resolute that Ruby thought her chest would crack in two. She felt Irene's foot touch her own under the table. The gentle pressure was intended as reassurance, but its effect was to emphasise the link between them. They had never spent a day apart. Where one sister ended, the other began. It had been this way for as long as she could remember.

The first seizure had come upon Irene when they were small children and playing together in the garden. She had fallen onto her side, then flat on the grass and begun her strange moving. Ruby had thought she was dying and shouted for their mother and then knelt on the grass beside her, calling for her to come back.

'I saw us,' Irene had said when she'd returned to them, her eyes cloudy. 'You and me, Ruby, holding hands while we ran down a hill and we were running so fast we couldn't stop. And I wouldn't let you go, and you wouldn't let me go, even though the world was rushing past us.'

Even in Irene's visions, the sisters were conjoined.

'So, what did Nancy say?' Hester asked, mopping her greasy mouth with her napkin, and looking at Ruby with a certain belligerence.

'She said I was welcome to stay with her,' Ruby answered, unable to look at Irene.

'Well then, you are denying yourself eternal life, but on your own deluded head be it. Stay with Nancy if you must. I cannot help thinking, though, that it is a terribly selfish decision, Ruby. It is just like you to think of no one but yourself.'

'Ruby must do what she feels is the best thing for her,' Irene said. 'I shall manage wherever I am, and Ruby can come and visit... She will be able to come and visit, will she not, Mother?'

'Reverend Peters said that only those people sanctioned by him are allowed to come into the community.'

Ruby looked at her mother's implacable, shining face. Was this what love did? Did it take people and make them suddenly unreachable? Is that what love had done to Ruby, too?

'Why do you begin all of your sentences with *"Reverend Peters says"*, Mother?' Ruby said savagely. 'You sound like a fool.'

'I think you should leave the table if you cannot be civil, Ruby.'

'I cannot sit here with you a minute longer in any case.' Ruby said, and stormed out, unsure of whether it was her mother or Irene she could no longer bear to be with.

Sleepless, and feeling more alone than she ever had before, Irene lay in bed trying to envision a life without her sister. Not even to be able to see her. It would be as if Ruby had died. She did not much care now where or how she lived her own life. There were times when she did not feel properly part of the world she inhabited. It did not accommodate her. Her illness made her unfit to bear witness in a court of law, or to work in any position of responsibility, even of the lowliest sort. She was unsanctioned as a wife or a mother. The love she had given had been rejected. Her pride was all that was left to her. She thought she may as well be hidden behind a wall as hidden in full view, but without Ruby, the guide that had always shown her the way home when she was taken away, who had always been the tapping finger on the compass, Irene would be completely lost.

Lying in the next room, Ruby could hear her sister's restless movements and could feel the weight of her sorrow through the wall. Throughout the long night, she changed her mind from slow hour to slow hour. How could she let Irene face the dim future alone? And yet, how could she allow herself to be kidnapped, which is what this proposed move amounted to? Who were these people she was expected to live amongst? She thought of the Reverend's burn, the way he had pulled her to him simply with one look. *The young woman who is full of grief* was how he had described her. He had seen what she thought had been a secret. He had the power to shed her skin. The thought of this made her breathless, as if she was already behind the wall, already locked up and under his attention.

By the time the light had begun to creep around the edge of the curtain, bringing with it the cold reality of her situation, she had moved from defiance to capitulation so many times, she was as wounded as if she had been in physical combat. They were always the worst battles – the ones when you had to fight yourself. She could not stay in Bridgwater. It wasn't only that she knew Irene needed her, she had also done her sister a great wrong. She had betrayed her in the worst possible way. She justified her actions on an almost daily basis, and yet she knew in the part of her that was too often in the descendent, that she was culpable. To be disloyal to her now, to let her go alone to face whatever awaited her, would only deepen Ruby's crime.

In the silver half-light, she looked around her room with its familiar things placed just as they had always been. The bronze lion on the mantelpiece, with which they had cracked open stolen walnuts, the tapestry cushion adorned with the lopsided tulips that Ruby had impatiently laboured over. They would leave all this behind. The possessions that had marked their childhood no longer belonged to them. Their father was dead, there was no possibility of imminent marriage and so, it seemed, they were to be placed in the hands of a stranger.

Chapter 7

BRIDGWATER TO YAXTON

Leaving Bridgwater had taken them longer than they had anticipated. Their house and its contents had already been sold – the pictures and linen and china, wrapped up and marked with the names of the new owners, but there had been decisions to make about exactly which of their possessions they should bring with them. Hester had been firm on the matter.

'Bring only what is absolutely necessary,' she had said.

Irene had made her choices quickly – her suitcase was packed and waiting in the hall in less than half an hour.

'When it comes to it, I find there is very little I cannot live without,' she had said, her slender white fingers resting in her lap as she waited on the swaddled hall chair for her older sister to be ready.

Ruby, on the other hand, had found the single piece of luggage allowance an impossible limitation. She had crammed the biggest trunk she could find, and then demanded that May, who should herself have gone the day before, but who had been left behind with the as yet unclaimed household items, sit on the lid until it was possible to do up the straps.

Ruby did a hasty farewell tour of the house, saying goodbye to her room, with its bed now stripped bare, and the place on the wall she had lain picking at the plaster when she was a child; the curtained window seat in her father's study where she had so often hidden when she had felt at odds with herself and with the world. She felt the same sense of dislocation now, but there was no longer anywhere to take refuge.

She had returned to Nancy's house with a far slower tread than before to tell her what she had decided. She had almost wavered at her friend's evident disappointment but had marshalled herself against the weakness. She had lain her head on Nancy's duck-egg-blue shoulder, wetting it with her tears, and said her goodbyes.

'I will write, and you must write back, and then I won't feel as if I am on an island,' she had said, although she knew it would not be enough. Perhaps it would be worse to receive such missives because they would only remind her of what she had lost.

All too soon, the river and the cone-shaped tower of the glassworks, and the grey steeple of St Mary's Church were behind them, and Ruby felt the movement of the carriage as if it was peeling her away. She tried to control the anxiety and frustration that threatened to engulf her. Perhaps living a peaceful life amongst the saved might allow her to atone and be restored, the way the root of the ash tree renews the sheen on dulled pearls. Perhaps, after all, the place would not be as bad as she feared.

'Isn't it beautiful!' Irene said looking out of the window, and Ruby, who had always taken longer than her sister to adjust herself to the moment, looked unwillingly out. It *was* beautiful – everything was suffused with a rosy glow – the fenced fields were striped red and green. The cows stood in maroon clusters beyond the bracken, which was crushed in rust-coloured heaps.

'What will our new home be like?' Irene asked her mother.

'It will be like being born again,' Hester said, her face infused with its newly acquired gleam, as if she had shed her old skin and found underneath, the ten years she thought she had lost.

As Irene looked out of the window at the haze over the fields, her vision began to focus on the particular – the intricacy of the cow parsley that laced the edges of the road and the exact curl of the dog rose petals in the hedgerows. At the very top of the horizon, she saw a line of red-jacketed hunters, racing towards the woods. Then, between one galloping stride and the next, she was amongst them. She could feel the warmth of the horses' pelts, hear the stinging hit of the crops, smell the sharp, urine odour of the fox. She felt her body start its familiar battle.

They had only been travelling for fifteen minutes, when Irene made the small, resigned sound that the other two knew heralded the beginning of a fit. Her skin had a light sheen of sweat on it and her eyes had the fixed, urgent look they both recognised.

'It is coming on me,' Irene said, and so they called for the cab to be stopped, and the driver wheeled the horses round and onto a rough track, which stretched out across a field of young wheat.

'The excitement of leaving has been too much for her,' Hester said as they helped Irene out. Ruby spread a blanket on the path so that she could lie down. In recent months Irene's fits had become less and less frequent, and both her mother and sister had hoped this was a sign that her affliction was easing and might eventually pass altogether.

Irene lay with her head on her mother's lap, and Hester and Ruby waited for the taking, for that was how these strange absences manifested themselves. It seemed to them that she was transported out of reach and went to another place altogether. Her limbs began their small tremors, and the movement built in her so that soon she was juddering helplessly, her eyes high in her head, her pale fists banging against her chin. The driver stood holding the horses, his head averted, perhaps to spare them the exposure, at such a moment, to the eyes of a stranger, although Ruby had seen other people make the sign of the cross when witnessing one of Irene's takings, as if to protect themselves, and so perhaps the man was not manifesting a kindness, but rather hiding a repugnance.

After her seizures, Irene told stories from the past, or spoke about things she had not seen before. They had decided as a family that it was best to keep these episodes to themselves. This type of infirmity was viewed with suspicion, even fear, and Ruby had always harboured an anxiety that Irene's affliction, if discovered, might be taken for madness by those ignorant of its true nature. Ruby had heard of people being put in asylums for all manner of reasons and was scared that this might happen to Irene too. This fear had always deepened her desire to shield her sister from public scrutiny. Irene had become adept at taking herself away from company when she felt the falling sickness coming on her, and her mother and sister were always quick to blame the heat, a too-rich supper, a weakness of the blood. And Irene's appearance seemed to confirm the theory to everyone who saw her that she was prey to illness – her skin was almost translucent, and her body had the slightness of a child's.

Ruby had the sensation, as she often did during her sister's fits that the world was holding its breath, and now it seemed the slight breeze had dropped and the clouds, which had just begun to blur into evening, had stopped their slide across the sky. Eventually, Irene stilled too, and lay looking up, as if trying to remember the place she had left.

'There, my darling, there, there,' Hester said, in soothing tones, wiping her daughter's face with a handkerchief.

Three or four pigeons flew suddenly from the hedge, their feathers making a loud ticking sound. In the distance came the grind of quick wheels and the single agonised whinny of a whipped horse. The open-topped carriage was upon them a moment or two later. The vehicle was moving so fast that they barely had time to see the occupant, but Ruby got a glimpse of the man she had seen in the marketplace. He was dressed in a red, fur-trimmed cape and was looking steadfastly ahead. Following behind were two riders on white horses.

'Behold who commeth, it is the Saviour,' one of them intoned – a man with red hair and bold features, who looked above their heads as he passed by.

'It is Reverend Peters,' Hester said, her face full of joy, and she moved Irene's head off her lap and almost ran to the edge of the lane so that she could watch the carriage until it disappeared over the crest in the road.

'He must be bound for one of his meetings,' Hester said, and clasped her hands together as if she was praying.

'You might spare a thought for Irene,' Ruby said. She had taken her mother's place and was stroking her sister's damp hair away from her forehead.

'It is a sign,' Hester said, 'a sign that we are doing the right thing.'

Irene sat up and looked around her.

'I saw the night light up,' she said, in the scratchy voice she always had after a fit, as if in the short time she had been away she had forgotten what words sounded like. 'It was the middle of the night and yet I could see all in front of me, and the birds started singing as if they thought it was dawn.'

Irene seemed suddenly agitated. 'It was as though the world had turned on its head,' she continued tremulously, twisting her hands.

'Don't upset yourself,' Ruby said, helping her to her feet. Ruby was accustomed to this transitional stage when her sister seemed to rest halfway between two worlds, as if the place where she had briefly been, was trying to claim her back.

The village of Yaxton was set on a sloping crossroads that looked out on the wide stretch of the Quantock Hills. There were only a dozen cottages and an inn set around a threadbare patch of a green. Towering over all the other buildings was a high, red-brick wall which Ruby assumed was the community's fortification.

Chimneys and crenellated ramparts and what looked like the roof of a chapel were just visible over the top. The chapel was crowned with a stone lion carrying a pendent flag which didn't have the decorous, blank look of other, similar emblems – but rather stood in growling, arched-back defiance, its legs planted firmly, its toothed, open mouth turned towards the village of Wynch, which was just over the next hill.

The women alighted from the carriage in full view of the drinkers sitting outside the Star Inn who looked at them with a kind of jaded curiosity, as if they couldn't quite break their rather weary habit of derision.

'There be three more of 'em,' Ruby heard one of them say to his companion.

'Like a trio of crows,' the other man answered, and they both laughed, and Ruby was aware of how strange they must look, dressed in black, landed suddenly in front of the cream wall of the inn on the white dust of the lane, like the shadow puppets she had once seen at a Christmas party, moving on wooden joints behind an illuminated screen.

Chapter 8

YAXTON

At the Star Inn, Philip found several men who claimed to have been drinking outside on Saturday evening a fortnight before. This was when he thought it most likely the baby had been abandoned. The little scrap of a thing would surely not have lasted much longer at the mercy of the elements. Many of the drinkers were quick to blame the inhabitants of the community, the entrance to which was almost directly in front of the inn.

'I've seen some comings and goings you wouldn't believe,' said one man. He tapped the side of his nose, which was tendrilled with livid veins.

'But did you see anything out of the ordinary on this particular night?' Philip asked.

'All I'll say, is that the folks in there are not like you and me. They're a different breed altogether,' he answered, raising his cup once more to his fiery muzzle. Philip edged away from his companion. The man smelt like rotting fall in an apple orchard.

No one else he spoke to had seen anything untoward. It seemed that whoever had left the baby had been quick about it, or perhaps it had happened later, after the regulars had staggered home. The innkeeper, keen not to bite the tankarded fists of the carriage drivers and the delivery men who stopped by when they were on community-related business, argued that the baby couldn't be the responsibility of anyone who lived there.

'They are all spiritual,' he said, his mouth small in his wide face. His hands were fast and angry as he dried the glasses on the counter. 'They live on a higher plain. The men and women are separate. Even the ones that are married.'

'High and mighty, you mean' said the apple-saturated man who had edged close to Philip once more.

The policeman declined the offer of a drink and made his escape. With the vague notion that he might find someone else to talk to, he walked down the lane that ran alongside the front wall of the community until he reached the point where it turned inwards. There was a small gate at the side, which he leant against, expecting it to be locked, as the main gate always was, but he was surprised when it opened easily. He hesitated for a moment and then went in. Living as he did only a mile or so from Yaxton, he knew of the community's reputation, but he had never been inside the wall before. The inhabitants did not encourage visits from outsiders. He walked past a farm building and a row of cottages into an area of the garden that was hidden from the windows of the hall which was the largest of the buildings, by a hedge and a mass of ferns.

He noticed a woman dressed in one of the pastel frocks favoured by the inhabitants sitting on a bench directly ahead of him, so he ducked quickly behind a tree. He didn't relish the idea of having the dogs that always guarded the gate set on him. Rumour had it that they ate intruders for breakfast. The woman sat with her legs slightly apart, her feet loose and pointed outwards in their neat shoes and pale stockings. She was pushing her hand down on herself through the material of her skirt. Her eyes were closed, her teeth biting into her reddened bottom lip, her breath coming fast. She looked as if she was trying to remember something of great importance or perhaps trying to forget it. Philip, who himself sometimes became moved by the curve of a breast or the thought of having someone warm in his bed, recognised the act for what it was and turned away in embarrassment and a measure of shock. *That is what comes from living a spiritual life*, he said to himself as he retraced his steps. The leader of this strange group of people might preach abstinence, but flesh had a way of rearing up and making itself felt.

He was walking back down the lane towards the front entrance of the community, just as three women were being helped down from a carriage by the driver. The older woman who was fussing with her bag, was clearly the mother of the two – they all shared the same fine-boned profile. One of the younger women had an unworldly beauty, with a mass of barely contained red hair, and skin so pale it looked as if all the colour of her face had gathered in her lips. The other, who was taller and had black hair and who he judged to be the older sister, walked over, and stared up at the roof of the chapel with an expression he could not quite fathom. Less obviously beautiful than her sibling, she nevertheless had a fierce vigour, a kind of boldness that made him want to look at her. His immediate impression was that she was as rooted to the ground as her sister was unfastened to it. By the time he was abreast of the party, this sister was banging loudly on the gate and demanding admittance. The guard dogs had begun snarling and rattling on the chains they were fastened to, and in all the noise and confusion, the mother, seeing his approach and in a tone he was very familiar with, addressed him without preamble.

'We do not seem able to get in. Do something.'

He stepped forward and using the end of his truncheon, knocked as loudly as he could. It was surely a coincidence, but the gate swung open almost immediately, giving Philip an unusual and fleeting sense that he had been useful. The mother walked by him with hardly a glance, followed by the ethereal sister who murmured her thanks. The third woman now seemed reluctant to go in, despite her earlier forceful attempts to enter. She stood outside the entrance, spinning the heel of her boot into the grit of the lane, whilst the driver manhandled their cases. Seen close to, he was astonished that he had thought her less attractive than her sister. She looked at him from beneath dark brows, her colour high, her mouth generous.

'It is reassuring to know that there is an officer of the law nearby,' she said. 'I may well need to be rescued.'

Her tone was mocking, and yet beneath her bravado he could sense her anxiety.

He bowed from the waist and felt his hat, which had been handed down from the previous incumbent who had clearly possessed a larger head than his own, almost slipped off. He made a humiliating clutch at it.

'Police Constable Philip Hodge,' he managed. 'If I can ever be of service…'

'What kind of a place have I arrived at, Police Constable Hodge?'

He hesitated, his recent, somewhat disconcerting sighting still fresh in his mind.

'Well, from the little I have seen, the garden is beautiful and by all accounts, the residents enjoy a peaceful, productive life,' he said.

She looked at him again with a direct gaze.

'Peaceful and productive … that sounds … if not fascinating, at least … improving.'

She righted her shoulders, as if in preparation for an ordeal, and then turned to go in.

On the way back to Bridgwater, mounted on his portly horse called Thunder on account of its propensity for wind and its slow gait, Philip Hodge tried to remember the exact colour of the woman's eyes. Dark blue? Dark Grey? He recalled that valiant little readjustment in her bearing and wished that she had at least given him her name.

Chapter 9

THE GARDEN KINGDOM

Ruby's first impression was of a dazzling brightness. On the village side of the wall, the evening had been drawing in, darkening the trees, making shadows of the birds that clustered on their branches, but this place looked as if it belonged under a different sky. Coming from the dust and dirt of the lane the contrast was almost painful – like the pull of ice-cold water on a parched throat. The lawn stretched round the main house as one long, unbroken sweep and she could see several neat lines of cottages and the arched wooden door of the chapel. Peacocks wandered across the grass and through the privet hedge. The fresh greenness of the lawn and shrubbery and the glisten of the fruit she could see pressing up against the glass of the greenhouses had the same saturated colour as rich oil paints spread on a white canvas.

A young man, selected to be doorkeeper no doubt on account of his wide arms and thick chest, beckoned them in.

'Do not worry about the dogs. They cannot hurt you now,' he said, in a low, musical voice, quite out of keeping with his brawny appearance. The five hounds were all of the same black, dribbling aspect and looked at the women with bloodshot, baleful eyes as if they had been cheated of the entertainment they were due.

'I am George,' the young man said. 'Welcome to the Garden Kingdom.'

He made no move to shake their hands, or greet them in any of the ways the women were accustomed to, and yet he did not have the bearing or attitude of a servant, rather there was an uprightness to his bearing and a thinness to the skin around his eyes that made the women think almost subliminally, so used were they to making a hundred daily judgements of this sort, that he was their equal, despite his plain jacket and the scarf worn loosely around his neck.

'Come with me,' George said. 'Someone will bring your luggage in for you.' And he set off without checking that they were following him. He led them up a flagged path to an imposing house accessed by a flight of steps, pushed the front door open, and then stepped aside to allow them to enter.

The interior was dim after the garden's acid glare. There were polished tiles at their feet and the walls were decorated with a paper patterned with twisted vines, which began at the skirting and snaked their way up the walls to the high ceiling.

'I will leave you,' George said. 'Sister Miriam will be here shortly to show you to your rooms.'

As her eyes became accustomed to the low light, Ruby saw silver candlesticks on a honey-coloured table, several high-backed chairs against the wall, and a blue glass vase of lilac which was just beginning to brown and tighten and had lost its first, clean scent. The wide, curved staircase had a newel post as large as a human head. They waited in silence for a few moments more.

'Is this the house in which we are to live?' Ruby asked at last, more to break the silence than from a desire for an answer.

'I believe it is considered to be an honour to be invited to live in the Hall,' Hester answered in a whisper.

'An honour commensurate perhaps with how much has been given,' Ruby said in a loud voice.

'Ruby...' said Hester reprovingly.

Just then, some small movement caught Ruby's eye and she

looked up to the shadowed top of the stairs. A woman was standing there. The top half of her body was in complete darkness, but Ruby could see her skirt and her feet neatly lined up with the edge of the tread. She wasn't moving and Ruby wondered how long she had been listening to their conversation.

'Mrs Hart?' the figure said, and Ruby had the unsettling sense that it had been her own glance upwards that had caused the woman to move, and that if the three of them had not arrived at this day, at this place, she would still be at the top of the stairs waiting to be set in motion by other visitors.

The woman was of an indeterminate age. She could have been in her thirties or forties, maybe even older. She had a graceful, contained way of moving, as if she seldom did anything without thinking carefully first. She had a small, purplish birthmark on her cheek, the tail of which just grazed the corner of her mouth. Her seed-shaped eyes were dark brown under black brows that swept upwards, giving her a haughty look. She was dressed in a plum-coloured dress, its plain fabric and simple style not disguising the quality of its cut.

'I am Sister Miriam,' she said, 'I have charge of the running of the Hall. I am sure you are eager to unpack and make yourselves comfortable.'

Her voice had a hiss of sibilance caused by her slightly overhanging top teeth. She indicated that they should follow her up the stairs. She didn't ask them any questions about where they had come from, nor offered the kinds of pleasantries usually given to guests by their hosts, and so it was difficult to make conversation and they climbed in silence. They went up a further flight of stairs and into a hallway with a blue-glassed window, which made the light look murky. Sister Miriam opened a door on the right and led them into a drawing room with heavy upholstery and a view out over the garden, and the cottages and fields beyond. It was not as well appointed as their old home which had been spacious and full of their father's books and treasures, but it seemed comfortable enough.

'This room is for your own use. There are two adjoining bedrooms. I hope you find the accommodation satisfactory,' she said, her face expressionless, as if she didn't much care if they did or not.

Miriam always felt slightly impatient with new community members. They arrived expecting some kind of instant transformation. They did not realise that miracles were things you made for yourself. They were not available to pluck like fruit from a low-hanging branch. What to make of these three? The youngest one was extraordinarily beautiful. Skin like the palest of roses. Hair the colour of the dark red weed Miriam had seen once at the edge of the sea when she had been living her other life.

'This is all perfectly lovely,' said Hester speaking in a slightly too-loud voice that revealed both her eagerness to please and a desire to make some impression on their inscrutable host.

'Supper is served at seven in the dining room. You will be required to change out of your mourning dress.'

Seeing Hester's involuntary recoil at her words, an expression of feeling entered Miriam's face for the first time since their arrival – her eyes widened, and her severe mouth softened into the beginning of a smile.

'This is not a place of mourning,' she said. 'Death has no dominion here.' And she left the room, closing the door gently behind her.

There was a moment of silence while the three women assessed their surroundings. The room was growing dark, and Ruby lit the two lamps placed on the chenille-covered table.

'You and Irene take the room on the left, I'll take the right,' said Hester, who seemed, now she had arrived at the much longed-for destination, to be curiously flat, like a child who had found the promised treat not as glorious as she had expected.

'I hope they send our clothes up soon,' said Irene, 'if we are to change in time for dinner.'

Hester went into her bedroom and stood looking at her reflection in the long mirror on the back of the wardrobe door. She surveyed herself anxiously, plucking at the bodice of her dress and smoothing the creases it had acquired in the carriage.

'I am not sure it is right to take off my black dress. After all, it has only been eight months since Arthur's death and besides, I have brought no other dresses with me.'

'I am sure that Father would not have wanted you to wear black for too long,' Irene said.

'He is still part of me whilst I am dressed as a widow.'

There was a quick knock at the door and Ruby opened it to find what she thought was a boy, since his diminutive stature suggested youth, but when she looked more closely at him, she saw his face was lined and his shock of surprised-looking hair was streaked with grey. He stood perspiring by their pile of luggage.

'Goodness! You haven't struggled all the way up the stairs by yourself?' Ruby exclaimed, thinking guiltily of her bulging trunk.

'I am Trench. The bringing of luggage and the cleaning of boots and shoes,' the man intoned by way of introduction. 'And on Sundays the polishing of The Beloved's special cup.'

To Trench the women still retained their outside world smell – oily and bitter, like burnt marmalade. The largest one had the blunt face and clumsiness of a bullock. The middle one moved like a horse that had been left too long in its stable. The little one had the same shine as the crimson head of a goldfinch.

He dragged their luggage into the room, breathing heavily and then disappeared.

'Is that person a saint, Mother?' asked Irene.

'Those that are saints have the title "Brother" or "Sister",' said Hester. 'So, I think not. It is Reverend Peters' choice who is honoured so.'

I have chosen nothing, thought Ruby, except for William and he hasn't chosen me. She shrugged the thought of him off and undid the straps of her case releasing a mound of fabric and the smell of home.

'It is fortunate that I, at least, thought to bring the best part of my wardrobe,' she said. 'You can wear my green poplin, Mother;

and Irene, the pink – and I'll wear this.' She pulled on her blue muslin dress, enjoying the smooth sensation against her skin.

'I'll help you, Mother,' Irene said, and Hester stood passively while Irene unbuttoned her, pulling the dark dress off her shoulders, letting it fall to her waist and then kneeling to pull it, all in one piece, down her legs.

'It is the last of him gone,' said Hester sadly, her face shadowed in the way it used to be before Reverend Peters had set her blood racing and allowed her to dream about the possibility of redemption. Irene nudged her gently, and Hester stepped out of her fallen dress, as if she was stepping onto uncertain ground.

Chapter 10

THE GARDEN KINGDOM

Dressed as they all were in similar, pastel-coloured unadorned frocks, and with their hair pulled back tightly into neat plaits, it was hard to tell the difference between the thirty or so women seated around the long table in the candlelit dining room. At first glance it seemed to Ruby that they were featureless, like the figures on the worn marble frieze that Nancy's husband had acquired on his travels, which stood in pride of place above the mantelpiece in their drawing room. *They look like phantoms don't they?* Nancy had said once, looking up at the plaque with a grimace. Ruby tried to dispel the image of her friend's dear face. Thinking about her only served to sharpen her anguish. Sister Miriam was sitting at the head of the table dressed in an ice-blue dress, and she nodded at them and gestured to the three empty seats next to her own.

'Please welcome the newest members of our community,' she said. 'Mrs Hester Hart and her daughters, Ruby and Irene. I will not introduce you to everyone now. You will get to know them all in time.'

She gave another of her queenly nods and four women, differentiated only from those seated at the table by the white aprons they wore over their dresses, moved from the wall against which they were standing and began to serve the food waiting on the sideboard.

The meal was plentiful but served only with water. Ruby, who had no appetite, took small mouthfuls of her vegetable soup, and in between stole quick glances around the table at her companions. She felt her mother's sharp elbow in her side and took this to mean that she should stop staring.

'Have you come far?'

This question was addressed to the three of them by a young woman with a pink-and-white prettiness and a smile that revealed small teeth and a wrinkle on either side of her nose.

'Only from Bridgwater,' Hester said.

'Not an arduous trip, then. I am Sister Angela. Welcome to the Garden Kingdom.'

'Sister Angela arrived with us five years ago and has been a saint for four years,' Miriam said. 'She is a valued member of the community.'

'So, you had to wait a year before you were made a saint?' Ruby asked, earning another dig in the ribs from her mother.

'Some have to wait even longer. I am Edith,' said a thin woman dressed in pale yellow at the other end of the table. 'I have been here for two years and am yet to be elevated.'

Edith had pockmarked skin and wide gums and an air about her of wanting to please. She brought her hands to her meagre chest in a way that reminded Ruby of the unfortunate mouse that Irene had captured when she was little and kept for several days in a cardboard box before it escaped through a gnawed hole.

'What earns those living here the right to be a saint?' Ruby asked, and this time Hester gave one of the warning coughs, she was all too familiar with. Hester had been coughing at Ruby for as long as she could remember.

'I am afraid my eldest daughter is unable to master her curiosity,' Hester said, and smiled around the table apologetically.

'Curiosity has its place,' Miriam said. 'You just have to know when to exert it and when to curb it.' She looked at Ruby with a neutral expression and then bent her long neck back to her soup.

'The decision about what is to happen to us is in The Beloved's hands. We do only what pleases him,' Edith said firmly and began nibbling on a piece of bread.

'Might I ask who lives in the Hall, and who lives in the cottages I saw when we arrived?' Irene asked. Ruby shot her a grateful smile. She knew the question had been asked as an act of solidarity. Irene disliked drawing attention to herself. It seemed that this enquiry was acceptable to Hester, since their mother failed to dispense one of her coded reprimands.

'The Beloved occupies a series of rooms on the ground floor, next to the chapel. The other floors in the Hall are for those members of the community, both saints and saints-in-waiting, who are not married. The cottages are set aside for married members of the community. I am Sister Eloise and have been here for six years, three of them as a saint.'

The woman who had furnished this explanation was elderly and had kind eyes and the same knotty fingers as Ruby's father.

'We mean, spiritual marriage, of course,' Sister Angela said, smiling. 'Men and women do not occupy the same cottages and, other than The Beloved and Trench, who does odd jobs and who does not matter, only women live in the Hall. Those who work most closely with The Beloved live in the largest of the cottages.'

'Goodness, it all seems quite complicated!' Hester exclaimed, shooting Miriam an anxious look. Ruby knew that her mother hated to feel as if she was not in full possession of the facts. It made her nervous in case, in her ignorance, she said or did the wrong thing.

'All will become clear in the fullness of time,' Miriam said soothingly, and at some invisible command, the women came forward to take the soup bowls away and replace them with plates of sliced pork, well roasted and served with apple sauce.

Ruby lapsed into silence for the rest of the meal. She caught the names of only two more of her dining companions – Hattie, a woman of indeterminate shape, who sat at the far end of the table, eating with silent and earnest attention, and Norah, whose arched eyebrows and slightly protuberant eyes gave her a look of permanent surprise. Ruby felt a wave of despair. None of the community members looked as if they had ever lusted after a hat or felt their hearts race. How was she going to live in such a place, among such people? People who seemed to be waiting for something strange and unspecific. Something she did not understand. She wanted to be back at home amongst her own things. She thought of her old living room with its familiar view out of the window, and the steady tick of the clock in the hallway, with such longing she thought she might cry. She felt Irene's hand on her arm and took what comfort she could from its warmth.

Chapter 11

The next morning, they were informed by the perspiring man-boy, Trench, who clearly should have added messenger to his list of duties, that Brother Martin was waiting for them in the office.

'The Beloved is still away. Brother Martin deals with all in his absence,' Trench said, standing with his eyes averted and worrying at his plume of hair.

Don't look directly at anyone. That was what Trench had been instructed. But he could feel the little one's vibration. It was the hum of this world and the next. He had miles of silver to polish. When it was laid out for Sister Miriam to see maybe he would be able to escape for a while. When you were almost nothing, your absence was not so visible.

Trench made a curious ducking motion and left them at the office door.

'I do wish The Beloved himself was here to welcome us,' Hester said. 'But I know he has matters of great importance to deal with.'

The room was furnished with a desk and chairs and a patterned rug and had a mantelpiece, above which hung a portrait of Reverend Peters. He was standing with his arms crossed, surveying a landscape that bore no resemblance to the one around them. He was dressed in a sweeping white robe and, to Ruby's eyes, a faintly ridiculous turban. Behind him there was a dun-coloured mountainside and goats with horns twisted like barley sugar.

Standing by the desk was the man that Ruby recognised as being one of the riders that had accompanied the Reverend's carriage when it had passed them the day before – the one with bright red hair and pronounced features, who had made his sonorous announcement. It felt much longer than a day since they had arrived. Something about the atmosphere of the community made judging the passing of time difficult, as if those who lived here operated a different system of minutes and hours.

'I would like to formally welcome you to the Garden Kingdom and explain a little of what life is like here,' Martin said. He stood for a moment looking at them as if unsure of what to say next. Ruby noticed the contrast between his heavy features and the lightness of his gaze. His eyes were such a watery grey that they seemed almost without colour, and he had a slightly unfocused, searching look that made her think that perhaps his vision was impaired.

'Although of course you will not be expected to do any heavy work, we prefer it if all the members of our community are gainfully employed. Have you any special talents you might employ to the benefit of the community? Mrs Hart, you have earned the right of exception from such duties, but perhaps your daughters?'

'I enjoy gardening,' Ruby said, thinking of the patch at home where she had grown vegetables and flowers in a corner that the gardener had left to her sole ministrations. Martin nodded solemnly at her.

'Any help you can give us would be gratefully received,' he said.

'I can sew,' Irene said, and blushed as she often did when addressing strangers. Ruby thought Irene was at her most beautiful when she was shy. Unlike the ugly blushes of other people that rose from their necks in ragged rashes, her embarrassment manifested itself as a kind of glow – the delicate pink suffusing her skin, making her shine. Martin looked at Irene and Ruby saw that just for a moment, his face lost its searching, vague look and became strangely intent and then, seconds later it reverted to its previous expression. It was as if a shadow had cleared, or he had become alert to something he thought he had seen and then decided he had been mistaken, after all.

'I'll show you round the house and grounds and explain what we need doing and you can tell me if it suits your skills and inclinations.' He led them back into the hallway.

'This is the chapel,' he said, indicating a door to the left. 'There is the main entrance accessed from outside, but this is the additional side door. This is where you will be initiated when the time is right. Until then, you are not permitted to enter unless specifically invited to do so.'

He pointed out the library, the drawing room, the meeting room, the dining room they had been in the night before; all spaces that were sombrely, yet richly decorated.

'These are The Beloved's rooms and are not ever to be entered,' he said, putting his hand against a door off the hallway, and holding it there as if to emphasise the seriousness of his words.

They climbed up to the second floor and Martin stopped at the first room off the corridor.

'Here is the sewing room,' he said, and ushered them in.

The room was full of sun that streamed in through three windows. Low wooden benches were arranged against the walls and lying across the carpet was a long stretch of fine-weaved canvas. Three large baskets of glossy thread were standing ready. They had such varied and sumptuous hues that Ruby wanted to put her hands through the rich skeins to feel their colours against her skin.

'The Beloved has commissioned an embroidery to depict *The Song of Solomon*,' Martin said to Irene, who was eyeing the canvas with trepidation.

'You are familiar with the text?' he asked. And when she shook her head, said, 'No matter. Someone will read it to you.'

'And who will work out the design?' asked Irene.

'There will be others helping,' said Martin. The design will come from within you.'

His words seem to make him inexplicably embarrassed, because he coloured and looked over their heads and around the room and then out of the window as if he didn't quite dare to let his gaze rest anywhere in particular. Finally, he coughed and turned his pale eyes to them again. Ruby wondered what ailed the man. He looked as if he had taken a bite of meat and found it to be nothing but gristle.

'It will be a lengthy task, but well worth the doing,' he said at last, and wheeled out of the room, leaving them to follow.

'I do not know how I will manage without a pattern,' Irene whispered anxiously to Ruby who was looking out of one of the windows onto the trees and the hills, which were gleaming with new green.

'There is a lot of ground to cover,' said Irene, staring at the blank canvas as if trying to fill it in her mind's eye with a prism of colours and shapes and all the ladders, the lattices, the lazy daisies, the leaves, the links, the loops, and other fancy stitches that would be required to complete the task.

'You will invent it,' Hester said. 'Something from the Bible, animals and flowers and such like.'

The women hurried down the stairs to catch up with their guide. As they descended, they met three young women coming from the opposite way, dressed in pale-coloured cotton dresses, their hair coiled over their ears. Ruby could not remember if they had been present at dinner the night before. They smiled and then lowered their heads as they passed by in a single file.

'We must get ourselves some new dresses. I favour a primrose colour, perhaps a lilac too,' Hester said.

Martin was waiting for them at the door of the house.

'Now to show you the gardens,' he said.

He seemed to have recovered his former manner, and all trace of the uncertainty he had demonstrated in the sewing room had disappeared. Ruby thought him as changeable as the device she had once seen in a shop window, which had by turns released from a tiny wooden door, a sparrow to indicate fair weather and a blackbird to signify coming rain.

The garden was as glorious as Ruby's first glimpse of it had promised. Much of it was laid out in formal alleyways of box and beech, but there were also areas that shimmered with colour. Banks of roses, just beginning to unwrap from bud with faint traces of gold and crimson, surrounded the lawn, and along the side of the Hall a fan-shaped pear tree stretched along the wall. Early summer flowers, in shades from misty blue to a purple that was almost black, bloomed in great stretches of unbroken colour that was so deep and rich that it seemed like the landscape of a dream.

Martin took them into the first of the greenhouses – a high-roofed ironwork edifice that was crammed from its bosky, damp-earthed floor to its top with orchids. As Ruby stepped inside, she was immediately assailed by the sudoriferous heat, which wrapped itself around her, as tangible as a length of sodden cloth. They walked down the dripping central pathway over which the bulbous tongues of flowers hung at eye level, and down below, clinging to the trunks of trees and insinuating themselves though the foliage were a hundred varieties of the flower; some veined and fleshy, others feathered, frilled, and spotted and stained at the edges of their open mouths with dark, inky shapes and blood-red markings.

'Look at this,' Martin said, stopping and taking a magnifying glass out of his pocket. He cupped a cerise, speckled bloom carefully in his hand and indicated that Ruby should look through the glass.

'It is a Lady's Slipper,' Martin said.

Ruby bent her head and had the sensation, as she looked through the thick lens, that the ground had become uneven, as if the magnification and the sudden change of perspective from wide to particular had destabilised her.

'Can you see where the insect becomes trapped?' Martin asked eagerly. His face was uncomfortably close to her own, as if in his excitement he had temporarily forgotten himself. The bulge of the labellum was grotesque – a violent green with fine, white hairs attached to it. Just above, hidden by what looked like a shield, was a column tipped with pale yellow pollen in a viscous mass.

Ruby drew her head away. The sight of the intimate heart of the flower made her uneasy.

'I am not familiar with such exotic plants,' she said. 'My little patch at home housed far more commonplace things. I do not know how to care for orchids.'

She wondered if she would even be able to touch such delicate, ornate flowers.

'George, who I imagine let you in yesterday, is an expert and will teach you all he knows,' Martin said. 'I am sure your green fingers will be a great advantage.'

He glanced at her hands. It was only a passing look, but it made Ruby feel strangely exposed, as if he was making an assessment of some kind. She laced her fingers tightly and placed them behind her body, out of sight.

They left the greenhouse and were given a tour around the fernery, which was situated in a shaded area of the garden under a chestnut tree, and the pineapple pit in which the peculiar fruit, with skin scaled like the side of a fish, grew amid pronged leaves.

'What do they taste like?' Irene asked, fascinated by the exotic sight.

'I shall give you a slice,' Martin said, 'and you shall judge for yourself.'

He went into a shed and emerged with a knife. He lifted the glass lid of the pit, releasing a fierce smell of fermenting manure, and cut a small fruit from its branch.

'This one is not quite ready, but it is ripe enough.'

He placed the pineapple on the stone pathway and sliced

through its crown and along its sides with a quick motion, and then cut a chunk from the top section of the fruit and handed it to Hester on the tip of his knife. She took it in her hand and gave a tentative bite and then absorbed the rest of it in a great gulping swallow.

'Quite, quite delicious,' she said.

'It tastes like sunshine,' Irene said of her own portion. Ruby's mouth was watering even before the fruit's plump pith hit her tongue. It was like nothing else she had ever eaten – sharp and honeyed, yielding and yet with a gritty edge. Her mouth filled with the juice, and she could feel it running down her chin.

'For heaven's sake child, wipe your face,' Hester exclaimed, waving a handkerchief in Ruby's direction. 'Brother Martin will think you quite a savage.'

'I think nothing of the sort,' he said, inclining his head. 'We are extremely fortunate to have you all in our midst.'

'And we in turn, are very glad to be here, are we not?'

'It is very beautiful,' Irene said, seeing the stretch of the garden and the wall that encompassed it. She thought that being separated from the world that lay just on the other side of the community's defences might be a good thing. It could be that these dreaming strangers, so absorbed in higher matters, would not dwell on what made her different and that she would be safe from scrutiny and the disappointments of the heart.

Chapter 12

Philip Hodge wished he were a braver man. There had been one, or perhaps two points in his life when he had been given the opportunity to take a chance, but although he had wavered, feeling the tug of all that he had not seen and felt, he had chosen to leave things as they were. Leaving things as they were was a side effect of having had an elder brother called Gareth, for whom danger had been like breathing. When they were both children, their mother Catherine had been terrified by his endless escapades. She had been widowed when Gareth was just a baby and had been left with a sense of the fragility of life, which took its expression in anxiety about her sons.

You stay here by me, she would say to Philip, pulling at his arm and averting her face to his brother's laughing walk along the top of a wall or his one-armed swing from the highest branch of a tree. And then, when Gareth had grown older and started staying away from home for weeks on end, returning eventually with a bloody nose or a debt they had no hope of paying and some complicated story of opportunities that had been near enough to taste but were then snatched away as a result of the duplicity of one or another, his mother would look at Philip and say *At least I can rely on you to live long enough to see me through*, as if, without his knowledge, Philip's contract to remain always by her side had already been drawn up and signed.

Gareth had eventually taken one risk too many and had been brought back to his mother's house at the age of nineteen with a chest held together by a stranger's torn shirt. He had lived for five flickering hours on the kitchen table and then turned his head to the open window. *So, it's just the two of us now*, his mother had said, as if she took a kind of pleasure in being right, although afterwards she cried so hard and long, he thought she might never stop.

'I slept almost the whole night through,' his mother said now, watching from her chair as he ate his egg-soaked bread. She was engaged as she almost always was in her embroidery – an account of her life sewn in red thread on a narrow length of cream linen, a task that seemed endless, although Philip couldn't imagine how she had so much to say. As far as he knew she had never been further than the five miles to Bridgwater, and then only on three occasions – once to marry their father, then to bury him and finally for the funeral of her eldest son. She had been born in the house in which they now lived, a cottage with mean dimensions and a sloping roof, as had her own mother before her. Nevertheless, her samplered story was now so long that its crimson length pooled at her feet like blood.

'What part of your life have you arrived at, Mother?' Philip asked, mopping up the last of the butter from his plate.

'The summer of 1814, when I was eighteen years old.'

'What were you doing then?'

'Making a braided loaf to take to my sister's wedding and a bee got caught in my hair.'

'You are telling a very detailed tale.'

'That is where God is,' she said, pulling the thread through without looking, as if she was stitching her life by touch alone.

'And the devil, too' said Philip, thinking again of the abandoned baby, who, at his own expense, he had placed into the care of a local woman who was already nursing and had milk to spare. She was still so small he did not like the idea of her going into the local orphanage which is what Jowler had suggested. Philip had named her Pearl, on account of her delicate, shining skin, not that he would ever tell anyone he had done something so fanciful. He could just imagine Jowler's look of derision if he heard about it, although this was unlikely since his superior never showed the slightest curiosity about him. There were people in this life meant for talking and others for listening and Philip fell firmly into the latter category. He knew his superior liked whisky, women with eyes the colour of conkers, a good piece of beef, taking walks with his plump, twin grandchildren, a landscape painting with plenty of sky, and an advantageous hand of cards. The chief constable, however, barely knew in which direction Philip set off for home at the end of a working day.

It had been almost a month since the baby had been found and yet he was no nearer to discovering how she had ended up in the lane. Nobody he had spoken to in the village had volunteered any useful information and the local doctor said he had been unaware of any recent pregnancies amongst his patients that hadn't led to happy births. The baby *had to* belong to someone.

'Still troubling yourself over that poor babber?' his mother asked, breaking off a thread with her teeth.

'Jowler says that I should let the matter rest. He says there are other, more important things I should be concentrating on. It was nothing to him at all that someone left her like a bag of rags.'

'Perhaps it's a fairy child?' his mother ventured. Philip bit back his impatience at her words. He wanted always to be kind to her.

'Only if fairies are made in the same mould as you and I.'

Catherine set aside her work, which Philip knew was the sign that she was about to launch into an important conversation, the subject of which was always roughly the same.

'Now, work's all fine and good—' she stopped to cough into her hand. He thought her cough had worsened lately and they would have to get the doctor out again. They could ill afford the expense, but it was his job to do the very best he could for her.

'I'm as proud as any mother can be,' Catherine continued. 'You work hard, you are kind, you are more than commonly handsome, although your hair could do with a trim… I'll see to that later… Now, where have I put the scissors? What was I saying…? Oh, yes, my point is that any girl would be fortunate to have you.'

'It must be terrible to have poor eyesight,' Philip replied, wondering when he could safely escape to the field behind the house where Thunder was waiting to be fed.

'There is nothing wrong with my eyesight! I've always been able to see close and as far away as I've a mind to look. What I am saying is that it's time you found yourself someone. I am seventy-three years of age. I'm not going to be here forever.'

'You make it sound as if there is a throng, just waiting for my attention.'

'Well, there was Mary's daughter, Enid … she used to come here all the time. Just dropped in when she knew you would be here, with all manner of things … some onions once, which was peculiar because Mary knows I can't manage them. Another time, a basket of scones, which were woefully short on salt. Or she'd come saying she needed a sharp knife or a claw hammer … and her father well stocked with all manner of tools! Keen as mustard, she was, but you would barely pass the time of day with her, and eventually she lost heart. She married a man from Bridgwater in the end, who, I've heard tell, walks in his sleep, which must be hard for her to manage…'

'Enid was perfectly nice. I just wasn't drawn to her. Her laugh was too loud.'

'And then, what about Kate? Pretty as anything, with that heart-shaped face and clever way with her hair. She would have had you in a snap, if you'd only let her.'

'Kate had no subject of conversation other than Kate.'

'The trouble with you Philip, is you are just too particular. There have been scores of girls, but you have turned your back on them all. You are seven and twenty, it's time you settled down with someone.'

'I just haven't found the right person, Mother.'

'Well, you'd better find someone soon. Loneliness is a terrible thing.'

'I'm not lonely,' Philip said, getting up and kissing his mother on her forehead, to forestall any further discussion.

In the field, with Thunder eagerly chewing his way through the fresh straw he had piled up in front of him, Philip rested his head against his horse's ample and comforting flank and considered the subject of loneliness. He didn't feel himself to be particularly afflicted with it, and yet, there were times, returning home after a long day, when he thought about what it would be like to have someone waiting for him. Someone who would take his coat, and dust it down, and tell him small, important things.

Chapter 13

Ruby had begun her apprenticeship in the garden and greenhouses under the tutelage of George, who had the dual roles of Head Gardener and Door Keeper. She was accompanied in this endeavour by Edith, the mousey young woman who had explained the hierarchy of the community members to Ruby at their first dinner, and Hattie who had not spoken that night, or indeed much since. Irene, along with knotty-fingered Sister Eloise, pretty Sister Angela, and perpetually astonished Norah, had started work on the embroidery in the sewing room. Irene was still much exercised in trying to work out exactly what the design of it would be and spent a lot of time sketching out ideas. Hester sat in their living room, looking out of the window, waiting for something to happen.

As July had made way for August, the three of them slowly became used to the movements of the community – the bustle of activity in the mornings when everyone set about their tasks, the silence in the evenings when they retired to their quarters, the way time seemed to stretch out, so that each day merged into the next, there was a sense for Ruby, who had not had high expectations anyway, that this was not the place that had been sold to them. Where was the much-promised salvation? What form was it going to take? Even Hester seemed rather bewildered.

'I understood that I would feel differently when I came here,' she said, as she was getting ready for bed, unbuttoning her recently acquired lilac dress with an air of despondency. 'Reverend Peters said I would be heard and understood. That I would become full to the brim with peace and thankfulness. But nothing has happened. I feel just the same as I did before. If anything, I feel a little worse, because at least before there was the anticipation of coming. If he was here, perhaps I would feel something new. I do wish he would come back!'

Irene made a soothing noise and unpinned her mother's hair and set to brushing it with even strokes, the way she knew her mother liked it to be done, although Hester stilled her hands impatiently.

'I miss May. She knew how to brush my hair properly,' she said.

'We have only been here a relatively short time, Mother. We cannot expect to feel any great change yet.'

'Or indeed, ever,' said Ruby who gathered up the cards she had been playing with and tossed them into the air.

Later, with sleep eluding her, Ruby heard crying. An almost childish keening, that rose, sharp and high, and then subsided. A minute later, she heard it again – the same rising note and then the descending sob. It was such a grief-laden sound that Ruby's impulse was to try and find its source, even though they had been told by Miriam in her customary frigid tone, that they all had to stay in their rooms at night. Her mother had said many times that Ruby's lack of obedience would be her undoing, along with her tendency to speak when she shouldn't and the way her hair could never be made to lie quite flat enough. Ruby sometimes wondered if her mother liked anything about her at all.

She crept out of the bedroom, leaving Irene deeply asleep, lit the lamp on the table and went out of their quarters into the corridor. She listened at each of the closed doors but couldn't hear anything. She thought perhaps the sound had not been a human cry after all, but instead the call of an animal – a fox's mating howl or the screech of one of the peacocks in the garden. This was an alleged paradise on earth after all, not a place of sorrow.

She stood still for a moment, with the light from her lamp illuminating the ivied wallpaper in narrow, wavering sections, tracing the creep of the tangled tendrils to the ceiling. Ruby, who was not given to flights of fancy, suddenly felt the skin on her arms and the back of her neck prickle. It was something about the quality of the darkness – it felt heavy and tangible, as if it might move, all in one overstuffed piece and pull her inwards. She was about to retreat to the safety of her room when she heard the cry again. It seemed to be coming from the floor below.

She went down the stairs. The door at the far end of the corridor was slightly ajar and the sound of crying was coming from there and so she walked towards it. She did not want to intrude on private grief, but it was possible that the person had been taken ill or had suffered a fall. She could not, in all conscience, ignore the sounds of such distress. She looked into the room, which was in complete darkness, then tentatively stepped inside, raising her lamp as she did so.

It took Ruby a few moments to understand what she was seeing. She had to pass her lamp across the space a section at a time. Hattie, her taciturn gardening companion, was standing on a chair in the middle of the room. Dressed only in her chemise, her exposed flesh pallid in the dim light, she was staring straight ahead, her face convulsed with tears.

'Hattie! Whatever are you doing?' Ruby said, and moved nearer.

Hattie simply continued staring at some point above Ruby's head and did not respond. Her eyes were wide and dark. There were what appeared to be scratch marks on her face. Her body was shaking with cold or fear or with the strain of standing on the narrow wooden chair, Ruby could not tell.

'Let me help you down,' Ruby said, touching the woman's feet which were chilly under her hand. This gesture seemed to bring Hattie somewhat back to herself and she looked at Ruby. 'Come now,' Ruby implored her, 'get down and tell me what the matter is. Has something happened?'

Hattie shrunk away from her. She wrapped her arms around herself and shook her head violently.

'Leave me. Leave me alone,' she said. Her voice was high and strained. Ruby could not reconcile its frantic pitch with the slow-moving silent woman that Hattie had always appeared to be.

'I cannot leave you like this. Is there someone you will talk to? Shall I go and get Sister Miriam?'

At this Hattie, began shaking harder and began making strange snarling noises. Ruby thought that she had perhaps gone mad.

'No. Go away. I have to stay where I am,' Hattie said, her mouth working, her nails digging into her arms. Her wildness scared Ruby.

'But why do you have to stand like this? You will make yourself ill. Let me at least get you something to put around yourself.'

All of a sudden, Hattie stopped shaking. Her hands went to her hair, and she smoothed its tangle away from her face. She spoke clearly and with such viciousness that the impact of it made Ruby step back from her.

'You do not understand. You do not understand *anything*. What would such as you know about what it is I have to do. What I have lost and how I must be tested to earn salvation.'

'I am only trying to help,' Ruby said. She could feel the arm holding the lamp begin to shake, although she tried to hold it steady.

'Get out and leave me be.'

Ruby felt the woman's spittle land on her face, and she backed out of the room.

She ran back down the hallway. Her lamp swung from side to side, and she couldn't see where to put her feet. She almost fell as she climbed the stairs. It was only when the bedroom door was safely closed behind her that she began to breathe again.

19th August

My Dearest Nancy,

It seems an age since I last saw you, although we left Bridgwater not much more than two months ago. I have been meaning to write for a while but have waited until I had a better sense of where we are. I find myself in a peculiar place. It is a community of people under the leadership of one Reverend Peters who has been absent since we arrived. I am told he is away gathering new members. His earnest recruitment makes him sound like the Pied Piper of Hamelin, leading the entranced away with a rat-wooing pipe.

I think that there are about 150 people living here, although we were led to believe there were more. I have a feeling the Reverend has a tendency to exaggerate. The high walls that enclose us surround extensive grounds, which include a farm and fields and woods, even a lake. Mother, Irene, and I reside in the main hall, along with the other unmarried members of the Garden Kingdom. There are at least thirty other buildings, some of which are inhabited by men and some by women. Our leader espouses spiritual marriage, even for those that were already married in the conventional way before they arrived at the community, a situation that might please our mutual friend, Lydia, who must by now feel the need to put some distance between herself and her husband's little balls of bread, but does not bode well for my own romantic future.

My fellow inmates are by and large odd. I came upon one of them standing on a chair in the middle of the night and she would not come down even though I entreated her to do so, but instead screamed at me to get out of her room. When I saw her the next day at breakfast she acknowledged nothing of the incident. She seemed exactly as she had before. Had she not had what I imagine were self-inflicted scratches on her face, I might have thought I had dreamt the whole thing. There is something about the atmosphere here that makes one doubt things one has seen with one's own eyes. It feels to me that there is what is happening on the surface – my work in the garden, Irene's sewing that she does for such long stretches of time that sometimes the tips of her fingers bleed, the meals taken in each other's company that seem civil enough affairs (although the housekeeper, Sister Miriam, is rather unpleasant), and what is really happening underneath. I cannot tell you why, but I sense a kind of strain. It is so hard to explain to someone who has not experienced it, even you, who always understands everything.

Despite my worries that we should be continually on our knees in some hard place, muttering abeyances, I have been informed there is no need for any of us to pray. Instead, Sunday is set aside as a day of recreation. The men solemnly line up on the lawn and then, at the sound of a whistle, scamper around with curious sticks shaped like shepherd's hooks, chasing a piece of rubber from one end of the garden to the other. They are like children. The women's favoured pastime is to have dancing lessons on the large, circular stage which is situated at one end of the meeting room. This strange edifice, which I am reliably informed was custom-made for just such a purpose out of special, flexible wood, rotates on an axis, presumably providing those pirouetting on board the illusion that they are spinning faster than they are. It is a wonder they are not thrown off the thing. I told you I was amongst strange people!

I think the villagers of Yaxton view us as their entertainment. They climb on each other's shoulders to peer over the wall and shout insults. They have lately taken to relieving themselves against our fortifications, so in the morning the smell wafts up, almost obscuring the odour of the flowers. The others tell me such behaviour is born of fear. Here, they view all who live outside as bound for hell.

Mother has instructed a dressmaker to deliver several dresses in the prescribed pastel colours. She sent a man called Trench, who is one of the few people allowed out of the community, with the instruction. The delivery boy threw the packages over the wall, so great is the terror of those around us of the hounds that guard the gate. Mother had to apply for the money to cover the expense, which only a short while ago had been hers to command. I now own three very plain dresses in pale blue. It hardly seems worthwhile changing since they are almost identical. We also have to wear ridiculous little shoes with straps, of the sort that the very young wear. They would not survive even the lightest shower of rain, let alone the muddy streets of Bridgwater. I suspect they are designed to keep us inside and discourage flight.

I miss you and so much else that belonged to my previous life. I feel as if I am slowly setting in aspic. We are not kept here against our will, but it seems that no one leaves or indeed, appears to want to.

Irene sends her love. After what happened with William, I think she feels that she no longer has a part in the real world. She seems resigned, even glad, to have left it all behind.

Please do write soon and spare me no details.

Your incarcerated friend,

Ruby.

Chapter 14

Philip was riding towards Yaxton when he came upon someone standing right in the middle of the lane, making hand gestures indicating that he should stop. The man seemed not to want to move, despite Philip's encouraging sideways motion, and so he was forced to dismount. He thought at first that the person, who was short in stature and had odd, indistinct features, was not in full possession of his wits. He could barely get his words out and kept shifting from side to side.

'Watch where you go, sir. Your horse might walk into it,' he said finally, ducking his tufted head. He spoke in small gasping groups of words, as if he was out of breath. The man took off his jacket and laid it on the grass of the verge and then picked up what looked to Philip like a dead fox from the edge of the lane and wrapped it up carefully.

'What will you do with a dead fox?' Philip asked.

The man shook his head with a serious expression on his face, which was neither young nor old, but something in between.

'I feel the life in him. I'll keep him warm.'

He clutched the bundle, from which limp legs and a matted tail protruded, and stood at the side of the lane silently, clearly waiting for Philip to be on his way.

'What's your name?' Philip asked. 'Where do you live?'

A wary look crossed the man's face. He grasped the swaddled fox closer to his chest.

'Trench,' he said and pointed mutely at the wall behind him.

'Oh, so you live in the community.'

'Must go now, sir. I have him to see to,' Trench said, indicating his parcel.

'You didn't see anybody in the lane a few weeks back, did you? A baby was found just about where we are standing.'

The man lowered his head and stared at the ground.

'I haven't seen anything at all, sir,' he said, his face still turned away.

'Are you absolutely sure?'

'It was deep dark, sir.'

'You can trust me, Mr Trench,' Philip said quietly, stroking Thunder's mane. He knew his skills were not of the elevated kind, but he was good at drawing out information from those reluctant to divulge it. 'The little thing was close to death, like your fox there.'

The man glanced around him as if he was looking for an escape route.

'I might have heard a cry. Could have been an animal. Could have been something else,' Trench said at last. When he raised his head Philip could see that he was agitated, maybe even scared. His eyes were wide and troubled.

'What time did you hear the cry?'

'Late Sir. Shouldn't have been out. It was awful tight in my room. The gate was open, so I just went through. The bolts are always across at night. You mustn't tell,' Trench said, and then set off down the lane as if he was being chased.

'I cannot understand why you are wasting your time and ours.

Your presence here is interrupting the smooth running of the community.'

The woman who had introduced herself as Sister Miriam, the housekeeper of the community, was clearly a dragon of the most ferocious sort. From the top of her stiffly braided head to the click of her sharp-toed boots, she exuded disdain. She would have seen him straight back out of the community gate if he hadn't been so persistent and held his ground. She eventually led him, with impatient exhortations to keep up, to the basement kitchen which was thick with the smell of something deliciously rich and savoury. A chicken and mushroom pie perhaps – good and salty with a thick, buttery crust. His stomach growled. He had not eaten anything all day except for the bit of bread and cheese his mother had wedged into the inside band of his hat that morning.

She opened the door to a room barely larger than a cupboard with sacks of potatoes on the floor and a string of pheasants hanging from the ceiling. There was a low stool against the wall, presumably for the maid to sit on to peel vegetables or pluck feathers.

'This will have to suffice as your interview room,' she said, with a derisive emphasis on the word interview. 'I will send people to you in small groups. You cannot possibly hope to talk to them all. Some are occupied with their work, others will be reluctant to see you, and I will not force them.'

Miriam disliked the man's bold glance. She had seen the same look of blunt incredulity in the faces of other outsiders – the tradesmen who smirked out of the corners of their mouths, the drinkers slathering for titbits at the inn, the indignant husbands who banged rudely on the gate in the middle of the night, demanding the return of their wives, as if they were possessions to be gathered up and tossed back where they belonged. What did the policeman know of what they had built here? Of the way that purposeful work could forge something strong and lasting. Of the power of belief. He was blind and muzzled to beauty and truth. She took in his worn-out boots and the dusting of pollen along the bottoms of his trousers and the way he held his ridiculous hat under his arm and decided not to offer him anything in the way of refreshment. His thick tongue could stick to the roof of his thick mouth for all she cared.

'Whatever you think you are looking for, Constable Hodge, I doubt you will find it here.'

'I have spoken to a witness who says he heard a cry. He also said that someone from the community was in the lane on the night in question. The gate had been left open.'

'I imagine you are referring to Trench. He has a habit of wandering. You cannot believe anything he says. He is half formed.'

'He seemed perfectly clear on the matter.'

'I will leave you to your … work,' Miriam said, with a curl of her lip. She looked as if she had opened the door to the pantry and found a side of rotting meat. He couldn't imagine her cold-eyed stare on any church painting. If she was any version of holy, then the whole world was bound for hell.

Members of the community trooped down to the kitchen in batches and stood gathered at the door. He asked the same questions, and by and large received the same replies. There were no babies in the community. They lived a life free from the sins of the flesh. They were chosen. They were going to be saved. They worked for the good of each other and for God. They lived in an earthly paradise in expectation of the greater one to come on the Day of Judgement. They all had the same polite but blank faces, the same, low, reasonable tones. Only one, an elderly woman by the name of Eloise with a gentle face had thought to offer him a drink. He felt foolish sitting almost at the level of the floor, looking up at them, his knees sticking out, scratching in his notebook.

The family he had met at the gate to the community came to see him at the end of the afternoon with a couple of other women who, he was told, worked in the garden. Hester, Irene, and Ruby Hart and the two others – Hattie Blackthorn and Edith Lambert. The name Ruby suited her, Philip thought. It reflected her dark shine. He didn't want to be caught in a cupboard with his feet planted amongst potatoes, so he got up, the cramp in his legs making him wince.

'I know it is unlikely you will have seen anything,' he said, directing his words at the Hart family, 'since you arrived at the community after the incident. But perhaps you others saw something material, pertaining to the matter in hand.'

He winced again, this time at the slight tone of self-importance he knew had entered his voice.

'It is Police Constable Hodge, is it not?' Ruby said, and he couldn't help being gratified that she had remembered his name.

'Yes, it is Miss Hart. Here to try and ascertain the identity of a baby left just outside the community.'

'Poor little thing,' Irene exclaimed. 'It must have been so cold. Did it survive the night?'

'Barely, Miss Hart. When she was brought to me, I thought at first that she had passed away.'

'The wages of sin,' said Edith, who had a pinched look about her.

Hattie, who had the shape of one of the sacks in the cupboard, stood with her eyes on the ground.

'How about you Miss Blackthorn?' he asked. 'Did you see anyone? Perhaps from your window?'

'My bedroom is at the back,' she replied. 'I have not set foot out of the community for more than four years.'

In the silence that followed this pronouncement, and much to his mortification, Philip's stomach emitted a long groan.

Ruby gave a low laugh which earned a glare from her mother.

'It is time we all returned to our duties,' Hester said. 'I am afraid you will have to look elsewhere for your answer, Constable Hodge. Or better still, let the matter rest. It *is* only a baby, after all.'

She swept out, followed by the others, and Philip sat back down on his stool with a sigh and perused his sketchy notes. Perhaps Mrs Hart was right that it was time to set aside this investigation. Jowler would skin him alive and hang him up with the pheasants if he discovered what Philip was doing. Just then, Ruby appeared at the door once more.

'I thought you might benefit from this,' she said, handing him a plate of chicken pie before placing a warning finger to her lips.

On his way back home, with Thunder raising bursts of golden smoke at each heavy step, he wondered what was it that possessed people to lock themselves away from the world and live a peculiar half-life without the comfort of proper companionship. It was all right for the more elderly members of the community who were clearly dozing themselves towards death under a blanket of dubious consolation, but women such as Ruby and even Edith with her shifting eyes, and Norah with her lumpy body, might actually be out in the world, living as they should. 'What a waste!' he exclaimed out loud and a cloud of white butterflies rose in the air in front of him.

Chapter 15

September

It was the sound of the birds that woke Ruby. She thought at first that she must have overslept, but Irene was still in bed and her sister invariably got up before she did. Disorientated and still only half awake, she went to the window and drew aside the curtains. The garden was lit up with what looked like the brightest of moonlight and yet Ruby could see only a pale crescent on the horizon. The birds were clustered in the tops of the trees in such great swarms that the branches were moving as if someone was shaking them. Their collective noise was louder than any dawn chorus she had ever heard. Ruby prodded Irene awake.

'There is something wrong with the sky,' she said.

'What time is it?' Irene asked sleepily.

'I do not know, but I think it is the middle of the night.'

Irene stumbled to the window.

'It is as I saw it,' she said. 'It is the same brightness, the same singing of the birds.' Her voice was anxious. Along the hallway, doors were being opened and there was the sound of raised voices and running feet.

'Perhaps we should not leave our room,' Irene said. 'I am not sure it is safe.'

'I want to see what is happening,' Ruby answered, and she pulled on her dressing gown and handed Irene hers.

'Should we wake Mother?' Irene asked.

But Ruby was already out of the door, so Irene followed.

By the time they got downstairs, it seemed the whole household had risen. The hallway was crowded with community members in various states of agitation. Norah was standing at the bottom of the stairs clutching the newel post as if she thought letting go of it would pull her into deep water.

'The clock shows the hour as only two and yet it is as if it is daytime!' she said, and began crying.

'Perhaps the Day of Judgement has arrived,' Edith said, wide-eyed, fretting at the neck of her night jacket.

'I am not yet ready!' Norah howled square-mouthed, letting go of the newel post and grinding her eyes with her fists. Miriam stood in the midst of all of this trying to maintain calm, although her words were falling on deaf ears.

Ruby and Irene went out into the garden where a crowd of people had gathered and were looking upwards. Others streamed from the cottages and the farm buildings.

'It is just as I saw it,' Irene said again and took hold of Ruby's hand. Ruby could feel the tension in her, it vibrated like a string pulled taut.

Above them a glorious canopy of colour was spread like vapour across the sky. Streams of yellow and orange met and crossed each other in great pillars and then melted away. Following after were curdled wisps of the brightest green, dancing towards the mountains where they fell in vivid shades of purple.

'Angels are arranging the glorious scenery of the heavens,' Sister Eloise said, her hands clasped.

At each shift and ripple in the folds of the sky, there was a corresponding shout from the crowd. A few had fallen to their knees, others were crying quietly. Someone in the crowd began singing and the hymn was taken up by others, so that it seemed that those on the ground and whatever was happening in the firmament were in some kind of battle for ascendancy. The voices rose as each luminous spectacle reached its peak of beauty. The dogs by the gate were growling deep in their throats and rattling their restraining chains. From the fields came the bellowing of cows, who should at this time of night have been in the barn. In the flower beds, butterflies fluttered with iridescent wings.

The Reverend's sudden appearance amongst them came as a shock to Ruby who had not even been aware he had returned to the community. She had not seen him since he had left in his carriage on the day of their arrival. It was as if the light had conjured him up. He was standing on the steps down to the garden. She recognised his tall outline and the upright way he held himself. She had the impression in that moment that he was as startled as any of them by the untimely arrival of the day. It seemed to her that he hesitated. She thought he might even have turned to take a step back towards the house, but then he paused and stretched his arms out above his head. Had anyone else noticed the slight revision of intent? Or thought, as she did, that there was something theatrical in his pose?

One by one, people noticed him and nudged and hushed their companions. They turned to face him. A waiting silence fell.

'It is the first sign,' said Reverend Peters, his voice deep and full of conviction. 'It is the coming of the Day of Judgement.'

Someone in the crowd let out a frightened shout. The noise was like a trigger and was echoed amongst the assembled saints.

'This is not something to be frightened of. This is the first indication that we are chosen. The sun has shown itself only to us who are safe within these walls. It touches us with its eternal light. I have brought these colours to shine on your faces, on your flesh that has been reclaimed here in this new heaven. The night will return at my will.'

He stood with his head raised to the sky. His arms moved as if he was spinning the dazzling strands or as if he was conducting music only he could hear. Everyone looked upwards with him. For a while nothing changed, the garden still glittered, the colours still shifted and turned. And then it seemed as if the heavens were obedient to him, because the last strands of pink and gold began to dissolve, as though water had been poured on them. The sky took on the most exquisite silvery whiteness, and then darkened. From their perches on the trees the birds rose all at once in an invisible rush. There were exclamations of astonishment and shouts of joy from the crowd and then they surged forward towards Peters, all as one, as if drawn to him by a magnet.

'Go now and take your rest,' he said. 'And when you rise again we shall have a day of celebration and give thanks for The Miracle of The Sacred Light.'

'It seems The Beloved has claimed a miracle,' Ruby said to Irene as they went upstairs, holding the candles that Miriam had lit and passed to each of them. 'It surely cannot be that it was only our patch of ground that was so affected. Such lights will have been seen all over, though what caused them I cannot imagine.'

Irene was still subdued and didn't answer her.

'Do you not think so, Irene?' Ruby persisted as they reached their room.

'I do not know why the sun touched the earth in the middle of the night, but only that in my taking, the darkness when it came was colder and deeper than it is now and was full of the sound of weeping,' Irene said.

'Goodness, how gloomy you are! You know full well that you see all manner of things in your takings. Why, you once told me that you had seen the whole congregation of St Mary's Church grow ears as long as a rabbit's, right the way through their hats, and that never came to pass, did it?'

'But I saw just such a sky, Ruby, I really did.'

Hester's bedroom opened and her tousled head emerged.

'Wherever have you been?' she asked.

'Witnessing The Miracle of The Sacred Light, Mother,' Ruby answered.

'You might have woken me up!' Hester exclaimed in annoyance.

Chapter 16

In the late afternoon, rugs and blankets were brought out by the serving staff and spread out in the shade. Men and women sat apart from each other on either side of the lawn. Bread and cheese and cold meat and cake and great urns of tea were set on long trestle tables. The atmosphere was festive – the garden was filled with chatter and laughter. Reverend Peters moved amongst his congregation, stopping to talk to one person and then another. Their devotion was palpable. Ruby could see it in the way their bodies stretched towards him like low-growing plants trying to reach the sun. His voice seemed to slake their thirst – they raised their half-opened mouths to catch the drops left by his words. His touch on an arm here, and a shoulder there, caused those that had been selected for this benevolence to twist and expand as if they had been waiting for just such a release. They moved as if they were suffering, as if they were too near a fire, but on their tilted faces she could only see longing. Where exactly was the comfort? All she could see was insatiable need.

'What is it that they want from him?' she asked Irene.

'They want love,' Irene replied. She had barely spoken all day and Ruby had caught her looking up at the sky as if she thought she could read an answer there.

'But what are they prepared to do, to win it?' Ruby asked, thinking of Hattie standing weeping in the darkness as if she was being punished. Had she been told to do such a thing? Or had her actions been caused by some derangement of her mind?

'I wish I had witnessed the miracle. I still cannot believe you did not come and get me,' Hester said. She was eating the chunks of cheese and slices of cold beef with what seemed to Ruby to be excessive relish.

'It was over almost as soon as it began, Mother,' Ruby said. 'We would not have had the time.'

'And you foretold this did you not, Irene? On our way to Yaxton. You saw just such as a sky as the others have described.'

'I am not sure,' Irene said. 'It is hard to remember exactly.'

Irene had been informed by an eminent doctor whom her father had found in London that her infirmity was caused by electrical impulses in the brain firing erratically, like a storm over the sea, but she knew that this was not widely believed. People, including most of the medical profession, attributed her condition to some sort of possession or the result of deviancy or suppressed desires. She had tried the proposed treatments – the ice-cold baths, the letting of blood, the ground-up concoctions of nameless animal parts, the hours spent in darkness – as if the very light itself might awake the devil – but the fits had remained part of her, the way a parasite glues itself to the flesh of its prey. She was not sure of what she saw or why she saw it, but she had the sense that in her absences she met her other self.

'Lie with your head on my knee,' said Ruby, and her sister obediently complied, and Ruby stroked her sister's copper curls away from her forehead, thinking about what had almost divided them. She saw William with his easy charm, sitting in their old garden, one arm stretched across the back of the bench as he waited for Irene to come out of the house and take a walk with him. Irene claimed she could see straight through Ruby's face to her mind, but Ruby knew she was better at dissembling than her sister realised. She had kept a secret for more than two years and had never spoken of it, although at times it had gathered in her mouth, like the juice that comes just before sickness.

She had loved William first. It had happened suddenly one afternoon when he was standing in the hallway – the world around him had disappeared so that he was all she could see. She thought at the beginning that she was ailing but the torn feeling in her chest had not shifted. He had caught on her heart like a hook through the flesh of a fish, and all the while he didn't have the slightest idea what he had started up in her.

She remembered the exact moment when she had understood he cared for her sister. Irene had stumbled over a root that had grown across the path and William had reached for her with a gesture as instinctive as a breath. Ruby saw in the way he briefly steadied her, and the answering movement Irene made towards him, so slight it was nothing more than a kind of softening, that they shared an understanding. William and Irene had not been officially engaged, but they had spoken of their feelings to each other.

'I think I may love him,' Irene had said one night, as she was getting ready for bed, winding her hair into a glimmering rope. Ruby had felt a nasty corresponding twist in the very centre of her body. If they married, she would be abandoned by them both. She would lose everything.

'What is it about him you like so much?' she had asked, the words bitter in her mouth.

'He is so sure. So certain of himself. When I am by his side I feel more distinct, too,' Irene had replied, smiling gently as if she had a secret Ruby was excluded from.

'Do you not think his certainty demonstrates a certain self-regard?' Ruby had said and then felt ashamed when she saw the light fade a little from her sister's face. Ruby knew Irene wanted her blessing for the union.

It had seemed for several weeks that the matter was decided, but then there had been that walk around the grounds of

William's home; a visit designed as a prelude to their engagement in which he showed her what was soon to be theirs to share.

'I'll move the fountain if you wish it,' he had said gaily when Irene thought its position so far from the house ill-judged, and her sister's face had lit up with pleasure. Ruby had been walking alongside them, wishing she were elsewhere. Then Irene had fallen. A sudden seizure with none of the usual warnings – no fracture of the light or taste of metal – and when William saw her move and found her so changed, he couldn't hide his horror. Like Ruby, he showed all in his face. The habit of secrecy about her condition was so ingrained that Irene hadn't told him, hoping, perhaps, that love might cure her.

When he hadn't come to the house the next day, Irene knew his feelings had changed, and then when he sent word that he was going abroad for a while, she knew for certain she had been discarded.

'Ah, the Hart family!'

Reverend Peters had approached now, without any of them realising. Hester scrambled hastily to her feet, shedding crumbs as she rose and made a frantic scooping motion with her hand to indicate that her daughters should get up, too.

'I am sorry not to have been able to welcome you until now,' he said, and held out his hand to each of them in turn.

'I am absolutely stricken not to have been present for the miracle.' Hester could hardly get her words out. She was breathing heavily.

'Even if you were indoors throughout, you will still have been touched by the beneficent light,' Peters said, and placed his hand on her head. She moved under his touch like a cat being stroked.

Ruby thought that in the blaze of the real day Peters had lost some of the dazzle that the celestial light show had lent him. He was less deity and more man now. There was something almost of the dandy in his sharp white cuffs and the set of his collar. He touched his hair frequently, raking it back across his head. There was no denying his obvious physical attributes and yet, beneath his courtly, almost old-fashioned manner, despite the firm lines of his face, Ruby felt an absence of something.

'Reverend Peters,' she said, 'I was wondering if what we witnessed last night was something that would have been seen by other people. Other people outside of the community, I mean.'

Hester made a low hissing sound.

The Reverend's eyes swivelled round to Ruby. Just for a moment she thought she saw something in the glitter of his gaze that looked like anger, but when he spoke it was in the most conciliatory of tones.

'When you have been here longer, Ruby, you will understand more. It takes time to recognise the prize we are striving for.'

'I only meant that the sky stretches further than the patch over the community,' Ruby said, unwilling to give way. There was something in him, some knot of hardness she wanted to push against.

'Ruby! Do not speak to The Beloved so!'

Hester looked as if she was going to expire with mortification. Her face had turned a deep pink.

'I take no offence. A mind that explores options is a mind I can work with,' Peters said. 'I will leave you now to enjoy the rest of the festivities,' and he wheeled off to stop at another group of worshipers.

'I do not know what on earth I am going to do with you, Ruby!' Hester exclaimed sitting back down with a complaining squeak. 'You are quite out of control.'

'She is just being our Ruby,' Irene said, threading her arm through her sister's.

'Well, *our Ruby* should watch her tongue.'

Hester resumed her ingestion of the picnic, tipping her head back to suck in a sliver of rare beef.

'When he touched me, I could feel my heart move in my body,' she said, with her mouth full. 'I knew that when The Beloved came back I would feel transformed.'

Chapter 17

'There has been an incursion,' Jowler announced. 'A serious theft that requires immediate investigation.'

The chief constable steepled his plump digits. Philip, who had been up most of the night listening to his mother cough, felt a wave of weariness. Jowler's announcements usually led to hours of mind-numbingly pointless work. The man would not recognise a proper crime if it leapt out of the night and hit him on his fat head.

'The community in Yaxton has been the victim of a burglary. More than thirty pineapples have been stolen from the garden. Reverend Peters was good enough to come himself to inform me of it.'

'Pineapples?' Philip had no idea what a pineapple was but guessed at some kind of fruit.

'A large, fibrous fruit with a fountain of foliage at the top. Quite delicious, particularly with a slice or two of ham and some cherry brandy. The Reverend, an unconventional man, I will admit, but nevertheless impressive in his bearing and the owner of substantial amounts of land and property, also informed me that the villagers have been terrorising the inhabitants. Peering over the walls and … relieving themselves against it. Even … you know … on a couple of occasions … actually, passing…'

Jowler pursed his lips, his beady eyes shining with incredulity.

Philip tried his best not to smile. His superior's constant astonishment at the vagaries of human behaviour was his only slightly endearing quality.

'Well, the villagers of Yaxton view those living in the community with a certain amount of suspicion. It doesn't help that they are continually railed at by some of Peters' henchmen and told that they are bound for hell.'

'That is not an excuse for disgusting behaviour and now someone has taken it a step further and actually entered the community and committed a robbery. It seems the world has gone mad since the night when the sky lit up. There has been all manner of foul play. Thefts and fires and fights – and it is not just people who seem to have been taking a wrong turn. I heard from a colleague who works in Burnham-On-Sea that a number of small whales lost their bearings and ended up on the shore. Something that has never in living memory happened before. They are lying beached and rotting.'

Jowler wrung his hands as if trying to remove a layer of grime from them.

'I wonder how the robber who broke into the community got the fruit back over the wall,' Philip said. 'I expect they threw them over one by one to a waiting accomplice.'

'Don't stand around thinking about it, Hodge! I want action. Now. At once. I assured Peters we would get to the bottom of the matter swiftly. I would lay money on it being that runt, Balch. It has all the hallmarks of the wretched creature.'

Thomas Balch, a man of no fixed occupation who lived with his two boys in Wynch was a thorn in Jowler's ample side. Rumour had it that the man had stripped whole orchards, leaving them looking as if locusts had passed through. People said he could clear a hen coop better than any fox and gathered gold watches and bracelets from the folks at Bridgwater market as swiftly as the movement of a rake though grass. Much to Jowler's frustration, Balch had so far avoided retribution, always managing to prove he was elsewhere at the time of the alleged crimes.

'And Hodge – as well as discovering the fate of the pineapples, I want you to make regular visits to the walled community. Stand outside the inn. Walk around looking official. When the villagers see a man in uniform, even if it is only you, they might think twice. I am keen to keep on the right side of a man of the Reverend's evident worth.'

'You will be sure to let me know when he returns,' Philip said. Thomas Balch's son, Archie, nodded at him solemnly, his eyes huge in his narrow face, his small fists by his side as tight as they would have been the day he was born. It was hard to tell the child's age beneath the dirt that made his skin the same ashy colour as his shirt and trousers. Philip had a fair idea that the boy's father was lurking in an upstairs room of their cottage in Wynch, or perhaps in the barn on the other side of the field, but he didn't have the stomach for further investigation. There was something so desperately brave in the child's gaze that he couldn't bring himself to push him any further. His father was a thief, but perhaps Philip would be, too, if he had two boys to feed and only occasional paid work. He would come back when the boy wasn't there. Maybe the chief constable was right, and he didn't have the right sort of character for police work.

'A wrongdoing is a wrongdoing and should incur a penalty. There is no grey area, no space for feelings,' Jowler had said in response to Philip's remark that there were some convictions that would punish the innocent more than the miscreant. As far as Constable Hodge was concerned the grey area was all too evident. It was standing right in front of him, staring out of its silvery face.

'Tell your father, I will be back,' Philip said, and the boy gave another of his cautious nods. PC Hodge looked around the mean room for evidence of exotic fruit, but there was no food at all, even in the pot by the unlit fire. He sighed and extricated his bread and cheese and handed it to the boy, who hesitated for maybe three seconds before snatching it and placing it inside his shirt with the practised move of a person who had learned from a master.

The house next door to that of the Balch family was where he had placed the abandoned baby. The woman of the house had recently given birth to her own fourth child. Some impulse he didn't really understand made him stop and knock. A green-eyed toddler opened the door to him. The cottage which listed slightly and had moss growing across its roof, smelt of new leather and mould. When Philip went into the front room, Minnie, fifteen years old and the eldest child of the family, was working at her sewing machine and at the same time rocking Pearl with her foot. The child had been placed in a low cradle on the floor. From the mewling cries coming from above, it was clear that the other baby was currently the focus of attention.

Minnie's work as gloveress provided the bulk of the family's income. Her siblings helped as much as they could, organising the cut-leather shapes supplied by the factory into piles and parcelling up the completed pairs, but they were too young to do much. The mother took in babies and washing. Philip had never met the father, but he had to be present some of the time, if only to expand his family. Philip tried not to make judgements. He knew life was hard, but he took a dim view of missing fathers.

Minnie smiled at him, her pretty face prematurely crumpled around her eyes from her endless close work, often done in poor light in the winter.

'Come to see the baby?' she asked. 'She's as good as anything. Never cries. Not like the other one.' She jerked her head upwards.

Philip bent over the crib. Pearl, who was only a little over three months old, already had an alert look about her. She stared at Philip with dark blue eyes. He ventured a finger and was surprised when she took it in her shell-like fist.

'She's a quick one,' Minnie remarked. 'Already holding on to things.'

The soft down on the baby's dented head, and the folds of her neck, made Philip feel tenderly towards her. She was perfect and yet no one wanted her or even seemed to miss her. He thought it was a terrible shame. The child's face gave a tremor, and the corners of her tiny mouth turned up.

'She smiled at me!' he exclaimed, delighted.

'That's just wind,' Minnie said.

'Well, it's clear, she is being well looked after,' Philip said straightening up. 'Tell your mother I have been by. We will have to find the child a permanent home in a couple of months.'

He picked up one of the finished pairs of gloves. The stitching was even, and the gloves lay flat in his palm. In the little extra patch below the thumb there was a small crescent moon sewn in the same colour thread as the seams.

'I wonder that you have the time for such embellishments,' he said.

'I always put a little picture in the querk of the glove,' she said. 'So as I would know them as mine if I saw them again.'

'I'll be on my way then,' Philip said, and she nodded and bent once more to her work, twisting, and manipulating the leather as if she was wrestling with a phantom hand.

When he arrived home that evening, he found his mother lying on the floor. She had tripped across the corner of the hearth and had been unable to get up. Her hands between his were cold and her breath came in shallow gasps. He called the doctor and between them they took her upstairs and settled her in bed.

'Her chest is troubling,' the doctor said. 'I do not like her colour, either.'

The words were delivered with a final sounding click of the clasp on his bag, which Philip took to mean that it was unlikely his mother would ever come downstairs again. He folded up her embroidery, trying to tame the length of it carefully so that it wouldn't get creased, and placed it by her side.

'I want you to rest and recover, Mother,' he said. His heart felt heavy. It was possible his mother would not now progress with her embroidery much beyond her eighteenth year of bread and a bee, and a sister called Clara whose name was always sewn with a little extra flourish on the tail of the 'a'.

Chapter 18

Since The Miracle of The Sacred Light, a new energy had consumed the community. Everyone worked harder and with more earnest attention. The daily gatherings on the lawn over which Reverend Peters presided, had taken on a louder and more fervent quality. The choir practised more often and later into the night. George marshalled his small group to take on elaborate plans for landscaping the garden. It seemed to Ruby, that despite this change in mood and application, despite the apparent vigour with which the members of the community went about their business, a kind of bewilderment and anxiety was also in evidence. Amidst the electric atmosphere of bustle and devotion there was a sense that the community members felt something approaching. Something they were not yet prepared for.

There were other signs that all was not well. The cows were not producing as much milk, and what milk there was, had a vaguely sour taste. The homing pigeons, who were the pride and joy of the saint who manged the farm, had flown off and never returned. In the garden, plants that should have just been reaching their peak, had bloomed, and withered almost as soon as they had come into flower. She wondered whether all this was connected in some way to the lights in the sky. Had the sun itself changed its nature?

Crossing the hallway on her way out to the orchid house, Ruby heard voices coming from the Reverend's office. She stopped by the closed door and listened. She heard Peters' smooth voice and Brother Martin's rougher, louder tone.

'How many more are joining?' Martin asked.

'A mother and daughter I spoke to in Bath are coming shortly, just as soon as their affairs are in order.'

'They have adequate means?'

Here, Ruby could not quite make out the Reverend's answer.

'We will need more and soon if you are to fulfil your vision. Our mission for salvation must not lose momentum,' Martin said.

'In a few months, the Hart sisters will be in an advantageous position.'

'Yes, we need to think carefully about future arrangements,' Martin replied. There was the sound of the clatter of glasses and a cupboard door being banged shut, so Ruby did not hear the words that followed, but something was said by Peters in a low tone and Martin laughed in response. More startling than hearing herself and Irene mentioned in the context of the money they were to inherit – Ruby had always understood that their place at the community had been bought – was the laugh itself. She could not imagine Martin, who she had never even seen smiling, making such a noise. There was about it a kind of uncontained, loose quality that chilled her. What were the arrangements the men were referring to? Did it involve their elevation to sainthood? But surely this would not be happening so soon. Some of the other community members had had to wait for much longer. She knew how much her companions longed for it. How, despite their piety and reticence, there was keen competition to impress The Beloved. To earn the right to be amongst his special army of the saved. There were times they jostled with each other to be chosen to do the small tasks that the Reverend had ordered, so that just for a few moments, they could be alone in his presence.

The thought that once sainthood was conferred on them they would be further entrenched into the community, hit her like a blow in her chest. She realised that all this time she had been hoping that their being there was somehow temporary. That their mother would come to her senses, or that someone would rescue them, although with no means at their disposal where would they go? She knew that the River Parrett would still be collecting its foaming debris and that the sails in the harbour would still be cracking and swelling in the wind, but such scenes seemed to be much further away than the five or six miles that divided them. It felt to her as if the bridge home had collapsed.

Still churning over these thoughts, Ruby went into the orchid house. Moisture ran down the glass and dripped in a steady rhythm onto the iron pathway. The smell of wet earth and vegetation was overlaid with a sweetness that was more marrow than floral, as if something corporeal had over-heated under the glass. George was digging out a large plant that had finished flowering and was showing nothing but spent nub ends. Ruby's, Hattie's, and Edith's job that day was to help him cut back some of the planting that had spread over the central avenue and was blocking the light from the lower growing specimens.

Edith was already hard at work and had sweat marks that reached down almost to the waist of her yellow dress. In the greenish light of the glasshouse, Hattie looked unwell. Ruby had been wary of engaging her in conversation ever since the episode in the night in case it provoked further distress. The women worked alongside in silence for a while, filling the wheelbarrow with cut vegetation and then taking it in turns to push it out to the bricked enclosure behind the barn, where the garden waste and vegetable leavings from the kitchen were kept in varying degrees of decomposition, the mounds still transitioning from plant to the rich, black mulch they would become, giving off a heat that Ruby could feel on her arms as she tipped the wheelbarrow of its contents.

'He is quiet, isn't he?' she said in an undertone to Edith, nodding her head in George's direction.

'We are not supposed to talk to each other more than what needs to be said,' Edith replied. 'Men and women, I mean. Women can talk together as much as we care to. In fact, The Beloved prefers it that we stay together in twos and threes. Safety in numbers, he says.'

'Being together is a protection from what?' Ruby asked straightening up and pouring herself a glass from the jug of water placed by the door. 'I can't imagine many people bold enough to challenge the dogs at the gate.'

'It is what The Beloved wants. He is the voice of God,' Edith said implacably.

'Who elected him to be so?'

Edith stopped her clipping and stared at Ruby, her little face drawn in fierce lines.

'You speak like an outsider,' she said.

'But where did he and his belief begin?'

'He was a doctor in London and felt his calling in the wards of the sick and dying. He was spoken to by God in the night. He describes it as the spirit entering his body and engulfing him. He was chosen.'

'And his doctrine of spiritual marriage. Did that come in the night, too?'

'I do not know where it came from. Only that it is the way we must live to ensure our salvation on the Day of Judgement. We repudiate the sins that might be committed by our flesh.'

Edith turned back to her work. The tips of her ears were red. Her uneven skin shone with perspiration. Ruby could feel the unpleasant trickle of her own in the small of her back. With a sigh that seemed to shake her whole body, Hattie took up the handles of the wheelbarrow and trundled heavily along the path to the exit.

'What special privileges does sainthood confer'? Ruby asked.

'You ask a lot of questions, Ruby. It might be better for you if you asked less.'

'I just want to know what it is that we are supposed to be striving for.'

'Sainthood confers immortality and the male saints form part of The Beloved's inner circle and are instrumental in making decisions about what happens in the community,' Edith said, and began poking at the earth with a trowel, loosening the compacted clods of earth with sharp, jabbing motions.

'So, you are saying that once we are made saints we will live forever?'

'Being a saint gives us the opportunity to live forever. If we continue on the right path and do not sin then we will be protected from death by our sainthood.'

'I have often thought that the definition of a sin is somewhat vague and depends on who is making the judgement,' Ruby said.

'I am not sure you have the makings of a true saint, Ruby,' Edith said, looking up at her with a frown. 'I feel there is too much resistance in you.'

For a while, the women continued to work without talking. The atmosphere in the glass house – its dripping noises and its heavy, foetid atmosphere made it seem as if they were enclosed in another world.

'You know my story, such as it is. Might I not know some of yours?' Ruby asked, as always unable to bear silence for extended periods of time. She was curious about the path that had led Edith to this place. Had she been converted the way Hester had, by a chance encounter?

'We are told not to dwell on the past,' Edith said in a low voice.

Ruby thought at first that the habit of discretion would prevail, but it seemed suddenly as if Edith wanted to unburden herself, because she started whispering in a tiny, feverish voice.

'There was a man,' she said, looking furtively around her, as if she thought they might be overheard.

'He ... he wasn't kind, and yet I was to marry him. He mocked my looks, my voice … everything. He said the blemishes on my skin signified that I was marked out. He said no one wanted me. I felt as if he was burying me with his words. Every day the burden of the earth grew greater, until I could barely breathe. He hurt me … in the night … after he had drunk and eaten, sitting at the table with my parents with a face as smooth and bright as a new penny, he would find me and when he did, he showed the other side of the coin. The one he didn't reveal to anyone else.'

'Did you marry him?' Ruby asked fascinated by the remote, almost blank look that had passed over her companion's face.

'I put a pillow over his face when he was drunk,' she said, stretching out her small, dirty hands, palms upwards, for Ruby's inspection. As if they were not part of her body and she was still surprised by what they had done. 'They thought he had choked in the night. They never found out that it was me who did it.'

Chapter 19

Ruby was in the sewing room when her sister's seizure came upon her. She had been admiring Irene's section of the embroidery. It stood out from the work of her companions as particularly fine – the veins and ribs and petioles of the leaf motif were picked out so carefully that they seemed almost to have the waxy surface of life. The pattern was similar to the wallpaper in the hall's corridors – it had the same twisted, sinewy quality. She wondered why its design had begun creeping across the main body of the canvas.

'Why have you not kept the leaf design just to the border as you intended?' she asked, and then Irene turned to her, and she saw the taking building in her sister's face. She put her arms around her and helped her gently to the floor.

'Whatever are you doing? Norah asked, looking up from her end of the tapestry.

'My sister has been taken unwell,' Ruby answered. Irene began to shudder slightly and her grip on Ruby's hand loosened. 'She needs air,' Ruby said, opening one of the windows.

'Why is she shaking like that?' Norah asked. She stood over Irene with her face agog. 'Has the devil taken her over?'

Sister Eloise put down the skein of silk she was winding and came over.

'Has this happened before?' she asked, her gentle face concerned.

'Yes, my sister suffers from an affliction.'

Ruby knelt by Irene, until she saw the movements in her body begin to slow and then stop. Sister Angela had been out and returned with a small basin of water and a soft cloth and knelt on the other side of Irene.

'May I?' she asked Ruby, and on receiving a nod, proceeded to wipe Irene's forehead with gentle strokes and soft, reassuring murmurs. Ruby was grateful for her calm, unshocked reaction.

'What is all this commotion about?' Martin came into the room. Ruby stood up and tried to shield her sister from his gaze. The habit of protection was deeply ingrained in her.

'Has she had another taking?' he asked, moving beyond Ruby, and standing looking down at Irene with a curiously avid expression.

'What do you mean?' Ruby asked, astonished by his question. How can he have known about Irene's infirmity? This was the first time it had happened since they had been at the community. As a family they had always been at pains to keep the truth of it to themselves.

'Your mother told The Beloved about it. She wanted to be sure that your sister's incapacity would not disqualify you all from sainthood. There are many people who consider such takings as a sign of sin.'

Ruby understood at that moment that Hester had given more than their money to Peters. She had given all three of them over, whole, to do with as he wished. The strength of this new devotion of Hester's had taken precedence over all previous discretion and loyalty. What else might she have told him? If she had so readily disclosed this secret about Irene, a matter that she had always said was to be kept strictly amongst themselves, what had she told Peters about her other daughter? That she was difficult? Hard to love? Perhaps her mother had witnessed her shame and told him about it.

'I believe she suffered a fit on the way to the community,' Martin continued. 'Mrs Hart said she conjured up a vision of The Miracle of The Sacred Light. She foresaw the same brightness, even the same singing of the birds.'

'Irene does not foretell the future,' Ruby said. 'Her seizures are the result of a condition. A medical condition.'

'I imagine that what you know about medicine is somewhat limited, Ruby.'

The dismissive tone in his voice and the absorbed way he was looking at Irene, unsettled her. There was some hunger in it that she did not understand.

Irene opened her eyes and Ruby knelt beside her again. She didn't want her sister to be exposed to the gaze of this man when she was at her most helpless.

'Ruby... It was cold. The same cold I felt before, but this time someone was there.'

'Be still now. Don't tire yourself with talking.'

'Let me hear what she is saying,' Martin said, bending closer.

Ruby looked at Irene and shook her head slightly and Irene looked back, her eyes wide.

'My sister needs to rest. She should be taken to her room straight away,' Ruby said as firmly as she was able. There was something about Martin that suggested he would not much like being contradicted.

She thought at first that he would prevent her, but then he nodded at Trench, who was hovering by the door.

'Help Ruby to get her sister back to their quarters. You go too, Sister Angela,' he said, and left the room.

Between them, they got Irene to her feet, Trench taking most of her weight.

'She's as light as a bird,' Trench said.

He wanted to lift her up in his arms and run with her. He wanted to put her in a goldfinch's woollen nest where no one would find her. He wanted to keep her safe so that her shine would not be worn off. In his head he had given her the name of Goldie since she was precious like the birds.

Later, when Irene had at last fallen asleep – she was usually exhausted after a fit, but this one had made her restless – and the community had subsided into silence, Ruby sat at her desk trying to write a letter to Nancy. The words she might have used before seemed to no longer be available to her. Her old life had already retreated and taken on the aspect of a dream. She was marooned. She did not even know exactly what the world outside the wall looked like. She had only had a quick glimpse of the village when she had arrived. How could she properly describe the community? She had no news of the kind she had shared before – no gossip about who was looking at who across the dinner table. No descriptions of new hats or shoes. No common ground. Only this place where time stood still and where she did not belong. She thought perhaps it was not completely new, this inability to say what she was truly feeling. Perhaps she had always stayed on the light, safe surface of things. She took up her pen again.

I ran after him, Nancy. I did not care who was watching me or what they might think. I could not stop myself.

She scratched the words out. It was impossible to say such things. Nancy would understand as little of that as she would of Ruby's fear at the way Martin had looked at Irene when she was having her seizure.

Chapter 20

The next morning, they were summoned to Reverend Peters' office for what was known in the community as the 'Undertaking'– an interview designed to establish whether or not a person wanted to begin their journey towards sainthood.

As Ruby descended the stairs, followed by her mother and Irene, she was beset by an almost overwhelming sense of fear. Her hands were clammy, and she felt nauseous. She thought she might collapse. She looked at the Hall's front door just ahead of her. What would happen if she simply opened it and walked out into the world beyond? Could she run fast and far enough to leave it all behind? She found she could not take another step. She stopped so suddenly that Hester almost toppled over.

'For heaven's sake, girl!' her mother exclaimed, clutching the banister. 'What did you do that for?'

'Why don't we delay our decision, Mother?' Ruby said. 'Just for a while.'

She hated to plead for anything, but her terror had weakened her. She tried to reach for her mother's hand, but Hester batted her away.

'Why would we do that?' Hester asked, staring at her in astonishment. 'This is our chance to live forever.'

'No one lives forever,' Ruby said. She thought of her father – the way he used to take her on his back when she was a child and run across their garden. She could still feel the happy clutch of her legs around him and the almond smell of the pomade in his hair.

'Once we are saints, we will,' Hester said, and pushed past her.

'We will still be the same, Ruby. The same you and the same me, regardless of what we are called,' Irene said.

She tugged gently on Ruby's arm. She was not concerned about whether she was a saint or not, only that once this status was conferred, they would have a mandate to stay. She was untouchable here. She'd had a taking and it seemed that her infirmity had been seen and accepted. She had thought that at the very least, Reverend Peters would have questioned her, but there had been no such request. As she had hoped, there was evidently a tolerance here that did not exist in the real world.

'Let us run away,' Ruby said. 'Let us just go, you and I, Irene. Let Mother become a saint if she wants to, but not us. I heard them talking. I think they have plans for us that we know nothing of.'

'I want to stay, Ruby,' she said. 'It is better for me in here, than it is outside.'

Her sister was looking at her so pleadingly that Ruby reluctantly took her proffered hand. She felt helpless. What choice did she really have about where to be?

In his office, Peters sat behind his desk, with Miriam standing by his side.

'This is an important day,' he announced, and placed his hands, which Ruby had noticed were always fastidiously clean, flat on his desk as if he was about to stand up, although he remained seated.

'Indeed, indeed, an extraordinary day,' Hester tweeted. She was always skittish in his presence, like a creature trying to establish the parameters of its enclosure.

'Once you have been selected to be a saint, when the transition will take place will be at my discretion; it is tantamount to a vow to remain with us forever,' he said.

The Taking of Irene Hart

Ruby thought that her legs might give way beneath her.

'Do people never leave?' she asked, earning a glare from her mother and an assessing looking from Miriam.

Miriam thought the eldest girl was one to watch. She was irreverent and swift to judgement and as hard on others as she was on herself. She was most unlike her delicate sibling who seemed so insubstantial that you could almost forget she was there at all, until she turned that limpid gaze on you and then you saw her strength. The mother was a goose. Miriam had met many like her in her years with Peters. She recognised the blank dazzle in Hester's face as relief at finding something she could believe in without having to earn that faith through sacrifice, or indeed any more complicated thought than she would expend over the choosing of a dress or the arrangement of her hair. She was of the type who was adept at finding justifications for her small acts of meanness and her self-indulgence. Miriam had seen the way she diminished Ruby; tried to repress the girl's fire with quenching coughs and dampening asides. She was also always last from the table and was already visibly plumping up on the farm's cream and cheese on which she gorged noisily. Miriam thought she would perhaps ask Reverend Peters if he might have a word with them all about intemperance.

'Those that leave have failed in their endeavour,' Miriam said. 'Everyone here is free to go should they wish to do so. This is not a prison. We offer salvation. Many people come here because they have lost their way or because they have been denied the right to lead full and productive lives, unburdened by judgement.'

'Do you wish to become a saint? To live by my teachings. To repudiate the sins of the flesh. To listen to God through me?' Peters asked.

His voice was at its deepest and most solemn. This is the voice he uses when he wants most to sell something, Ruby thought, noting the way his words seemed to fill him up as he spoke, so that he appeared to swell in size. It was like a magician's trick. Ruby had a wild desire to laugh. Perhaps he could pull rainbows out of his pockets and coins from his ears, too. She remembered how she had felt when she had first seen him. He had mesmerised her in some way then. How else to explain the feelings of elation and distress she had experienced at the time? Had his influence on her simply been part of his act? She knew he was only a man, but there was still a part of her, a part she found hard to repress, that felt the force of his authority.

'We do. We most sincerely do. On this day and on every day. Forever and forever more.' Hester could barely get the words out in her excitement. Ruby thought that her mother was looking at The Beloved as if she wanted to eat him.

'Very well. I have to tell you, that it is possible you will not all become saints at once,' Peters said. Everyone has their own journey towards sainthood. Some achieve it more quickly than others. It often depends on the depth of their understanding of our mission.'

His eyes met Ruby's. She saw a flicker of what might have been censure there, and then thought she must have imagined it, because he gave her one of his rare smiles. It made him seem as if he thought there was some understanding between them. For a moment he appeared almost approachable. The smile disappeared as suddenly as it had come.

'There are some that are held back by their desires,' he said, and this time there was no mistaking the antagonism in his tone. He sees my guilt, Ruby thought. He sees straight through me. The thought made her shiver.

'Of my daughters, Irene is the one most likely to deserve sainthood,' Hester said. She had started to look concerned when the Reverend had intimated that their passage to immortality might be delayed, and now spoke fast, with an eager look on her face. 'She is a most *spiritual* person. She has special powers, you know.'

Irene made a sound of objection and then fastened her eyes to the floor. Ruby felt shame flood her. Their mother was trying to use Irene's infirmity as a bargaining chip. She hated the way Hester's hands fluttered around her as if in supplication. She tried

The Taking of Irene Hart

not to speak. She knew it would stand against her if she did, but she could not help herself.

'It might be, Mother, that Irene does not want to be made a saint. Have you actually asked her? We do not know, after all, exactly what comes with the supposed elevation.'

Peters stood up behind his desk. He bristled with a fierce energy.

'We will talk more in the days to come. This is only the first stage. I suggest that you spend some time thinking about how you might behave in a way more befitting a sister, Ruby. It is your job as the elder to ensure the very best for Irene.'

The Reverend's words brought a hot flush to Ruby's face.

'I have always taken the greatest of care of Irene!' she said, but even as she spoke, she felt herself faltering. Did he know of her perfidy? It was not possible, surely. He had no access to her thoughts and her longings. Believing otherwise was a kind of madness.

Miriam ushered the women out. Hester had taken hold of Irene's arm and she turned her head determinedly away from Ruby.

'There are times Ruby, when I wish I had never had you,' she said.

Hurt and angry after their interview with Peters, Ruby felt the need to escape the confines of the house. Irene was happy to remain inside reading, and her mother had gone to the farm. Hester had developed a fondness for the goats they kept there and had taken to visiting them daily.

It was Sunday, and so most of the community members were either in their rooms or engaged in a Reverend Peters endorsed activity. Some of the men were playing cricket in the big field behind the hall. A group of women were having their weekly dancing session on the large rotating stage in the meeting room.

When Ruby glanced through the window as she passed by, she saw them lined up around the edge of this edifice with their arms linked, their feet placed at right angles, their heads all turned in the same direction. They looked like some sort of a toy.

She heard her name called out and turned to see Edith and Angela approaching.

'There you are!' Angela exclaimed. 'We are going for a walk to the lake with some sandwiches and a slice or two of Sister Rachel's sponge cake. We have just been to your room to ask if you would like to accompany us.'

'Yes, thank you,' said Ruby, though uncertain.

The women walked past the farm where Ruby caught a glimpse of her mother, sitting on a stool, surrounded by goats, then across two meadows and on into the wood. The trees grew close together, forming a thick canopy, and the light fell dimly on the narrow path that wound its way through. Ruby was startled by the quick motion of a red squirrel that shot up a nearby trunk and then stopped, quivering, in a cleft between branches. It was astonishingly vivid. It burned in the gloom, like a creature from a fairytale. At their feet, the roots were spread so lavishly, it was impossible to tell which tree they belonged to. In the spaces between their tangle, delicate white flowers that Ruby thought might be wild orchids, stood in spiked clusters.

She might have passed by without noticing anything if she had not heard a voice. It came from a little distance away. She was walking slightly behind her two companions and stopped and looked to her right which was the direction she thought the voice had come from. Here the light was a little brighter, as if the trees were less dense. Why she stepped off the path, she could not say, only that the voice with its tone of command seemed out of place in the quiet of the woods. She pushed her way through the branches and across some fallen trunks. Although she was still hidden by the trees, she had a clear view of a small clearing. The ground was somewhat hollow, as if it had been dug out to provide a sheltering rim. Hattie was standing in the centre of this depression. She was dressed in a white, high-necked gown and her hair was wet and hung down her back; she held a large stone, circular in shape and pierced with a hole wide enough to get your hand through. Ruby could see that Hattie could barely keep her grip on it. Her whole body was shaking with the effort of keeping it elevated. She buckled and it looked for a moment as if she might drop her burden.

'Do not let your weakness master you. STAND UP!'

She had been so focused on Hattie, that Ruby had not seen Martin. He was sitting above the hollow on a trunk of a tree, leaning back against one of its protruding branches, his legs spread wide, his arms crossed. He had the relaxed air of a man who had simply stopped on a walk to have a rest and take in the view. On hearing his words, Hattie forced herself upright and lifted the stone. Ruby could see the effort this cost her in the desperate clutch of her hands and the slide of her bare feet. She could barely get purchase on the ground.

Ruby heard one of her companions calling out and Martin looked in her direction. His previously relaxed body was suddenly alert. She was not doing anything wrong, but the thought that Martin might find her there, spying on him filled her with fear. If she retreated back to the path she would surely be seen. Martin got to his feet and looked as if he was going to come and investigate, but then the red squirrel she had seen earlier appeared in the tree she was hiding behind. It ascended the trunk. She could hear the scratch of its claws. It stopped on the end of one of the branches and began chirping. Then its call changed to a kind of mewling, warning sound that was louder than Ruby would have imagined such a small creature could make. Martin looked up at it and then turned back to his seat. As soon as he was facing the other direction, Ruby crept back to the path.

Edith and Angela were waiting for her a little distance away and she walked quickly to catch up with them.

'Wherever did you get to?' Edith asked. 'We thought you were behind us and then you disappeared!'

'I saw something in the clearing,' Ruby said. She was out of breath and could feel her heart hammering in her chest. 'Hattie was there, dressed in white, holding an enormous stone and Brother Martin ... Brother Martin was telling her she had to keep holding it up, even though it was heavy, and she was struggling.'

'It is always best to keep to the path,' Edith said.

'But what did it mean? Why was he making her do that?' Ruby asked.

'Hattie is being prepared for sainthood,' Angela said.

'Will we all have to undergo such tests?' Ruby asked, thinking of Irene standing as Hattie had done, trying to hold up such a great weight. Her sister would not be able to bear it.

'The nature of the tests vary from person to person. Such things are designed by The Beloved and only he knows the pattern they must make. You have twigs and leaves in your hair, Ruby!' Angela said laughing and plucking at Ruby's head.

'But she was so distressed!' Ruby said. 'She was shaking as if she was cold.'

'Sainthood has to be earned and Hattie fights all manner of demons. Come now, forget it. Let us go on to the lake while the sun is still shining,' Angela said.

'Surely Sister Eloise was not made to do such a thing' Ruby exclaimed. 'What tests were you subjected to, Sister Angela?'

'It could be that Sister Eloise had a less problematic journey,' Edith said. 'She is so good, she was born to be a saint.'

Angela linked her arm through Ruby's. 'Sister Rachel's cake is calling to me through the basket,' she said.

Only a little further on and the wood opened out onto the lake. The women walked a little around its edge, until they found some flat stones. Edith spread out the blanket and they sat down. The view was like a picture in a story book – turn the page and there it was – sky, clear blue, grass, paint-pot green, and swans drifting so slowly on the surface of the water they seemed fixed there. Despite the balminess of the afternoon and the chatter of her companions,

Ruby's unease still lingered. In their smooth, untroubled faces Ruby found a kind of heedlessness that disturbed her. Were they not even a little worried about what Hattie was suffering only such a short distance from where they were sitting? Did nothing penetrate their apparent equanimity? She thought of Hattie's anguished face and of the strange, almost savage look on Edith's when she had told Ruby about what she had done to her betrothed. Perhaps they all had two faces. The one they showed around the community, and quite another when they thought themselves unobserved. Maybe they hid their true feelings, just as she did.

'How are you settling in, Ruby?' Angela asked, unpacking the basket. 'Are you pleased that you are here amongst us?'

Ruby had been at the opening of the station at Bridgwater and had stood in the crowd on the platform to witness the arrival of the first train. Its bellow and smoke had made her feel both aghast and exhilarated. She had thought of it moving on, through the town and on to the next, blundering through valleys and curving its heft around lakes and woods, unstoppable, like a great beast being chased by its own tail as the track fell away from under it. When she glimpsed it in the distance, as it moved towards the Mendip Hills, she had felt a shiver of longing to be taken. That would never happen now. The train and everything that she might have seen from its windows was the world they had eschewed.

'I am not sure exactly how I feel,' Ruby said, wary of sharing her misgivings. The others were fervent in their belief that they were where they were supposed to be. Ruby did not think they would understand her feeling that life was passing her by.

'It takes a while to truly understand the full meaning of what we are doing here. It crept up on me slowly, until I was full of the glory of it. To the glory of eternal life,' Angela said, her peachy complexion shining in the sun. She took a dainty bite of her sandwich.

'When you talk of eternal life,' Ruby said, 'do you mean the eternal life afforded by heaven? The place allotted to the good after they die?'

'On the Day of Judgement, whenever that will be, those outside the walls will die, but those who are saints will live on,' Edith said.

'But surely, we will age and become infirm and even the most devout cannot hope to avoid what the evidence shows us. We wither and perish. It is what science, and the church tells us.'

'God will strike the sinning world but keep us in the community safe in His grace. We will be like an ark,' Edith said, her mouth full of sponge cake.

'In time, Ruby, you too will understand,' Angela said, and then got to her feet. 'How about a paddle?' She kicked off her shoes and swiftly rolled down her stockings. In a matter of seconds, she had hoiked up her dress and was knee deep in the water.

'Do try it! It feels wonderful,' she said, smiling.

Edith gigglingly followed suit, tucking the hem of her dress into her bloomers and squealing as the cold water met her thin thighs. The women's combined exhortations forced Ruby in, too, and soon they were splashing each other and laughing. Edith lost her footing and ended up totally submerged and had to be dragged, coughing and spluttering, to the shore. Exhausted by her exertions, Edith lay flat on the grass.

'Why, Edith, your modesty is quite gone!' Angela exclaimed gleefully, plucking at the folds of her companion's dress which had wrapped themselves around her slight body like a second skin.

Later, as they walked back across the fields, feeling the residue of sun and water on them and the power and pleasure of being young, it seemed possible, even to Ruby, that living forever might indeed be a possibility.

Chapter 21

'Have you seen Hattie?' Miriam asked Ruby who was washing her hands at the kitchen sink, trying to get the soil from beneath her nails.

'No, she hasn't been in the orchid house all day, Sister Miriam,' Ruby answered. 'It has only been Edith and I.'

'She is not in her room, either,' Miriam said.

'Perhaps she has joined the others in the sewing room or is in the library. Hattie tends to disappear. She did it only the other day. I turned around to speak to her and she was gone,' Ruby said. She was always provoked to talk more than usual in Miriam's presence, as if her chatter would show her to be amenable, but she knew it had the opposite effect. Miriam had a habit of looking at her closely as if inspecting her face for smudges and wrongdoing.

'Hattie has hands like trowels and has never been known to pick up a book,' Miriam said, as if she thought Ruby was trying to trick her.

'I don't know then,' Ruby said lamely.

'I am watching you, Ruby. I think you have a bent towards secrecy,' Miriam said ominously. Ruby thought it was entirely possible that Miriam had powers of perception that went far beyond the usual. It was as if she could smell guilt as powerfully as she sniffed out the flowers that had been standing too long in water, and sheets that had not been pounded sufficiently.

'She is probably lurking in a corner somewhere. I have tried to cheer her up, but Hattie is determined to be sad,' Angela said.

She was at the kitchen table, vigorously flattening some pastry with a rolling pin, lifting it, and turning it with quick, deft motions, raising flour around her in puffs so that it looked like plumes of breath on a cold morning.

'Well, please let me know if you see her,' Miriam said, lingering at the table and watching Angela work. 'You are getting very skilled, Sister,' she said approvingly, as Angela lifted the pastry off the table and laid it on top of a meat filled dish and plucked the edges with nimble fingers.

Miriam reflected on how very far Angela had come since her arrival at the community five years before. Reverend Peters had found her wandering around Bridgwater, half naked and dazed and unable even to string a sentence together. They still hadn't been able to establish exactly what had happened to her, but the old bruises and the new ones mottling her arms and legs had told their own story, as had the way the girl used to flinch every time anyone came too close. It had taken Miriam days to persuade her into a bath and even longer to cajole her into sharing a meal with them at the table. Miriam took pride in the way she had been able to chafe her back to life with each rub of a warm towel, each kind word that had slowly restored the light to her eyes. Restoration was what she did best. It was due to her efforts that the community worked in the way that it did. She had cured the roses in the garden of their blight, set the silver gleaming, schooled the choir in the purity of their voices, monitored the souls of each and every person who lived there. Sister Angela was a living testament to her efforts. The saint had journeyed from abandonment to belonging and was now so full of God's grace that it shone from her. There were times, when seeing Angela going about her business in such a purposeful way, that Miriam was assailed by an old desire, beaten back and largely dormant, but felt occasionally, like weak sun on her skin.

'I will leave you to your work. I have much to do,' she said, in a tone of voice that suggested that they had been the ones delaying her.

Ruby poured herself a glass of water from the jug and sat down at the kitchen table, where Angela had begun work on the pastry for a second pie.

'Is Sister Miriam right, Ruby? *Do* you have a bent towards secrecy?' Angela asked, looking at her with a smile.

'She is wrong. I am an open book,' Ruby replied, taking a long drink of water.

'Secrets have no place here. The Beloved knows all. He can see into our hearts.'

Ruby thought of the moment in the office when Peters had looked at her as if he knew what lay under her skin. She bent her head and traced the patterns of knife marks on the table. She had a secret that she had never shared with anyone. Nobody but William knew how she had behaved that day at his house. The day when he had seen Irene fall and turned his heart against her. Caring nothing for her sister's humiliation and abandonment and seeing only her advantage, she had run after him. *Don't go, stay for me*, she had said to him and touched his arm. *I care for you more than I can say. Attend to your sister*, he had replied, looking at her in such a way that she had felt her body grow hot under his hard eyes. *I have none of her weakness*, she had said, pleading, not yet ashamed enough to let him go. *You have none of her strength, either*, he had said, and she had felt anger then and the creep of jealousy, bile-coloured and warm, winding its way around her.

'Well, if our leader can see into my heart, he would see nothing more than its ordinary beating,' she said lightly.

'Hattie is still missing,' Ruby said to Irene that night, as they were getting ready for bed. 'Miriam has searched everywhere for her.'

'Maybe she has run away,' Irene answered. 'I believe community members do from time to time. Sometimes their relatives come and claim them back and they have little say in the matter.'

'Perhaps she has, although she is an unlikely candidate for escape. She is bent on the path towards sainthood. I told you that in her room late at night and then again in the woods, she was undergoing what Edith and Angela call tests, although they seem to me to be more like punishments. Surely, you do not want to expose yourself to such things, Irene. They seem to me to be strange and unnatural.'

'They say that those who leave the community and give up the prospect of sainthood, immediately become sinners,' Irene said. She was dipping the tips of her fingers, which were always sore after a day of sewing, in witch hazel to sooth them.

'Do you believe this to be true? Surely you do not. Was I a sinner before I entered the gates and would be so again if I left?'

Churches for Ruby had never been much more than places for imposed reflection. She had been known to quail at the thought of hell when its sulphurous prospect was delivered particularly vividly by the vicar and coincided with a sense of her own shortcomings, but she had never thought of herself as truly bad. She thought that there was even a measure of goodness in her. Had she not always put Irene first? After all, she had given everything up and come to the community because she would not leave her behind.

'They all seem so sure, don't they?' asked Ruby, drawing the brush through her hair as she sat at the mirror, thinking, not for the first time how much better it would be if her mouth was not quite so wide and her brows so heavy. She disliked this vanity in herself, but couldn't master it.

'It would be wonderful to believe, really believe that our journey has only just begun,' Irene said softly, taking her fingers out of the liquid and wiping them dry. 'I think there are many worse things to be than a saint. There is sense that we are all the same and share the same endeavour. There is a power in that.'

'It seems to me that Peters and his inner circle are the ones with the power. Everyone else behaves as if they have no agency at all. They are simply waiting to be told what to do.'

'There is peace in letting go of all the things that troubled us in the outside world,' Irene said, unbuttoning her bodice. Her shoulders gleamed. She was so very beautiful, and since being at the community it seemed to Ruby she had become even more so. The little frown that had sometimes marked her forehead was seldom in evidence now. Ruby remembered the way she had thought Hester less hunched, smoothed out in some way after her first sighting of the Reverend. It felt to Ruby as if she was being left behind. Her mother and her sister seemed to be adapting to their new life. It was only Ruby that remained as she always had been.

'How is the embroidery developing?' asked Ruby, changing the subject since it was making her anxious.

'Sister Angela has been charged with reading *The Song of Solomon* aloud to us as an encouragement. She says it is intended to inspire our work. It is full of the most peculiar things,' said Irene, slipping into bed. 'It is supposed to be from the Bible, but I've never heard it read in any church I have been to.'

'What do you mean?'

'It is a poem about love. There is a lot about gazelles and stags on a mountain of spices and—' Irene broke off and started giggling.

'What are you laughing about?'

Irene put her hand to her mouth and spoke through her fingers.

'There was something about myrrh lying between a woman's breasts, which looked like twin fauns.'

'Fauns?' Ruby exclaimed. 'I suppose in profile they might be described as such.'

Irene looked at Ruby and started laughing again.

'And a bit about lovers entering locked gardens and tasting fruit,' she said, and both the women exploded into mirth. They laughed so hard that Ruby thought she would never be able to stop. Her body ached with the convulsions of it. The old Irene seemed restored to her, and Ruby felt the relief of this. Each time they subsided into hiccupping silence, one or other of them would start up again, until they laughed themselves still and fell asleep at last.

Chapter 22

'She was found where?' Miriam asked, sitting down at the desk suddenly as if she could no longer quite trust her legs to hold her up. She looked terribly pale. It seems she has a heart after all, Philip thought, for all her attempts to disguise the fact.

'In an orchard a little way from here,' Philip said, looking above Miriam at the painting of Reverend Peters standing on top of a strangely shaped mountain. The man looked foolish in his archaic robes and with his all-conquering stance. In the matter of faith, Philip had always placed his trust in what he could see in front of him, rather than what lay beyond. It was perhaps the real reason why he had never ventured further than this small area of Somerset. Despite his incredulity that Reverend Peters could have become the object of such veneration, it was becoming clear to him, after spending a little time in the community, that anyone could be whatever they chose to be. He wondered why this same rule did not extend to himself.

'She used a red cord. The man who guards the door, George, I believe he is called, showed me round. I discovered there is one missing from the chapel curtains,' he said, unwilling to spare Miriam the details. He was still smarting from his banishment to the pantry.

'How dreadful,' Miriam said, so softly that he could barely hear her. She touched the birthmark on her face as if she was trying to trace her way back to something familiar.

'Are you sure it is her?'

'She had a note in the pocket of her dress,' he said. 'I recognised her from my previous visit, but the letter confirms her identity.'

'What did it say?' Miriam asked as if she did not really want to know. He took the piece of paper from his pocket and laid it on the desk in front of her.

I have lost the chance to enter the gates of eternal life.
There is nothing in this world for me now.

Hattie

'And this was all there was?' she asked, looking at him at last.

'There was also a note pinned to the bodice of her dress, with the word "saint", written in ink and then crossed out. Have you any idea why she would have done such a thing?'

His question seemed to rouse her to some approximation of her previous superciliousness. She squared her shoulders.

'I have no idea at all,' she said. 'It seems she must have lost her mind to commit such a grievous sin.'

It was important to try and keep the ship steady. She had seen the policeman furtively stealing radishes from the kitchen garden when he had first arrived. She had been tempted to bang on her window to make him jump – it would have amused her to expose his theft and catch him at a disadvantage. She wasn't fooled for a minute by the polite incline of his head, nor his studiously abstracted manner. He knew nothing, understood less and yet he was ready to force his way in and tarnish their guarded beauty. They had built something worth having. A place that offered protection for herself and for others. 'You can't lock yourself away', Emily, her dearest love, had said, holding Miriam's hand as if she was dangling from the side of a cliff, her skin patched red from crying. 'I can't bear the thought of you hiding from the world because of me.' It was *a long time ago, but she could still remember the way pain had scraped away at the inside of her as she had walked away for the last time. 'At least they won't have won', Miriam had said to her. 'At least I will have some peace.'*

'Were you aware of her evident unhappiness?' Philip asked, and she was brought back to herself and the importance of not letting the fissures widen.

'The last time I saw her, she was exactly as she always was. She was not a woman given to merriment and she was never talkative, but I thought her quite contented.'

'Had she formed any particular attachments?'

'Her attachment was to us, to her family,' Miriam said. Even though she seemed to have regained her usual poise, Philip thought he heard a note of pleading in her voice, as if she was trying to convince both herself and him of something.

'Are there relatives that I should inform?'

'As far as I know, Hattie had no one other than us.'

The office door opened, and a tall, russet-haired man walked in. Philip had not seen him before and wondered where he had been when he had talked to everyone during his previous visit.

'This is Brother Martin,' Miriam said, now fully back on her guard. She rose to her feet. The other man inclined his head slightly in Philip's direction.

'Who else knows of this business?' he asked without preamble. 'Have any of those mongrels at the inn got wind of it?'

'This is a very small village and there are many people keen to find something to pin their prejudices on,' Philip said. 'A suicide in their midst is bound to shock and distress people, especially so when the person was living amongst the so-called saved.'

'This has nothing to do with us,' Martin said. 'All we can do is offer safety and consolation. If people choose to reject the advantages they have been given, it is no fault of ours.'

'And yet, you must surely feel some regret that one of your own has ended her life in this way?' Philip said.

'She stopped being one of our own, when she chose to countenance death,' Martin said.

'If I may say, sir, that shows more than a little lack of sympathy.'

He had seen dead people before, even a couple that had met violent ends, but the sight of Hattie's long body hanging from the tree had distressed him more than he would have imagined. It was the solitary nature of her death that affected him the most. The thought that she must have walked out of the community alone and kept walking until she found a place where she could be confident that she wouldn't be discovered, made him intensely sad. How lonely the night must have felt to her and how resolute her intention must have been. He remembered the way her childish shoes had lain discarded in the grass at a happy angle, as if she had kicked them off to feel the cool dampness on her stockinged feet. As if, just for a moment, there had been joy.

He saw Miriam glance at Brother Martin who had removed himself from the conversation and was standing by a large open drawer in which lines of orchids, pressed and labelled, lay under glass. There was something strange in the pair's arrogant rudeness and lack of feeling. He thought perhaps it was the way they always spoke to people who were not of their clan; but underneath the bluster he sensed something almost furtive about their behaviour. He had felt it in Miriam's involuntary glance in Martin's direction and the way she pulled at the brooch at her neck. Martin's too-studious perusal of the specimen chest also struck an odd note. Philip was almost certain that they knew more than they were willing to admit. That did not mean they had anything to do with Hattie's death, and yet it made him wonder.

'It is not your place, Constable, to say what does, and what does not deserve our sympathy,' Miriam said. 'You have done all that you needed to do by informing us of the situation, the matter is now in our hands. I will escort you out.'

The Taking of Irene Hart

As he passed a greenhouse, Philip caught a glimpse of Ruby, her head stretched upwards, her long, white throat exposed, her hands busy amongst the foliage. But for his icy companion, he would have stopped and talked to her. It was just possible that she might have heard something about Hattie. Perhaps even been aware of the woman's state of mind. He thought there would be little those dark eyes of hers didn't register, which was something he knew would not play to his advantage. Philip Hodge had few illusions about himself or his place in the world. He knew his coat that was worn under the arms, and his still untrimmed hair, were unlikely to provoke the admiration he wanted from her. She deserved someone altogether finer than a local constable with nothing much to offer other than a small house with damp walls, a horse who generated an excess of gas, and a stubborn personality that wearied even him.

Chapter 23

Although those who were not yet saints were not generally permitted in the chapel, Ruby, Irene, and Hester had been invited to witness a Ceremony of Taking. This was when someone officially became a saint, a much-anticipated day, about which the community members talked with great longing, as if speaking of a distant and wonderful land.

When they entered the chapel door, Ruby stopped still with astonishment. The building bore no resemblance to the stark arches and simple oak of the churches she was accustomed to. Apart from the wooden pews, which were arranged at the back of the room, nothing else was familiar. A wide plum-coloured Persian carpet covered the floorboards and red damask curtains hung at the windows. Along one wall stood a scarlet velvet sofa littered with coral-coloured cushions. Amid the easy chairs and antimacassars, stood a pile of hymn books and ornate candelabra. Two of the high lancet windows were filled with gaudy stained glass, the other two bore Reverend Peters' crest of a lion standing on a bed of roses, flanked by a lamb and a dove. In front of the altar, almost hiding it from view, was a billiard table, with the cues neatly lined up in a rack on the wall. In the centre of all was a lectern, carved with The Beloved's motif and bearing the words –

'All Hail, Holy Love!'
This was not the spartan self-denying place of worship that Ruby knew. The chapel felt like the hidden centre of something, and its crimson, secret richness was like a beating heart. Ruby had a sudden panicked impulse to retreat – to close the door on this strange place where the focus didn't seem to be on prayer, or at least no prayers that Ruby was familiar with, but instead seemed like a place for show; an indulgence designed to celebrate something she did not understand. She thought of the church she had attended sporadically in Bridgwater – the cool, hard stone under her knees and the taintless light that shone through the windows, which lent even Father Landy's dull sermons a kind of beauty.

'I don't like it in here,' Ruby said, turning to her mother and sister, and Irene looked as if she too was getting ready to flee. Hester, however, gazed around her with a delighted air.

'Every day is the Sabbath. That is what He says. The playing of billiards is a celebration of our Lord as much as prayer is.'

'But the playing of billiards in a church, Mother?' Irene queried in a soft voice, looking uneasily around her as if she thought that she might be overheard, although they were alone. The women were still hovering uncertainly when there was a sudden, loud trumpet fanfare and a saint Ruby hadn't seen before, a tall man dressed in ceremonial robes, entered the room followed by others similarly attired, who walked in a line and gathered around the pulpit. A moment or so later Peters himself appeared, dressed in the crimson robes he had been wearing in his carriage and the trumpet player stopped suddenly as if he had dropped his instrument. Ruby had an impulse to laugh at the squeaking end to the flourish, but the laughter died in her throat when Peters looked in their direction. Despite the poor trumpeting and the chapel tricked out like a parlour, it was impossible to take your eyes away from him. The room faded and he seemed to absorb all the colour around him so that he shimmered. A few other community members came in and sat down on the pews and so the three women did, too. A man Ruby had seen once or twice was then led in by Martin and took his place at the front of the chapel.

'This is a day of great celebration. The day your flesh becomes sanctified. You are made of base tissue and common sinew and hampered by the limitations of your human needs and frailties, but the word of God told to you, through me, will set you free.'

Reverend Peters spoke to a point somewhere above the man's bowed head.

'Saint Matthew, you are blessed' he said. One of his company handed him a goblet, which he put to Matthew's lips. After Matthew had taken a sip of the wine, Peters wiped his mouth with his hand which struck Ruby as the way one might touch a child.

'Only in the denying of our flesh can we hope to meet the Day of Judgement with our bodies transformed and our souls unblemished. We are here to fight the battle against our baser selves so that we might live forever.'

It seemed that Matthew's passage to sainthood was complete because a moment or two later, Peters summoned up a bowl of water and a cloth and washed his hands carefully, taking time to dry between his fingers, and then the querulous fanfare began once more, and the saints trooped out behind him.

'We were present at the wonder!' Hester said. 'The excitement of it all has given me a terrible hunger. Do you think it's time for lunch?'

She and Irene led the way out and Ruby was about to follow when she saw a door at the back of the chapel that she had not noticed before. Curious to see where the door led, she turned the metal-ring handle. The room was dimly lit and larger than she had imagined it would be. A curtain on a narrow, arched window let in light around its edges. Ruby was immediately assailed by the odour of roses, not the fresh syrupy smell of the outdoor version, but rather a dense, oily perfume that was so strong, it was almost suffocating. A narrow bed took up the length of the wall beneath the window. In the centre of the floor, which was carpeted in the same dark colour as in the rest of the chapel, stood a large bath, wider on one end than the other. Floating on the surface was a length of muslin, looking like the skin that forms on milk. A pair of shoes of the kind the community members all wore were lying discarded.

She was so absorbed in her perusal of the room, that his sudden appearance by her side made her start violently.

'What are you doing in here, Ruby?' Martin said.

The room which had appeared spacious before, seemed to shrink. She had not realised quite how big the man was. Broad and slack armed, like a bear, he filled the space around her so effectively that for one wild moment she wondered how she was going to get out. He stared at her impassively. The heavy way he held his body gave him an unfinished look, like something half-stuffed waiting to be shaped into a living thing.

'I was just curious about what was in here,' she said, humiliated by the wobble in her voice.

'This room is always locked,' he said. 'Only The Beloved and I are allowed in here.'

'Well, it was not locked today,' Ruby said, regaining some of her spirit and looking as squarely as she could into his strange, unfocused eyes.

'I will have to reprimand Sister Miriam for leaving it open. She should have checked.'

For a couple of moments, it seemed that he was not going to let her pass – the bulk of him loomed over her like a wall – but then, at last, he stepped back.

'Your curiosity will be your undoing, Ruby. Your mother has spoken of it to me. You would do well to try and keep out of things that do not concern you.'

Outside, Ruby found that she was shaking. She walked around the garden to try and ease her agitation. The sheer abundance of what was around her, its detailed and specific beauty, should have calmed her. Instead, it seemed only to intensify her sense of alienation. In the past, she had sometimes chafed against where she found herself, but she had always understood the parameters of her world. Here she did not even know the rules. She thought of her father, whom she had barely had time to mourn properly. She thought of William – the line of his smiling mouth and the way his arm had snaked around Irene's waist when he thought no one was watching, and she felt the old grief that would not leave her, even though the trees were moving softly, and the lawn was a cool green.

Chapter 24

Miriam stood up at the lunch table and cleared her throat. The women looked at her expectantly. Rumours had been gathering in the community about Hattie's whereabouts. Edith had announced to Ruby and Irene as they were walking down the stairs that she thought Hattie had been taken up by God in a chariot. Norah, who was behind them, suggested that it was more likely that Hattie had been snatched away by Satan.

'Hattie turned her face from the light,' Norah said, her own face glowing with the prospect of disaster.

'Norah!' Edith had exclaimed with a purse of her thin lips, 'You know full well, we are safe from the machinations of the devil here!'

Miriam coughed again. It was clear that she was reluctant to start talking. It wasn't like her to be so hesitant.

'I am afraid that I have some unpleasant news to share with you this morning,' she finally said. 'Hattie was found yesterday outside the community, hanged by the neck.'

A ripple of consternation spread around the table. Norah gave an alarmed squeak.

Ruby felt her stomach roil. *Hattie. Poor Hattie.*

'This is what happens when people leave us. We can no longer protect those who go beyond the walls. They become prey to the same sadness and the same sins of those who live on the outside.'

Ruby noticed that Miriam's usually immaculate hair was hanging down a little on one side. In anyone else, the slight disarrangement in her appearance would not have been particularly significant, but it seemed to Ruby that in Miriam it indicated a disturbance far greater than she was willing to show. She thought it was probably the shock of the news. It took a while to reconcile the fact of death when you are still assuming life. The first instinct is always denial. Ruby herself, although she had barely even known Hattie, felt the horror of it and a kind of disbelief that under the woman's stolid, slow face there had all along been this intent. She thought of Hattie's struggle in the wood. The way her bare feet had almost slipped beneath her and her scrabbling hands on the stone. What had happened between then and now? It had been only a few days, after all. Had she decided that she was not cut from the necessary cloth? Had she failed the test that had been set her?

'I want you to do as I have done since I heard the terrible news,' Miriam said. 'I want you to use this loss to our community as a lesson. Do not dwell on the death but think rather about the life you are earning here.'

'Would she not have died if she had become a saint and chosen a tree within the community walls to hang from?' Ruby asked into the uneasy silence that had followed Miriam's pronouncement.

Irene shot Ruby a warning glance. She loved the defiant angle of her sister's chin and the straight way she was looking down the table at Miriam and yet it made her heart quail. Being within the embrace of her fierce sister's protection had been one of the great treasures of her life. Irene herself came and went, but Ruby had always been resolutely there. She would not change it, but sometimes she feared where it might lead them.

'She died because she was outside, Ruby. That is all you need to know,' Miriam said.

'So, am I to understand that it is simply a matter of geography then? Inside the wall we are immortal, and two steps beyond the gate, mortal?'

Two patches of colour appeared on Miriam's pale face.

'You should take the time to really listen, instead of being so quick to jump to judgement, Ruby. You think you see everything so clearly, but in fact you are befuddled by your own limitations.'

She would have to ask Reverend Peters to talk to the woman. The community depended entirely on the secure binding together of all. Any weakening of the fastening would cause it to fall apart. She had known as soon as she had sworn allegiance to Peters all those years ago that there would be no going back. She had never been consumed by the fervour of his doctrine as most of the others were. Before she had met him, she had always thought of religion as immutable – faith written down in stone which might weather as the years passed when life threw challenges and doubts in your path, but was, nevertheless, always there to turn to for reference and consolation. The Beloved had a more flexible theology. His words seemed to her to be always in a state of flux – by turns narrowing and then widening to accommodate new thoughts and fresh impulses. Indeed, recently she had felt yet another shift was taking place, and that he was brooding about what he was to do next. There had been some talk of uniting spirit and flesh, which she did not quite understand since it seemed to contradict what he had always preached. Regardless, she would turn in the direction he showed them. She would focus only on the things she needed to. The community was her life. It was all she had.

'I suggest you leave the table and go about your business, Ruby,' Hester said. Despite the gravity of Miriam's announcement, her mother had barely looked up or paused her ingestion of smoked haddock, eggs, and several slices of bread, thickly spread with butter. 'You are making a spectacle of yourself and causing me great embarrassment.'

'I will come with you,' Irene said and rose and accompanied her sister out of the kitchen.

'Ruby, you really should not share your thoughts so readily, nor ask so many questions,' she murmured as they walked up the stairs.

'Tell me, Irene, would our father have wanted this for us? Think of the hours he spent with you, showing you the way things worked. All those illustrations in our encyclopaedias of the organs of the body. All those explanations of steam engines and the way the sun moves through the sky. He told us about those things because he wanted in some way to make us part of the world we live in.'

Ruby, furious, stalked ahead.

'Here is where we find ourselves, Ruby. We have to make the best of it… I am afraid I am becoming indisposed…'

Ruby whipped around to see Irene holding onto the banister.

'Have I time to get you to our room?'

She held Irene in her arms and could feel the rapid beat of her sister's heart.

'No just lay me down,' Irene managed.

Irene's gaze followed the pattern of leaves up the wall to the very top. As she stared, they seemed to move – the twists of ivy turning in on themselves again, so that the stems became more and more tangled. Then there was the fall, which did not land but rather spread, feeling something like flying in its hurtle and its sudden sense of time and landscape opening up.

The seizure inevitably attracted the attention of the others. They seemed in some way drawn to what was happening. They stood silently on the stairs, gazing at what they clearly imagined was some kind of spectacle. Martin appeared in the hallway and shooed the others aside so that he could get closer.

'In a couple of moments, my sister will be well enough to be moved to her bed,' Ruby said, to forestall the questions she could see gathering in him.

'Has she spoken of what she saw?' he asked.

The Taking of Irene Hart

'No. She has only just returned.'

'Is it true?' Norah, who had stared enthralled throughout Irene's seizure, asked. 'Does she see the Day of Judgement?'

'No, she does not,' Ruby replied. 'It would be helpful if everyone would go and leave us in peace.'

'But she saw The Miracle of The Sacred Light. What else might she conjure up?'

Ruby turned back to her sister and saw from her absent gaze that Irene was holding on to wherever she had been – not a place, surely, certainly not a vision of the kind that fool Norah was implying, but rather fragments of a dream of the sort that drift across at night when you are not sure whether you are awake or asleep.

'There was so much water, Ruby. Rising and rising and unstoppable and in it all manner of things were floating…'

Irene's voice was hoarse.

A wave of twittering excitement spread though the spectators.

'A flood!' someone exclaimed. 'She is foretelling a flood!'

'All of you leave now,' Martin ordered, and the others dispersed reluctantly.

'Ruby, once Irene has recovered, I would be grateful if you would both make yourselves available to speak with me,' he said.

20th September

Dearest Nancy,

Thank you for your letter. You write in such a way that I was able to conjure up the wedding – Cousin Anna's complacent look beneath her pearly tiara, Mrs Feather's tumbling bosom, almost escaping its confines as she scampered her way through the Virginia Reel, Mr Tootrue cornering Limp Lucy and breathing his fishy breath full into her face. Your descriptions made me feel as if I was there.

Life in the community continues at the same deathly pace. It started to rain heavily yesterday, and it has not stopped since, making my work in the garden impossible just now, and so I generally remain in the greenhouses. Being inside the glass when it is being lashed with rain is like being in a boat at sea.

Sister Miriam keeps me under her beady eye. She always creeps up on me at the very moment I have taken a break from my labours. I swear the woman has wheels under her skirt – she seems to glide rather than walk. Brother Martin rules over all of us. Although the others seem to admire him, I find him strange, even frightening (and you know I am not easily frightened!). Do you remember that blind man who used to beg in the market square, the one with the shoes that flapped like tongues? You always said you thought his blindness was an act to elicit sympathy and pennies. We used to dare each other to get as close to him as we could (the poor soul, children are so cruel and thoughtless!). I have something of the same feeling with Brother Martin – it is as if he is pretending not to see and yet somehow (you will call me fanciful) I think he is a watcher.

I have yet to find a friend who matches me the way you do. Edith, who works with me in the greenhouse, is an odd little creature who has decided to fasten herself to my side and be my spiritual guide. Angela is kind about helping me with household tasks. You know how clumsy I can be. There was another gardener called Hattie, who sadly took her own life. I am told that it is because she was sinful that death came to her, but she was trying so hard to earn her salvation. Her struggle for sainthood took a terrible toll on her. I had been led to believe our path to salvation was marked out and ready for us, but it seems it has to be battled for. I think Reverend Peters uses the promise of sainthood as a way of making people do what he wants.

Irene is blossoming. She has had two takings, but rather than spurn her, as people in the real world might, the community seem almost to welcome her indisposition. They gather round her as if they are at the theatre. She is working hard on an embroidery that has been commissioned by Reverend Peters for some, as yet unspecified, event. She thought at first that she would not be able to work out the pattern, but now she tells me it is as if her needle has a life of its own.

The Taking of Irene Hart

I must go now. It is almost time for dinner. Tell that husband of yours he needs to pay you more attention. If I cannot be a mother, I want at least to be a loving, almost aunt.

With great affection,
Ruby

Chapter 25

It seemed to Philip that the space occupied by his mother in the bed was becoming smaller every day. He thought that the morning would surely come when he would lift the sheet and find her gone. She had always been illusive – caught up in dreams or examining regrets – and now her illness seemed simply to be a continuation of this withdrawal. The day before she had sat up and asked that he bring her the embroidery, and for a while she had plucked restlessly at it.

'I have so much still to say,' she had exclaimed, her lips so dry that they stuck to her gums giving her the look of a child, even though she also seemed to him beyond old.

'There is no one now to tell my story.'

'I shall tell it, Mother,' he had said, trying to moisten her mouth with the cloth he kept in the bowl of steeped chamomile, but she turned her head away from him.

'But you don't know it. Only *I* know it.'

Later, as he was dozing by her bed, glad that she was sleeping at last, she spoke again and startled him awake.

'I need to be able to lay down the reasons why I loved and didn't love and all the ways I told myself that the things I did wrong were not so bad. All the times I made excuses for myself.'

'I am sure you have nothing to blame yourself for,' he said.

'If I cannot see clearly now, when will I?' she asked, sparse tears on her face, as if even crying was now beyond her.

'Shall I ask the vicar to come?' She had never been a church-going woman but for the big occasions that demanded such ceremony, but he thought perhaps she might need someone now.

'What good would that do?' she said. 'No one can absolve me. I wanted to set it all out, clear, so you could see the pattern and the places I dropped a stitch because my heart was hurting and the times when I sewed as if I had the wind in my fingers. Before I go, I want to tell what I have kept tight inside me and told no one.'

Philip touched her head, the shape of it painfully clear now and soon she fell asleep, and he went out, not because he had anywhere particular to go, but because he couldn't stay in the house any longer. He roused a neighbour, Mrs Grawler, a glum woman who only seemed to come alive when death was imminent, to sit with her.

Philip decided to leave Thunder behind and walk to the inn. At least there he would find some ready company to distract him. As he marched along by the river, he barely noticed the rain that punctured its normally smooth surface, nor how wet his jacket was becoming. It wasn't just his mother's illness that was preoccupying him, although that was uppermost in his mind, it was also that Jowler was on the war path. A sudden surfeit of pineapples had appeared at Bridgwater market and although Philip had at last tracked down Thomas Balch, he claimed to have been ten miles away from Yaxton on the night in question. In addition, there were at least three other people willing to testify to the veracity of his claim. Jowler had expressed his disgust at Philip's failure to bring the man to justice.

'I was horrified to discover,' the chief constable had almost shouted at him, his whole head sliding from side to side in agitation, 'that not only have you failed to solve the matter of the pineapple burglary, but you have been implying that there has been some wrongdoing at the community. As if its leader is responsible for the terrible sin of one of his flock.'

'I simply went to report the death,' Philip had replied. It had taken all his strength not to wipe the spittle from his face that his superior had discharged across his desk.

'Imagine my mortification. I had to hear it from the man himself. He very graciously invited me to dine with him at the community. A very nice spread it was too – a fine Julienne soup, trout with horseradish, a roasted pheasant and a cream-topped meringue… He told me that you had suggested that the right amount of *sympathy* had not been shown following the news of the death. Why should the leader of the community feel sympathy for someone who has chosen the devil's path?'

The upshot of it all was that he had ordered Philip to be on almost permanent duty outside the community. Philip felt ruefully he would do better to join the pack of hounds at the gate, since a guard dog was more or less what he had been reduced to.

The drinkers were already at their allotted places in the Star Inn, and they shuffled aside to allow him to sit on the bench next to them. His immediate neighbour introduced himself as Giles Yardley.

'Are you here in an official capacity?' the man asked, indicating Philip's uniform.

'No, my working day is over,' Philip replied. 'I've not seen you around before. What brings you here?'

'I am a writer. A writer looking for a story and the community over the road has captured my interest.'

He had an engaging, open manner and a wide, friendly gaze. Necessary attributes, Philip thought, for a man in his profession.

'I gather,' Giles said, 'that there was a suicide a week or so ago and it was not the first.'

'Is that so?' Philip asked noncommittally, taking another pull on his beer, and looking around him as if he was not much concerned, although the information that Hattie's death was not the first had provoked his interest.

'Yes. About a year ago.'

This was around the time that Philip had started his job and would perhaps explain, if it were true, why he had not been privy to the information.

'Another young woman from the community, found hanging in near enough the same place as this latest one was found.'

'Who told you this?'

'The man who discovered her – he drinks here sometimes – came upon her when he was picking fruit. He is clearly not squeamish, because he extracted the suicide note from the pocket of her apron.'

'What did he do about his discovery?'

'He was with his son – poor lad – at the time, and he sent the boy to inform the community. He says a couple of them came late at night and took her away. The man wasn't supposed to be on the land, much less stealing fruit, and a churn of butter, and so kept it to himself.'

'Do you know the man's name?'

'I doubt he will welcome me snitching to a policeman, but it is Thomas Balch.'

Philip half smiled at the thought of the buttery apple pie the Balch family would have enjoyed that evening. Martin had said something along the lines that Hattie had forfeited her sainthood. Perhaps a crisis of faith had been the cause of this earlier death, and Hattie's, too. It would be devastating for a person who truly believed in an immaculate hereafter to find herself excluded from the Garden of Eden.

'Don't worry about exposing Thomas. I am already aware of his habits,' Philip said.

'I would like to know exactly what is happening in the community,' Giles said.

'So, what is your theory?'

'I think it a place where the inhabitants only see what it is they are supposed to see. Understanding anything other than the stated doctrine would cause the whole edifice to topple.'

'Faith is surely a matter of personal choice.'

'Indeed. There is no set of beliefs too strange that there will not be people who will swallow them whole and what is more, persist in believing, despite all evidence to the contrary. There have been such places and such leaders since the beginning of time, and no doubt there will be others in the future.'

'Not, perhaps, so much of a story then,' Philip said.

'It is the Reverend himself who interests me. I have done a bit of digging around, and the man has a very murky past. He trained as a doctor but was in practice barely three years before he fell ill with some mysterious ailment. Thrown on to his own devices, he took to reading aloud to his mother's elderly lodger who, it is claimed, was so enchanted by his mellifluous voice, reading from *The Song of Solomon*, of all things, that she fell in love with him and told him that she was willing to do anything he wanted. Peters asked her to pay for fees at a theological college, which she duly did. In gratitude, he married her, although she seems to have died shortly after, so the union was short-lived. At theological college, he was unpopular for his extreme religiosity, in particular his tendency to condemn his superiors for drinking wine.'

'He still preaches abstinence,' Philip said, 'although judging by the meal my chief constable recently enjoyed, perhaps not in all things.'

'The tale gets even more tangled. After college he was dismissed from one and then another curacy, reportedly for whipping up his congregations, which were largely made up of women, into a frenzy. He decided to strike out on his own and after an energetic recruitment campaign, in which many people, again mostly women, felt compelled to part with large amounts of money to finance the building of the community.'

'He certainly appears to be a very persuasive man,' Philip said.

'Particularly where the fairer sex is concerned.'

'I could only wish for a similar influence,' Philip said, smiling.

Over the shoulder of his companion, he saw the cider-saturated man making his way lurchingly towards him and hastily draining the last of his beer, he got to his feet.

'It is time I went home,' he said. 'I wish you luck with your story.'

As Philip passed the community, he heard the sound of singing coming from a distance, perhaps through an open window. He wondered if Ruby Hart was amongst the choir. He could see her there, sitting with the others, yet quite alone. Her hands crossed in her lap and her lovely, restless face moving with the song.

Chapter 26

Unable to work in the garden due to the continuous, torrential rain that was turning the flower beds into a bog, Ruby had been charged with replenishing the vases in the Hall. She had run outside with a shawl over her head to collect waterlogged blooms, her feet squelching across the lawn, her scissors slipping on the damp stalks, and had gathered a wet basketful of pink dahlias and lilac-coloured asters. Miriam had also instructed her to change the flowers in the chapel in a tone of voice that intimated that Ruby should consider the task a rare honour.

She collected a bucket from the kitchen and made her way there. When she pushed the chapel door open, she was surprised to see Reverend Peters sitting at one of the pews with his head bowed. He was not usually about so early in the day, and it was unusual to find him in an attitude of prayer. She considered leaving and returning when he had gone, but Miriam's instruction had been delivered with a great deal of firmness, so she quietly began emptying the vases by the door into her bucket, hoping to accomplish her task without drawing his attention.

'Good morning, Ruby.'

The Taking of Irene Hart

His voice startled her, and the vase she was holding slipped from her fingers and crashed to the floor. Ruby bent down and started hopelessly picking up the shards of glass and placing them in the pocket of her apron. Her haste made her clumsy for a second time, and she cut her hand in the soft part between thumb and forefinger. She was bleeding profusely down her arm – an insistent flow that dripped onto the floor and mingled with the muddle of water and glass and flowers at her feet. She pulled up the hem of her apron and wrapped it around her hand.

'Let me see what you have done to yourself,' Peters said, appearing beside her.

He unwound the apron that was already stained dark red. Ruby tried to pull away. She had never stood as close to him, or indeed any man, except her father. She felt overwhelmed by his proximity. She tugged again, but Peters held her hand firmly. This pressure caused her wound to bleed even more, and she could not repress a sound of distress at the way the blood was pulsing from her.

'I need to go and attend to myself,' she said. She had wanted to sound calm but could hear the note of entreaty in her voice. She knew he had registered it, too, because his eyes widened. He looked at her with what she thought was an expression of amusement, and then, as if he was challenging her to object, he raised her hand to his mouth. His gaze on hers was steady, assessing. Before she realised quite what he was doing, and still holding her hand firmly in his, he placed his lips around the wound, his mouth on the softest part of her palm, and sucked softly. This action was so strange and unexpected, that she froze. The sensation of his skin against her filled her with a kind of fearful repulsion. She tried once again to pull away, but he persisted. His lips were fastened to her so avidly, it felt as if he was taking more from her than blood. She stared mutely at him, noticing at these close quarters the details that were usually hidden. There were broken veins around his nose and his face was speckled with sharp, emerging grey hairs that dulled his skin. She could smell him – the incense on his clothes and the soap with which he washed his hands so fastidiously, but beneath that, and stronger than the rest, was his human sourness. He let her go at last and looking down she saw that he had temporarily stopped the bleeding. He took a handkerchief from his pocket and tied it tightly around her hand – binding thumb and fingers together.

'You should sit for a while,' he said, indicating the pew. 'Keep your hand raised. Doctor's orders.'

'I need to clean this up,' she said indicating the floor.

He shook his head.

'You have had a shock.'

She wanted to get away from him and wash her hand in some cool water and find Sister Eloise with her soothing voice and box of ointments, but she let herself be led and Reverend Peters sat down at her side. The crimson chapel seemed to be shifting and stretching in front of her eyes.

'When you found me, I was in conversation with my Master,' Peters said. 'He was telling me what I must do next to ensure our salvation.'

'I thought we were already saved,' Ruby ventured.

He turned and looked at her gravely. His shoulders stretched and he did that uncanny thing she had seen before of growing somehow in stature as if he had been fed by the power he had been consulting and it had strengthened him.

'The word of God through me is not set, but rather a discourse.'

'What did He tell you?' she asked.

'He told me that only when the body and the soul are united can we finally purge the community of all sin.'

'And how are you to do that?' Ruby asked.

They sat in silence for a while, Peters seemingly transfixed in thought and Ruby with bent head watching her blood creep stealthily through The Beloved's handkerchief.

'I intend to find a way,' he said at last.

Ruby wondered when she could safely get up and leave.

'I feel that there is much in you that wants expression that has not found its channel. You are yet to take your first, proper, full breath. You are waiting for your life to start.'

Ruby was surprised to find herself suddenly close to tears. His was a strange power that pushed you and pulled you almost at the same time, so that you no longer knew exactly where you were.

'How is your sister? Has she recovered from her latest taking?'

'Yes, she has. She is accustomed to having seizures. She has had them since she was a child.'

'I gather this time she saw some kind of flood.'

Ruby felt the implacable will in him. It was as hard to breach as the wall that surrounded them. She marshalled her resistance.

'She sees only parts of things. They are more like dreams than visions. My sister dislikes notice being taken of her condition.'

'Nevertheless, I want to know what she has to say. Guidance can come from the most unlikely sources. In the meantime, I have instructed Brother Martin, who knows a great deal about the healing power of plants, to mix up a tincture that will help your sister to build up her strength. I look to you to help me with this.'

'I will always do what I feel is best for my sister,' she said.

'So, you will not stand in her way? Not become an obstacle in her path to redemption?'

His questions felt like a command.

'We stay together. We always will,' she said, lifting her head, trying to keep herself steady.

She felt him relinquish her, as if he had won an unspoken battle and she left the chapel.

On her way back to her room, nursing her hand, she met Martin coming along the corridor towards her. He seemed a little dishevelled and out of breath.

'I have just knocked on the door to your quarters and received no answer,' he said, stopping in front of her.

'I expect my sister is sleeping,' she said, trying to keep a distance between herself and his bulk. 'And in any case, she is alone. My mother is at the farm.'

He looked at her and smiled. The sudden joviality of his expression made Ruby uneasy.

'Irene is fortunate to have you as her protector. I find your devotion touching, even inspiring,' he said. 'I will let you get back to her.' He stepped aside and Ruby held herself in as tightly as she could as she walked by, as one would when passing an open fire or a thorned bush. She did not want any part of her to touch him.

'You should perhaps close the window, the rain is soaking the curtains,' he said.

Irene was indeed sleeping when Ruby went into the drawing room but opened her eyes as Ruby bent over her.

'How are you, my darling?' Ruby asked.

'Feeling much better,' Irene answered.

Ruby looked at the window and the limp fall of the damp curtain. How had Martin known that it was open? She did not want to shut it at his command. A little rain would not hurt anything. The sound of peacocks filled the room. Penned into the small walled garden by Reverend Peters' quarters to stop their wanton destruction of the flowerbeds, they were giving vent to their ugly song.

'They sound like women in the pain of childbirth,' Irene said.

'I hate them,' Ruby said. 'I could pull out their feathers one by one.'

'They are prized by Reverend Peters as a symbol of immortality. Their tails never fade like those of other birds but remain the same vibrant colour.'

'I still dislike them,' Ruby said. 'They have nasty darting eyes, and as for what they leave behind, I have never smelt anything quite so disgusting.'

'I love it when you pull faces. You look just like the little girl you were only a few years ago.'

Just then there was a brisk knock at the door and Miriam came in.

'I have brought the tincture recommended by The Beloved for Irene.'

All traces of her previous disarrangement had been smoothed down – her hair was arranged in two firm coils above her ears, from which dangled dark red stones that looked like drops of blood against her pale skin.

'What is in it exactly?' Ruby asked, looking doubtfully at the bottle of milky liquid.

'It is not my place to query the recommendations of The Beloved, nor is it yours, Ruby. Two drops in water, twice a day. Once on waking and again before sleep. I'll leave you now.'

'It seems to me that Sister Miriam is exactly like a peacock,' said Ruby under her breath as they listened to the woman's retreating footsteps.

'I am surprised you think her so,' Irene said, settling back in her bed. 'She is not in the least showy. I have rarely seen anyone wear plainer clothes.'

'Her tail feathers may be disguised, but they are there, nonetheless,' Ruby said. 'She keeps them tucked down between her legs.'

'Ruby!' Irene said, trying not to laugh. 'You will get us into trouble speaking so.'

'She didn't hear me,' Ruby said, shrugging her shoulders unrepentantly and throwing herself down on the sofa so heavily that its frame shook.

'Talk to me,' Irene said.

'What would you like me to talk about?'

'About what it was like when we were children, and it was summertime.'

And so Ruby described their walks to the park in Bridgwater, the picnics they used to take with their mother, the times they visited their father at the factory when they were sometimes allowed to help the men to fill the brick moulds; a doll lost and never recovered in a field of corn, a pet rabbit who had munched its way through its enclosure, the way the sun seemed as if it would never set, the sweet, rank smell of river and the dragon flies that hurtled over it which they used to try and catch in their hands. At some point in her narrative, Irene fell asleep again, and Ruby found, when she turned towards her, that she had been talking into the empty air.

Chapter 27

'There is someone asking for Irene at the gate. He is waiting for her now,' George called out to Ruby. She was trying to push a wheelbarrow laden with saturated compost that had already toppled over twice. Despite the rain, George had insisted that they try at least to do some essential work in the garden. Ruby found this and many of George's other requests unreasonable. She was soaked through and the cut on her hand was hot and sore. She thought it had become infected, despite the cream that Sister Eloise had carefully administered and the soft bandage she had wound around it.

'Shall I send Trench to get her?' George asked.

'Are we allowed to receive visitors?' Ruby asked.

It had never been explicitly said by anyone that interaction with friends and relatives from outside was forbidden, but like so many other things in the community, Ruby had understood from things she had overheard, that it was strongly discouraged.

'They cannot come into the community without the express permission of Reverend Peters,' George said carefully, 'but he understands that it sometimes happens that we have to explain the situation to people who do not know how we live.' He averted his eyes from Ruby.

'Did they say their name?' she asked, wiping her muddy hands down the sides of her dress, and pinning back her hair, which had come loose during her exertions. She couldn't imagine who had come to the community to see Irene. Ruby was even beginning to forget faces that had once been familiar to her. Living at the community caused you to turn in on yourself.

'What are we to do while we wait for the final day?' she had asked Edith as they were crouched down, clearing the drain that ran alongside the orchid beds which had become blocked with pieces of bark.

'We are to do nothing at all,' Edith had answered peaceably, looking at her companion with an untroubled face.

'So, we are just supposed to wait for the end?' Ruby had asked.

'We are waiting for the beginning, not the end,' Edith had answered.

'He said he was William. William Everett,' George said now.

At the sound of his name, her heart rose into her mouth. She felt suddenly unsteady.

'I will deal with it,' she said.

Her instinct, as she reminded herself afterwards, was to turn for the house and her sister, but she stopped halfway across the lawn. *Irene will be made upset by the sight of him. I should protect her from that.* And so, she went alone, past the battered flowerbeds and the saturated dogs. The gate, which had been left slightly ajar was heavy to move, even with both hands, and the hinges creaked like Eloise's knuckles once they were freed from their manacle of thread.

He was as he had been before. She did not know why she had expected him to be changed. Now that she saw him again, she knew that although living at the community seemed to have so quickly blurred her past life, she could have drawn his likeness from memory – the exact colour of his eyes that rested perfectly between green and brown, his ears with their slight, loveable protuberance, his full, spoilt mouth, his air of owning all he looked at.

'Nancy told me where you all were,' he said, and his voice rubbed against her. 'I have come to see Irene.' The sound of her sister's name brought Ruby back to herself.

'Where have you been all these months?' she asked.

'In India. Dealing with an uprising of farmers refusing to grow the indigo they were paid for. Crooked troublemakers all of them.'

As he talked, his face had adopted a petulance she remembered. He had always believed himself to be right.

'Where is Irene?' William asked.

'She is unwell.' Her voice emerged as weaker than she wanted it to be. 'She is resting. She is asleep,' she said more loudly, and she found herself leaning against the gate for support.

'What is this place?' William asked, looking beyond her into the garden.

'It is a community of people who are aspiring to live forever.' In her shock and nervousness, she felt a wild desire to laugh. Seeing him in this new context deepened the strangeness of her situation. She must look deranged standing at the gate to this place, her clothes soaked through. Her hair sticking to her face and neck, her hand in its grimy bandage, talking about salvation.

'Are you here against your will?' he asked, looking at the wall, the crenelated chapel roof, the slathering dogs.

'Our mother brought us here,' Ruby answered. 'She was taken with strong feeling. It brought her back to life after Father died.'

'So, you can leave at any time you choose?' William asked. 'Nancy seemed to think it was some sort of a prison.'

'We can come and go when we want to,' Ruby said, surprised to find herself defending what had so recently become her home, although she did not feel it to be so.

'It seems to me to be a very strange kind of a place.'

'Why have you come?' she asked William, noting the way his face moved at her words, their chill tightening his skin. 'You have done damage enough.' She thought maybe she had managed to muster anger because he flinched.

'I want to speak to her,' he said. 'I want to explain.' His voice trailed off and she was glad that she had weakened him.

'I doubt very much that she will want to speak to you.'

'I've had time away, to … to reflect,' he said, avoiding her gaze and looking up again at the statue of the lion. It seemed to fascinate him.

'As has *she*,' Ruby answered.

'It is not entirely my fault. You must grant me that. I had no knowledge of her … illness. The change during her taking was … was so great. I had thought her the perfect woman … until then… Her face was like that of a saint. She seemed to have such gentleness.'

'She is the gentlest person I know!'

'Could you at least tell her that I have been here?'

His eyes darkened so that they looked less green and more brown. His wet jacket and trousers clung to his body.

'I think it will only serve to distress her.' Ruby's hands rolled into tight fists, whether in defence of her sister or herself, she could not tell.

'Tell her that I will come again in a few days. Perhaps she will be able to see me when she has recovered from her illness.' He put on his hat and turned away.

'Do not come again,' she said, although she knew that she wanted him to.

Ruby closed the gate and walked back to the vegetable garden. Her skin was sore as if she had been subjected to the sting of blown sand, and her chest and throat felt tight. She picked up her discarded wheelbarrow and pushed it along the edge of the garden until she reached the last bed. She tipped its claggy load with an effortful shove and her hand throbbed in response.

'Did you speak to your visitor?' George said, looking up at her.

'I did,' Ruby said. 'I would be grateful if you would not mention the fact that he came here. There is a history too complicated to explain that means if my mother and sister knew he had visited the community, it would upset them greatly, even threaten their ease with living here. If he comes again, please be sure to call for me and not trouble them with it.'

George hesitated a moment, but then he nodded.

'Your secret is safe with me.'

'It is not a secret,' Ruby said, reluctant to put herself at the mercy of this taciturn man. 'It is simply something I feel I should manage myself.'

George nodded again and plunged his hands in the earth as far as his wrists.

Chapter 28

'It came creeping and creeping in the night. In the end I must've gone to sleep and when I woke, it'd got right in.'

Archie Balch was knee deep in what was once the kitchen of his cottage, but which now resembled nothing more than a thoroughfare for the flood water that had driven through it. A chair, knocked onto its side, was almost submerged. The table had only half of the length of its legs showing, and straw and leaves and items of clothing floated on the brackish, oily surface. Philip, who had witnessed similar scenes all day in several of the villages and hamlets, and who was himself, soaked through and chilled to the bone, tried to comfort the boy as best he could.

'They say it is subsiding. It crept in and it will creep out again, and then you will be able to make all good again.'

Archie cast a despairing glance around him, and Philip regretted his choice of words –'making good' was an unfamiliar concept for a boy who had spent most of his short life dealing with what was almost exclusively bad.

'The sun will come out, and everything will dry. In the meantime, stay in the upstairs room and don't venture too far afield. There are parts where the water is quite wild. There is a boat with food and water coming for those most in need and I will put you on the list.'

Philip extricated his soggy notebook from the pocket of his jacket and his pencil from where he had kept it dry inside the lining of his hat. Although he was only one of half a dozen constables who had been sent from Bridgwater to deal with the destruction left in the wake of the floods, he was exhausted by both the miles he had covered and the sense that he had little to offer in the way of help to those afflicted. His own home had managed to escape the worst of it. The water had lapped at his doorstep, but luckily had not gone further.

Floods were not common in this part of the county. When the River Parrett burst its banks, it was usually the areas to the east and south of Bridgwater that were affected, but this time, the spread had been more extensive. Three days of unceasing and torrential rain had caused the river to rise higher than ever before, and filled the smaller rivers and fields, so that now parts of the landscape looked like quite another place. Some roads were completely impassable and familiar trees that had acted as landmarks, had been diminished to only their higher branches. Philip had seen the carcasses of chickens and lambs float past him. He only hoped that no human creature had met a similar fate. Thunder had flatly refused to venture into any water that came higher than his fetlocks, which meant that for much of the day Philip had had to leave him tied to any available and still-visible fence and make his way onward on foot. Unknown, underwater things knocked at his ankles or slithered past him as if he was moving through some kind of horrible stew. There was a strange, eerie silence everywhere, similar to the muffling wrought by a heavy fall of snow.

The front door of the house where Pearl was being nursed was open and when Philip sloshed his way up what had once been the path and put his head inside, he saw to his dismay that the water level had reached even higher up the wall than it had in the Balch cottage. Here nothing was visible except for the cut-out parts of Minnie's gloves, which floated on the surface like disembodied hands. When Philip shouted out, answering voices came from upstairs. He took a deep breath and waded through the soup. The family were all crammed into the bedroom, sitting on the bedding they had managed to keep dry. At the sight of him, one of the younger children started to wail, which set off one of the babies, so it was a while before Philip could make his voice heard to reassure them that some help was on its way.

'In the rush, we almost forgot the babber,' Minnie said, her eyes wide. 'I went back down when I remembered and… It was hard to see in the dark. I had to feel for her … her cradle was floating.'

Philip wondered at Pearl's resilience. She had survived birth. She had withstood abandonment and the cold night air. She had persisted in living, despite being forgotten in flood waters. He looked at her lying in the crook of Minnie's arm, her gaze untroubled, her skin so pale it seemed to shine in the gloomy room. There had not been much opportunity in Philip's life for the luxury of self-expression, and yet now he felt an almost unbearable affection for the child. His eyes filled with tears that he had to cough to disguise. After a weary, cold day full of distress he had been able to do little to assuage, the baby seemed to him to be as close to a miracle as he was ever going to get.

'The machine and the gloves are all spoilt,' Minnie said. 'What shall we do? I shall be driven to find work elsewhere.'

Though she was undeniably a bonny young woman, she looked much older than the child she still was, he thought.

'The machine can be repaired, and you will get more gloves from the factory,' Philip said, but they both knew that this was a blow the family would have difficulty recovering from. Such means of earning money relied on daily and regular endeavour and would not likely survive the interruption that this flood had brought. He promised he would visit relatives who lived in the next village and let them know of the family's plight, and after repeating that food was on its way and that the water levels were already subsiding and asking when they thought the father of the house would be returning – a question that was met with blank looks – he waded back out.

Although the lane leading into Yaxton was running with water, it was shallow enough to be acceptable to Thunder's finicky hooves, and Philip was relieved not to have to walk any further. He could barely feel his feet in the stirrups, and his trousers were wet to the waist. His mind was running to such matters as hot soup and a warm bed, when he saw Trench walking ahead of him with his scurrying gait. He was a curious person – not boy and yet not quite man, hovering instead somewhere in between. He was carrying a basket over his arm.

With Jowler's exhortations to keep the community under his eye ringing in his ears, Philip greeted Trench, and then, with some reluctance since his leaky boots had only just dripped their water out, dismounted and began to walk alongside him. Thunder, no doubt as disposed towards food and warmth as Philip was, pulled his black lips back in disgust. His horse reactions were so human, that Philip half expected that one day, the creature would open its gummy mouth and emit a perfectly formed sentence.

'How has the community fared in the floods?' he asked.

'One dead fox, five dead hedgehogs and a deal of dead rabbits,' Trench replied, plodding on with his head down.

It was the kind man. He was as determined as a robin and had the same brightness in his chest. He opened mouths like the rush of water over high stones. He wanted to tell this sturdy, buttoned person why he felt scared. Why in the night the darkness swelled. How the Lamb was much weaker than the Lion.

'But what of the house and inhabitants? Did the water get in?'

'No, sir. Only the garden.'

'That is welcome news,' Philip said. They carried on walking for a while, Philip thinking about how strong walls and money protected people from all manner of things, even the forces of nature.

'Tell me, Mr Trench,' Philip said, 'How long have you been living in the community?'

'Almost five years, sir.'

'Do you know about another woman who died? Not Hattie, but one before? About a year ago.'

'She used to sing. She had hair the colour of a blackbird's wing.'

'And she took her own life, just as Hattie did?'

'She was found in the orchard, sir,' Trench replied.

'And did you see her? Afterwards, I mean.'

Trench fell silent.

Don't talk. Don't speak of things seen and heard. The turn of the key in the door of the cold place. The smell of what happened there in the floor and the cracks of the walls.

'I do not want to cause you distress,' Philip said. Noticing the same agitation in the man as he had before.

'I am not allowed out of my room at night,' Trench finally said in a quiet voice.

He thought of her tiny little hands. How she used to move them from side to side when she was singing. They had watched her, too, the way they watched Goldie.

'You know you will not be in trouble with me if you were to tell me what you know.'

'I don't know anything.'

'But if you *had* been out of your room when they brought her back, what *would* you have seen?' Philip said, trying another tack.

'I was sleeping.'

'So, you did not go for one of your walks, that night?'

'I expect I was dreaming,' Trench said.

'Yes, that is it. I am sure you were. What did you see in your dream?'

'Two of them carrying her in. Her hair all awry. Her face strange to me. I think they dragged her. Her clothes were muddy. A piece of paper pinned to the front of her. It had a word on it and on top of that a cross. Not a Christ cross. The cross like the sign at Four Forks, where the roads meet.'

'You are quite certain of this? I mean, you are certain of what you saw in your dream?'

They had reached the gate to the community, and Trench stopped.

'I dreamt it. In the morning she was gone.'

Chapter 29

'Has the flood subsided yet?' Irene asked, fastening the buttons on a pale green dress that gave her an otherworldly look, like a creature who belonged in the mist.

Ruby looked out of the window. The lawn was still under water. The Hall had been spared an incursion, but she knew that when the flood eventually soaked its way onward and downward, the garden would need a lot of work to restore it. Flower heads and stalks drifted around slowly, as if someone had cast them onto the water in commemoration of a death. The sun had finally come out, turning the wetness on the ground into a mirror in which the trees and the wall and the roof of the chapel were reflected. It made her feel anxious to see the extent of her world shown so, as if her enclosure had shrunk.

'I think it is receding,' she said.

The community had been summoned to the chapel, an occurrence which was unusual enough to provoke a feeling of alarm, and the sisters and their mother made their way down the stairs with trepidation. The men and woman were divided down the middle with Peters' inner circle of saints, all men, who Ruby seldom saw since they largely kept themselves apart, at the front. As soon as they had all taken their seats or found a place against the wall to stand, for there were far more people than there were chairs, Peters began to speak from behind his ornate pulpit. Ruby could see that his mood was a black one. This was not the gentle leader, but rather a tighter, darker version of the man.

'I have gathered you together to tell you about something that shames us all. Two of our number have not been living as I have asked you all to live. It has come to my attention that the people in question have been spending nights together, under one roof.'

The saints murmured and hissed with a sound like heat against wet stone as his eyes passed over them, as if he had touched them with hot hands rather than words.

'Spiritual marriage, as you all know, is central to our work here. This is the Garden of Eden before Adam took the wormed apple from the snake, before Eve showed her wanton flesh and tempted him. Daniel and Anne come before us.'

At his words Martin led the couple in. Anne, a little woman with an open face and a marching walk who Ruby knew looked after the cows at the farm, was followed by her husband who was holding his hat between his constantly moving fingers.

'Uncover your head,' Peters said. He came from behind the lectern holding a pair of scissors. With trembling hands Anne untied the string around her chin and pulled off her bonnet.

'Let your hair down,' he commanded, and the woman whose normally ruddy face had turned as white as the mid-section of the Sheeted Somerset cattle under which she laboured, raised her arms, and unpinned a fall of corn-coloured tresses that reached down below her waist in spirals of curls. Peters raised his scissors, and the crowd gave a kind of moaning sigh.

'Bend your head,' the Reverend said, his voice low, almost caressing. There was a movement of dissent from Daniel, then, a kind of desperate lurch towards his wife. But Martin, who was standing next to him, took hold of his arm to stop him. Anne bent slowly from her waist as if she was bowing, and her hair hung down to the floor and gathered in a great mass at her feet. Peters took hold of the weight of it in his fist and began slicing through it, cutting large chunks at a time. The noise was surprisingly loud in the chapel. Each bite of the scissor's blades made a grinding sound like a cow chewing on grass and set Ruby's teeth on edge. Soon Anne was left with uneven tufts like someone who had been bitten about the head by a dog. The sisters exchanged wide-eyed looks.

'Put your head up,' Peters said, and she obeyed him. She looked like a completely different person – as if her head was on the wrong body. Ruby remembered a game she had played as a child, where a set of cards had to be placed above and below each other in a certain way to correctly make up various characters. It looked now as if Anne's cards had been placed against the head of quite another person. Standing bent double for such a length of time had obviously made her dizzy, because she staggered slightly. Again, Daniel made a move towards her and was restrained by Martin.

'Sister Miriam, can I ask you to finish shaving Anne's head,' Peters said.

A chair was brought for Anne, and Miriam rubbed some sort of ointment on her scalp and then moved the razor in smooth, unhurried movements. The woman took on yet another incarnation from wild waif to moon-headed baby.

'Anne and Daniel,' Peters said as Martin began shaving Daniel's hair in sections, so that the shape of his head was slowly revealed. 'You have transgressed, but you know your sin. Be on constant guard against the beatings and pulses of your bodies. Command your flesh to your will and to mine.'

Peters indicated that a bowl of water should be brought to him, and he washed his hands slowly, spreading the soap between each of his fingers and rinsing twice and then wiping himself dry with the towel that was draped over the arm of one of the saints. The congregation remained watching in silence, as if the ablutions of their leader were part of the spectacle.

'What will happen to Anne and Daniel now?' Ruby asked as she walked back to the sewing room with Irene and Angela. She had been unsettled by what they had just seen. Angela, on the other hand, seemed in good spirits; she was talking ten to the dozen and she plucked a sprig of salvia from the vase in the hallway.

'It has such a lovely, peppery scent,' she said, waving the flower in front of Irene's face.

'What will Reverend Peters do?' Ruby asked again. 'Other, that is, than cutting off their hair.' She thought it quite punishment enough to be so exposed, thinking of the way that Anne had ducked her head as she had walked from the chapel as if she had mislaid her sturdiness and found instead a new, trembling shame.

'The shaving of the head is the first warning. There will not be another after that,' said Angela.

'So, they are able to remain in the community?' Ruby asked.

'For now, although they know that The Beloved is watching them for further transgressions,' Angela said. 'And it will take them longer to attain sainthood, if they ever do.'

'But they could, of their own free will, leave at any time of their choosing?'

'Yes, of course,' Angela answered, 'but who would willingly renounce the chance of salvation?'

'And to think only a few months ago Irene and I, and our mother, too, were heedlessly wading our way through the mire of depravity beyond these walls!' Ruby exclaimed. Her tone was light, but Angela turned her head sharply and sniffed, as if she could smell something less pleasant than the salvia.

'Indeed, you have been fortunate,' she said. 'You left it almost as late as it was possible to leave it. Those outside will die terrible and lonely deaths and be damned to eternal, burning, torturous pain.' She said this as prettily as if she was reeling off the recipe for pastry or talking of where a vase of flowers might best be placed in a room.

'And you care nothing for them?' Irene asked quietly, her head bent.

'They have made their choice,' Angela said, 'and I have made mine, and that is all there is to it.'

For a moment she looked peevishly at them, but then her face broke into her usual wide smile, and she leant over and placed the flower behind Irene's ear and stepped back, her head on one side to consider its effect.

'Blue in the red,' she said, still smiling, 'like a flame.' And she turned and led the way up the stairs.

'You've made a lot of progress since I saw it last,' Ruby said, in the sewing room, inspecting the embroidery. A mountain range in shades of green and grey and several towers with roofs shaped like shells had attached themselves to the sky. Ruby could see Irene's delicate hand in a line of what looked like animals that snaked their way through the landscape. They were so intricately rendered, so small, that she had to examine them closely. She saw that they were not the creatures she had at first assumed them to be, but rather a series of naked babies, crawling in a single file, the feet of one almost touching the head of the next, and making up a chain.

'This is a strange procession, Irene!' she exclaimed. Her sister shrugged as if she did not herself know how such an oddity had come to be represented there.

'I simply sew as Sister Angela reads,' she said.

At the bottom of the embroidery was the beginning of a wall, the mortar studded with dark red bricks which were placed sloping to the left and the right in the distinctively haphazard style of the community's own fortification. Ruby had been told that many hands had been involved in the construction of the wall and she had walked round its entire circumference one day noting, in the sudden changes of slant and texture and the new careering paths the roughly cut bricks suddenly took, the junctions where one workman had been replaced by another.

'You've put our wall into the picture!' Ruby said, surprised. 'I understood that *The Song of Solomon* was set in landscape further away than this patch of Somerset. Mount Gilead, isn't it? Not that I know exactly where that is.'

'The text speaks of a garden enclosed,' Eloise said, raising her head from the painstaking work of untangling skeins of thread in shades of yellow that ranged from the pallid ash of curdled cheese to a vibrant ochre only a breath away from gold, and laying the freed lengths across her lap.

'And what exactly is the text about?' Ruby said mischievously, catching Irene's admonishing eye and hiding a smile.

'It tells of God's love for us and of our yearning expectation that we will one day be worthy of that love,' Eloise said, looking over their heads at the half-opened window as if she expected the word of God to come flying into the room on the kind of written scroll that adorned the frames of some of the paintings on the walls of the sewing room; pictures of pale women in attitudes of devotion with bitten, maroon lips and hooded eyes, holding lilies between long, pale fingers, and cupping doves.

'It is an allegory,' said Eloise, bowing her head to her task once more, weaving her fingers in and out of her aureate strands. 'It describes symbols that represent our union with God.'

'So, the fauns and suchlike do not actually refer to parts of the anatomy?' said Ruby, unable now to stop.

'They refer to the spread and glory of God's Kingdom,' Eloise said and sucked one end of a piece of silk and held a needle close to her eye and attempted to thread it, although it was clear that her hand was shaking too hard to accomplish the task.

'Let me do that,' Angela said, taking the thread and needle from the older woman and sitting back down. Just then there was a brief knock at the door and a young woman who Ruby did not recognise came in.

'Who are you?' Angela asked. 'I have not seen you before.'

'I'm the new maid, miss,' she replied. 'My name is Minnie.'

She made an awkward ducking motion. Ruby was struck by

both her beauty and her youth. Golden curls were escaping from her loosely tied bonnet and her eyes were a wide, guileless green.

'There is no need to curtsy!' Angela exclaimed sharply. 'We do not show such subservience here.'

'I'm sorry, miss. I didn't know. I've just come to say that Reverend Peters has asked that Miss Ruby and Miss Irene come and see him in his rooms,' she said.

Chapter 30

Ruby's heart sank at their summons. She had very little doubt that Peters and Martin wanted to question Irene about her seizures.

'I hope Ruby and Irene are not being called to see The Beloved because of some misdemeanour,' Angela said, giving her tinkling laugh. 'I would hate to see Irene shorn of all that beautiful hair.'

Martin then appeared in the doorway. He had come to escort them.

'No fault has been committed,' he said, and Norah who had been glancing avidly between him and the sisters, gave an almost disappointed look and turned back to her work.

Martin led them down the stairs and entered Peters' room after knocking briefly. It wasn't at all the space Ruby had been expecting. The windows were draped with sprigged muslin and the sofa was covered in lace and littered with silky pillows. It wasn't the kind of room she would have imagined for any man, least of all him. If pressed on the matter she would have guessed that his would be a darker, more masculine quarters, in keeping with his plain dress.

Ruby then realised with a start of surprise that their leader was lying stretched out on the sofa, his shirt partly unbuttoned, his head propped up by cushions, his feet bare. This strange informality in someone usually so meticulous in his presentation alarmed her in a way that she could not define – it suggested a kind of intimacy that made her uncomfortable. She remembered the sensation of his mouth on her hand, and she felt a wave of nausea. Despite the apparent relaxation of his pose, it seemed to her that as always, he was trying to contain some great feeling that was continually in danger of escaping him, the way the boiling contents of a saucepan push up against its lid.

He indicated that they should sit down. Martin remained standing by the door, like a sentry who thought someone was about to bolt.

'You look like you belong in a painting, Irene,' Peters remarked. 'One of those women who have an expression halfway between sleep and exaltation.'

'I *am* rather tired,' Irene said. 'The sewing I have been doing is hard on the back and on the eyes.'

'But are you fully recovered from your last episode?'

'Yes, thank you, quite recovered.'

'And have you been taking the tincture I recommended?'

'I have, Reverend Peters,' Irene said.

'It is your takings that I want to talk to you and your sister about.'

Ruby could not take her eyes from his feet. He flexed them as he spoke. His toe nails were yellowish and slightly too long.

'It is a medical phenomenon, the result of faulty connections in the brain,' Irene said, plucking at the fabric of her dress.

'I am trained as a doctor,' Peters said somewhat loftily, 'so I am conversant with the workings of the brain. This, however, seems to be something other.'

'Something other, indeed,' Martin said.

Ruby thought she could smell Martin from where she was sitting – a kind of warm, woody smell, that put her in mind of dark, enclosed places.

'What I am interested in is that you seem to be able to see into the future.'

'I have never claimed to be able to do so,' Irene said.

'And yet you foretold the night sun, and then the flood, in which sadly, I hear four people died.'

'She only sees portions of things,' Ruby said. 'She has reported all manner of happenings that have made no sense at all.'

'Perhaps the sense depends on who hears it,' Martin said.

'I was wondering, if you might act as a guide to us,' Peter said, ignoring his companion. 'You might be able, for instance, to foretell the nature and time of the Day of Judgement'.

His words, delivered as they were with such calm equanimity, as if he was talking about the vagaries of the weather, astonished Ruby. She had thought that they might have persuaded themselves that Irene had some sort of power as a soothsayer, which was, in itself a misguided notion, but at least within the realms of common misconception. That they seemed to think that her sister might be able to predict their day of salvation, made no sense to her at all. They had advertised the community as some kind of vessel, captained by Peters, on its charted journey to its final destination. Now it seemed that they were hoping Irene was to be their navigator. What of the much-vaunted special relationship with God? Was not the narrative he had spun that he already knew the way? The Beloved gave a luxuriant stretch and his feet fanned out against the sofa.

'I thought that the Day of Judgement was something you were to identify, Reverend Peters,' Ruby said.

Peters looked at her. She saw the sharpness in the glance.

'I would not presume to recognise the Day of Judgement,' Irene murmured.

'Nevertheless, Irene, I want to know all that you see. It could be that your visions simply need to be interpreted correctly. Who better than I to recognise the word of God, even though it may come in an unlikely form?' Peters replied, swinging himself languidly into a sitting position. 'I think you have strength far beyond the usual. I think you are a true Spiritual Bride.'

'Oh, yes indeed, indeed,' Martin said, his voice low and distracted as if he was unaware that he had spoken out loud.

'And you are well on the path to sainthood, Irene,' Peters added, giving Ruby another glance that she refused to meet.

'I think lunch is being served,' he said then. They all rose to their feet. As she was passing the large table in the centre of the room, Ruby saw a map spread out and held in place at each corner with a paperweight.

'What is this?' she asked bending over it.

The document was a representation of the community exactly as it was – the lion-topped chapel, the main house, the triple line of cottages, and the farm with the fields beyond. Even the lake with its swans was marked out in its improbable blue. Diminutive people in pale dresses and waistcoats populated the garden and she could see others leaning out of windows or drawing curtains. Tiny greenhouses were full of vividly rendered tomatoes and geraniums.

'I drew it myself. It helps me to see what I have accomplished and have yet to accomplish,' Peters said. 'You see this here?' He indicated a whole stretch of land beyond the wall and to the north with unfamiliar houses drawn with a sketchy stroke and not yet coloured. 'This is what we will be working on next. This is the second phase of the community.

'How many more are to join us?' Ruby asked.

'As many as have the sense to stop and listen and recognise God in me. There is still some time.'

Martin tried to usher them out, but Ruby bent closer to the map. She was fascinated by its detail and accuracy. In the miniature sewing room, Irene, who was distinguishable by her mass of red hair and white skin, was bending over the canvas. Sister Angela was distinct in her pink dress. Sister Eloise, crowned with thin tufts of hair had her arms held up and bound round with skeins of kingfisher-blue thread. In the orchid house the figures within were surrounded by a filigree of blooms. She thought she was the one with a tiny spade, dressed in the blue she favoured, and yellow-frocked Edith was at her side holding a watering can. As she scrutinised the scene she noticed the area near her own portrait had the diffused, watery look of some recent adjustment. It took her a moment to realise that Hattie had already been painted out. At the back of the Hall, beyond the lawn and the fernery was a small, oddly-shaped building, Ruby had not noticed before.

'What is this?' she asked, pointing to it.

'Sister Miriam dislikes late arrivals,' Martin said, swiftly moving aside two of the restraining weights so that the map suddenly rolled itself up.

Peters nodded his dismissal.

'It seems you are on the brink of sainthood,' Ruby said as they walked to the dining room.

'I shall not become a saint if you are not made one, too,' Irene said, scurrying after Ruby who was striding ahead. 'Are you angry that it seems I am preferred?' she added anxiously.

'I do not want either of us to become saints,' Ruby said. 'Look what happened to poor Hattie who has already been painted out of The Beloved's great plan. Why is it that they are so eager for you to become one? Other people have far longer to wait for the dubious honour to be conferred on them. I feel they have some plan for you, perhaps for both of us, although I do not know what it is. They want our money, I know that.'

'They think that I will be able to offer them some guidance,' Irene said.

'Do you believe this to be true?' Ruby asked stopping and turning to her sister.

'I did see water in the last taking, Ruby. I saw a flood thick with creatures.'

'You cannot call rising water and the loss of some farmyard animals a *flood thick with creatures*. Remember what our father told us. He said it was superstition to view an illness as somehow imbued with magic. I have always thought that what you see in your seizures is similar to what is created by a fever.'

'It was not just animals who died in the flood, but people, too,' Irene protested.

'What magic are you talking of?' Angela appeared alongside them. As always, Ruby was struck by Angela's animation. There was a vitality about her that belied her soft, pretty looks.

'Only that there is no such thing,' Ruby said.

'Why, sister Ruby, there is magic everywhere! Is it not magic the way the bud grows to a flower? Or the way the moon swells and then diminishes?'

Angela accompanied her words with a kind of dancing twist, as if she was demonstrating her own part in the enchantment.

'Some might call those things *magical*. But they are part of the real workings of the earth and skies,' Ruby said.

'How very solemn your sister is!' Angela laughed and linked her arm through Irene's. 'Let us go in and eat some of Sister Rachel's *magical* rabbit pie.'

Chapter 31

Quite what the chief constable imagined Philip would achieve by patrolling the circumference of the community was unclear, but nevertheless here Philip found himself at the beginning of another week of law enforcement. The flood waters had largely subsided, leaving the fields and villages askew – fences were lying on their sides, uprooted trees rested across lanes, apple crates and cooking pots had journeyed across the landscape and ended up where they didn't belong – as if some huge hand had shaken everything in its fist and thrown it down. The sun was inhaling the moisture from the ground, making a haze of steam over the horizon.

Philip had discharged his one other required duty that morning, a visit to Farmington, a village to the south of Yaxton, where it had been reported that the innkeeper of The Globe had been serving up short measures. He had had dealings with the man before. He was exactly the type of individual Philip most disliked – he had a hearty, forceful affableness that was always a wink away from belligerence. Philip rubbed his hands across the front of his jacket. The innkeeper's damp paw had clutched his too closely and for too long as they had parted, more in threat Philip thought, than with any fellow feeling.

'All they have to do is ask me to fill their cups to the top, if they really want to be spilling beer down their greedy fronts,' had been his answer to the policeman's enquiry about short measures.

He was thinking, in a halfhearted kind of way, about lunch, knowing there was only some sausage and a lump of cheese in his pocket – since his mother's illness he had had to fend for himself – when a familiar figure appeared in the lane. It was the gloveress, Minnie, dressed in one of the community's pastel frocks under her apron.

'Good morning, Minnie!' he exclaimed. 'I did not expect to see you here.'

'I work in the community now,' she said. 'My machine couldn't be mended after the flood. I lost my job.'

She cupped her hand across her forehead and squinted up at him. Her dress was too large for her – the cuffs hung down and the shoulders were set too low on her arm. Despite her youth and the weight of responsibility she had to bear, she had a fortitude, that Philip found admirable.

'I am sorry to hear that' he said.

'Don't worry, my mother is looking after the babber and the oldest of the little ones does his share, bless him.'

'What is it like working at the community?'

Minnie shrugged her narrow shoulders.

'Fireplaces and floors and privvies are the same everywhere. I just do my work.'

'But how do you find the people? Is their way of life strange to you?'

'I don't say anything above what I have to. There are parts of the community I am not allowed to go into. She shrugged again. 'Suits me. Means I've less to do.'

'And have you had any dealings with the leader?'

'Thinks a bit of himself with his fancy shirts and cloaks and what have you. Not quite as holy as he makes himself out to be, either. They are all supposed to abstain. Caught a glimpse of him through his office door, taking a great big glass of wine. I'd have guessed in any case. If there is one smell I know, it's the drink.'

A shadow crossed her face, giving Philip a clue as to why her father was so often absent.

'I'd better go in. That Miriam will eat me alive otherwise,' she said.

'Yes, perhaps not a person you want to get on the wrong side of.'

Minnie made a funny cross-eyed expression and laughed and went on her way.

A little later, as his perambulations took him to the entrance of the community, Philip saw that two people were standing by the gate waiting for admittance – an older woman and a younger. Philip, who was used to noticing the differences in people, saw their privilege in the shine of their dresses, in the details of hair arrangement and the age and quality of their luggage.

Once they had gone inside, and stuffing his cheese into his pocket, he approached the carriage driver who had been left with their bags.

'Some new members of the community?' he asked in a light tone, hoping that the man was not of the reticent variety.

'Good riddance to them,' the man muttered, giving the pile of luggage a bad-tempered shove.

Philip was pleased to see that he was clearly consumed with ill feeling. In his experience, people in the throes of resentment were generally at their most voluble.

'Your previous employers? I take it that they were people you found it difficult to work for,' he said, taking off his hat, the wearing of which sometimes had the effect of stemming the flow of information, and which he was, in any case, finding rather warm.

'Difficult!' the man exclaimed, wiping his nose on the back of his sleeve. 'They got rid of the lot of us! This is my last working day. Years of loyal service and dismissed like we was nothing more than kitchen scrapings. The master takes a few more drinks than he should have, sets off after a fox and ends up thrown over a bridge, dead. And then *she*, Mrs Vantage'— here the man accompanied his words with a well-aimed kick at the largest trunk —'she decides to move into this place. She handed over her entire fortune to someone she has known for barely a week.'

'How inconsiderate,' Philip said in his most encouraging voice.

'Inconsiderate! It was like she was enchanted out of her right mind. The daughter is being offered into "spiritual marriage", whatever the hell that means, with one of the so-called leader's henchmen, with a hefty sum no doubt attached.'

'It does seem a drastic measure to take.'

'Drastic! It is downright wrong. *She* talked about salvation and everlasting life, but it seems to me the place is nothing more than a business. One designed to line the pocket of its leader. Have you seen him in his cloak? Parading around like a popinjay.'

With that, the man delivered a globule of spit to the ground and thumped on the gate.

Philip walked on and finding a tree to lean against, took out his lunch again. As he contemplated the vaporous sky, he mused on the conversation he had just had. Most of the things he dealt with were about money in some form or another – arguments about unpaid debts, thefts from those who had become drunk and unwary, transactions which were not as they had first seemed. Money was what drove most people to do things they shouldn't.

He had also expended a lot of thought on the matter of the messages pinned to the dresses of the two suicide victims. Unless there was some sort of acknowledged stricture within the community that those who took their own lives should adorn themselves in this way, it seemed to him distinctly strange that the pieces of paper had been exactly the same; each bearing the word *saint*, which had been crossed out. It was surely more than a coincidence. In his opinion, and Philip tended to arrive at opinions in a slow but thorough fashion, this could only have happened in one of two ways. Either writing such notes was one of the community's strange rules, or someone other than the unfortunate victims had penned them. If someone else had been involved, it threw into doubt whether the young women had died at their own hands. There was a third option, which in the cause of approaching the matter in a systematic way Philip was forced to contemplate: Trench had indeed dreamt up what he had seen. He thought this last possibility very unlikely. The man might be a little out of the ordinary, maybe even not razor-sharp in his wits, but he had an air of honesty, in the manner of a child, when it hasn't grown enough to develop adult wiles. His account of seeing the dead woman returned to the community had a veracity that was compelling.

Perhaps if it was finance that drove the motivations of the community's leader, the deaths were somehow linked to this. Maybe Hattie had expended her usefulness in this regard and could no longer pay her way. If spiritual brides were chosen on the basis of what they could bring to the coffers, it could be that her currency had expired and that of the other woman, too. Maybe it wasn't about a crisis of faith at all. Whatever the reason for the deaths, Philip was determined to find it out. The mystery had in some way renewed his sense of purpose. Jowler could bluster all he liked about priorities, but surely this was what Philip was *supposed* to be doing as an officer of the law. If there was wrongdoing at the community, he wanted to be the one to bring it to light. The fact that Ruby Hart with her slices of pie and her animated face was living within its walls, did nothing to dent this intent.

An almost immediate diminishment of Philip's new sense of confidence and conviction was provoked, however, by the sight of Thomas Balch sauntering down the lane towards him. The man tipped his hat sardonically in Philip's direction.

Chapter 32

4th November

Dearest Nancy,

It seems my longing for home is becoming unspecific. It used to be that I missed tangible things – the swing in our old garden that used to take me so high that I could touch the leaves with the tips of my toes, the freedom of being in a house where I could get up at night and eat hunks of buttered bread without notice, the walks along the river, arm in arm with you, talking our comforting nonsense. Now I just have a sense of longing without having anything particular to pin it to. It is as if I am forgetting who I am or even what I used to want. I looked in the mirror the other morning and it seemed to me I had a whole other face – it was watchful and narrower, somehow, although this thinning might be due to the fact that my hair always has to be pulled back in plaits so tight they give me a headache. I am sorry to complain so. Please do not worry about me. Your old, noisy, self-centred Ruby is still in there somewhere. You do not get rid of me so easily!

Irene has gained much notoriety within the community. They have all become convinced that she will foresee the day we are to be saved during one of her takings. I sometimes think that she has begun to believe it, too. I fear I am losing her. Every day that passes, she seems a little further away. She is taking some kind of a medicine that I am told is to build up her strength and yet I see no evidence of any positive effect. If anything, she seems more tired and remote. Perhaps it is simply the atmosphere of the community, which seems to make dreamers of us all. It is difficult here somehow to hang on to the things that you think you know.

Love, Ruby

Ruby was alone in the kitchen trying to clean the water marks on the glass vases when Trench came hurtling through the door, caught up as always in a whirl of motion. He stopped short halfway across the room and tugged at his hair as if operating a brake.

'George said that I was to come and find you… There's a gentleman at the door…' He stopped as if he had run out of words.

'Thank you,' Ruby said, continuing to dry one of the vases to give herself a little time. Her hands and feet felt as if she had passed them across the tops of new nettles. Although she had told him to keep away, she had known he would come back. She had been expecting him for several days. The right thing to do would be to go to her sister. She could explain that she hadn't wanted Irene to come down to the gate on the occasion of William's first visit in order to protect her. Irene would believe that to be the truth because she always spoke the truth herself. It was possible still to reverse the damage, but there would be no way of explaining why she hadn't reported his return.

Her sister would most likely send William away. *He isn't worthy of my thoughts* she had said. She would surely tell him he had missed his chance and that she wanted nothing more to do with him. And yet, she might not. It could be that she would see the shame and the hope in William's face, and she would soften. Her sister was always one kind word away from offering love.

Ruby thought of their bodies leaning towards each other and how the curve of William's arm around her sister's waist had felt to her like the cruellest of exclusions.

Irene will have a life outside and I will have to stay here with my mother, tending to the orchids and pushing wheelbarrows around until my knuckles are knots of wood, like those of Sister Eloise.

With her face firmly turned away from the house, hoping that her sister wouldn't choose this very moment to lay aside the embroidery to lean out of the window, she went across the lawn.

'My sister does not want to see you,' she said as soon as she opened the gate. If she was to do the deed, she wanted the blow struck quickly and squarely so that she didn't have the chance to change her mind. William looked at her without speaking, in that assessing way he had, as if he took pride at accepting nothing at face value. He had always had this arrogance and it should have repelled her, yet it had drawn him to her in a way that greater humility would not have. She knew that it was a weakness in herself to be so attracted to his swagger and confidence. She tried to keep her heart steady and cold and to look for things in him she didn't like. What was he after all but a boy who had wavered at the first sign that things were not exactly as he wanted? He had loved the Irene that he had invented, not the woman she actually was, who for all her physical frailty was worth a hundred of him. The surface of her had shifted and it had sent him running.

'Might I speak with your mother?' he asked.

'She is right the way over the other side of the community. It would take too long to fetch her.'

'I have plenty of time at my disposal,' William said. 'I can wait for as long as is necessary.'

Ruby began to feel agitated. It was simply luck that until now nobody had noticed William's presence at the open gate. Before too much longer someone would surely come and find out what was keeping her there so long. She half turned to check that there wasn't already somebody approaching and saw Trench hovering in the background. She indicated he should come closer.

'I wonder if you might accompany me and my friend while we go on a short walk,' she said to him. 'Keep a little way behind us. We won't go far.'

As she stepped through the gate she was aware of a stab of disquiet. The stretch of the sky seemed too wide and the road ahead too long. The narrow dimensions of the community had begun to hold her in their thrall. She would not have thought she would be affected so. She hesitated and almost decided to retreat, but then reminded herself that if she did, she would be left with the problem of how to deal with William.

Unprotected by the wall and the fragrant screen of the garden, the yeasty, faecal smell from the inn was almost unbearably strong and she saw how quickly she had become unused to the eyes of strangers, all of whom were now looking at her with varying degrees of curiosity.

'Looks like someone's made a bid for freedom,' a man sitting at a table outside the inn said, looking at Ruby from top to toe in a way that made her flush furiously. His companion, a young man with dark hair and a friendly face got to his feet.

'Giles Yardley at your service, miss. I wonder if I might have a word. I'd like to ask you a couple of questions,' he said.

'Keep your questions to yourself,' William interjected coldly.

'What kind of a man is Reverend Peters? What exactly is a spiritual marriage? Is it true what they say about a member of the community committing suicide? Surely people of such deep faith would not countenance such a sin.' Ruby and William passed by him with their heads averted and after starting to go after them, the young man changed his mind and fell back with an exclamation of annoyance.

'You'll not get any of them to speak,' Ruby heard his companion say. 'They are all bewitched.'

William unlatched the gate to a path across the field in which the horses were kept, and Ruby and he walked in silence for a while. Trench kept speeding up and then slowing his steps as if he was finding it hard to keep a measured distance behind them.

'You have missed your chance with Irene,' Ruby said. 'She has shut her heart to you completely.'

'I would prefer to hear the words from her own mouth,' William said stubbornly. 'I want to explain what happened.'

'What happened was that you deserted her when she was at her most vulnerable. You found her indisposition to be ugly. You left without a single word.'

'I was wrong. I behaved in an unforgivable way,' William said.

'That is exactly it. It was unforgivable,' she said.

'Irene has a softer heart than yours, as we both know.' He looked sideways at her.

'It isn't kind of you to refer to what I said then.' Ruby felt a flush of mortification much deeper than that elicited by the man at the inn.

'It seems neither of us is very good at demonstrating kindness,' William answered, slashing at the vegetation with his stick as he walked.

'At least I have never abandoned her,' Ruby said.

'Have you not?' William answered, and Ruby found herself unable to reply. She hated the fact that he thought ill of her, but she couldn't take back what she had done, and she was now adding to her tally of deceit and disloyalty.

'Are you certain of what your sister wants? What were her exact words when you told her of my last visit? Can you assure me that you have made my case well and not discouraged her? I would not put such behaviour beyond you.' He looked at her with a hard expression on his face.

'I have to go back. They will miss me if I am gone for any length of time.'

They stopped under the overhang of an oak tree and Trench ground to an abrupt halt and squatted on the edge of the path waiting for them.

He smelt fruit on the man – the sweetish smell of strawberries left too long in the sun. The woman, Goldie's sister, was enchanted out of her mind. She had the heat of longing on her. Too distracted to see what was happening. To see where it was heading. His heart felt heavier than a stone. What could he do? He had been found when he was a day old on the edge of a pit. A stray foot could have kicked him over. He had been nothing then and he was nothing now. He was like the baby in the hedge.

'I will write her a letter,' William decided, and Ruby's heart sank at the thought of having to monitor the post every day to intercept the missive.

'It will not make any difference,' she said, turning away from him. 'In any case, all such things have been taken out of our hands.'

'Such things as love?' William answered, and for the first time his voice had a kind of softness in it, or perhaps she was mistaking puzzlement for concern.

'Reverend Peters has care for our flesh now.' She found there was a relief in having this justification for her actions. She told herself she wasn't betraying her sister but rather keeping her safe in their new world, where ordinary love was meaningless.

The walked back in silence, and with an abrupt goodbye when they reached the community, William went on his way up the lane. Trench slipped through the still mercifully unlatched gate, but Ruby stood looking after William. She could not help that she wanted him. She had no control over her heart or her body, which felt bereft at his departure. Would he come back? When would she see him again?

'Good morning, Miss Hart.'

She turned to find the policeman standing beside her.

'Goodness! You made me start, PC Hodge. I imagine being able to lurk is a useful skill in your profession.'

'Lurking is my main qualification.'

'Well, what are you doing lurking here?'

She was amused at the way she seemed to have discomfited him. The man had flushed almost to his ears and couldn't seem to take his eyes away from his own feet.

'I have been charged with patrolling the community.'

'I had no idea we were privileged enough to have our very own guard.'

He looked up at her then. His eyes were an unambiguous brown and his hair, which was curly and somewhat unruly, fell over his forehead. His face had a disarming openness.

'Well, there has been a theft and the chief constable seems keen to make a good impression on your leader.'

'Do you mean the *pineapples*?'

Ruby could not help laughing as another look of embarrassment crossed the man's face. PC Hodge might be good at surprising people, but if having a poker face was a requisite of his profession, he was lacking in this particular facility.

'Yes. The *incursion* into the community of someone who might have stolen anything at all.'

She saw that despite his somewhat scruffy appearance and an inability to control his blushes, the man had an air of firmness and resolution. She saw it in the solid way he stood and the way his chin went up in reaction to her words.

'Yes, of course. One has to take such things seriously.'

PC Hodge, looked down at his feet again. Ruby did not know how so much scrutiny of his dusty boots had not prompted the attentions of a brush and some polish.

'I understood that community members are not encouraged to leave the community, and yet, you have just been out, Miss Hart.'

It was Ruby's turn to feel at a disadvantage, although she did her best to hide the fact.

'We are not manacled to the walls, Constable Hodge. I am entitled to come and go as I please.'

Her words were defiant, but she couldn't help an involuntary glance through the gate, which she was sure he would have noticed. His eyes might be friendly, but she suspected that there was not much that passed him by. She wondered if his disingenuous air was in actual fact a kind of disguise.

'Can I ask you, Miss Hart, are you happy living here?'

Ruby hesitated. She didn't want to talk about what she felt to someone who was almost a stranger to her. She thought it was even possible that the policeman's close patrol of the community's walls had been at the behest of Miriam, or even Peters himself. Perhaps, seeing her as an impediment to their plans for Irene, the policeman had even been sent there to monitor Ruby's own movements. Living at the community had made her wary in a way she had never been before.

'It is comfortable enough and my mother and sister seem happy here, but it is not what I would have wished for.'

'What *do* you wish for?'

'Good heavens, Constable Hodge, that is a very personal question!'

'Forgive me. Do not answer if you do not want to.'

'It is almost as if you are questioning me because you suspect *me* of being the pineapple thief.'

Hodge looked almost comically stricken at her words.

'Oh, no, of course not. It is simply that I wondered why someone such as yourself. Someone so … so … young, would choose to spend her life walled up.'

'You might have the freedom to roam the streets and go in and out of places without anyone thinking anything of it, I, on the other hand have very little choice of where to be.'

She had noticed his hesitation when he was trying to describe her and couldn't help wondering what it was that he had really wanted to say. She found herself hoping that he thought well of her and wasn't sure why. What did a country policeman's opinion of her matter, after all? It was only that there was something so earnest about him and it had been a while since anyone had asked her what she felt about anything.

'I see. But surely this cannot be the only option available to you?'

'There are ties with family and the small matter of duty, officer,' Ruby said, in as haughty a tone as she could manage, despite the fact that her loyalty towards her family had not been well manifested lately.

'Do you feel that the community is a good place to be? Is it at least some kind of refuge?'

'Many people feel it to be, but I am not sure… Recently I have been feeling something is wrong, although I could not really tell you what.'

'Wrong in what kind of a way?'

Ruby heard voices and was brought back to a sense that she was not where she was supposed to be.

'I must go,' she said.

'I am often here, Miss Hart, if there is anything you ever need,' she heard the policeman say, as she slipped through the gate.

Chapter 33

There were two new arrivals seated at the breakfast table. Miriam introduced them with a stately nod of her head. Mrs and Miss Vantage. A mother and daughter who demonstrated the passage of time with cruel exactness. Although unmistakably related and of similar colouring and stature, where the mother drooped and loosened, the daughter curved and blossomed. Sitting side by side at the table with their arms pressed together, the younger had the air of a creature that had come into being by sucking the life from her host.

'Welcome to the community,' Ruby said, as she took her seat opposite them and the mother gave a watery smile, while her daughter revealed symmetrical dimples.

'Call me Delia,' she said, 'and this is my mother, Eva. We are to be sisters after all so should call each other by our proper names. I've always wanted a sister.' She looked around the table as if she was contemplating selecting a sibling immediately.

'You will gain a great many sisters and brothers,' Edith said, as eager as ever to make newcomers feel at home.

'I shall take you to the farm and show you the animals,' Hester said. 'There are two new kids that will steal your hearts.'

'Being here is not about how *you* are going to benefit, Delia,'

Norah put in sourly. She gave the young girl an aggressive stare over the top of her glass of milk. The creamy liquid had gathered on her top lip, and she licked at herself with a narrow tongue. Ruby suspected that Norah, whom nobody ever referred to as comely, was jealous of the young woman's good looks. Delia coloured and then recoiled as if she had been slapped.

'Forgive me. I have only just arrived and do not know yet how things work,' she said, lowering her glance to her plate.

'If you have any questions, I will be happy to answer them,' Norah said, passing a finger around the inside of her bowl and sucking on it.

'Since you are so adept at cleaning the crockery, perhaps you would be good enough to clear the empty plates and take them to the kitchen, Norah,' Miriam said, and Norah's complacent smile vanished and was replaced by a look of resentment, but she got to her feet obediently.

'For those of you who do not yet know, Sister Eloise has been taken ill and is being cared for by The Beloved,' Miriam announced, and then calmly sat down and began eating her porridge.

Ruby had been in the sewing room when Sister Eloise had been carried out after collapsing to the floor. The relaxation of her body, its sudden shapelessness, had made Ruby think that death must surely be near. Eloise was very old and had been born in the distant past. She had known a time when there had been no steam or electromagnetics, or friction matches or even shoelaces. Though insignificant compared to big machines, even shoelaces were a step forward for the human race, indeed they were essential for any steps forward, Ruby thought and smiled to herself. She caught Angela's eye.

'Will she recover soon?' asked Edith looking anxiously at Miriam.

'Of course she will,' Miriam replied. 'She is a saint and even though she is temporarily indisposed, her faith will protect her. As long as she believes and does not sin, she will not die.'

Edith nodded and seemed reassured, and her relief was transmitted down the table so that they all began to chatter and laugh. Sister Eloise was a popular member of the community – the person to whom everyone turned with their small physical ailments and worries. Feeling the ache in her bones during the chilly spell before the floods, she had come to the orchid house for some warmth and had sat watching Ruby work. Often restless herself, Ruby had asked her companion how it was that she always seemed so calm and never prey to the same anxieties as others.

'I am anxious all the time, Ruby,' Sister Eloise had said smiling.

'What about?'

'About whether the remedy I provide for a stomach ache is the right one, or if the guidance I give is thoughtful enough, or how to hide my lack of appetite at the sight of one of Edith's stews, or whether it is saintly to feel so irritated by the sound of Brother Colin's tapping stick, that I want to snatch it up and snap it in two. I could go on. My weaknesses are legion.'

'But you feel you are in the right place?'

'Here we have to do what we can for each other and that makes us better than we might be otherwise.'

'But what of your faith? Do you believe that The Beloved is leading us to salvation?'

'It is this belief that gives me the strength to fight my weaknesses,' Eloise had said.

'It is wonderful, is it not, that dear Sister Eloise will soon be better and will be able to be amongst us once more?' Angela asked now.

'It is indeed,' Ruby answered turning her attention to her poached egg, which wasn't as well cooked as she liked and had a sickening snarl of red in it.

Just as she was about to leave the table, there was a loud crash. She saw that her sister had fallen from her chair, taking a length of the table cloth with her. Ruby got up and rushed to her side. If she had known it was coming, Irene would surely have left the room sooner. She had clearly been felled by a taking that had come with absolutely no warning. Pushing aside the broken bowls and cutlery that littered the floor around her, Ruby knelt down. Hester stood to one side, but did not approach her daughter. Miriam left the room saying she was going to fetch Martin. As was now their custom, everyone clustered around. One of them, Ruby could not identify who, made a sound of chanting encouragement of the kind a midwife might make at the birth of a child, and this low sound was taken up by a few of the others, so that Irene's movements were accompanied by its strange, murmured rhythm.

The fit was the most violent and sustained that Ruby had ever witnessed. Irene's poor body seemed to be thrust this way and that so strongly, that it seemed at times as if she would leave the ground, and foam gathered around her mouth in a way that Ruby had not seen before. In distress, she tried to wipe her sister's face with a napkin and to say the things she knew had calmed her in the past, but Irene still continued to move with the same terrible force, until Ruby began to think she would never stop.

'What shall I do? She will hurt herself against the floor,' she said, looking up at Miriam and Martin, feeling alone, despite their presence. If she had been able to, she would have lifted Irene up in her arms and taken her to safety. From her position on the floor, Miriam and Martin loomed above her, their eyes fixed on Irene. It seemed to her that they were willing her sister on. The longer the fit lasted the more intent they became. Ruby could feel their breath on her face – hot and tainted with egg and milk.

'Just let it take its course,' Martin said.

'But this is much worse than other fits! We should summon a doctor.'

'What could another doctor do more than The Beloved has already done?' Martin asked.

'I want you to go and see if the policeman is outside, and ask him to get help,' Ruby said, in as firm a voice as she could manage. She thought Constable Hodge, with his calm good sense and understanding eyes, would surely know what to do.

The Taking of Irene Hart

'I do not think we need to involve anyone from outside,' Miriam said implacably, her arms crossed in front of her. Ruby thought to go and find the man herself, but didn't want to leave her sister alone, even for a moment. There was something covetous in the way that Martin was watching Irene that chilled her.

'It is strange, is it not, that in the throes, your sister quite loses her beauty?' Martin said.

A panicked rage suffused Ruby. She felt her body shaking. She felt so savage that she wanted to sink her teeth into the man's leg.

'My sister's illness is not a spectacle for you to gawk at,' she snarled at him.

'Ruby!' Hester said. 'Do not speak so to Brother Martin!'

'Mother, will *you* not send for a doctor?' said Ruby appealing to her.

'I think it is best that we do as Brother Martin tells us to.'

It seemed to Ruby that her mother had become a stranger to her. All her impulses to protect, even to assert herself, had gone and had been replaced by a kind of indifference and the same unblinking gaze she saw on many of the saints' faces. The latent child in Ruby felt the pain of this.

Just when she thought that Irene might die, Ruby saw her sister's body begin, at last, to slow its movements.

'You see! She is coming back to us!' Hester said, gazing at Martin as if it had been him who had wrought this change.

After a few more gentle spasms, Irene lay still. She was as white as the scattered crockery, and she had livid, purplish shadows under her eyes. Ruby bent down and was relieved to feel her sister's breath against her face.

'I must record every word she says.'

Martin had moved forward and was poised over Irene with his notebook and pencil.

Irene opened her eyes and looked up into Ruby's face.

'Save me,' she said, her voice indistinct, as if it came from a long way away.

'She is talking of salvation!' Martin exclaimed.

'Shh, Irene… Shh now,' Ruby said.

'Oh, Ruby, I could not get out, even though I tried so hard.' A single tear welled in the corner of one of her eyes.

'What could you not get out of?' Martin asked.

'There were rats. Hundreds and hundreds of them with long, fat tails.' Irene's body shuddered with revulsion, as if she could see them still. 'They ran everywhere in one great mass, like a river.'

'Let me help you up,' Ruby, said, desperate to get Irene away from her audience, but when she tried putting her arm around her sister, Irene's body was heavy and inert.

'I could not open the door, though I threw myself against it over and over.'

'Did you recognise the place?' Martin asked, but Irene closed her eyes again and seemed to be drifting into sleep.

Trench appeared in the doorway of the dining room looking anxious, and Ruby waved him over.

'Help me get Irene to bed.'

By putting her arms around their shoulders, Trench and Ruby managed to get Irene from the room and slowly up the stairs. Ruby expected Martin to come after them and press Irene into further revelations, but it seemed that for the time being, he had got all he needed.

Chapter 34

'When the wind is strong, it seems to me I can detect the odour of Bridgwater and of home,' Irene said, sniffing the air.

The half-opened window in the bedroom rattled on its latch. In the garden below the trees were unsettled. The tall chestnuts swayed, dislodging their flaming leaves in showers.

Irene was arranging her hair, but she paused midway through her slow combing and rested her arms on the dressing table. Ruby, who was sitting in the corner of the room mending the sleeve of a dress that had caught on a stray curl of bramble, didn't answer. In truth, she was finding it hard to even look at Irene. She kept thinking of William's face when he had said her sister's name and her throat sealed up.

'You are fearfully quiet,' Irene said.

'I don't have to chatter all the time.'

'In actual fact, Ruby, you mostly do,' Irene said, smiling at her. It was painful to Ruby to see her sister's once lustrous skin now as white as heated alabaster, and her slender fingers, playing now with a discarded brooch. Ruby pricked her finger on her needle and made an exclamation of annoyance.

'That is more the sound I am accustomed to!' Irene said

looking fondly at her. 'The world does not seem quite right when you are not noisy. It is as if a river has suddenly fallen silent.

'Are you calling me a noisy river?' said Ruby in mock outrage.

'You are a wonderful, wide, swift-moving one, with glittering curves and waterfalls. The sort of river you can hear singing though trees and in valleys.'

'Hmm,' Ruby said and dipped her head once more to her task. She didn't have the same facility as her sister with a needle and her stitches were uneven, by turns too wide and then too small and tight, so that the patch she had mended was puckered like the mite-riddled spinach leaves in the vegetable garden.

'I know you do not like to talk of him, but do you ever wish you could see him again? William, I mean.'

Irene allowed herself a brief image of William's face as it had been that day when she had finally returned to her other self, lying on the lawn of the garden that was to have been theirs. It wasn't that she mourned the garden itself, only the loss of the time they might have spent in it together. The walks they would have taken with their arms against each other, observing the detail of things. When she had come back, he had been looking down at her as if she was a stranger. All the loved lines of his face had turned outwards, like something being peeled and she had watched while what had been revealed was not tenderness, nor even pity, but rather a horrified disappointment, as if he had examined a half-eaten fruit and found it ridden with worms.

'I thought he was someone who saw beneath the surface of things. Someone who loved all the parts of me, even the inconvenient ones, but it turned out he did not,' she replied.

'Might he perhaps have changed his mind by now?'

Ruby felt like the most perfidious person in the world. It seemed to her that being at the community was deepening her ability to dissemble. She was always on her guard now against something that she could not quite describe. She thought of Peters' expression when he looked at her – its singular combination of persuasion and aggression and of Martin's vague, watchful eyes. Her hand throbbed and she glanced down at what had become a raised weal between her thumb and her first finger. It was strange, she usually healed quickly.

'Please do my hair for me. I am too tired to do my own and you always do it so well,' Irene said.

Ruby got to her feet to find that she had sewn the sleeve of her torn dress to the skirt she was wearing. She made another exclamation of annoyance. Irene looked at her and laughed.

'You see! You are so distracted that you are sewing yourself into a pickle!' She came and knelt at her sister's feet and cut carefully through the stitches with a pair of small, golden scissors.

'I'll mend the dress for you later,' she said, still laughing.

Once liberated, Ruby brushed Irene's hair. She could feel the weight of it against her hands and smell its slightly oily, perfumed fragrance. It had more colours in it than she would ever be able to describe – gold and copper and a flaming orange and an almost purplish red.

'How do you want it done?' she asked, and Irene's reflection shrugged at her from the glass.

'Any way you wish,' she said, and so Ruby pulled the heavy fall of it up in a twist and fastened it with pins, rebelliously eschewing the prescribed plaits. She noticed that Irene's neck had a rash around it, just where the collar of her dress met her skin.

'Is this causing you discomfort?' Ruby asked, tracing the line of small, blistered spots with her finger.

'I have had it for a couple of days,' Irene answered, putting her own hand up to her neck. 'It itches a little.'

'I'll speak to Miriam about an ointment to sooth it,' Ruby said. The scant, white girth of Irene's neck smote her heart and made her feel ashamed and contrite. It was always this way with her. She never could settle to being good, nor yet embrace her baseness, but rather fluctuated between the two. It was exhausting.

When Ruby had finished, Irene got to her feet.

'I must start work,' she said. 'The others will already be there.'

'Well, do not strain your eyes again,' Ruby said. 'Tell Brother Martin if he wants a machine, he should get one propelled by steam and coal, not blood and sinew.'

After looking for her in the house, Ruby eventually found Miriam in the garden despite the fact that there was a chilly wind blowing. Her facility for stillness was more in evidence than ever. Her face was in shadow, and she stood looking at some point in the middle distance. She turned as Ruby approached.

'I am sorry to disturb you,' Ruby said. 'Irene has a rash, and I was wondering if you perhaps had something to ease it.'

She was discomfited by Miriam's indifferent gaze. She looked as if she was still absorbed in her own thoughts and Ruby was nothing much more than a bee that had flown out of its allotted sphere of flowers and sunshine into a place it didn't belong.

'I'll ask Brother Martin to prepare something,' Miriam said, and then looked at Ruby enquiringly.

'Was there anything else I can help you with?' she asked.

'I was wondering if we are allowed to go out,' Ruby said in a rush, not knowing that this was what she was going to ask. Miriam didn't immediately reply, but instead sat down on the bench and indicated the space next to her.

'Is there somewhere particular you want to go?' she asked after Ruby had settled herself.

'No, it's not that I want to go anywhere specific, it's just that I was wondering if I could. In theory I mean...' She trailed off under Miriam's unblinking regard.

'You can go through the gate right now and walk away and never look back.'

'I am not planning on leaving for good,' Ruby said hastily. 'I simply wanted to establish whether or not I could go out for a short while. To take a walk, for instance.'

The Taking of Irene Hart

Miriam had shaken off her blank look and was studying Ruby's face with minute attention.

'You have so much spirit,' she said, and her voice was low and warm and without a trace of its usual superciliousness. The wind was picking up power. It rocked the trees so that their roots creaked and from the far side of the main house came the furious cries of the peacocks, the sound now part of the wind. Ruby pictured the gusts sending their gaudy tails into disarray, even plucking the feathers from their pallid flesh and sending them drifting over the wall.

'You are stronger than you know,' Miriam said, and Ruby was surprised by the look of sadness, or perhaps longing, that passed across the other woman's face.

'I was strong once, just like you, but my strength was taken from me.'

Ruby looked doubtfully at Miriam. She could not imagine that she was or had ever been anything other than completely sure, like a practised arm that pulls back and lets the arrow fly, knowing, without even looking, that it would reach its target.

'It is often difficult for women out in the world, unless they get what they want, or are happy to accept what they are given. Reverend Peters has provided an alternative. He has given us something to build and call our own. I passed my money to him gladly, knowing it would be used for good. Better him than some other man who would not.'

The two women sat, while the garden shuddered and shook around them, and Ruby had the sensation that at any moment, she would be plucked up along with the peacock feathers and thrown over the wall and set tumbling across fields, on and on until she reached the water.

'I will see that Irene gets the salve she needs,' Miriam said, breaking the silence and getting to her feet. Her face had adopted its habitual silky blankness and her tone was cool.

Reluctant to go back to her room straight away, Ruby walked on beyond the fern garden, into a part of the grounds she had not yet explored. There were days when the area available to them seemed to her to be enough, even generous, and others when she felt the restriction of being walled in, keenly. The latter feeling had been more in evidence recently. It was the nature of all confined places she supposed, to become smaller than they seemed at first, as if the barriers between the space within, and without, grew more evident over time. She came upon what she had always assumed, from a distance, to be simply an irregularity in the ground, but when she went round to the other side of the grass-covered mound, she saw that it contained a steep flight of steps down to a door. This entrance was masked by the shrubbery that grew around it, so that it would have been easy to miss it altogether. She thought this was perhaps the building that she had seen on the map. She wondered why the Reverend should have marked such an insignificant-looking edifice when other outhouses were not represented.

Ruby descended the steps and opened the latch on the door, expecting it to be locked, but it opened easily, the dark, windowless space immediately flooded with light, like a closed eye, lifting its lid. She left the door open, both to allow her to see the interior and also with an instinctive feeling that this was not a place she wanted to be trapped in. With the door jammed she doubted anyone would be able to hear cries for help. The roof was domed, which would explain its shape in the ground, and she guessed it to be an abandoned ice house of the kind that were no longer much used. The walls were made of thick stone and studded with knapped flint, the floor was wooden and stained, probably from the constant drip of ice onto its surface. There were a few iron shelves mounted into the wall and a metal table to one side and not much else. Ruby was about to leave, finding the atmosphere of the place dank and unpleasant, when her eye was caught by what appeared to be scratchings on the wall. She bent lower to take a closer look, and after a moment, was able to make out words in what had first seemed random markings. *Save me* was written over and over again at various heights and depths of incision, as if someone had scraped the words into the wall over a passage of time. *Save me. Save me. Save me.* In a reaction that seemed to Ruby to be out of proportion to what she had seen, she felt a great wave of coldness, that started in her hands and arms and then seemed to spread into the very centre of her body, and which propelled her out of the room as fast as she could go. She banged the door shut behind her and stumbled in her haste as she scrambled back up the steps.

Chapter 35

Philip had finally been granted an interview with Peters. It had taken two more visits to the community to bring this about, but his persistence had paid off and George had informed him the previous day in a somewhat less than enthusiastic fashion that should he return on Monday morning at eleven o'clock, The Beloved would be prepared to grant him an audience. At the allotted hour, Philip made his presence known and was admitted through the gate and then into the man's office.

Peters was sitting at his desk, his head bowed over sheets of paper on which he was writing in a hasty, almost frantic hand. Philip coughed to announce himself and Peters looked up.

'Ah, the man of the law,' he remarked, putting down his pen. 'I wonder whether your colleagues share your single-minded sense of purpose. If so, criminals everywhere must be quaking in their boots.'

His scorn was so evident, despite his smile, that for a moment Philip felt himself falter. He could see now in the direct gaze and presence of the man what it was that made people attach themselves to him. His portrait did not show his strength, nor the will that seemed to run through him where blood should be.

'Please do take a seat,' Peters continued. 'You must need a rest from all your tramping around.'

'I have some questions for you,' Philip said.

'I am fond of questions,' Peters remarked. 'We all should question ourselves daily to ensure our motives are pure.'

'Are your motives pure, Reverend Peters?' Philip asked, which was not at all what he had planned to lead with. Peters surveyed him and then leant forward across his desk.

'I can see you are beyond redemption, Police Constable Hodge. There is in you a fatal stubbornness that prevents you accepting anything other than what you think you already know. It makes you lonely. You are crying out for love, but you do not know where to find it.'

'This interview is about you and your community, not about me,' Philip said evenly.

'Well then, ask me whatever you like,' Peters said, with a complacent air of a man who knew his target had hit home.

'I want to know about a baby that someone from this community left in the lane and two apparent suicides. It seems the community has things that it wishes to hide.'

'Does the chief constable know you are here?'

'I am simply doing my job, Reverend Peters.'

'So, if I were to go to your superior's office and ask if this interview was sanctioned by him, he would answer in the affirmative?'

'It seems to me that you are avoiding the subject under discussion,' Philip said, glad that the man's arrogance was beginning to anger rather than intimidate him.

'What is it exactly that we are being accused of?'

'Well firstly, since you, or rather your housekeeper, Miriam, claim that no babies could be born in the community because of the nature of your faith, why it is that a member of the community was involved in the near death of a child? A child who was left in the lane just outside the community. And secondly, to what do you attribute the deaths of two young women, both members of this community, whose bodies were found in a nearby orchard? How could two such apparently devout people countenance such a sin?'

'The thing about the devil,' Peters remarked in a conversational tone, 'is that he can get through even the slimmest of cracks. Even *I* cannot keep everyone safe.'

'Is there some kind of twisted rule amongst your congregation that states that those contemplating suicide should pin the word "saint" – crossed out – to the front of their dresses before launching themselves from a tree?'

'I do not know what on earth you are talking about, Constable Hodge. You must excuse me. I see that I have ink on my fingers. I must wash it off,' Peters said and got up and poured water from a jug into the bowl and began scrubbing at his hands with a bar of soap. Philip had the distinct impression that this was a diversionary tactic. It was clear that his questioning was discomfiting the other man.

'I have reason to believe that both the dead women had identical messages attached to them. Does that not strike you as strange? *Is* there such a custom here?'

'It is not a rule I have stipulated, but then I would hardly think to cover such an eventuality. Our faith ensures eternal life. I have hundreds of souls under my care and cannot be aware of every small detail. It is possible that the one found out that the other had done it, and it became something of a fashion,' Peters said, drying his hands with a towel. He seemed to be fully in control of himself, but Philip detected a slight faltering. It was nothing more than a new tightness of the shoulders, but it was unmistakably there. Philip took courage from it.

'A *fashion*, Reverend Peters? Is that how you would describe the unfortunate deaths of two of the souls *under your care*?'

'Regret makes people do all manner of things,' Peters said.

'I understand that advantageous matches – I think you refer to them as "spiritual marriages" – are made by certain members of your circle to young women who are able to swell the community's coffers. Is this some kind of reward for those closest to you?'

'Have you come here to question our beliefs, or have you come to investigate the deaths?' Peters asked, and now he seemed almost rattled, although he did his best to hide this by toying with his pen.

'It is only that I am trying to understand the hierarchy of the community.'

'There is no hierarchy in the Garden Kingdom.'

'And yet you are clearly the king, are you not?'

Peters had reached the end of his tolerance. He stood, holding on to the back of his chair with a white-knuckled grip. He wasn't, after all, Philip reflected, very different from the landlord of The Globe; he just had a more sophisticated way of controlling his anger.

'You cannot know, how could you? The level of sacrifice I am willing to make to ensure I lead my flock to redemption. Soon, you and others will understand how far I am prepared to go.'

The words were delivered in a tone of fervent intent. He believes what he is saying, Philip thought. That is the terrible nub of it. He is possessed by his own dogma. This must be what kept him pushing forward, collecting his disciples, and ensuring that faith remained vivid in them. The danger was that a man such as Peters, who wrote his own narrative and the narrative of those around him, would have absolute control over the way the story ended. As its author, he could justify almost anything and would always be able to shape things to fit his own purposes. Philip, who tended to deal with things as they arose and prided himself on a realistic and practical approach, felt an unfamiliar sense of dread.

'I have spared you all the time at my disposal,' Peters said, and Philip got to his feet.

At that moment Martin entered the room. Philip suspected he had been primed to interrupt in case he outstayed his welcome. Martin was dressed for riding in a jacket and hat and with a crop in hand. As he silently held the door open for Philip, he saw that on the small patch beneath the thumb of his glove was a tiny, embroidered eye. At first he could not remember where he had seen such a motif, and then remembered the little embellishments that Minnie used to add it to her gloves. *So as I would know them as mine if I saw them again*, she had said. Martin must therefore have made Minnie's acquaintance, or at least been at her house before she started working in the community.

Philip made his way out, thinking about the implications of what he had just seen. Had Minnie been identified as someone that Martin wanted in the community? She brought no money with her, but what she did bring was her youth and beauty. He felt another pang of the dread he had felt when he was with Peters. As he walked through the garden, he noticed Ruby through the glass of the greenhouse. Ever since their exchange a few days before, he had been thinking about her and what she had said about being in the community. It had also not escaped his attention that just before they had spoken she had been in the company of a man who had set off down the lane at quite a pace after they had parted. Someone who clearly did not live amongst the saved. He hoped it was a relative of hers come to check on why she was living in such a strange place. He did not think he liked any of the other possible alternatives.

The sight of her now made his heart beat. I am not designed at all for sainthood, he thought and found the entrance and went in. He was glad to see that surly George was not there and that Ruby was by herself.

'Good morning!' she exclaimed when she saw him. 'At least I think it is. I rather lose track of time when I am in here.'

She was flushed and little beads of sweat traced her hairline. Her dress was marked at its hem with soil, and she had placed her implements – a pair of scissors and some secateurs – into the ties of her apron. She looked so heartily alive, that afterwards, Philip thought of this view of her, standing smiling amid the orchids, as the exact moment he fell in love. As it was, this switch in him was manifested only as a temporary loss of vision and speech.

'Why are you here? Have there been more thefts?'

'I was finally granted a meeting with Peters,' he managed at last.

'You were fortunate to get the opportunity. He has not been much around. He keeps to his rooms.'

'There seems to be quite a lot of mysteries attached to this place. Are you aware that Hattie's death was the second, almost identical death to one that happened a year before?' Philip asked.

'I was not. I think about Hattie quite a lot, even though we were not close. She did not seem to me the sort of person who is moved to such extremes of passions as to take her own life. But I suppose we never really know what is happening under the skin of other people.'

'I cannot help feeling there are many things we do not know about what is happening in the community.'

'And you mean to follow the clues and reveal all.'

She spoke in a slightly teasing tone and Philip's newly tender feelings were a little hurt. He tried to stand taller and look more authoritative.

'I do my job to the very best of my ability,' he said. And then thinking he probably sounded pompous added, 'Although I often find myself not quite as skilled at it as I would like to be.'

He was pleased to hear her laugh. She showed her amusement without shyness, rather as a man would – opening her mouth wide and titling her head back so that he got a glimpse of the redness against the white of her teeth.

'I think you notice more than most, Miss Hart. If you do discover anything that concerns or worries you, I would be grateful if you would let me know,' he said.

He wrote his address in his notebook and tore out the page and handed it to her.

'If I am not at home, tell the messenger to knock at the door of my neighbour, Mrs Grawler, who usually knows where I am. You could also speak of any concerns to the maid called Minnie who now works here and is an acquaintance of mine.'

She took the proffered piece of paper and put it in the pocket of her apron.

'Tell me, Constable Hodge,' Ruby said. 'Was there a night a few weeks ago when the sky lit up with colours?'

'There was indeed,' he said. 'There has been talk of something called a solar storm. I am not sure of the science, but it was in the newspaper. Apparently its effects were seen in many parts of the world.'

'I thought so,' Ruby said, almost absently.

'Why do you ask? You surely witnessed it yourself.'

'I did. Reverend Peters claimed it was something conjured up by him.'

'If I were you, Miss Hart, I would take much of what Reverend Peters says with a pinch of salt. Now, show me some of your finest specimens,' he said, and she led him round the greenhouse, bending here and there to cup a favourite flower, making him stretch up to get a clear view of the petals and what they hid inside, or pointing out a particularly vivid shade of yellow or green. He tried his best to demonstrate a keen interest and to ask the right questions, while all the while he was totally distracted by the much more appealing attributes of his guide.

Chapter 36

When Ruby came downstairs the next morning, she saw to her relief that the mail still lay in an unopened pile on the hall table. After looking cautiously around her, she picked up the handful of letters and fanned through them quickly. William's handwriting with its long loops and wide gaps between words was immediately familiar to her and she crammed it into the pocket of her dress.

George had not yet made an appearance in the orchid house to issue his instructions, so Ruby made her way to the fernery and sat down on the hidden bench. Of all the places in the community, this was where she felt the safest, because the others seldom ventured further than the landscaped areas of the garden. She knew as she sat there, feeling the chill in the air, she still had a choice. It was still possible for her to do the right thing. She could go upstairs and place the unopened letter on the table for Irene to discover. It would mean that she would have to explain why she hadn't told Irene about William's previous visits, but she could probably make a convincing case that she had not wanted to upset her when she was indisposed. There was nothing strange about a sister wanting to protect her sibling. But Ruby also knew that if she did read the letter and keep it from her sister, there would be no going back. She would have moved further into the thicket and further from knowing how to return. Ruby took the letter out, looked at it, and put it back in her pocket. She did this twice. The third time she tore it open without allowing herself to think any more. *I can't help myself. Something is making me do it.* As she began to read, she felt her body clench as if readying itself for a blow.

10th November

My Dear Irene,

I write to you not knowing how else to tell you of my feelings since I seem unable to see you. I deserve nothing more than contempt for the way I treated you and yet I hang on to the notion that there might be traces yet of the affection that I inspired in you, and then dismissed so cruelly. It will forever be a source of shame to me that it needed so little for my love to waver. It was I, not you, who was taken that day, my weakness being so much greater than yours.

Ruby says you don't wish to see me and if that is true, I will accept what I deserve. But might I not visit you just one more time? Might there not be something still of the old feeling to allow me at least this? Regardless of what you decide, you will always be the person to whom my poor, unworthy heart cleaves. This will never change.

Trench, from that strange place in which you reside, has been primed to bring any communication from you to me, and I wait for this miracle with faint hope and repentant love.

William.

Ruby's hand curled round the paper, and she pushed it down into her lap. She felt his words like a slice to her heart – as if the paper itself had used its edge to cut deep inside her. She folded the letter up and put it back into her pocket.

'How is Sister Eloise?' Irene asked that evening. Ruby was feeding her soup as she sat in bed, propped up by pillows. She'd had another taking, and this time it had weakened her to such an extent that she had remained in bed. Irene thought Ruby looked strained. Although her sister continually bemoaned her looks and picked fault with them, Irene had always thought Ruby was beautiful. Everything about her was vivid – her navy-coloured eyes, the distinct, bowed outline of her mouth, the flare of colour in her cheeks that appeared when she knew she was saying something she shouldn't. You could tell the weather of her moods in the bloom of her skin and the way she moved. She was so perfectly clear that to Irene, she seemed indestructible.

'There has been no sign of her since she was taken ill,' Ruby replied, aware that Irene was only eating the soup to make her feel better, she could barely keep her neck up. Irene's frailty enraged Ruby. It seemed like a reproach. Irene gazed at her.

'Are you all right, Ruby?'

'I am fine. Just tired.'

Indeed, she had worked like one possessed in the garden all day, digging out the dead plants and transporting great shovelfuls of earth in heaped wheelbarrow loads to the other side of the garden, where George was proposing to build a rockery.

'You should not work so hard.'

'It helps me not to think so much.'

'What are you trying not to think about, Ruby?' Irene asked, putting out her hand as if to stroke her sister's face. Ruby busied herself with the soup to avoid the caress.

'I am still wondering when my life is to begin,' Ruby replied, knowing that the familiarity of her response, always given in the same old way, would reassure her sister, who, sure enough, settled back into her bed with a smile.

'It has already begun, you silly thing,' Irene said, and shut her eyes.

Despite the exhaustion in her body, Ruby could not sleep. Her mind kept turning to the letter in the pocket of the dress that was hanging on the wardrobe door. She needed to dispose of it before it was discovered, but she wasn't sure how this could be safely done. She couldn't leave it in the bin in their room, tearing it up into small pieces would only draw attention to the fact she was trying to hide something. She would have to bury it among the kitchen waste the next day. But what if she was discovered in the act? Miriam seemed to have eyes in the back of her head. She would not put it past the woman to creep up behind her. In the darkness, the letter seemed to take on monstrous proportions – stretching and swelling – the words dancing under her eyelids.

In the end, if only to stop the madness that was consuming her, Ruby got up and put on her dressing gown and shoes, all the while holding her breath in case she woke her sister. Taking the letter from the pocket of her dress, she crept out into the corridor. The house was heavy with silence. Outside, the full moon was a smooth disc, Its lustrous light lit up the pathways and the iced edges of the privet. She made her way silently across the lawn towards the fernery, checking from time to time that she was unobserved. At the very far edge, near the wall, she swept aside the foliage to find a patch of loose earth. She used a stick to dig a hole and lay the balled-up letter in it. She crammed the soil back in with the heel of her shoe making sure to settle the ferns again so that they hid the place from sight.

I loved him first she told herself. *It is not wrong if I loved him first.*

She was about to turn back to the house when she heard voices and ducked down. She recognised Martin in the way his arms hung by his sides and his curiously hunched bearing, but the other two men were strangers to her. They were in a lamplit huddle on the edge of the large field. It was a miracle that they had not spotted her since she had been in direct line of sight. A spade was standing upright in a mound of freshly dug earth. She could smell the soil's mortal sweetness. Martin stood watching as the two other men bent down and lifted what she at first assumed was a box, until the moonlight caught its edges and revealed its hexagonal shape. She heard a muffled gasp of effort from one of the men as they tipped the coffin vertically, so that its narrower foot-end entered the earth first. After some further grunting and manoeuvring, it disappeared into the ground, bolt upright.

As soon as it was dispatched and without words, Martin took hold of the spade and began replacing a portion of the soil. The other men gathered the surplus in their hands and sprinkled it around and stamped it down. What were they burying? Was it perhaps an animal? The coffin looked larger than that required by one of the guard dogs. The quiet way the men were talking, and their slow, careful movements suggested that they did not want observers. She saw that they had finished their task and were walking in her direction. She held her breath, terrified that she would be discovered.

'Sister Eloise will be able to walk straight out on the Day of Judgement if she is still amongst the saved,' one of the men remarked as they passed by, but was shushed by his companion.

'I think that unlikely,' she heard Martin say, his voice careless. 'It seems she was not the true saint we thought her. I have had reports of stolen jewellery and in any case, a wealth of tangled thread was found under her mattress. She was secreting it there as if she was making a nest.' He made a kind of snorting noise that might have been a laugh.

Ruby's legs were shaking with the effort of staying still in her crouched position and she could feel sweat gathering in the hollow of her neck. She was horrified by the idea that Eloise had been placed so that her face, which must still have the completeness it had held in life, was without the protection of a proper heft of earth above it. So, this was how inconvenient death was to be explained away. It was to be sold to them as a shortfall of belief. Sister Eloise had died and therefore it stood to reason that somewhere along the way she must have allowed evil to beset her soul. It was the perfect and incontestable rationalisation against doubt. It wasn't that she had simply become ill and old and died in the sad but natural way of things.

Was it a mercy that Eloise had lived convinced that the snags in her ageing body would one, glorious day, be straightened out? Or would it have been better for her to have known her frailty and been able to properly prepare for death? Maybe it would have made little difference. There was not a person alive who really understood, even in their most rational part, that there was always an ending. Ruby could not imagine it for herself. She closed her eyes and blessed the thistle-downed head resting so near the surface of the earth. When she finally left her hiding place, she looked up at the house and was sure, although she could not make out any recognisable features, that there was a watching face at one of the windows on the second floor.

Chapter 37

'We need to hurry if we are to be at the front,' Norah said, pulling on Edith's arm and hustling Irene and Ruby into the meeting room. A large number of saints had congregated by the door, as if waiting for permission to enter. Ignoring such politeness, Norah squeezed through them, urging her companions after her and made for a place by the circular stage. Peters was standing in the very centre of it, like the handle of a spinning top. He was black capped and dressed in a red velvet cape, which was cut across with a blue sash, emblazoned with the words: **The Lamb Of GOD**.

'I saw something in the garden last night,' Ruby whispered to her sister who had dragged herself from her bed and was still looking very pale.

'What were you doing in the garden?'

Ruby was about to reply but stopped talking as Angela jostled into position by her side.

'I think I know what is going to be announced,' Angela said.

'With the greatest respect, Sister Angela,' Edith said timidly, 'only The Beloved knows.'

Angela shot her an irritated look.

'As a saint I am privy to certain information, that you are not, Edith.'

'He is about to begin,' Norah said in an undertone. 'Stop talking or you will miss a part of it.'

While they had been chattering, the others had gathered, and Miriam shut the door quietly behind the last of the stragglers. Peters raised his arms and the room fell silent.

'I shall not keep you long, but I have something very important to tell you,' Peters said. 'I have spent long hours in tortuous reflection. I have sat deep into the night examining the best way forward. I have looked intently into the heart of God, and I have come to a momentous and extraordinary decision. I have decided to take a bride. A special bride.' Peters glowed with a hectic flush.

There was a murmuring noise from the saints who did not at all understand what this meant, but who felt they should react to what was clearly an announcement of great significance.

'It will be for the greatest of goods. Over the next weeks, I shall be selecting someone. This will be a great honour for the person I choose. There is no higher approbation possible. Be assured, I will make my selection very carefully. In the meantime, go about your business as usual – work hard, do the best that you can. Keep the devil from the door.'

Ruby happened to be looking in Miriam's direction and she was surprised by the look of consternation, even bewilderment that crossed the woman's face. So, their leader's announcement was news to her, too. Without saying anything more, Peters walked from the stage and the saints made a pathway for him.

'I wonder who will be chosen,' Edith said excitedly as they made their way from the meeting room back to their allotted tasks.

'He will choose someone with beauty who has demonstrated exemplary service,' Angela said.

'What did Reverend Peters mean by a *special* bride?' Ruby asked. 'Will it not be a spiritual marriage like any other?'

'I am sure all will become clear,' Edith said. 'For myself, I am just happy to wait, confident that whatever The Beloved does will be the right thing for us all. Perhaps he will choose amongst those of us who are not yet saints.'

'Edith, I would give up all thoughts that it might be *you*,' Angela said, tossing her ringletted head.

'I have no such thoughts. I know my own shortcomings,' Edith said.

'I think it might well be Irene. She is the most beautiful amongst us and in addition, possesses special powers. Or perhaps Delia, who is lovely too and is by all accounts to be shortly made a saint. I have seen The Beloved in conversation with her,' Norah said, with a malicious glance in Angela's direction.

'I think the selection should be made from the saints who have been here the longest,' said Sister Margaret, a woman known for her industry and a perpetual, rasping cough.

'I have no desire to be the chosen one,' Irene said hastily before the jibbing grew into a full-blown war.

'We must all accept what He wants.' Angela spoke with decision.

'Well, in the meantime, I intend to take particular care of my appearance, just in case The Beloved's eye should fall upon me. In fact, I am going to my room now to put on my best frock,' Norah announced, running up the stairs.

'You would do better, Norah, to concentrate on your work rather than waste time embellishing yourself. Are you not supposed to be helping with lunch today?' Miriam called up to Norah's retreating back. She stopped, gave an exaggerated sigh, and unwillingly began retracing her steps.

'You would all do well to keep your heads and remember what it is you are here for,' Miriam continued, her eyes scanning the group, and they all dispersed hastily.

'I think you should rest, Irene,' Ruby said when they were back in their rooms. 'You are not properly recovered. You should not even have gone to the meeting this morning.'

'I cannot let my illness master me, Ruby.'

'It will master you if you do not heed the signs in your body. Have you taken your tincture today?'

'I have, Miss Bossy.'

'Have you felt any benefit since you started taking it? It seems to me that it makes you sleepier than you were before.'

'I am not aware of any particular difference, but The Beloved is keen that I should keep taking it and so I shall.'

Irene took off her shoes and lay on the bed, while Ruby fussed around, folding sheets, and pouring water.

'Why are you so eager to do what Peters says?

'I believe he has our best interests at heart, Ruby. I really do.'

'Well, they can do without you in the sewing room today. It will not help your condition to spend so many hours poring over such fine detail.'

'Now, tell me what you started to tell me before,' Irene said, settling herself against her pillow. 'What did you see in the garden and what were you doing roaming around at night?'

'I could not sleep,' Ruby said. 'I thought it would help if I took a walk. I saw something that I found most disturbing. Martin and some other men were burying Sister Eloise on the edge of the big field. They buried her upright as if she was a piece of luggage. They said no words and there is no marker. I went to check this morning. The earth has simply been stamped down.'

Irene absorbed this information in silence, a stunned look on her face.

'So, she is dead! Her sainthood did not save her.'

'Irene! Sister Eloise was old and ill. No faith can keep what is mortal, alive, not on this earth, here, where we live and breathe.'

'Perhaps she sinned, and we did not know of it.'

Ruby sat down on the end of Irene's bed and stared at her.

'This is Sister Eloise we are talking about...Where have you gone, Irene? Where is the girl who always had such good sense? The one who tried with every fibre of her being to get our father's heart beating again and then laid her hand on his dear head and told me it was over? Do you truly believe he was a sinner?'

'We never know what is happening in the hearts and minds of others.'

'But we know, do we not, that hearts and minds wear out.'

'I want, above all other things, to believe that what is here is good. That it is worth something. That what we have given up is a fair exchange for what we have been given.'

'If we ask about what happened to Sister Eloise, what do you think they will tell us?'

'I do not know.'

'Well, I *do* know because I heard Martin talking about it. He said that some jewellery was missing, which may not even be true – and even if it is, may have nothing at all to do with Sister Eloise – and that she had been secreting thread in her mattress and *that* is why she died. She committed the major sin of thread theft.'

Irene stared at Ruby, aghast.

'I think maybe what was hidden in her bed were the skeins she couldn't untangle into balls. Her hands were getting so stiff. I told her it did not matter, but she hated not being useful,' Irene said, her eyes filling with tears. 'I should have helped her more.'

'I am sure you did all you could,' Ruby said, more softly, seeing her sister's distress. 'The point I am trying to make is that Sister Eloise did not die because she put some thread into her mattress. Will you not at least acknowledge that things are not as they seem in this place.'

'I cannot believe that Reverend Peters would lie to us,' Irene said, wiping her face with the sleeve of her dress.

'It seems to me that if you believe enough and want to keep on believing, then there is nothing that cannot be explained away. Faith, or at least the one they share here, seems like a shell that grows so many layers that it becomes too hard to crack. Irene, I do not want to be here until I grow my own shell. We could escape. There is really nothing stopping us.'

'What about Mother?'

'She has made her choice, and it was never *our* choice, Irene.'

'Maybe Reverend Peters is not lying, he simply believes what he feels to be true and wants to share that belief with us.'

'He is certainly fervent,' Ruby replied. 'Forgive me, for going on so. You must rest.'

'What is the time?'

'I never know. I used always to know,' Ruby said fretfully.

'I love you, Ruby,' Irene replied, rolling over wearily to face the window and tucking her hands under her chin in the way she always did when she was about to go to sleep.

Before going back down into the garden, Ruby sat at the desk and started to write a letter. She had nothing if she did not have this. Irene had slipped further from her. It was barely as if she needed Ruby any more, at least not in the way that she used to. She seemed to belong in the community. They seemed to worship her, and she had clearly begun to believe what they all believed. Ruby resisted the thought that this distance between her and her sister suited her just now. She wrote the words quickly so that she did not have to think about what she was doing.

12th November

Dear William,

Irene has asked that I write to you since she has had another spell of ill health. Although she is still of the same mind and no longer has feelings for you of a romantic nature, she is prepared to speak with you one last time since you have been so persistent in your attentions. We will be at the spot you and I walked to when you last came, at five o'clock, on Sunday evening. I will send Trench with this message. I trust it will find you well.

Ruby Hart

Chapter 38

'I fear she has very little time now,' Doctor Pontifex said, washing his hands in the bowl in the sink. 'You should start to prepare yourself.'

Philip, who was sitting at the kitchen table, wondered exactly what preparing himself would involve. He supposed the doctor meant that he should try to imagine what life would be like without his mother. How it would feel to push open the door of the cottage and not find her sitting where she had always sat, her hands moving across linen, the window damp with stew and her breath. The nights he would spend in the company of ghosts – hers and his brother's and his father's, too, although he had only a dim memory of the latter and he thought his phantom form would be indistinct. How was it he had found himself in a life where nothing seemed ever to be added, only taken away? Maybe it was the same for everyone. Maybe he just wasn't very good at counting his blessings. His mind found its way to Pearl. It could be she was a fairy child after all, just as his mother had suggested. How else to explain the way she tugged at him, even though she was really nothing to do with him at all.

'Is there anything I can do … to make Mother more comfortable?' he asked.

Despite the fact that he had barely touched Catherine other than to take her blueish wrist briefly between two fingers, the look the doctor gave Philip now had a professional compassion. He was not his mother's usual doctor and he had never met Philip before, so there was not even a shared history. This was just another imminent death of a stranger.

'All that could have been done, has been done,' he said, glancing around for a cloth to dry his hands on, and Philip felt a kind of shame to only have the dirty rag that was hanging on the door to offer. Since his mother's indisposition he had rather let the cleanliness of the kitchen slide. Perhaps that was the best way to occupy himself, instead of sitting listening to his mother's ragged breaths, he would set the place to rights. Make it look as she had always made it look – the chipped sink shining, flowers in the jug on the table, the two pans clean and hanging on their hooks.

'I gather you have someone with her when you are at work,' Doctor Pontifex said, rolling down the cuffs of his shirt. 'You must tell whoever it is that they should be prepared for the end.'

Philip could tell he was already halfway to the next sick child, the next dying parent. He wondered what it would be like to go from house to house presenting his certain face to those who felt only uncertainty.

'My neighbour, Mrs Grawler, is very well qualified,' Philip said. 'She is fond of a crisis.'

'I expect you are as busy as I,' the doctor said, indicating Philip's uniform. 'Were you not the policeman who was called out when that poor woman from the community in Yaxton took her own life?'

Philip nodded.

'I thought I had heard your name. I was the doctor on duty that day. I understood the community members in that unorthodox place do not indulge in the usual marital relations, and so I was surprised to discover that the unfortunate woman had just been delivered of a child.'

Philip stared at the man. How was it that he had not talked to him before? He thought he had interviewed everyone that might possibly have been involved.

'Are you sure?'

'Yes. And fairly recently, too. I would not have thought twice. It is simply my responsibility to establish death, not look into the background of the circumstances. It was only that I wondered about her condition in the context of where she had been living.'

'How recently?' Philip asked.

'I would say approximately three weeks, perhaps a month before her death. I mentioned it to the chief constable, in case it was pertinent, but it seems he did not pass the information on to you.'

Philip saw the doctor to the door and then sat back at the kitchen table. He thought about the woman he had met briefly in the pantry. He remembered the way Hattie had looked at the ground when he had spoken to her and the shape of her heavy body. What was it she had said? *I have not set foot out of the community for more than four years.*

Chapter 39

She stood waiting for him. She could feel a pulse flickering fast in her neck. The sun was beginning to go down, and in the distance the gathered starlings flew in swollen clouds, shapeshifting their great mass in smooth, bulbous motions across the sky. She could hear church bells – a practice ringing that stopped and started – the clamouring peels by turns ominous and merry.

It had taken subterfuge to leave the community undetected – she had claimed a headache and a sore throat, and with Irene still in bed and Hester largely indifferent, there was no one to check her whereabouts. She'd had a moment of fear when the dogs had started growling as she approached them, but a lump of cheese strategically thrown into their slavering midst had diverted their attention for long enough to get the gate open and then closed behind her.

She saw the shape of him at the other end of the path, approaching on horseback. The low sun was burnishing his outline so that she couldn't see him clearly. She wondered at exactly what point he would understand there was only one person waiting for him and not the expected two. Her heart was beating so fast, she thought she might fall.

The sun relinquished him, and he was no longer a longed-for and dreaded prospect, but a real person she had summoned and brought to this place under false pretences. She could see the detail of him – the sure lines of his face, the tight hold of his legs against the sides of his horse, and one bare, luminous arm holding the front of his saddle. He dismounted and led his horse towards her.

'Where is she?'

'She is not coming.' She thought her voice would fail her, but it came out surprisingly strongly.

'Is she still unwell?' he said, frowning and stamping his feet as if his ride had chilled him.

'She is often tired, especially after her takings.' Ruby knew her perfidy. She had hoped invoking Irene's affliction would remind him of his first aversion.

'Too tired to walk barely half a mile?'

She saw the discontented line of his mouth. She knew his weakness and his lack of imagination. He flew over the surface of things and changed direction on a gust of breeze, and yet she couldn't shake him off. He was an illness, like one of her sister's takings.

'She says you are not what she needs or wants.'

'Why did you write to say she was willing to meet me?'

He wound his reins around his hand, as if preparing his fist to administer a blow. The horse, sensing his master's mood and reacting to the new tightness against his mouth, tried to pull away.

'She told me she would come, but then she changed her mind at the last minute. She said it would serve little purpose.'

'In the absence of Irene, I would have thought Mrs Hart might at least tell me herself.'

'Mother is set on our salvation. She is full of fervour and no longer aspires to the things she did before. She would not countenance marriage to a person who lives outside the community because it would mean having to leave and in doing so, sacrifice immortality.'

'She has been brainwashed! Does Irene believe this, too?'

'Irene is content to be where she finds herself.'

Ruby could feel her body become hot under the weight of her deceit. The light was turning hazy, and she, too, felt herself becoming less distinct. This is what sinning feels like, she thought. This is what it is like to become lost to oneself.

'Content to remain locked up for the rest of her life?'

'Her indisposition marks her out. You know as well as I. The community provides a safe place for her.'

As she anticipated, the reminder of his own weakness in this regard, hit home.

'I have lost her, then,' he said, and she wondered, and took terrible heart at the lack of fight in him. Would not true, unswerving love inspire more determination? If he really loved Irene, would he not knock down the wall and claim her? Although she knew him, it still surprised her how easily he had accepted what he had been told.

'I think you would be better off giving up all hope of her. There will surely be someone else who will love you.'

'And what of you, Ruby? Are you content to remain behind walls, without prospect of love?'

'I am made of different stuff,' she said.

'You are indeed,' he said, and she was surprised to see what might even have been a smile on his face. 'We both know of what stuff *you* are made.'

'At least I am constant in what I want,' she said, with her chin tilted for battle but terrified by her own words, which sounded so shameless.

He looked at her closely, then, scanning her face as if trying to work out a riddle. It seemed to her that his expression softened. She took a step towards him. He looked at her mouth with his eyes half closed. He inclined his head towards hers. She stretched up to meet him. His sleek gloved hand inserted itself into hers. For a moment, she felt a terrible panic, almost a revulsion, and then she stilled, and folded in on herself.

All she was aware of was the soft pressure of his lips against hers and the beating of her body. His mouth firmed, he pulled her head to him, and she matched the pressure. The evening with its birds and bells fell silent and there was only heat and longing and her skin which seemed to stretch and tighten, and then rest against his, as if it was meant to be there.

She had reached the hallway, sure she had escaped detection, her body still holding the warmth of William's imprint, when Martin and Miriam were suddenly standing in front of her. It was as if the darkness had invoked them. She stopped in her tracks, her flesh immediately cooling.

'Where have you been, Ruby?' Miriam asked. She was holding a candle and its light flickered across their faces. Ruby could see the hard set of the woman's mouth, the glitter of Martin's eyes. She was slow to make the adjustment. For a moment she could hardly speak. She could feel the rapid pulse of her heart which just a short time ago had been suffused with joy.

'I went out to get some air.'

'I had understood you were unwell,' Miriam replied, moving the candle closer to Ruby's face as if to examine the truth of her words.

'So very unwell, that you were nevertheless able to go out to meet a man, which in itself is revolting and against our faith, but is made all the more so, since the man in question is someone for whom your sister once had feelings.'

How did he know about William? Ruby had the panicked sense that all her movements were being monitored. Who had seen her go out?

'Your mother told me about all of it. She said you tried to get him for yourself from under your poor sister's nose.'

The Taking of Irene Hart

Martin's voice was triumphant. She could feel his horrible force.

'It seems you are extremely well-informed, Brother Martin,' she replied, trying to speak calmly and as if what was happening was of no consequence to her. She dug her nails into the palm of her hand to keep herself from shaking. In the distance the voices of the choir rose in perfect unison.

'There is nothing I do not know, Ruby. You were foolish to imagine otherwise. Now...' and here the man drew in a breath which seemed to make the flowers in the hallway vase, even the ivied wallpaper itself, move in response, 'I know your sister is already in a weakened state. Finding out about what you have done might very well cause her further damage. I am not an unreasonable man. I want to protect Irene from the sorrow of your betrayal. I am willing to pretend I do not know anything of this matter, but it is also reasonable for me to expect something in exchange.'

Ruby knew that she had brought this entrapment on herself. She would now have to dance to his tune.

'I want you to report every single word that comes out of your sister's lips,' he said. 'Every sigh, every movement, every vision is to come directly to me.'

She nodded. She had no choice.

'And if I find out that you have disobeyed me, I shall tell your sister what you are really like. To think one such as her, should be saddled with someone like you!' he exclaimed, and they turned and left her. Standing in the dark hallway Ruby remembered the day they had arrived at the community. While they had waited to be shown to their rooms, she had imagined that their presence there had somehow triggered Miriam's walk down the stairs. She had set something else in motion now and she knew that what she had started, could not be stopped.

Chapter 40

Ruby lay on her bed. She had unbuttoned the front of her dress and pulled it to her waist in an attempt to cool down. She was not sure what had come first – the intolerable heat, so strange and unnatural at this time of the year, or the Reverend's announcement that he was going to choose a bride. It seemed that the two things had happened simultaneously. It felt as if the intensity of the younger members of the community's longing to be the chosen one, was itself creating the burn.

They sponged and fanned and blew down the front of their dresses and drank water from greedy, cupped hands, as if they needed cooling from a heat even greater than that of the sun. Torpid and yet curiously avid, they stroked and pampered themselves – twisting curls around fingers and mixing up chalky concoctions to render their skin white. They rubbed cologne behind their ears and marked their brows with burnt cloves. Earlier that day Ruby had come upon Amelia and Alice spreading melted lard into each other's feet – the one stretching out luxuriously, the other kneeling on the floor and carefully working the fat between each toe. The elderly amongst them sat dazed in the shade, their softening flesh more pliable in the sun, so that it seemed they were melting to exactly fit the shapes of the chairs that had been pulled across the lawn and placed under the trees that now offered precious little shade.

As she lay with sweat gathering in the hollow of her throat, the place where William had kissed her, her feelings for him seemed part of the collective yearning that was consuming the community. The open window brought not air, but some other, muffling element which took up the space within – all the cracks in the walls and in the floorboards, even her own tender openings – and filled them to the very top. She went over every detail of the time they had spent together. The firmness of his mouth on her own. The sensation of his hand on her skin, the way, as he held her close, he had pulled at the little hairs at the back of her neck, the exhilarating, terrifying feeling of his body tight against her own. She was full of sensation. It was almost painful to feel so much – her feet on the floor fell heavier, her corset dug into her flesh making sore ridges around her waist and arms. The food in her mouth tasted too salty, the choir sang with such sweetness it brought her to tears. In the blazing heat of the glass house several panes of glass had buckled and then shattered with a bursting sound, sending shards through leaves and blooms, leaving her ears ringing.

Irene had suffered a series of seizures in their bedroom, each one harder and longer than the one before, until it seemed that her frail body could not bear much more. In terror that word would get to Martin of this, and feeling craven and ashamed, Ruby had duly gone to see him, and reported Irene's sightings. She had tried to keep the information she passed on to the barest details, despite the fact Martin kept prompting her for more. There hadn't been, in any case, much to say. Irene seemed to go further away each time she left them, but now when she returned, the words did not come readily. It was almost as if there was less difference for her between the world she saw when she was away, and the one she lived in. Ruby had told Martin of Irene's repeat sighting of rats and of being imprisoned, and also of a bright light behind a curtain. Then, in a spirit of resistance, added some invented embellishments all of her own. She spoke of golden gates and slaughtered lambs and a plague of moths. Martin seemed to accept all with alacrity, writing it solemnly down in his notebook.

'Is that you, Ruby?' Irene's creaking voice came through her shut bedroom door and Ruby got up and went in.

'It is,' she said, sitting down next to her sister. 'How are you feeling?'

'More tired than I have ever been,' Irene said. Her eyes were barely open, and her mouth was edged with a white crust. Ruby fetched a bowl of water and a cloth and began to wash her face.

'You are so kind to me!' Irene said. 'You have the gentlest touch of anyone in the world.'

The veins in her neck were a purpled blue and Ruby saw that the rash had extended further, so that it now traced her upper chest and shoulders.

'Have you been using your ointment?' Ruby asked.

'It doesn't seem to make any difference. I've grown almost accustomed to the sting and itch of it.' Irene said, her silvered eyelids closing.

'Is there anything I can get for you?' Ruby asked and Irene struggled to open her eyes again. Ruby's heart clenched with love and fury as she looked into their soft, luminous shine. Irene was the fair end of the child's toy they had once shared – a doll of which they had both been fond – a shock-haired witch with a wart-studded nose and dangling arms who, when turned upside down, revealed underneath the cobwebby skirt, a frail princess with a rosebud mouth and a pink petticoat.

'Do you remember Gloria and Grunter? Ruby asked referring to the childhood name they had given the doll.

'Yes, I do. What made you think of that now?' she asked, smiling at her sister.

'You were always Gloria, and I was Grunter,' Ruby said.

'I don't think that is right, Ruby,' Irene said. 'I always thought the doll was both of us. We were Gloria and Grunter in turns depending on how we were feeling that day.'

'Perhaps,' Ruby said, emptying the used water back into the jug to take downstairs.

'I saw a little more in my last taking,' Irene said 'It was the same room as before. The one I could not get out of, but there was someone else in there with me.'

'Who was it?' Ruby asked.

'I do not know. They had their back to me and just as they were about to turn, I was pulled away into darkness.'

'I want you to rest and not dwell on any of that.'

'Just because you are older than me, doesn't mean you are my mistress, Grunter,' said Irene, and she looked suddenly like the gleeful little girl Ruby remembered. The one who had run all the way home with a tadpole in her clenched fist, who had sobbed to find the creature still and dry on her palm and who had defiantly smuggled a custard pudding in the lining of her skirt when Ruby had been sent to bed without supper.

'I have always known what is best for you, Gloria,' Ruby said, her eyes filling with tears.

'Why are you crying, dearest?'

'I do not know. I am not myself. I feel all out of sorts,' Ruby said rubbing at her eyes crossly.

'Has anyone in the community asked what has happened to Sister Eloise?' Irene said.

'I think they assume she is still being looked after by Peters.'

'You must not tell anyone what you saw, Ruby.'

'Why not? It might make them think twice before accepting all they are told.'

She spoke defiantly, but the thought of confronting Martin made her quail. She could imagine his pale eyes passing over her.

'It will just upset everyone,' Irene said. 'What good would it do?'

'I no longer know what is good and what is not. I wish we were children and could start all over again,' Ruby said.

'Every day is a new start, Ruby. And as for knowing what is good, there is no one like you for seeing into the heart of things. If you really insist on me staying in bed, would you be kind enough to bring my book?' Irene said settling back on her pillow. 'I left it in the sewing room.'

It was lunchtime and the saints had abandoned their work. It was too hot to pore over an embroidery. Ruby placed the jug on the floor and searched around for Irene's book. She found it half-hidden beneath a pile of thread. Almost three quarters of the canvas was now complete. Parts of the text of *The Song of Solomon* had been picked out in black stitches in the silky sky.

Place me like a seal over your heart, like a seal on your arm, for love is as strong as death, its jealousy unyielding as the grave. It burns like blazing fire, like a mighty flame. Many waters cannot quench love and rivers cannot sweep it away.

Ruby knelt on the floor to get a closer look at the pattern which was so detailed that the animals and figures stitched into the landscape looked as if they might step out of the canvas and into the room. By a foaming river, right at the bottom of the canvas and added almost as an afterthought, were creatures more curious than any Ruby had ever seen – the shoulders of a bear bore a stag's horned head, a robin, ten times its proper size, had the feet of an alligator and held an engorged snake in its beak, a frog squatted on a rock with the haunches of a baby, and a cat with lashed, human eyes prowled in long grass.

Chapter 41

Philip was nursing a swollen jaw as he rode towards Wynch. Earlier in the day he had tried to intercede between warring neighbours – the one claiming the other had stolen the tiles from his roof, the other hotly denying it. He gave his face an exploratory poke and thought ruefully that being knocked to the ground in the blur of fists had at least had the effect of bringing about a truce. All thoughts of missing roof tiles had been diverted into sudden mirth, as the erstwhile enemies joined forces to pull him up and dust him down and rescue his hat that had rolled into some mud.

He intended to visit Minnie's mother to tell her that she would have to look after Pearl for somewhat longer than the agreed time. Philip had been unable to find a family to foster or adopt her permanently. The home for orphaned children near Bridgwater made his soul shrink whenever he was unfortunate enough to find himself there. It was the hope he saw in the faces whenever a stranger arrived, that brought him low, that and the rows of mean beds, barely a foot apart.

Archie Balch almost ran into Thunder's path as he hurtled out of his house and into the lane, preceded by his father's shouting voice. Philip stopped as abruptly as his horse would allow.

Thunder had his own views on the proper location for any unscheduled stops, most of which involved full troughs or bales of hay.

'Where are you off to in such a hurry?' he asked, dismounting, and tying Thunder to the fence. The boy looked even more grubby than he usually did, but Philip was relieved to see that following the flood, the house was back to its normal level of disorder.

'Pa's angry I dropped the bowl of stew on the floor,' Archie said, rubbing his stomach and the top of his head at the same time, as if he was performing some kind of party trick. From the bag on Thunder's flank, Philip extracted the muslin-wrapped slice of cake he had been given at one of the warring neighbour's houses as a token of apology, and handed it over. He stood watching as Archie inhaled it.

'Who did that to you?' the boy said through a cake-filled mouth, indicating Philip's fast-developing bruise.

'I just got in the way.'

'I do that, too,' he said mournfully.

'Tell me, Archie,' Philip said, leaning on the fence, 'Do you remember finding an unfortunate lady in the orchard, some time ago now. You were with your father.'

A cautious look crossed Archie's crumb-strewn face.

'You are not in any trouble. It is simply that I wondered if you could remember anything at all about it.'

'The butter churn did'na belong to anyone,' Archie said, scraping his bare foot through the dust of the lane.

'I am not interested in the butter churn, only in the lady.'

'It was 'orrible,' Archie said. 'Her face was all blue and her head was dangling down.'

Here Archie acted out the angle of the deceased's head.

'I did'na think she was dead at first, but Pa told me she was. Dead as a fox in a trap, he said.'

'What did your father do?'

'He did'na take nothing. He just looked in the lady's pocket.'

'Do you remember anything else?'

Archie stuck his hands into his armpits and then looked up at the sky.

'I think maybe … don't know… someone else was there, too. In the orchard.'

'Besides you and your father? What makes you think that?'

'I saw a shape just over from where we was. I think they was watching.'

'Was it the shape a man?'

'Could've been … I couldn't exactly see.'

'Not an animal then? A deer, perhaps?'

'Not a deer. I know their shape. Too big for a fox or a badger.'

'Archie! Come inside!'

The master of the house had emerged, red faced. His fury apparently deepening to see his son talking to Philip.

'Good afternoon, Mr Balch,' Philip said.

'Unless there is something that I can help you with, you can bugger off,' Thomas replied, stepping forth and hooking his son in a stranglehold.

'No, nothing to concern yourself with, that is unless you have something to tell me about some roof tiles that have disappeared a mile or so from here.'

'I got all the roof tiles I need,' Thomas Balch said, indicating his bowing roof.

'Of course you have, Mr Balch,' Philip replied, knocking on the neighbouring door.

After a short delay, Minnie came to the door with Pearl on her hip.

'Oh, I thought you would be at the community,' Philip exclaimed when he saw her.

'It's my day off. Though you'd not know it,' Minnie said.

Have you got a couple of moments to spare? We could perhaps sit under the tree,' Philip said, indicating the beech which was the only apparently living thing in the patch of ground in front of the house. Minnie nodded, disappeared back inside, and re-emerged with a moth-eaten blanket. Philip took the child while she laid the blanket out. Pearl nestled her soft, humped shape against him.

'My, how she's grown!' Philip exclaimed.

'If there's one thing Ma's good at, it's making milk,' Minnie replied with a roll of her eyes.

'I think she will have to stay with you for the time being. I have not found anywhere else for her.'

'We'll be glad for the money, and she's no trouble.'

She reached out and stroked Pearl's head. The child had grown wispy, pale hair which lay in a parting across her head, making her look older than she was. She reached upwards towards the tree with one of her star-shaped hands, as if she thought she could touch the branches, and made an unmistakably covetous grunt. They both laughed.

'How are you faring at the community?'

'If it wasn't for the wages which are fair, and the food I can take home for the little ones when there's leftovers, I'd be happy never to set foot in there again,' Minnie said, her voice uncharacteristically sharp.

'Are they unkind to you?'

'It's not that. They are polite enough. It's just not right in there.'

'What do you mean?'

Minnie looked up at the tree and then leant over to stroke Pearl's head again. She seemed to be searching for the right words to say. This made Philip suddenly alert. Minnie was not usually reticent. Her tendency to speak her mind was one of her most admirable qualities.

'There's one rule for some and another rule for the others,' Minnie said, her little face quite transformed from its usual expression of stoical equanimity with the kind of censure that can only be expressed by the young.

'The leader preaches … you know…. no marital relations … and the men and women are kept separate and all, but when I was on nights last week, I saw one of them ... a young girl, ever so pretty, dressed all in white with her feet bare, being taken into Reverend Peters' room by that Martin. And he gives me the creeps, too. All holy on the outside but with eyes ... you know ... eyes that wander all over a body.'

Philip trusted Minnie instincts more than he would those of many other people. Her life had not protected her, and so she had the ability to see the truth. He had suspected that something of this kind was happening at the wretched place, particularly now that he knew Hattie had given birth, but the fact that Minnie who was still just a child had to work there and be exposed to whatever was going on, disturbed him. His second thought was for Ruby. He had a feeling, that despite her lack of years, Minnie would be able to take care of herself. It might be quite another matter for the Hart girls and some of the others, too. And with sainthood dangled as the prize, there would presumably be added pressure on the women of the community.

'I do not like to think of you there, Minnie. I think there are bad things happening. I think that the baby who, as you know was left in the lane, was the child of one of the community members, the one that died a few months back.'

'Poor mite,' said Minnie, her forehead creasing as she glanced at Pearl. 'You don't need to worry about me,' she added. 'I keep a sharp eye and I have sharp knees and fists, too.'

'I wonder if you would do me a favour and keep that sharp eye of yours peeled and let me know about anything else you see.'

Chapter 42

Ruby had been out of the community to meet William again. This time in the early morning, before even the maid on breakfast duty had set the big pot on the stove boiling or gathered the straw-stained eggs from the coop and before the heat had had a chance to gather. She had walked out into the stolen air, her anticipation heightening her vision, so the silky swathes of cobweb linking branch to branch with beads of dew, even the way the hills in the distance seemed to lean towards her, made her feel as if she had conjured up the morning just for herself.

He had been waiting in what she had already started to think of as their place – a spot hidden by hedges where the field dipped into the ground, so that when she walked towards it, the hem of her dress damp, her breath rising and falling, she had at first thought he had not come. There was enough time to contemplate this possibility and to experience the corresponding dip of disappointment. It was only when she was almost upon him that she saw that he had taken off his jacket and was lying on it in the grass.

'Good morning,' he had said, smiling up at her.

They had lain side by side, the grass high around them, the sky threaded with pink. They turned to each other from time to time, his lips against her ear, her mouth on his throat. There was a certain point during all this munificence, in the grandeur of the morning and its fresh, rich smell and the wonder of being together, when it seemed to her that her vision wavered. She was confiding in him about the community and how it was making her feel anxious and constricted, even afraid, but when she looked at him, she saw his thoughts had taken him elsewhere and that he wasn't listening to her, at all. It seemed to her that his mouth had adopted the spoilt softness she had seen before and the way he had his arms behind his head in such a relaxed, carefree way, did not at all reflect the seriousness of what she was saying. For a while it seemed to her as if the morning had lost its burnish, and she had a sense that she no longer quite knew who she was or what she was doing there with him. Then he looked at her and his hand reached for hers, and her heart opened again.

Walking back across the field, taking the same crushed-grass route she had made on her way to meet him, it seemed strange to her the way her attraction to him had faltered, like a sudden cloud over the sun, and how it had been restored only moments later. She wondered if this was a sign of a lack of proper feeling in her, that she could change so quickly. She had nothing to compare it to. She did not know how love manifested itself. He had told her that he was going to be away on business for some time and so they had not arranged another meeting yet, but Ruby thought of little else. The memory of the graze of his skin against hers made her heart beat so quickly, she thought it would escape from her body.

The members of the community choir had taken to gathering outside the Hart family quarters in small groups to sing, rather as children used to do on doorsteps at Christmas time. Unlike the childish carollers, this was not done in expectation of caraway biscuits or twists of toffee, but rather in the hope that their voices might somehow inspire Irene to further revelations. When she heard them, Ruby usually opened the door and told them in brisk tones to go away, but whenever she did this, Irene remonstrated with her.

'Let them be, Ruby. They mean no harm and I rather like the sound of it so close. It is like a lullaby.'

It seemed to Ruby that most of the time these days, her sister was in a kind of trance. Not quite asleep, nor yet quite awake, she hovered somewhere in between. Most alarming of all, was that Irene seemed to be having what Ruby thought of as waking dreams, since they came upon her when she wasn't having a seizure but was simply sitting on a chair looking out of the window or lying on her bed. As before, she spoke of things that made no immediate sense but now these sightings were intermingled with the daily life of the community, so it was hard to work out what was a vision and what her sister had already seen.

The musical tributes from the saints had started shortly after the discovery of the first rat. Coiled nose to tail in the pantry and already reeking, it had been brought forth by Sister Angela and placed in a dish on the kitchen table, as if in preparation for one of her pies. Ruby had at first protested that there could be few houses in the land which did not have the occasional rat. Indeed, they had been quite regularly discovered in the outbuildings of their old home in Bridgwater, and when hunger or the weather had driven them in desperation to scratch their way into the living accommodation, they had even been spotted scuttling around the skirtings.

'This is hardly the river of rats Irene claimed to have seen,' she said, knowing that her words were falling on deaf ears. They all wanted to believe, and there was nothing that she could say or do to curb this longing. Barely two days later, the second rat was found, this time, alive and under Norah's bed. The woman had rushed down the stairs, her mouth theatrically agape, to report the sighting and had spent a good hour shivering in relish and recounting how its eyes had gleamed out at her from the darkness.

'It had horrible feet!' she kept wailing, clutching at her throat, and gulping. 'It made a ghastly noise against the floor, as if it was trying to dig its way out. Irene warned us of this!'

When another rat was spotted making its way between the feet of some saints in the chapel, the plague of rats was officially underway. Although, since the subsequent breathless accounts varied from, 'It was barely larger than my thumb' to 'It had teeth like sabres', Ruby could not help thinking that perhaps they had summoned the creature up from the crimson carpet just because they had wished for it. Plague of rats or no, Irene's status as a visionary was firmly established, and like everything in the community, quickly became an incontestable truth. There were times when Ruby thought Irene enjoyed the notoriety – the puddings brought to the door under muslin, the cool drinks placed carefully on saucers, the way her chair at the dining table was pulled out for her at supper time by one or other of the saints. Irene did not speak often, but when she did the saints immediately turned their heads to her and put down their cups and listened with the kind of rapt attention only Peters had hitherto been able to command.

'Two more saints have fainted,' Irene said, coming into the bedroom. 'Flora went first, sliding down her seat and onto her knees, and Effie just moments after. I think Effie didn't want to be outdone by her companion.'

'None of them are eating properly. The heat and the excitement about the upcoming wedding has have taken away their appetites,' Ruby said. 'Mine, too, for that matter.'

'What is it all about, do you suppose?'

'I have absolutely no idea.'

Irene's hair had come loose and lay in a coil against her neck. Her face was serene. She put her hands in the bowl of water by her bed and left them resting on the bottom.

'I wonder that you have the strength to continue working, Irene.'

'The embroidery needs to be finished within the week and

without … Sister Eloise, who used to keep us to the task, and with my own periods of indisposition, progress has slowed of late.'

'Could you really spend the rest of your life in here?' Ruby asked.

Irene took her hands from the water and rubbed them along her dress.

'I do not think of things in such absolute terms. I do not know what is to happen. We are here for now, and after all, there are worse places to be.'

'And there are many better! I fear that unless we take charge of our own lives, we will die here. When the gates open to admit us, or when the sun goes down and does not come up again, or indeed, as is most likely, when we are found chilled on chairs under the chestnut tree, we will take what grace we have earned and nothing we have been given.'

She reflected that her own portion of grace was likely to be meagre.

Hester came into their room in her usual barging fashion. Her face was ruddy from her exertions at the farm, and she had a distinct smell of goat about her person.

'Do not let The Beloved hear you talking about death, Ruby! Your chatter will lead to trouble.'

'What manner of trouble?' Ruby asked.

'The kind of trouble that would get us sent away from here,' Hester said. 'The kind you seem to attract all the time, Ruby.'

'I would be glad to be sent away,' Ruby said defiantly, although she caught a stricken look on Irene's face and felt contrite.

'Well, you can do what you like, Ruby,' Hester said. 'It is your sister that is destined for great things.'

'What things, Mother?' Ruby asked, suddenly anxious.

'You will find out,' Hester said and plunged her whole head in the basin of water so that it overflowed and sloshed across the floor.

'I'm going out,' Ruby said.

The Taking of Irene Hart

She went and sat in the garden. It was dark, and the heat of the day was dispersing. Ruby felt the relief of this blessed coolness on her throat and shoulders. What had her mother meant about Irene's future? She remembered standing outside the Reverend's office and hearing Martin laugh, and she shivered at the memory. As she sat looking out over the field she saw a figure in white, walking slowly across it. She thought it was Delia, from the shine of her golden hair and her willowy height. She was pulling a cart behind her which was laden with something – stones, perhaps, and earth. Ruby was reminded of when she had seen Hattie in the woods, just a day or two before her death. It must be that Delia was undergoing a similar kind of test. Something about the downward slant of the woman's head and her plodding walk filled Ruby with dread. Fear had prevented her from interrupting just such a spectacle last time, she could not fail in the same way again. She got to her feet and began walking fast towards the field; Delia was some distance away and she would have to be quick if she was to catch her up.

'What are you doing here after dark?' Reverend Peters said. He had come alongside without her noticing his approach.

His face had a sheen to it, as if he had been moving fast.

'I want to talk to Delia,' she said, pointing towards the field.

'I do not see her,' Peters said, staring in the direction of her finger.

Ruby looked, too, and saw that Delia was no longer there.

'I saw her ... only a moment ago,' she said.

'Are you quite certain of what you saw? It is dark, after all. Come with me,' Peters said, his hand on her arm. He led her back and they both sat down on the bench. She could smell wine on his breath. She had understood that abstinence was part of what he preached and so was surprised, when she looked at him more closely, to see that he had the slack look of someone who had drunk a great deal. The corners of his mouth were stained the same dark red as the dahlias that were now listing in the borders.

'The garden is still beautiful is it not, despite the heat?' Ruby asked, feeling awkward to be sitting so close to him.

'The mandrakes give a smell, and at our gates are all manner of pleasant fruits, new and old, which I have laid up for thee, O my beloved,' Peters said.

Ruby was made uneasy by his vacant stare and the way he was breathing so fast. He put his head up as if he had caught the scent of something. Perhaps the winter jasmine just beginning to reach and twist over the ivy in the walled garden, or the warm skin of the horses, locked up now and breathing through wet nostrils in the stables, or something even more allusive – the way an animal is alert to a scent from miles away.

'You desire something that you should not.' He turned his eyes, which were rimmed with red, as if he had been rubbing at them, towards her, and her chest jumped at the shock of his words. It seemed as if he had detected her deceit on the air. 'We all fight against the impulse to have what we cannot,' he said.

'Do you fight this in yourself?' Ruby asked and then wondered if perhaps her words had been impolite or too personal, but he didn't seem to take offence.

'When I was a doctor and working in the hospital, sometimes, especially at night, I would become overwhelmed by the stretch of flesh around me. The way it suppurated and sweated. It turned my stomach. There were times when it was all I could do to touch the patients, to cut and bandage their skin, to witness all the degrading secretions and lesions caused by living a godless life. And yet, despite my repulsion there was always in me a half-feeling that I wanted to give myself to it. To participate in the very thing that would bring me down, lower even than those others who had never heard the word of God.'

He fell quiet and Ruby had the sense he had disclosed more than he had wanted to, because he got to his feet, as if he had remembered he had somewhere else to be.

'You know my wishes on sitting, or standing for that matter, unaccompanied. It is the solitary who run the greatest risk of letting Satan in,' he said. She sat and watched him walk away. He looked as if he wasn't quite sure of the way back.

5th November

Dearest Nancy,

What happy, happy news! You cannot know how delighted I am at the prospect of a small you, perhaps with the same blue eyes, the same loose-skinned elbows, the same tendency to laugh at the least appropriate moments. Make Henry wait on you hand and foot and make sure to eat green-leafed things that are full of iron. I wish I could send you some of my chard from the community garden. It grows so quickly, we barely have time to eat it.

I hardy know what to tell you about my life here, nor of what I have done. I fear you will not consider me someone to admire when you know of it, and yet it burns in me so fiercely, that I feel I must tell someone, and you are my oldest friend and the person I have always told my secrets to, although, in those far off days, the secrets were much less significant. You must promise never to disclose a word of what I tell you to anyone.

William came back from India, where it appears he had a change of heart about Irene. He came to the community to talk to her twice, and each time I turned him away, saying that Irene did not want to see him and that her feelings for him had been extinguished. She has been unwell lately and some of my black heart thought there was a measure of protection in this, but if I am truthful, and I am trying to be truthful to you, I did nothing to test this notion. I did not tell her of his visits. I have always loved him. I have sincerely tried not to for my sister's sake, but I have not been able to give the thought of him up. I went to meet him, Nancy. I went to meet him when he thought that Irene would be with me. You know a little of him, how for all his charm, or maybe because of it, he changes so quickly. When I offered myself to him (I can scarcely believe I am writing these words, much less that I actually did what I did), he kissed me. The world stopped when I was in his arms. We talked and watched the sun go down and it was the most wonderful and most awful two hours I have ever experienced. I know all he is. I know all that I am, too, and yet in that unremarkable field, terrified that I might be discovered, I felt my life beginning. Since that first time, I have seen him once more and I felt the same wonder. It was as if we were in a world all of our own making.

We have not met for the last three weeks, since he is otherwise occupied, but I think of him constantly and every morning I go down to see if he has sent word to me to come to him. Adding to my tumbled thoughts and tumbled heart is the feeling that something awful is about to happen. Not just that I will be discovered in my perfidy, but that there is a punishment in store that in some way will be of my own making. I am worried about Irene who often seems so unwell, particularly after one of her takings. Mother has intimated that her sainthood is imminent, but I fear what this will mean for her. This place is full of shadows.

Forgive me.
Your friend Ruby (I hope)

Chapter 43

Ruby could not understand William's long silence. It had been more than a month since she had seen him last and there had been no word from him in all that time. In her desperation she had even taken Trench aside and asked him if he was sure he had not been given a message for her, but he had shaken his head from side to side and looked at her with those sad eyes of his.

'You best be careful,' he had said in his gasping voice. 'The Lion and the Bear, they see everything.'

In the orchid house, the smell of the sweltering blooms and the earth they rested in – a mixture of cinnamon, vanilla, citrus, and metal – was so strong it made a sound, a swelling, roaring tone that filled Ruby's head. She opened the windows and began splashing the flowers with water as if she was extinguishing a fire. The red-fluted orchid she had grafted onto a small white variety the previous week, hoping to make a pale pink mixture of the two, had thrived in this foetid atmosphere. Its closed buds had opened to reveal a dark purple centre. The rooted plant on which it was growing had shrivelled and fallen away under the stress of bearing its invader. Some of the less heat-tolerant plants had developed white patches circled by dark rings on their leaves and had already begun to rot, so Ruby cut these carefully from their stems and gathered them in the pocket of her apron. At the heart of a trumpet-headed bloom, the name of which she had now forgotten, a tiny butterfly lay moving gently amid the confetti-splattered petals. The orchids revealed their veins – more delicate and intricate than those on a human wrist – and their moist lips and folded, intricate crevices had a slimy, silvery shine. Underneath some large leaves, hidden from her until now, she discovered the first bloom of the ghost orchid – a newly acquired specimen. George had brought it in when it was just a few grey tendrils in a pot, but now it had attached itself by the roots to the base of a large trunked fern. When she touched its floating, frog-like legs, it seemed to drift under her hand. *I can see you*, she thought. *I can see you completely.* Tears came to her eyes at the sheer beauty of it – the way it showed itself so quietly and perfectly.

She heard a sound and raised her head. She did not at first understand what she was seeing. There seemed to be a shape attached to the glass. As if something had been thrown against it, but she had not heard the impact. Then she recognised it as a face – the features were spread out and monstrous. Forehead impossibly wide, nose squashed sideways, eyes wide, mouth stretched into a grimace that could have been a smile. She thought she screamed. She could feel the fear running through her body as if it was made of liquid. The face was so near to her own, it felt close enough to rest against her cheek.

It pulled away, grinning, and she saw that it was Martin. He rapped on the glass with his knuckles and indicated that she should come out. Ruby got to her feet, her legs almost giving way underneath her.

'There has not been an update on Irene's visions this week,' he said when she emerged. 'I want you to come to the office so that I can make a note of all you say.'

'There is really nothing new to report,' she said, but she began to walk with him towards the house. Her skin shrank at his proximity. One of his long, loose arms almost brushed her own and she stepped away from him.

'I had no idea you had such a sensitive nature, Ruby,' he said, looking sideways at her. When he caught her gaze, he stuck out the tip of his tongue as if he was testing the air.

'Wait a moment, until I finish this,' he said when they arrived at the office, 'and then you can begin.'

He had four or five samples from the orchid house and placed them carefully on blotting paper and caressed them down. He placed the wooden lid of the flower press on to its pegs and began to screw each corner down. Ruby imagined the trapped flowers between the layers of paper beginning to feel the mounting pressure and then spreading helplessly under their rigid roof, flattening out and exposing themselves bit by bit so that the whole of them would be open to scrutiny next time the press was released.

'Now settle yourself and tell me what our visionary has shared with you,' he said, sitting down at the desk and opening his notebook.

Ruby embellished and invented for half an hour, talking of a fall of snow and then another flood for good measure. She took comfort from the fact that at least she was not telling Martin anything that Irene had actually said, although she was terrified that he would somehow know that she was lying.

Afterwards, she climbed up the stairs to her quarters and found Hester at the dressing table staring at her reflection and darkening her naturally sparse eyebrows with the end of a burnt clove.

'Mother, this place is not what you think it is.'

'Oh, do stop rushing around, Ruby! You startled me and my hand shook.'

'Will you not at least listen for once as to why I believe we should not be here? Do you not wonder where Sister Eloise is? Are you just happy to accept what you are told that Peters is looking after her? I saw her buried in the grounds in the dead of night in a coffin that went in the ground, feet first, and Martin is a cruel man, he—'

'I always knew you would not find what you needed to find, Ruby,' Hester interrupted, turning from the mirror to look at her daughter. 'Even as a little girl you were always so impatient, so ready to rush ahead with your own little plots and schemes. There was no stopping you. You are no different now. You are still heedless and careless, still unwilling to listen to what you do not want to listen to. You take what you want without thought of the consequences.'

'But, Mother! I am only trying to explain…' Ruby expostulated, trying not to feel the sting of the words she had heard some version of all her life. Her mother had decided long ago who she was, and there was nothing Ruby could do now, no combination of words she could say that would turn the picture of herself that her mother had drawn into something Ruby felt was closer to who she really was. If she allowed herself to really dwell on this, she felt a kind of panic to think that if her mother, the person who had known her all her life, believed her to be a certain way, perhaps there was some truth in it. Perhaps she was someone forever trapped in the mould in which she had been cast, unable to change or develop or become better. After all, her mother was right to say she took what she wanted. Had she not done this very thing with William? It was just that she wished there was some small part of her that her mother could admire. All that was really left between them was a reflex of the kind elicited by a hammer blow under the kneecap – a jerking up of familial duty and the necessity to keep up appearances. It seemed to have little to do with genuine feeling.

'You and your sister are as different as silk and hemp.'

'Which am I, Mother? The silk or the hemp?' Ruby said.

'You know perfectly well. Irene is going to elevate me and help me earn my salvation. Now, why do you not wash that smudged face of yours and brush your hair so that you do not look quite so much like a mad woman,' Hester said placidly, turning back to the mirror.

'At least hemp has a resilience that silk does not have. Give me a rope of hemp over one made of silk any day,' Ruby said unable to stop herself from resorting to the childish retort.

'A rope you will hang yourself with, Ruby, if you are not careful.'

Despite it all, Ruby felt a kind of exasperated affection for her mother, sitting with her lopsided brows and her hair teased up into a complicated plait. Perhaps she thought she might be chosen as Peters' bride. She was so very hopeful. It had taken courage for her mother to rise from her bed and begin another story.

'You look nice, Mother,' was all she said. She splashed some water on her face and pushed the brush through her hair twice and left to find Irene.

Police Constable Hodge was in the downstairs hallway with Brother Martin, who was clearly trying to persuade the man off the premises. He was looming over him, his hands fisted, as if he was contemplating pushing him out of the door.

'The Beloved is not here,' Martin was saying. 'I have strict instructions not to answer questions and to forbid you access to the community unless you have an official warrant, which you do not.'

Martin's bullying manner seemed not to be affecting the policeman, at all. He stood with his hat under his arm, his posture relaxed, a half-smile on his face. It made Ruby's spirits rise to see Martin confronted in this way by someone who was not intimidated by him. Constable Hodge was so very steady, so persistent in his endeavours and it seemed to her, looking at the way he did not flinch or drop his gaze, that his strength was powered by goodness. His very presence in the community seemed in some way to dispel its shadows.

'I will be back,' Constable Hodge said. 'There are matters that your leader needs to address.'

Martin made an exclamation of annoyance and retreated into his study, slamming the door shut.

'Good afternoon, Constable Hodge,' Ruby said, descending the last of the stairs.

He smiled at her and as she approached, she saw that the eyes she had first thought a simple brown, had little flecks of gold in them.

'Good afternoon, Miss Hart,' he said, and she noticed that some of the confidence that he had exhibited in the face of Martin seemed suddenly to desert him. He moved his hat and lodged it under his other arm and smoothed down the front of his jacket.

'Still investigating the suicides?'

'I am doing my best to, Miss Hart.'

'And have you made any progress?'

'I believe I have,' he said. He seemed to hesitate then, as if he wasn't sure of what he should say.

'Miss Hart, have you seen anything that has made you think that all is not as it quite appears in the community?'

'Let me walk you to the gate,' Ruby replied, unsure herself of how to explain to him what she had seen and how it had made her feel. Perhaps she would just be reporting things that were only to be expected in a place such as this. After all, how would he be able to help if she told him about Hattie and Delia being tested, or of the way that Martin scared her. He was concerned with the law, and she could not say any crime had been committed. All the other community members seemed to accept the things that she wondered at. Even Irene, who had always been so sensible, had not reacted to her disclosures in the way she had expected. Her mother had utterly dismissed them. Perhaps she did not feel the same grace the others did, because she was a sinner. She had the sense she often had in the community, that it was hard to unpick exactly what was true and what was not.

'Although I never believed, and still do not, that being here would earn me immortality, I had understood that all those who do believe have an equal chance, but it seems to me that some must suffer more than others. I saw Hattie being terribly tested, and then she was found dead. And last night, I saw another woman called Delia undergoing a similar trial,' Ruby said, as they walked together through the garden. 'Martin seems to be the moving force behind all of this, although I believe he only does what Reverend Peters tells him to do.'

'There certainly seem to be some strange rituals here,' Hodge replied. 'I am not sure whether to tell you of this ... it is of a delicate nature, but I have discovered that Miss Hattie Blackthorn had recently been delivered of a child.'

She stopped dead in her tracks and stared at him. She felt her face flush with the shock of what he had said. It took her a couple of moments for the information to sink in.

'Do you think Hattie had an ... entanglement ... with someone outside the community? Perhaps a husband she abandoned to become a saint? She said she never left the place.'

Another thought struck Ruby. 'The baby that was left in the lane. Was it perhaps hers? Was it left by her because it would not be allowed to stay with her in the community? It is so sad. I can hardly bear to think about it.'

Ruby felt bewildered. She thought of Hattie's slow, heavy body and her silence. The surprise of it all brought tears to her eyes.

Philip put a hand out to her, and then seemed to think better of it and put it firmly in the pocket of his jacket.

'I have not been able to fit all the pieces of the puzzle together yet, Miss Hart,' he said gently, 'but I would strongly advise you to be wary. Remain with your sister and your mother. Do not go anywhere on your own.'

Still stunned by what she had learned, Ruby opened the gate for the policeman and after he had again said he was available to her at any time, he left. After his departure, Ruby felt the walls of the community shrink around her.

Chapter 44

'It does seem rather as if there is a pattern emerging,' Jowler said ponderously as he and Philip walked along Salmon Parade in Bridgwater. The two men were on their way back from the Bridgwater Infirmary where the body of Delia Vantage was laid out in the back room that served as a mortuary. She was attended now only by her weeping mother who refused to leave her. When Philip had pulled back the sheet that covered Delia's poor face he had been struck by how untouched she seemed – her curls lay around her head as if they had been arranged so, and he could almost imagine her curved mouth opening to speak. Her hands were folded quietly on her chest. If it had not been for the livid marks around her neck, you might have thought she was sleeping.

'It is indeed a sorry business,' Jowler continued with a distracted air.

Philip wondered if this was his first sighting of Jowler's feet in actual motion. They were usually firmly ensconced beneath his desk. He was struck by their diminutive nature – they were almost dainty in their button boots, making the chief constable, with his considerable girth, look like an inverted triangle. The river was its usual murky brown, and busy today with boats arriving for the fair. The whole town was animated by the visitors who had come to trade cattle or to buy goods or to partake of the peep shows and tented entertainment. Philip himself was tempted to go and see the much-acclaimed strong woman, who was said to be able to lift a horse onto her shoulders and wear it like a cape. He very much doubted though, that the horse would be of Thunder's dimensions.

'This is the third member of the community to be found dead by apparent suicide in little more than a year,' he said.

'It is a shame. She was a good-looking young woman. It suggests to me a high degree of hysteria amongst the female community members,' Jowler replied, picking his way around a horse deposit.

'But as I have said to you, sir, I do not believe the deaths were suicides. Someone other than the deceased was sighted by a witness, hiding at the spot where the second victim, Miss Blackthorn's body was found. Then there is the matter of the notes pinned to the dresses. This last tragic woman had the same crossed out message attached to the bodice of her dress as the other two. On what may be a related matter, sir, I have found out from the doctor who attends on my mother that Miss Blackthorn had recently had a baby. Doctor Pontifex said he mentioned this fact to you at the time.'

'I have no memory of such a conversation,' Jowler said, shaking his head in a reprimanding fashion at a small boy who was standing in a rowing boat at the water's edge and rocking it violently from side to side in an apparent attempt to dislodge a smaller boy who was clutching onto his seat and roaring in terror.

'The mother, Eva, said that her daughter had been somewhat quieter than usual and complaining of feeling unwell, but there was absolutely nothing to indicate that she would be moved to commit such an act of violence against herself.'

Vivid in Philip's mind was Delia's mother's face when she had been summoned to the hospital and told of the death. It had been as if her features, her very self, had been hollowed out, and she had fallen forward into Philip's arms with a cry so loud it had made the hairs on his arms rise up.

'And was the young woman found in the same place?'

'It was a little further away from Yaxton, but everything else was the same. She was hanging from a tree, with a cord around her neck.'

'I suppose we must be seen to be doing something, if only to put a stop to some of the more lurid stories that are being disseminated,' the chief constable said. 'Although I am loathe to disturb Reverend Peters again. The Coroner is of a mind to cite suicide. He sees nothing to indicate otherwise.'

They crossed the bridge and turned on to Fore Street where the police station was located. People had congregated in large groups outside the Bridgwater Arms, making the most of the holiday spirit in noisy fashion.

'Might I at least have a mandate to go to the community and interview Reverend Peters again and some others?'

'If you must. But tread carefully, Hodge. I do not want to offend the Reverend. Do not suggest that any crimes have been committed unless you have hard evidence. Much of what you have gathered seems to be based on hearsay. It is not the stuff of proper policework which I suspect is rather above your level of skill to accomplish.'

'Yes, sir,' Philip said, biting his lip to prevent a more voluble response.

'I intend to go shortly into this tavern and check that everyone is behaving themselves,' Jowler said. Philip left his superior standing with his gaze fastened to the window of the nearby boot and shoe shop where the new range was on full, tempting display.

'Have there been any occasions over the last few weeks when you have noticed members of the community absent from where they were supposed to be?'

Miriam was chopping apples on the kitchen table. Her knife sliced with ferocious regularity. There was a large pan bubbling violently on the stove, emitting a smell of spice and vinegar and sugar. She had her sleeves rolled up, and Philip could see the glisten of sweat on her arms.

'Perhaps, for instance, people not being present at meal times or at the beginning of their working days?' he persevered, despite the fact she was refusing to look at him. The heat in the room was extraordinary. Who in their right minds would choose to labour so in such a temperature? Her evident anger added to the ferment, and it seemed to him that moving so fast and so fiercely, she must surely soon wear herself out. The way she doggedly kept at her task put him in mind of a character in one of those tales who, confronted by an impossible pile of straw to be spun into gold or a monster with a hundred tails to slay, still attempts what they know to be impossible.

She hated his thick boots on her clean floor. The way he leant so far back in his chair that the front legs rose, and then landed again with a scraping sound that made her want to bite him. He would befoul their sanctuary with his smell of horse and hay, with his nails rimmed with something unspeakable and with his dull notions of right and wrong. She would ignore him and keep working until there were thirty jars of chutney, tightly lidded and clearly labelled in a line on the pantry shelf. If she kept busy, she could keep herself steady. That The Beloved had remained away and had left her to deal with everything felt like an unfair burden. She remembered Delia's excitement when she had first arrived in the community, and her throat constricted.

She thought of the clean, early days of the Garden Kingdom when everything had still been ahead of them. She could remember her own vigour and the way her blood used to sing through her. No task had been beneath The Beloved then. He had toiled on the last section of the wall, his hands rubbed raw, working long after the others had retired. In the end, she had gone out to him in the evening light and insisted he come and eat. *We are almost safely in*, he had said, as she had led him back to the house. *When it is done, we will be complete, and we will be happy.* His faith still burned in him, but she thought it had acquired a new shape, something she could not help but feel was less than true, like glass blown along its length too forcefully, so that it acquires a distention beyond its original conceiving. Recently she had felt that he had become unduly influenced by Martin, a man who did not and had never had, the same purity of purpose. Martin was a different kind of a man, altogether. She had thought on many occasions that it had been a mistake to let him come to the community, but Peters had insisted on it. *I cannot do all I need to do by myself. I need a right-hand man*, he had said.

'You must surely feel some disquiet at this latest death? It must mean that something in the community is not working as it should. Do you not want to know what has been happening?' Philip asked.

She moved over to the pan and began stirring it so fast that its contents threatened to spill over.

'What has been happening, Constable Hodge, is that you have come blundering in here, without any understanding, determined to ferret out something for your own edification. What is it you are after? Some kind of promotion perhaps?'

She turned to him, then, her dripping wooden spoon pointed in his direction, her body so tightly held that he found himself feeling something like compassion. For all her rude haughtiness, he could sense her fear.

'Miss Delia Vantage,' he said, 'was due, I believe, to be married to a member of the community. Who was this and when was the marriage going to take place?'

'For you, marriage is a dirty shackling. A transaction of bodies and then a lifetime of narrow grubbing and resentment. Here, we respect each other. There is nothing of the selfish clutching that erodes potential and takes away freedom.'

'That is as may be,' Philip said, wondering who it was that had once hurt her. Her damage was visible in the corners of her mouth, in the way she moved as if she could not allow herself to rest. 'But please, answer my question... Who was Delia due to marry?'

'Delia was to enter into a sacred union with one of the founding members of the community. It had not yet been decided who. She was glad of the privilege.'

'Are you sure Miss Vantage was as enamoured of the proposed union as you suggest?'

'You are clearly too stupid to understand, or perhaps just determined not to.'

'But for a beautiful young girl such as she was, would there not have been at least some disappointment to find herself shackled, to use your terminology, to someone old enough to be her father? Maybe it was her mother that wanted to secure her place here, and the daughter was a casualty of this determination?'

'I think this conversation is pointless,' Miriam said, taking up her knife again. Despite the fact he had been feeling something close to pity for her only moments, before, Philip was aware of a rising irritation and a desire, he was half ashamed of, to try and hurt her.

'And how much did Mrs Vantage have to pay, to secure everlasting life?'

'It is time you left, Constable Hodge. You prod away into things you can never be part of.'

'What happens to the saints who can no longer pay for sanctuary? Are they asked to leave? Driven out perhaps? What happens to them when their Day of Judgement comes early?'

She felt a terrible desolation. The man was an oaf, but he had said something amongst his ignorant shots in the dark that had hit home like the blow of a hammer against her skull. Every part of her fought against the thought of it, but now that he had planted it there, she could feel it growing inside her with sharply thorned tendrils.

'Will you tell your leader, when he returns from his travels, that the chief constable has decided on a full investigation.' This was not strictly true, but he knew it would have more effect if those in the community believed it to be. 'I, and another officer will be back in due course to talk to each and every member of this community. We will also have to search all the rooms.'

'Do you really think that the suicides of some lost, sinning girls warrants all this fuss? Is it not simply that the community is the focus of people's prejudice and suspicion, and this provides an opportunity to meddle? People are made small by what they do not understand.'

She drew herself up, strengthened by this argument, which had, after all, always been true. They were viewed as not belonging to life, as being strange and unknowable. It was this difference from others that had always sustained her and made her proud.

'You can think what you like about our motivations. But three women have died; a fact that seems inexplicably beneath your interest. I do not believe they killed themselves. Something, or rather someone, in this supposed paradise on earth brought about their deaths.'

He took the opportunity of her sudden shocked silence to rock back on his chair one last time and then got to his feet.

'I will see myself out.'

After he had left the room, Miriam stood looking after him for a moment. She put the knife down on the table. She no longer had the strength to hold it. She walked over to the pan almost in a dream and put her right hand into its still boiling contents.

Chapter 45

Ruby had overheard several whispered conversations expressing puzzlement and disquiet about Delia's death. There were other community members, though, who seemed curiously unaffected, as if what had happened had nothing whatsoever to do with them. Edith had simply remarked that it was unfortunate that Delia had failed to earn the salvation she was only a matter of days away from. Norah talked in her usual way about the devil. Armed with the information Philip had given her, Delia's death filled Ruby with fear. She lay awake at night listening for footsteps in the corridor. She had even begun to imagine, in the absence of anyone to talk to about it, that by witnessing Hattie and Delia's struggles, she had in some terrible way contributed to their deaths.

Irene was recovering from another major seizure and seemed barely able to register what had happened. Ruby sat in the room by her bed, gazing at her sister's white face. Each taking pulled Irene further out, like a raft caught in a tide. Each absence seemed to rub a little more of her away. Even if Ruby could plan some way of leaving the community, how would she be able to take Irene with her? Her sister's periods of strength and lucidity seemed to get ever shorter, so that there was barely time for her to recover before she was taken away again. Ruby looked out of the window at the fields beyond the community and longed to be there again. Away from all this. She wished William would come back so that she could lie again with her head on his chest, the sky pink above them.

As had become her habit, Ruby had held back from opening her most recent letter from Nancy until she could be alone. These missives from the outside world were her only link with what she thought of as reality, although the descriptions of parties and flirtations that Nancy described had begun to feel more and more remote to her. She even wondered if she would be able to behave as she had before in the company of those she had left behind only a few months ago. Maybe being in the community had conferred a permanent mark on her that would set her apart amongst people she had moved amongst so easily before. She was also worried about Nancy's reaction to what had been revealed to her in Ruby's last letter.

It wasn't until after the evening meal, which for the first time since she had arrived at the community, was not attended by Miriam, that Ruby found the opportunity to slip away to the fern garden. The envelope contained only a single sheet which was unusual, since Nancy always wrote at length and in great detail. It took a while for Ruby to understand what she was reading. She had to read the sentences several times before she could make sense of them.

25th November

My Dearest Ruby,

I can hardly bear to tell you what I know I must. My words will surely hurt you more than any I have ever delivered. I only wish I could be with you to try and ease the sting, although I fear, my comfort would be woefully insufficient.

I had been gathering myself to reply to your last letter, wondering exactly what advice I might give you – whatever you have or have not done, you will always be my dear friend – when I heard some news about William. Lucy Bourne knows William's sister well and when she called upon her yesterday, she was told that William is engaged to be married. The girl is called Kate Roxenbury and has been living until recently in Switzerland with her parents. They returned home following the death of a relative who has left Kate a considerable amount of money. If it is any consolation, and I know it will not be much, she was pointed out to me in the park this morning and she is so plain and small and unattractively insubstantial, she almost blended into the shrubbery.

What can have changed his mind, I cannot imagine. I do not like to think that this was his plan all along and that you were simply some kind of diversion. I have never held William Everett in high esteem since his treatment of Irene, but this would be low, even for him. I can only think that he has somehow been forced into it by that father of his who I have always despised since the day I saw him almost twist the ear off his groom for no apparent reason other than the fact he was in Mr Everett's line of sight.

Be assured that nothing of what went on between the two of you will ever cross my lips and I doubt William will be spreading his perfidy abroad. Remember that I am always here.

Love, Nancy

Ruby felt as though she had drifted up to the top of the chestnut tree and was sitting on one of its branches looking down on herself. She saw the pitiful slope of her back, her white neck, her hands holding the letter, her feet planted side by side in their childish, buckled shoes. How was it possible to feel such pain and yet still remain intact? How could the garden still offer up its perfumed beauty, as if nothing at all had changed? Her tears fell on the letter and made the words indistinct. She wished the reality of them could be undone as easily. He did not love her, then. He likely never had any feelings for her, at all. She had been an amusement or a solace. Maybe tricking her, making her put to one side what she knew to be right, had even been a kind of revenge – a way of exerting his power when he had felt himself diminished. She thought of his mouth on her throat, of the push of his legs against the side of his horse and her body moved with a terrible, shameful friction. All of it for nothing! The betrayal of her sister, her capitulation to Martin's demands, the way she had deceived herself, had ended just in this – sitting in the dark, feeling lower than the things that crawled through the grass at her feet. Lower even than the worms that laced the earth and made a meal of dead things. She tried to muster anger, to feel the cauterising burn of it, but it would not come to her. She only felt the loss. The pain lodged itself under her ribcage and would not let her go. She pushed her feet against the ground and held on to the bench, trying to get purchase. Trying to gather what was left.

'It is my fault,' she said out loud. 'I tried to take what was not mine and told myself that I could not help it. I told myself that my love justified anything.'

It was late by the time Ruby had composed herself enough to go back in. She wondered how she was going to get through the days. I will never be the same again. I will always feel this terrible, heavy weight in my chest. Always feel the abandonment. The moon was only a sliver – a closed, silvered eyelid – and she had to feel her way across the lawn and down the privet pathways with careful feet. She practised the face she would present to Irene in case her sister was awake. It was an approximation of the empty mien of her fellow community members. This was what they all did – disguised their pain and fear and feelings of smallness underneath a mask of composure – their faith lending them the ability to hide in full view.

When she reached the house, she saw that the lights were still on in the meeting room. One of the curtains had not been properly pulled across the window and there were a few inches emitting a shine at its edge. There was music coming from inside, and although all she wanted to do was get to her bed and hide herself under its covers, she could not help wondering who might still be up and apparently celebrating at such a late hour. She stood flat against the wall and peered through the gap. She could only see small sections of the room and had to readjust her position several times to get a wider perspective.

The circular stage used for Sunday dancing and for standing on when people were making announcements was being utilised in quite another way. There were four women sitting evenly around its circumference, like the quarter and half-hour markings on a clock. Two of the women lived in the hall, but the other two were unknown to her. All were young, one particularly so – she was just a girl and had a soft-edged face. They were dressed in white, as were the women standing in a line along the wall who seemed to be waiting for their turn. Their hair was wet as if they had recently bathed.

Ruby was puzzled. No one had ever mentioned such an activity. Perhaps it was a ceremony of some kind that she had not yet participated in. Or some kind of a game?

She stepped back and almost cried out when Martin suddenly crossed her field of vision. He bent down and pushed the edge of the stage with his enormous arms. He began a scampering run around its edge, still holding on, so that the whole edifice began to turn on its central pivot. He ran faster and faster, his legs bent, his red hair agitated by the motion, his great head glistening with exertion. The women on board tried vainly to remain sitting upright, but the wooden surface was slippery, and they had nothing to hold on to, and so they were cast this way and that. The youngest of the women toppled over completely and had to scramble to her knees. Ruby could see her mouth moving piteously like a child who had found a fairground ride more taxing than she had expected.

There was a small group of watching men standing to the left of the stage. They were mostly members of Peters' inner circle – some had been present at the taking ceremony, but there were some she did not recognise – a policeman, older and larger than Constable Hodge and with more buttons on his uniform, was standing right at the front. They began a rising chant that grew louder and louder as the stage began to slow. A kind of whooping, warning sound. The noise was so great, it drowned out the music. She could see the black hole of their rounded mouths and the shine of their eyes and the movement of their fisted hands beating out a rhythm. This noise ended abruptly when the stage came to a final stop and then there were cheers and laughter as the youngest girl was lifted down by Martin.

Dazed by misery and now by a new kind of fear, Ruby turned away. She imagined going into the room and demanding to know what was happening. An earlier version of herself might have attempted it but she felt weak and without the necessary stature. She thought of all those shining eyes turning towards her, and Martin's blunt, assessing stare. He might even use the opportunity to tell them all exactly who she was. *This is the woman who sneaks out of the community to meet a man. She lies in fields with him and allows him to touch her. A man who does not care for her at all.* What if they directed their rising chant at her and moved their fists over her body? In any case, the door was almost certainly locked against intruders. It was clear that whatever was happening in the room was a secret only for those in the inner circle.

Chapter 46

Philip's mother died in the night. He wasn't with her at the time. He had been sitting with her earlier but had gone to bed to get some sleep, leaving his neighbour in his stead. He had returned to the room in the early hours of the morning and found her already cold and Mrs Grawler busily doing things with sheets. She had even placed a plank of wood at his mother's feet, *to help with the stiffenin'*, and had called the doctor.

'Why did you not come and get me?' he asked her.

'She would p'rhaps not 'ave passed with you there,' she had answered, her face alight with a sense of a pleasurable duty well done.

Once the doctor and Mrs Grawler had both gone, Philip had sat beside his mother for a while, wondering at her emptiness. Her face had hollowed out and her features had slackened into an approximation of what she had once been. A desolate longing to see her again caught him by surprise. He cried over her hand, moving the loose skin back and forth as if he was trying to rub her back to life. Her embroidery was on the floor at the side of the bed, and he picked it up and unfurled it. Her last instalment was picked out in an unsteady hand, the words sloping downwards – *I take it with me, as we all must.*

Now the undertaker had been and had slid the shell of her onto the back of a cart and the house was quiet. He had not realised how much she had filled it, even when she was sick. There is now only me, he thought, making a pile of her things. He would keep the embroidery and give the rest to people who might be glad of her good black coat that she had worn so seldom, and her two dresses in the same dark green with the buttons tightly sewn and the hems stitched carefully, as if she imagined that one day someone might turn them up to inspect them.

He needed to go somewhere and do something. He could not bear sitting in the empty house feeling the phantoms gather. He put his mother's clothes and her mirror and comb and a small, silver-plated dish that had held her hairpins, in a bag. His brother Gareth had given her the dish. Pilfered by him no doubt, but received by her with such wondering gratitude, the memory of it made his eyes fill again. She had placed it carefully in the very centre of the table in her room so she would be able to see it from her bed. She should have had more. She should have had a whole shining service of plates and bowls and goblets.

He left Thunder behind and set off on foot. Walking down the lanes he knew so well, past the river, lower and darker than it had been a few weeks ago but still moving round its familiar curves and straight lengths with the same comforting slide, he began to feel calmer. He thought about all the beautiful things that anchored him to the earth – Thunder's tawny, sweet-smelling flank, the colour of the corn when it was at its most golden; Ruby's laughing mouth, the soft give of Pearl's cheek. There were things left. He just had to count them.

At Minnie's cottage, the door was open and emitting a cacophony of voices.

'She ain't here,' Minnie's mother said, as soon as she saw him. It was strange to see the woman upright. In his previous sightings of her she had always been spread over the mattress and fastened to children. She moved slowly and creakily, like a boat trying to find its mooring.

'I just brought some things,' Philip said, placing the bag on the kitchen floor. 'I thought perhaps you might have use for them.'

She bent stiffly from her waist and poked an arm into the bag and pulled out one of his mother's dresses.

'She's gone then?' she said.

'Yes, early this morning.'

'She's better off out of it,' she said waving her arm to encompass the kitchen, the three children noisily consuming their greyish soup and the whole heedless world beyond.

'Is Minnie at work?' Philip asked, not taking offence at her apparent lack of sympathy. It was easier to deal with indifference than kindness. When you were grieving, which he supposed was what he was doing, kindness broke you apart.

'Yes. Told her not to go there, them being strange people with peculiar ideas, but the money is better than she could get elsewhere. And well…' She made another of her expansive gestures.

'And the baby?'

She pointed a finger upwards, and for one awful moment he thought she meant the child had died.

'Sleeping,' she said. 'Along with the other one. First bit of peace I've had all day.'

She nodded her permission when he asked if he might go upstairs, and suddenly finding her docking place, turned to whack the fingers of the eldest boy who had crept his hand stealthily towards the loaf of bread.

Pearl was lying in the cradle she was already almost too big for. Her arms were flung out above her head in an attitude of surrender. He watched her for a while, finding his own first bit of peace of the day in the way her rounded chest rose and fell and in the tiny, flickering fluctuations of her face.

Chapter 47

Ruby climbed the steps to her room slowly. She felt so tired, she had to stop halfway up and rest. Since reading Nancy's letter, she had hardly slept. She had lain awake for two long nights examining the details of William's abandonment and her part in it. She saw his face turning to her, felt the slide of his gloved hand and the insistent pressure of his lips on hers. At what point had he decided he did not want her? Was it even before he had kissed her that first time? Was it when he had lain in the grass with his hands behind his head and a stem of grass in his mouth, looking up at the flushed sky? She understood that the hope of him, the thought that he might love her, had sustained her until now. Now there was nothing left except a space in the very centre of herself and the shame that engulfed her every time she looked at her sister. To think she had so readily put Irene aside, without a thought of the consequences. Without considering what Irene would have felt if she had left the community to be with William. She had thought herself to be above others, more aware of herself, but now she knew that she was more stupid than the people she had always despised – the ones who fooled themselves they were someone they were not; the members of her erstwhile circle who had a misguided sense of their own attraction or power. *Who does he think he is?* She would say to Irene about a man who had talked long and boringly at dinner, or, *Does she really imagine that she is fooling anyone by the way she clutches on his arm? Anyone can see that she is only holding him so that he cannot get away.* Even the community members with their blind hope of an impossible dream had at least something they held fast to. Ruby had been more deluded than all of them. It was no wonder she was impossible to love. She did not deserve to be.

She opened the door to her quarters and froze. Martin was standing in the room. His loose stance and the shambling, unstuffed shape of him that had always made her skin shrink, was not apparent now. It was as if he had inhaled the air around him and it had coursed through his body, making him taut, intent, filled out. He was looking at Irene who was asleep on the sofa. The stays of her dress were unfastened, and her bodice was pulled down, so that a portion of her pale chest was visible. She lay with her neck extended across the back of the chair, her hair loosened and spread out behind. Despite her weariness, Ruby was suddenly and overwhelmingly terrified. She must have made a sound, although she was not aware of doing so. He shifted his shape, so that when he turned to face her, he had adopted his customary soft, yielding bulk.

She found her voice.

'What are you doing?' she asked. 'Why are you in our rooms?'

'I was delivering a message to your sister about the embroidery. It needs to be hung in the chapel tomorrow. Finding her asleep, I decided not to disturb her.'

His voice was too loud. It seemed to reverberate against the walls. He moved towards her. She could smell the warm mould of him. The apparent lack of control in his swinging arms and heavy legs stopped her breath. He is going to hit me, she thought. He is going to raise one of his bear paws and claw me. She backed out of the room slowly. She could hear her father's voice – *If you are ever confronted by a creature in the wild, do not run. Walk backwards without making any sudden movements. Try not to show your fear.*

He followed her out. She reached the top of the stairs and stopped, still facing him. She held tightly to the banister. What if he pushed her? She could see the fall – the scrabbling movement of her feet as she lost balance, the tumble of her dress, the impact of her body as it hit the hallway floor. For just a moment she thought he would take hold of her, but he just made a growling noise in the back of his throat and passed by. She stood for a moment holding on to the rail. The danger was still there. It felt like a moving thing that could run at her and take her down and hold her there. She went back into the room on unsteady legs.

'Irene!' Ruby touched her sister on her shoulder, and then when she did not respond, shook her gently.

'Irene, wake up!'

Irene turned her gaze to Ruby. Her eyes were cloudy, her lips dark red – the colour of damson jam – and sore looking. She looked down at herself and plucked at her bodice.

'Were you getting me undressed, Ruby? I cannot remember,' she said, in the creaking voice that belonged to her other self. 'Where have you been? I was spinning round and round, faster and faster. I could not hold on. I called out for you, but you were not there.'

Ruby's heart banged in her chest. Had Irene seen the spinning stage for herself? Or only dreamt it up? Could it be that she herself had been on the edifice?

'What do you mean you were spinning?'

'Do you remember that toy, Ruby? The one where you pulled a string and the top spun so fast all the colours joined up. It was like that.'

Ruby stared at her sister. There was something about the way her arms rested, the pull of her skin, the smoky shade of her eyelids that made Ruby feel icy cold, despite the heat. Irene was slipping away. While she had been preoccupied with herself, her sister had been slowly becoming invisible.

'Did you not see Martin here just now?'

'No, I have been quite on my own.'

'He was watching you, Irene. I came in just now and he was here.'

'You must be mistaken. I did not see him, Ruby.'

Ruby sank to her knees by Irene's chair and took hold of her hand. It rested in her own so calmly, so trustingly, it broke Ruby's heart.

After she had sponged Irene's arms and neck in cool water and made her drink a glass of lemonade she did not want, Ruby shut the door firmly behind her and went downstairs to find Miriam. It was not that she thought the woman would be a source of protection or even comfort, but she could not think of anyone else she could speak to.

Miriam was in none of the usual places such as the office or the kitchen or even the fern garden, so Ruby went to her room which was situated to the left of the chapel. She knocked and waited, and then knocked again more loudly and at last heard Miriam's instruction to come in.

She was sitting at her desk, but got to her feet as Ruby came in. The change in her appearance was startling. She held on to the back of her chair as if she was having trouble standing upright, her skin was ashen, her eyes dull. Her hitherto rigidly arranged hair was tied back carelessly and her dress was wrongly buttoned up. The reason for this dishevelment became evident when Ruby noticed that one of her hands was thickly bandaged.

'What happened to your hand, Sister Miriam?' Ruby asked.

'I had an accident in the kitchen. I was … careless,' Miriam answered, her voice subdued. 'Is there something I can help you with?'

'I hardly know how to tell you, but I came upon Brother Martin in our quarters and Irene was there. She did not know she was being watched. He is so … strange in his attentions to her. He did not actually do anything, although I thought he was going to but … he makes me afraid…'

Ruby broke off. How to explain how Martin had made her

feel? Or how being in the community was bearing down on her. She had nothing definite to pin her anxieties on.

'And the policeman, you know, the one that has been coming here, told me that he thinks that Hattie was murdered, which means that Delia might have been, too.'

Under Miriam's unblinking stare, Ruby felt herself falter again. It all sounded almost fanciful when said out loud.

'And you believe the words of a nobody in worn trousers? A policeman with dirt under his nails who steals radishes from the garden?'

Miriam's words, though bitter, were delivered without their usual force. Ruby thought it was as if someone had taken a spoon and scooped her out.

Miriam wondered how she still continued to breathe. How she was able to walk around the community looking at all that had been so precious to her, now turned to dust. To continue to issue instructions, even though none of it mattered anymore. At what point had the taint begun? It seemed to her now as if it had been sudden, but it could not have been. It must have crept in despite her efforts to keep all the cracks sealed. It must have happened when she was looking in the wrong direction. Her love had been terribly misplaced, although she thought, even now, if they were to come to her, she would talk to them as if to a lost child. This was not goodness in her, only the longing to cherish and be cherished.

'I do not know who or what I believe any longer,' Ruby said, 'Only that I am scared, and I think that Irene may be dying. Can you at least ask for a doctor to come to her?'

'Ruby, if I were you,' Miriam said, and as she spoke she wished she was indeed the young woman in front of her, still fiercely intact, with her mistakes still redeemable, with her life still ahead, 'I would take your sister and go as far away from here as possible. I would go and find your salvation elsewhere.'

On her way back to Irene and filled with the renewed sense that they must leave the community as soon as it could be arranged, Ruby saw the new maid, Minnie, standing in the hall. It seemed to Ruby that the girl had been waiting for her, because she put her finger to her lips and indicated that Ruby should follow her out into the garden.

'Miss Hart, I must tell you something,' Minnie said, speaking in an urgent undertone as soon as they were a safe distance from the house. 'The tincture that your sister has for her takings, it's bad for her.'

'What do you mean, Minnie?'

'I heard Brother Martin talking with the Reverend when they thought I wasn't there. They was saying about making the medicine stronger. I couldn't understand all the words. It is made of some special flower and makes your sister's takings deeper, or longer, or some such.'

Ruby's body tingled with shock.

'Are you sure?'

The maid nodded firmly.

'Philip ... Constable Hodge said I was to look out for anything wrong and tell him. Seems to me wrong to make someone weaker not stronger.'

'Why would they do such a thing? Do they think that Irene will reveal more of their salvation in her seizures if she is given something to make them more intense?' Ruby was talking more to herself than to Minnie. She still could not quite believe that that they would treat Irene so.

Minnie put her hand on Ruby's arm.

'They want her visions, but they also want her soft so as she can't put up a fight, Miss Hart.'

'A fight against what?'

An expression Ruby could not quite understand crossed the girl's face. She suddenly looked much older than her years. She seemed to be trying to find a way to explain something.

'I don't know. Not for sure. It could be they want her as

Reverend Peter's special bride. The one he is planning on marrying in some kind of ceremony. Martin watches her like a dog over a bone.'

'Although I am sure Irene would not want it or agree to it, being Peters' bride is considered an honour. The women are fighting amongst themselves to win the role. Why would Martin poison my sister to accomplish what many want so dearly?'

Minnie seemed to hesitate again. She lowered her head and began twisting the hem of her apron.

'It may be that this is a different kind of a union Miss Hart,' she said, finally, her eyes wide and anxious.

Ruby was about to question her further when they heard voices approaching.

'I have to go' Minnie said and walked away rapidly.

Ruby ran back into the house and up the stairs, taking two steps at a time. In her haste she almost tripped on her skirt but caught hold of the banister just in time. Her heart hammered in her chest, and she could barely breathe. There was no rational reason for this haste. Irene had been taking the tincture for months and one dose more or less was unlikely to make much difference, and yet she felt a frantic urgency. She burst through the door, but Irene was no longer in the drawing room where she had been when Ruby left her. Her shoes were lying discarded on the carpet. She went through to the bedroom, but Irene's bed was empty. Ruby was panting. Irene would surely not have left the room by herself. She had just come out of a seizure and could barely walk, and in any case she would not go out of their quarters in stockinged feet. Ruby went over to the window and hung out of it, scanning the garden. Nothing looked out of place. People were moving around in the same, purposeful, dreamy way, looking just as they did on The Beloved's map.

Chapter 48

By the afternoon, when Ruby still hadn't been able to find Irene, she began to feel terrified. Nobody she asked had seen her sister and Ruby had looked in all the obvious and not so obvious places. Miriam claimed that she had not seen Irene for at least two days, and when Ruby demanded to see Peters, told her that both he and Martin were out of the community and would not be returning until late that night. Ruby's stomach churned. Could Martin have taken her sister somewhere? She opened the gate to the community and looked up and down the lane. There was no sign of Constable Hodge, who she knew was often to be found patrolling the wall. Where was he when she needed him the most? One of the drinkers outside the inn noticed her standing half in and half out of the gate and raised a glass in her direction in a mocking kind of a way, so she went back inside.

She knew that Irene would have had neither the strength nor the inclination to walk any great distance, but nevertheless Ruby ran to the farm, stumbling over tussocks in her haste, pulling at grass stems as she went in an attempt to comfort herself. Please let her be with Hester. Please, Ruby prayed. Please let her be fast asleep on a pile of hay or sitting watching Mother churn the butter.

Hester was stroking the head of a goat who danced under her hand. She looked up at Ruby's running approach.

'Mother, have you seen Irene?' Ruby said as soon as she was near enough to be heard. She was gasping for breath and her skin was clammy with sweat.

'Ruby, you look quite deranged!' Hester replied. 'Come and see. I have made a collar of berries and ivy for the little one. Doesn't she look pretty?'

Hester's face was wreathed in smiles, and she indicated her handiwork. Ruby could see a few other of the goats were similarly adorned.

'I want them to look their best. They are God's creatures, and they travel on the ark with us.'

'I cannot find Irene. I have looked everywhere for her. Tell me you have seen her. Has she been here?'

'I saw her this morning,' Hester said, sitting down on a stool and beginning to weave a new collar.

'But not since then?'

Hester shook her head, her fingers moving through the foliage at her feet.

'Which do you think would look better? The snowberries or the rosehips?'

'Mother! This is serious. I am afraid she has been taken somewhere and she is not well and would not be able to fend for herself.'

'Honestly, Ruby, you are always so dramatic! Who would have taken her?'

'Well … Martin for one … or maybe Peters.'

Hester stilled her fingers and stared at her daughter.

'Firstly, you should not refer to The Beloved as Peters, and secondly, if she is under their care then no harm will come to her.'

Ruby felt a wave of despair. Her mother was as unreachable as the clouds that lingered over the Mendip Hills or the creatures that populated the bottom of the ocean.

'I have been trying to tell you for a while, Mother, that there are things happening here that frighten me. I believe that Irene might indeed be harmed. Will you not come with me and try and find her?'

'I have been told that there is a plan for your sister. We just have to wait and see what that is. I have a feeling that all will become evident very soon.'

'What exactly have you been told?'

'Nothing specific, but I believe that her visions are going to lead to a great honour.'

'Are you saying that you think Irene has been selected to be Peters' special bride?'

'It is not for me, or indeed you, to know. I suggest you go back to your work. You must resign yourself to being the second-best sister, Ruby, but that does not mean you do not have your own part to play. You can support Irene and try not to stand in her way.'

'Irene can barely walk. It appears that for all these weeks, she has been drugged with some sort of terrible potion. She will not be able to stop whatever is happening to her.'

Ruby felt herself swaying. The smell of the farm and the sweetish odour of crushed stems was overpowering. In her exhaustion, all she wanted to do was sink into the ground and be covered by earth. This was all her fault! She had looked the other way, expended her attention and energy on justifying her selfishness, and all the while Irene had been in danger. The darkness Ruby had felt in the corridor had moved, and sucked her in.

'Why would she want to stop what will be for the greater good? She is not like you, Ruby. She thinks of more than just herself.'

Hester's words hit Ruby in the chest with a blow so hard she thought she might die from it. There was nothing more she could say to her mother, so she turned and walked back, her legs heavy, her heart so sore, it was as if a hand had reached inside her and twisted it.

For the rest of the day, Ruby alternated between increasingly frantic searches of the hall and the cottages and watching at the window of the meeting room for Peters' and Martin's return. She looked around their room again for clues of what might have happened to her, but there was nothing that seemed out of the ordinary. Irene's dresses still hung in the wardrobe, her book was still by her bed, the bottle of tincture still stood on the window ledge. Ruby picked it up and smashed it against the washing bowl, and then got to her knees to pick up the fragments of glass. What if Irene was to come back and cut her feet on the shards? She longed for the door to the living room to open and for her sister to walk in, but as the time passed this seemed less and less likely. The brush on her dressing table had a tangle of Irene's hair and Ruby extricated it and held it in her hand.

At dinner time, Ruby waited until everyone had assembled and asked them each in turn if they knew of Irene's whereabouts, although she had already asked the same question of most of them already.

'Why don't you sit down and try and eat something?' Miriam said. She looked terribly ill and was pushing her food around with her undamaged hand, the other rested on the table gingerly, as if just this pressure was causing her pain.

Miriam did not know where Irene was, but she felt a mounting sense of dread. What had they done with her? Was it something to do with the wedding ceremony? There had been a time when The Beloved had told her everything, but it seemed that she had been cast out. She thought of Martin's eyes, that greedy look she had seen herself when he most wanted something, and she felt what little she had eaten rise in her throat. How had the man been able to take so much power? The other thing, the thing that bit into the very centre of her, she could not even bear to think about. She could not look at the others in case she caught their eyes. She was scared that she would not know what to say, or what to do if she did. It seemed that something had been let loose in the community that could not be stopped. Something solid and hot and angry... And so, she kept her eyes fastened to her plate, on the pink slivers of meat and the skinned gravy and prayed in a way she had not prayed for a long time.

'Maybe Irene has gone with The Beloved and Brother Martin on one of their recruitment expeditions,' Angela said. 'I think an explanation of your sister's powers would greatly impress, particularly if they could see her in person. She looks like a visionary, don't you think?'

Angela looked around the table and many of the others nodded their agreement.

'But has that ever happened before? Ruby asked. 'Has anyone ever been taken out of the community in such a way? In any case, Irene is so weak, she would not be in a fit state to be amongst strangers.'

'It could be that Irene's health took a sudden turn for the worse and The Beloved decided she needed care, although, of course, she really needs no extra protection...' Edith said, the expression on her pointed little face anxious. She got up from the table and put her arms around Ruby. 'Try not to worry. If your sister is with them, she will be safe.'

Ruby allowed herself to be held but felt no comfort.

Chapter 49

Ruby must have fallen asleep during her vigil in the meeting room, although she had been determined to stay awake. She had placed a chair close to the window so that she would be able to see Peters' and Martin's return. She woke suddenly and was, for a moment, completely disorientated. The room was dark, and the community silent. Then she heard the sound of footsteps and voices talking quietly. A door opened and then closed. She held her breath to listen but couldn't hear anyone going upstairs.

She felt her way across the room, navigating the edge of the revolving stage and the chairs. Out in the hallway there was faint light coming from the bottom of the chapel door. She put her ear to it and could hear whispering and feet moving across the floor. She slowly pressed the latch down, but the door would not open. She heard someone come into the hallway, and she quickly moved to the small landing at the top of the kitchen stairs and peered cautiously round the wall. She recognised the man as being one of Peters' inner circle. He knocked quietly and after a moment, Ruby heard the bolt being pulled back and he was admitted. She listened intently but there was no sound of the bolt being pulled across again. She waited a moment and then crept to the door again. This time, the latch descended under her careful pressure.

The Taking of Irene Hart

She held her breath and pushed the door open a little way. Just enough to be able to see what was happening inside.

The chapel had undergone a transformation. The pews had been pushed to the walls. A length of thin cloth had been stretched and fashioned into a screen and attached to one side of the billiard table, so that from where Ruby was standing, the table was obscured. Lamplight glowed from behind the material, but the only other illumination came from the candles placed on the floor. Peters sat on some kind of throne, white fur around his neck. A small group of men stood to one side. She saw that Martin was with them. He was dressed in a dark robe. Ruby felt a jolt of fear at the sight of his face, solemn now, with not a trace of the creature that lay inside him. Peters stood up and shrugged off his cloak. Ruby was astonished to see that beneath his regalia, he was wearing just a shift that grazed his ankles and slid off his shoulders. One of the group stepped forward and walked over to the wall where two curtains hung. Ruby had not noticed them on her first perusal of the chapel. The man pulled a cord which parted to reveal Irene's embroidery. Even in the dim light, the stitches she had made gleamed with the sinuousness of life. In the enclosed garden, the animals slithered and crept through the flowers. The fields and hills, seemingly without end, spread across and were made up of the hair and naked body of a woman. What ritual was this? Ruby wondered. Was it some kind of commemoration of the new embroidery? Why on earth do such a thing at night, and with such secrecy? It was clear in any case that Irene was not here. She was about to close the door and leave them to whatever strange ceremony they were participating in, when Peters spoke in a low voice. She had to strain to hear him.

'It has become clear to me that our salvation as a community, our pass into eternal life, relies on finding a way to join spirit with flesh. A way to reconcile God with man. My taking of a bride will be the means by which we will be absolved of all sin.'

Martin walked to the door of the anteroom that Martin had once told her she should never enter. How long ago had that been? It seemed to Ruby that years had passed. He went inside and came out again accompanied by a slightly built figure. Unmistakably a woman. She was dressed in white and shrouded in a thick veil. She moved slowly, as if she was not sure where she was putting her feet. At one point she almost fell and had to be pulled upright by Martin. Ruby's breath caught in her throat. Fear spread through her whole body as if she was being filled with ice. Was that Irene? What were they doing with her? Without thinking, she pushed the door open and ran towards the woman. She had almost reached her when she felt someone take hold of her and knock her to the floor. She lay winded, looking up into Martin's furious eyes.

'You are coming with me,' he said, his teeth bared, his breath foetid on her face. He was lying on top of her. The skin on his face rippled, as if there was something underneath trying to get out. She struggled to get free. If he took her she would not be able to save Irene. There would be nobody to protect her sister. The panic induced by this thought gave her strength. She tried to push him off and then to wriggle out from under him, but he held her firmly under his huge bulk. His great paws were on her face, then on her mouth. He was prising her lips open. She got an arm free and reached for him. She felt the tear of his flesh under her nails, and he yelped. She heard Peters speak but could not make out his words. She felt something cold and hard being pushed against her lips and then liquid in her mouth. It was glutinous and bitter. She tried to spit it out, but Martin held her mouth shut. She could smell the sourness of his hand. She saw the faces of the other men standing above her. She saw the slender shape of the shrouded woman. Run! She wanted to say. Run! But she couldn't speak, and then her vision narrowed to a single point of light, and she felt herself slip into darkness.

The Taking of Irene Hart

When Ruby came back to herself, she was lying on grass. The ground was cold and hard beneath her. It seemed the winter had come at last. Above was a lacing of trees, their branches black against a grey, early morning sky. She could hear birds and smell the vinegary odour of rotting apples. Her first thought was for Irene. How much time had passed? Several hours perhaps. She tried getting to her feet, but her body did not seem to be working properly. Her arms were not strong enough to push against. She tried again, and this time managed to sit up. Her vison swam and she felt nauseous.

'Awake at last,' Martin said. Although she couldn't see him clearly, his shambling frame was unmistakable. He was squatting in the grass. He jumped and caught hold of a branch of a tree and began swinging himself to and fro. He moved almost merrily, his great big feet going up and then down. She had a sudden memory of her swing in Bridgwater and of her own feet straining upwards, trying to reach the very top of the old chestnut tree.

'Nice and strong,' he said, dropping back to the ground with a grunt.

She saw him move a stool underneath the tree and her heart began beating so fast that it seemed to her that its drumming must be audible. She thought he would be able to hear her fear.

He looped a length of rope around the branch. She scrambled to her feet. She could feel her body swaying. She looked around her for a way to escape. How far was she from the lane? She tried to move, but her legs failed her, and she fell hard to the ground.

He gave the same laugh she had heard through the office door – its uncontained sound terrified her.

'Where's Irene?' she managed, although her tongue felt swollen and the inside of her mouth dry.

'Do not concern yourself,' he said. 'It is not any of your business.'

He approached and picked her up under her arms and dragged her across the grass. She could feel her body bumping against the ground and the squelch of apples under her. She bent and bit into one of his hands, causing him to shout and then briefly drop her, but in seconds he had taken hold of her again with an even more ferocious grip. He lifted her onto the stool. She felt its legs sink slightly under her weight. In a second more, he had pulled a noose of rope around her neck. Its roughness scratched against her throat. He was breathing heavily. She looked down. If the stool was taken away she would not be able to stop the drop. The rope would tighten around her throat. She screamed then. Perhaps someone would hear her. She felt the stool move from side to side under her feet. She fought to stay upright.

'If you do not stay still. You will dislodge the stool and save me having to do it,' he remarked.

Ruby thought of Hattie and Delia. They had stood just as she was standing now, their feet sliding on the surface of the stool, feeling the helplessness of being alone. Knowing there was no one to hear their cries. She felt a great, implacable rage. It was as if some other force had taken hold of her. He would not dispose of her so easily. She would not go without a fight. Irene needed her. She swung her body as high as she could and caught the branch above between her legs. She wrapped herself around it and held on tight. She turned her head to look down on him.

'You are the devil,' she said. 'Irene had a vision of the Day of Judgement…' It was a terrible effort to speak. 'You were being ripped apart by the dogs at the gate.' It took almost all of her strength to keep holding on, and all of what was left, to smile at him. She knew it was mockery that would inflame him the most. He gave a great bellow and moved towards her. She felt her arms weaken. She closed her eyes. It was her and Irene she saw. Hand in hand, running down a hill.

She heard a crashing sound and opened her eyes. Trench was standing over Martin, who was lying in the grass. He was holding a piece of wood above his head as if contemplating bringing it down on Martin again. Ruby let go of the branch, her feet scrabbling for the stool. Hands were holding it steady. Minnie was looking up at her.

'We must be quick,' Trench said. He untied the rope and helped her down.

Minnie put her arm around her shoulders and Ruby sank gratefully into her.

'Have you seen Irene?' she asked.

'Shh now,' Minnie said. 'Let's get you back.'

'Is he dead?' she asked indicating Martin's still body. Trench shook his head.

'The evil's still in him,' he said.

Between them they helped her through the orchard and onto the lane. She kept looking back as if she could hear his great lumbering steps coming after them.

Chapter 50

Philip wondered what the copper urn was for. Despite the name of the painting, Christ was not in the process of being taken from the cross but was already on the ground – his flesh yellow, a lank and despairing St John the Baptist bent over him, the Virgin Mary alongside, in a pallid, sweating faint. Philip's knowledge of painting was limited to this one, in St Mary's Church, Bridgwater, surveyed three times, including his view of it this morning, and the picture of two pink babies hovering over a plate of ripe fruit that adorned Jowler's office, but he thought perhaps the urn, being an ordinary, everyday thing was there to demonstrate that this was a death like any other. He speculated that the vessel might contain water to wash the body, or spices to mask the smell of death, or even salty, moistened bandages to ready Christ for the tomb. He almost smiled. He couldn't help looking for clues. Perhaps he was a better policeman than he thought.

This preoccupation with the details of the altar painting served to distract him from his mother's coffin – the best he had been able to muster – but still as unadorned as the cross from which the painted Christ had been taken. He had expected more people at the church. There was his mother's sister Clara, who, having travelled fifty miles and therefore in tragic disarray, looked seven lifetimes away from the young bride for whom his mother had plaited bread. There were a couple of men he did not recognise, two or three elderly ladies that she had been kind to and some neighbours, marshalled there with excitement by Mrs Grawler. It didn't seem a lot to show for a whole life, but he supposed that getting older meant the inevitable falling away of witnesses to your days of beauty and triumph. He knew she had possessed the former – there was a small, crumpled drawing she had kept in the kitchen drawer, which showed an unblemished gaze behind curls, but of the latter he was not so sure. She had not been a woman who had thought too much of herself or remarked on pleasures, although he did remember a day some years ago, during the floods, when she had walked through water up to her chest, the cutlery box held above her head, laughing as if it was all an adventure.

The vicar, who knew almost nothing about his mother other than the few details Philip had supplied when he had arranged the funeral, struggled through some words about compassion and family that could have applied to anyone. He had a disconcerting sliding left eye, which occasionally darted off into a corner of the church, as if he thought inspiration might be lurking there. Phillip struggled to contain his irritation and longed for the whole thing to be over. Who was it for, this clumsy ritual? It left him dry-eyed and horrified by his own heartlessness. Mrs Grawler cried with noisy relish on the front row and one of the elderly ladies began to cough into a handkerchief. The words of the hymn tied themselves in his throat, 'Change and decay, all around I see...'

The coffin, carried by him and five strangers, was lighter than he had imagined. He thought perhaps they had forgotten to lay his mother in it. The sun hit him full in the face and he stumbled down the steps from the church. Everyone gathered round and peered into the grave. Philip had noticed this tendency before – there wasn't a hole, anywhere, which a person could resist looking down. Making an assessment of just how deep things went seemed to be a universal need. There was a moment when his mother was lowered in, that caught his heart at last. She was gone from him.

The others left quickly. He didn't blame them; no one liked dawdling in graveyards and it was freezing cold. He stood for a long time looking at the dusted coffin, although his vigil was only for form's sake. What he really wanted to do was launch himself down the green slopes of the dyke they used to walk along when he was a child. He remembered tumbling down it, his arms tightly at his sides as his mother had instructed, faster and faster until he couldn't tell exactly where he was. The sight of Ruby, hastening towards him across the graveyard, interrupted his thoughts.

'I am so sorry to disturb you at such a sad time, Constable Hodge, but I do not know where Irene is. I am so terribly worried. I think I saw her in the chapel last night, but I am not sure.'

Her hair was falling down, and she was out of breath, as if she had been running. He also noticed, though inwardly chastising himself for doing so in the presence of his dead mother, that her dress fitted her so exactly that he could see her long, sleek curves and small waist. He had an almost irresistible impulse to put his arms around her, but clenched them at his sides as if preparing for the roll down the slope he had been thinking of just moments before.

'I took a horse from the farm and rode to your house. I do not know how I dared without a saddle. I spoke to a neighbour, and she told me where you were, and seeing my distress her husband kindly drove me here in his cart.'

'I'll get a cab to take us to Yaxton,' Philip said. 'Do not worry, we will find her.'

She came to me. She was scared, and she turned to me!

'I think that they have taken her somewhere. She is weakened by the tincture she has been taking. What if it was her I saw last night in the chapel? Maybe they have killed her, like the others, and like Martin tried to kill me.' She twisted her hands through the fabric of her dress and paced backwards and forwards, as if being still was impossible.

Once in the cab, she told him about what had happened the night before and earlier in the day, her words faltering as she came to certain parts of the account. He could feel her shock and panic and could not this time keep himself from taking her hand and holding it. While trying to comfort her, he felt incredulity and an anger he knew not to be professional, but he could not completely repress. Martin was an evil brute and Peters almost worse. He had a very good idea of what the man had been up to in the chapel. He hoped that the woman Ruby had seen had not been her sister. But even if it had not been her, somebody had been taken there. Some unfortunate young woman had fallen prey to the man. Peters had committed the cleverest of conjuring tricks – inventing the dogma that best suited what he most desired, and persuading others that they too would gain from his actions.

'I have just remembered something… I saw a policeman at the community a little while ago. He was with Peters and Martin, and they were spinning women on the revolving stage in the meeting room. It sounds completely absurd when I say it out loud, but it is true,' Ruby said. 'He was part of the watching crowd. If Peters has the law on his side, how will he ever be stopped?'

Philip was astonished by her words.

'Describe him to me,' he said, a mixture of fury and dread taking hold of him.

'I could not see him clearly, but he was a large man. Wide faced. His uniform had more buttons on the jacket than yours does, and I think he had some kind of braiding on his shoulders.'

Was it possible Jowler had discouraged Philip's investigations because of his own interests? He had not passed on the information told to him by the doctor about Hattie's pregnancy and had been resistant to Philip's suggestions for further investigation. The matter would have to be addressed, although he suspected the man would somehow wriggle out of any culpability. If confronted, he would no doubt bluster about being there to do his own checks and measures. Philip could see Jowler's face in his mind's eye – his wobbling, self-righteous indignation. Implacably sure of his position and the many ways he would always be protected.

'I can trust *you*, can I not, Constable Hodge?' Ruby asked, her face anxious.

She was so resolute and beautiful. He thought he would like to kiss the frown line that had appeared between her eyes, and then had to remind himself that he was engaged on urgent business that required his complete attention.

'Of course you can, Miss Hart,' he said. 'I will not stop until I have got to the bottom of it all. You can be assured of that.'

She scanned his face so intently, that he felt somewhat abashed by her scrutiny. He sincerely hoped that he had not left traces of his breakfast egg around his mouth.

'I believe I *can* trust you,' she said. 'You have a certain … nobility in your countenance. You rest securely in your skin.'

Philip was pleased by her description of his physiology, although he wasn't quite sure what she meant about his skin. Perhaps there were vestiges of egg on his chin, after all. He rubbed furtively at his jaw.

Ruby hung out of the window, as if trying to propel the vehicle forward and as soon as they arrived, she jumped down and began banging at the gate. When George opened it, she rushed past him, and Philip followed behind.

Chapter 51

Philip found Peters in his office. He must have changed from the robes that Ruby had described to him, because he was dressed as he usually was and sitting calmly at his desk, a pen in his hand and a pile of papers in front of him.

'Have you seen Brother Martin?' he asked, looking briefly up at Philip before resuming his writing.

'No, I have not, although I am looking for him myself,' Philip answered. 'I am also looking for Miss Irene Hart. Do you know where *she* is?'

'I have no idea. She will be here somewhere,' he said shrugging slightly.

'I would be grateful if you would stop whatever it is you are doing and give me your full attention,' Philip said.

'I have no time spare to talk to you. I must set it all down so that people will understand.'

'So, you are writing your confession?'

'Whatever are you talking about?'

Peters put down his pen and stared at him. Philip thought his expression strange – there was perhaps something approaching guilt there, or at least some kind of acknowledgement, but there was also a kind of impatience. The arrogance that Philip had seen in him before.

'I am talking about what has been happening in this place. The suspected murders of at least three young women and the attempted murder of Miss Ruby Hart. Not to mention the disappearance of her sister. Was Irene forced to take part in some kind of ceremony last night in the chapel? Her sister witnessed what seemed to be a wedding.'

'Ruby Hart should not have become involved in things she does not understand. She only has herself to blame for refusing to abide by our rules. I tried to explain it to her… I thought she had understood … but clearly not.'

'She understands very clearly that crimes have taken place, not least on her own person at the hands of your henchman, Martin.'

'All that I do and all that is done on my behalf, comes directly as an instruction from God.'

'How very convenient to have such a mandate,' Philip said, wondering whether what afflicted the man was faith, or madness, or evil. Perhaps all of those things in some measure. He felt unqualified to make a verdict. He was simply there to establish wrongdoing.

'You will present yourself at the police station in Bridgwater within a day to answer questions. Until then, you will stay within the walls of the community.'

Peters shrugged again.

'I will see nobody but the chief constable himself. Shut the door on your way out.'

Ruby was pacing in the hallway and rushed up to Philip as he came out of Peters' office.

'Does he know where she is?' she asked. 'Was Martin in there with him?'

'Martin was not there, although I would sorely like to get my hands on him,' Philip replied. 'Peters claims not to know of your sister's whereabouts. Try not to worry, she will be here somewhere.' He tried to speak with as much reassurance as he could, although he had grave misgivings. He had sent word to the station and an officer had been dispatched to look in the same area where the other women had died. Not that he had told Ruby about this. It would not help to put what might be unnecessary fears into her head. She was already terrified enough already.

'The best thing for you to do, is to go and sit somewhere quiet and perhaps have something to eat and drink. I would guess you have not eaten for some time.'

'I cannot eat anything!' Ruby exclaimed.

She was still full of fear, almost dropping on her feet with shock and exhaustion and she knew nothing would be right with the world until Irene was found, but Ruby was aware of the comfort of the policeman's presence. He expressed such quiet confidence that all would be well, she allowed herself to believe what he said. She saw his gift was to take what was bad around him and absorb it so that it would not travel further, but would stop only with him.

'Call me if you find anything. I will be in my room,' she said.

He began his search of the Hall, being as methodical as possible, feeling for all possible looseness in the walls, any discrepancy in the tread of the floor beneath him. He took one room at a time, looking into the cupboards and behind furniture. The women who occupied the rooms he entered on the first floor made way for his search without dissent, some even offered to help. He marshalled the volunteers, sending one group to look in the garden, one the farm and another to the fields beyond, while he carried on in the Hall by himself. The first floor had yielded nothing out of the ordinary, and he climbed to the second, beginning at one end of the corridor and working his way down. Most of the rooms were almost painfully tidy, with similar plain things arranged in the same ways on dressing tables and on window sills, but he was struck by the state of one of them. Here was all confusion – clothes were scattered everywhere and the bed, in contrast to the neatly made beds in all the other rooms, was in disarray. There was half-eaten food stiffening on plates and paper strewn on the floor. He went over to the desk where there was a pile of books amongst other random objects. He picked up one of them, hoping to find the identity of the owner of the room inscribed inside, and as he did so, a couple of pieces of paper fluttered to the floor. They were marked with the word 'saint', written boldly in dark ink, and then crossed out. He picked one up and stared at it for a few moments and then went out of the room and looked along the corridor. A young woman was approaching, he thought her name was Edith. He remembered her from the day he had conducted his interviews in the pantry. The one with the pinched face and yellow dress. She had been crying. Her eyes were red and there was a smudge on her face from where she had wiped her tears away with a dirty hand.

'Excuse me, miss, would you mind telling me whose room this is?' he asked.

'This is Sister Angela's room,' Edith answered. 'I was just coming to see her.'

Chapter 52

There was a loud bang on Ruby's door, and she opened it quickly, hoping it was Philip with good news. Trench was standing outside, tugging at his plume of hair.

'I know where she is. I know where Goldie is,' he said. 'Come.'

He ran down the stairs and she followed after him. He led her out into the garden and then beyond the fern garden and round the bend in the wall that obscured the dome of the ice house. He pointed mutely at it.

'What makes you think she is in there? Ruby asked, wondering how she had forgotten this place. She now remembered its dank walls etched with prayer or plea.

'Bad things have happened here,' he said. 'There were babies … I would not go near there after I heard the women crying. It made me scared.'

Ruby went down the steps to the ice house with Trench hovering behind her. She tried the door, but it was locked. It hadn't been when she had been there before. She banged and shouted Irene's name, but there was no answer. She picked up a stone and knocked more loudly, but there was still no response.

'Do you know if there is a key?' she asked Trent.

'Keys are kept in a box on the top shelf in the kitchen. Must not be touched.'

Ruby thought that there was little chance that whoever had locked Irene in here, if she was indeed inside, was unlikely to have replaced the key in its original place.

'We will have to break the door down,' she said, and Trench nodded and went running off and returned moments later with an axe.

'George was not there. I took it. He might be angry.'

'I do not much care what George thinks,' Ruby said and took a swing at the door with the axe. The wood splintered and she tried again. Trench stepped in front of her and took the axe from her hand and swung it high above his head. Ruby would not have imagined that such a small man would have had such strength, but Trench administered two blows and the door was soon hanging off its hinges.

There was someone lying on the floor. Ruby rushed in and crouched down. It was Irene. Ruby called her name and touched her on the shoulder and her face. She felt chilly under Ruby's fingers. Her eyes were closed, and her face was so white, it looked blue in the dim enclosure. Her heart in her mouth, Ruby bent closer and could feel a faint breath on her face.

'She is alive!' she said, tears of relief springing to her eyes. 'We must get her out and call a doctor.'

Trench came into the ice house a little tentatively, as if he was not sure he was invited, then bent and picked Irene up in his arms and carried her up the steps and across the lawn. The face he turned to Ruby after he had lain her carefully down on the sofa in the living room was unrecognisable and Ruby realised that it was only that he was smiling.

When Ruby asked for a doctor to be called, she had half expected that Miriam would resist, but the woman had simply

The Taking of Irene Hart

taken one look at Irene and disappeared, and had returned half an hour later accompanied by a Doctor Pontifex who, upon hearing about Irene's seizures and the tincture she had been given, had examined her and said that he thought she had probably suffered a major fit and the effects of that, combined with the cold of the ice house and dehydration, had caused her to fall unconscious.

'You did well to find her when you did,' he said. 'A couple of hours more, and who can say what might have happened?'

He told Ruby to keep her sister warm and that when she awoke to give her small amounts of water on a teaspoon. He said he would come out again if he was needed.

Now Ruby sat by Irene's side and watched her sister's breath come and go and held her hand as if she would never let go of it again. She sent Trench to find Constable Hodge and tell him the news, and he came quickly. His face was so pleased and relieved, she wondered that she had ever thought him unremarkable. Seen like this, with his hair, trimmed no doubt for his poor mother's funeral, she saw that he was handsome, with a finely-shaped face burnt by the sun.

'I am so glad she has been found. We owe much to Trench. When she is recovered, we will find out how she ended up locked into that place. I will leave you now since I have another matter to attend to. You have not seen Angela anywhere have you?'

Ruby said she had not and so he left, and she was surprised by the realisation that she had very much wanted him to stay.

'Ruby?'

Irene had opened her eyes and was gazing around her in much the same way that she used to do after one of her takings. Ruby gave a cry of pleasure and put her arms around her sister. How frail and small she felt!

'Have I had a seizure?' Irene asked.

'I think so my dearest one. But you are all right now. You are safe. Can you remember how you ended up locked in the ice house?'

Irene frowned and looked around the room again, and then her face took on an expression of fear.

'Sister Angela ... she ... took me there. I think ... I cannot quite remember. She said she wanted to show me something ... so ... I went with her to the domed place and then she pushed me down the steps and I was so weak already, I could not fight back.'

Irene seemed so distressed, Ruby thought perhaps she would wait before pressing her sister any further, but Irene carried on talking.

'She said ... she said that she thought The Beloved had chosen me as his special bride and that she was going to stop that happening because she wanted to be the one. She told me I was to stay with the ghosts of the babies. I did not know what she meant, Ruby, but when she locked the door and it was dark, I could feel them around me.'

Tears came to her eyes and poured down her face and gathered in her hair. Ruby tried to wipe them away.

'Do not talk anymore just now, Irene. Just stay quiet and take a little of this water,' Ruby said putting the spoon to Irene's mouth.

'I could hear crying, Ruby, just as I did in my taking and the cold... It was so cold.'

Chapter 53

The chapel door was slightly ajar. He pushed it open with his foot. He stood looking into the room. Because the light from the windows was so bright, Philip was briefly dazzled by its hard fall across the floor. The crimson room glittered with an ominous, lacquered shine. It was the smell he noticed first. Honey and rust. He recognised it straight away but could not see its source. He could feel the wrong. It saturated the place with the kind of gathering swell that comes before a storm. He went forward, subduing the instinct that was telling him to turn and get out as fast as he could. He told himself to breathe. In and out. Feet steady on the floor. An alignment of body and heart.

His policeman's eye noticed the missing curtain cords. From behind the sofa, neatly arranged with its line of coral-coloured cushions, a leg protruded. Philip edged round, keeping his gaze as wide as possible. He did not immediately recognise the body. The face was turned to the floor, as if the person's last movement had been to avoid a blow. The white-shirted chest was scored, like cuts across the fat of meat that has been made ready for roasting, and all around the glaze of red spread from the body and on through the cracks in the wooden floor. He knelt and placed two unnecessary fingers on the neck. No pulse. Only wide eyes and a beard of blood from the mouth. How small he seemed! It was as if death had stolen his stature. The promised salvation was not visible in Peters' emptied face. As Philip looked, the colours of the lamb and the rose depicted in the stained-glass window were cast onto the man's wide forehead. The white and the red lay on him briefly, like a benediction. Then the light dimmed, as if a cloud had passed over. Philip turned just in time.

Angela was standing over him with her arm raised. She brought the knife down with a sudden, vicious blow. Philip moved quickly but still felt the slice and sting of the blade in his side. He got to his feet. She stood swaying in front of him. Eyes darker than the night. Mouth loose with sorrow or anger, he could not tell. Her pale dress was splattered so widely, it looked as if blood had been thrown over her from above. He found his voice.

'Give me the knife, Sister Angela.'

She made a sobbing sound then, as if his words had loosened her breath. She jabbed the knife several times in his direction, and he stepped back.

'Be still … be still.' He spoke as if he was on Thunder's back and his horse had reared after being startled by a sudden sound.

She made another noise. This one more distinct, more like a word. She spun round, her knife held out in front of her as if she had heard someone coming up behind. Philip caught hold of her and tried to dislodge the weapon from her hand. She twisted in his arms as though she was burning. The knife glanced across his cheek. He could feel the beat of her heart against him, the shake of her body, the heat of her skin.

'It is all right,' he said. 'You can stop now, Sister Angela.'

There was what seemed to him to be a long silence as they stood linked, as if they had just been dancing, or were waiting to begin. The light fell in shards of colour. She gave a sigh so deep it had a musical resonance. He heard the dull thud of the knife on the carpet. He let her go and kicked it away across the floor.

'I did all he asked of me. All of it. But even so, he never chose me. Why do you think that is?'

Angela's face was distracted. Her mouth worked, as if she was trying to dislodge something from her teeth.

He guided her down to a chair, wondering if the chapel door had a lock, thinking about how he was going to arrange for her to be taken away. He would send Trench. Did the man ride? Perhaps Miriam could arrange it. He tried to approach the matter methodically in his mind, although his thoughts were scattered and the pain in his side had deepened. He glanced down and saw to his surprise that his jacket had a dark patch. Angela seemed to be in some kind of dream and oblivious to his stealthy move to the door, his call out across the hallway, the sound of running feet and his quick instruction.

He sat down in the chair next to hers. He was, in truth, glad to take the weight off his legs. The room swam in front of his eyes. Despite the streak of blood that bisected her face from her mouth to her ear, he could see her beauty. She was like a doll, with her round blue eyes, the painterly diameter of the pink in her cheek, the tidy set of her ears under the blonde coils of her hair. She gave a small shrug and turned herself away from him. She spoke in a voice devoid of all expression, as if she was saying words that had been said many times before.

'I cannot say what when it began. It might have been a long time ago. The time I have schooled myself not to remember. But then ... I do not know. It seemed to me I was saved and brought to paradise. Soft cloth against my skin. Softer words. I was reborn.'

She stopped and seemed to be considering what she had just said.

'Or perhaps I was reshaped out of the same ugly stuff, but no one could see it. I loved him... It was the most love I have ever felt or been given. I gave myself to him to do what he wanted because I knew it would be for my good. It would shore up the saving of me and of what he dreamt. Life eternal.'

She fell silent again. Dust rose from the floor and was caught up in the arms of the light and sent shining. Philip could hear commotion outside, but Angela seemed oblivious.

'And then…' he prompted. Pressing his arm against his side, feeling the warm creep of his blood.

'He told me that I must do all that Martin instructed. Martin … who watches and cannot do, became his mouthpiece. *My words come directly through him*, is what The Beloved said. So, when Martin told me that it would be the end of all I had come to love, if it came to be known that there was … what he called spawn … devil's spawn in the community. He meant babies…'

Angela turned to him then. Her eyes wide and unfocused. She had an air of someone who had forgotten something essential. Philip fought to stay sitting upright. The edges of the chapel seemed to be bearing down on him.

'He told me I had to dispose of them. Three times I had to do it. Two were dead when they arrived early in the ice house, because of the tincture Martin gave the women. The last baby was complete. Hattie being big already … it did not show much on her. I could not bear to put my hand over the baby's mouth and nose and stop her. I took her into the lane in the night and left her there. Hattie's spawn.'

'And what of Hattie herself, and the other women who died?'

'Martin and I took them. Hattie was sent quite wild over the loss of her baby and was threatening to disclose all and the other two … the one before and the one after. He said they had the spawn in them. We told them to come to the orchard and if they survived hanging it would show that they could become saints and live forever. We told them it would be a test of faith…'

'But how did you manage such a thing?' Philip tried not to think about the long swing of Hattie's body and her discarded shoes or of Delia's small, folded hands. Angela looked at him for the first time, straight into his eyes, as if she could not believe he would ask such a question, as if she was surprised that he could not understand.

'I could do it because they believed,' she said. 'Martin tied the rope, and they fastened it around their own necks. I took the stool away. It is the one we keep in the pantry.'

Philip inwardly shuddered at the thought that she was referring to the stool he had sat on when he interviewed the community members.

'Did you believe that they would survive? That their faith would keep them safe?'

Some part of Philip still wanted to believe that this was a blindness not an intent.

'I thought maybe the first time ... but then when she died, I saw that she was not a proper saint. That she had become spoilt. They had all become spoilt.'

Her doll's head tilted. He thought she might even have smiled.

'And Peters?' His words were beginning to escape him. He felt so tired. More tired than he had ever felt before.

'I thought that after all that I had done he might have chosen me as his special bride. But he chose another. I thought at first it would be Irene. They prized her so highly and planned to elevate her. Martin was bewitched. He could not take his eyes from her. But in the end it was a girl from outside. Nobody even knew her!'

She sat straighter then, still astonished at being overlooked. He closed his eyes.

He could not say afterwards, how much time passed between that moment, and the next time he regained consciousness. Angela must have made a sound because something brought him back to himself. He saw that the knife was in her hand again. He tried to stand, but he had no strength left in him. He shouted out, but she seemed not to hear. She stood by the window. The light fell on her with all its colours. Her lips moved, as if in prayer. She held out her arm, and cut across the wrist with a quick motion and then did the same to the other. She showed no hesitation. She made no noise. He saw the plume of her blood. She swayed for a moment, and fell, and then he descended into darkness.

Chapter 54

In the kitchen, Miriam was scrubbing the table. It helped her to think clearly when she was engaged on such a task, and it was soothing to see the familiar markings on its surface – the grooves where knives had gone in too deep, the dark crescents where hot pans had briefly rested. After the policemen had done whatever it was they had to do, she had carried Sister Angela's dead body from the chapel. She had lain her on the sofa in her own room and bound the wounds on her wrists where she had cut herself, even though her blood had all been spent. She had not wanted anyone to see the marks on her perfect skin, nor to leave her blemished. Miriam could tell herself that love had blinded her, as if it had been some outside force that had prevented her from recognising who Angela was, or rather, what she suffered from, but in the days that had followed, Miriam had chosen not to justify herself. She had known in some part of her that the damage wrought on the girl before she had arrived, bruised and mute, at the community, could never have been chaffed away with warm towels. She knew she should have seen it.

She felt nothing but an intense, hard rage towards Martin. It was just like him to have left his dirt and run away, like the cowardly creature he was. They had said he would be found and brought to justice, but Miriam thought it likely that he would simply disappear. He was a man without a core and could therefore always hide in plain sight. About Peters, she could barely even formulate her thoughts. The maid, Minnie, and the policeman had come and told her what had happened during the wedding ceremony. If such a travesty could be called by that name. She had not cried for years, but the tears had poured out of her uncontrollably when she heard what they had to say. A village girl, barely more than a *child*, had been brought to the community, drugged, and dressed in a veil and taken – Miriam couldn't think about it without wanting to be sick – *taken* on some kind of makeshift altar fashioned on the billiard table. As if it had been the man's sovereign right to do so. She understood now that this is what Peters had meant when he had talked of reconciling flesh and spirit. He had made his lust explicit by making a spectacle of it, sanctioning it in front of those who were also complicit. What faith she had invested in him! Despite it all, she still hung on to the notion that he had not started out with such intentions. She could not believe this had been his plan all along. The young man she had known had burned with such clean fervour. His dreams had aligned with her own and provided shelter and direction. He must have lost himself. He had started following a thread that had become tangled along the way, forcing him to find ways to explain and exonerate himself. She did not know. Perhaps she and him were not so very different. She had chosen to see only what she wanted to. She had known nothing of what Angela and Martin were doing at his behest, but she knew she had not looked hard enough. It had suited her not to.

Despite Peters' and Angela's deaths, and the rumours that were flying around, she had been surprised by how relatively few people had chosen to leave the community. From her window she had seen those that had decided to do so, make their departures from the Garden Kingdom. Each had hesitated, just for a moment, as they went through the gate, as if something still pulled on them to remain. Or maybe it was simply that the sky above and fields beyond were without boundaries, and they had become fearful of the unfettered freedom they had once chosen to live without. She heard the ones who had remained, in the hallways or in the garden, weaving what had happened into a new story, incorporating it into the language of their faith, so that as time passed she knew that the fabric would knit up and be seamless. She had resolved to stay, too. It was not that she had nowhere else to go, but rather that she wanted to save what had been good. She would marshal them all, the waifs and strays, the dreamers. If she could not offer eternal life, she could at least make the wall and those within it, strong again.

Chapter 55

'I am giving my dresses to Norah, I could not bear to ever wear them again,' Ruby said, pulling them from the wardrobe and placing them on her bed in a folded pile.

'I have given mine to Edith, since she is the only one small enough,' Irene replied.

She was sitting watching Ruby pack her things into her trunk, her own suitcase was already waiting at the door. Ruby was pleased to see that her sister looked almost as she had done when they first arrived at the community. The lustre of her hair and skin had returned, and her eyes were their old, calm grey. It had taken a few weeks, but without the effects of Martin's tincture, she had been restored to them. If you looked closely you could see a difference in the cast of her mouth which, in repose, gave her a look of sadness that had not been there before. You had to know her face intimately to see it. Most people do not, Ruby reflected, look closely enough at people to notice such small changes.

She had waited until she thought her sister was strong enough to tell her what she knew she must, choosing a time when they were alone. She had knelt on the floor beside her bed and gone through every shameful part of what she had done. When she had finally come to the end of her sorry recitation, she had raised her eyes to Irene's and found her sister gazing at her with such an expression of love, it had taken her breath away.

'My dear Ruby,' Irene had said, 'I knew. I knew almost from William's first visit. How could I not? You are my sister who wears all she feels full on her face.'

Ruby had stared at her astounded.

'But ... but why did you not say anything?'

'I wanted you to do what it was you felt you had to do. I did not want to stand in your way. I hoped that since you are so good at reading people, that you would see for yourself what he is.'

'But I did not. I did not,' Ruby had said, tears pouring down her face.

'You see it now, that is what matters.' Irene had wiped Ruby's face and held her in the same way she always had. Providing the same comfort, showing the same belief in their power to overcome anything, as long as they were together.

'Nancy is more than happy to have us both,' Ruby said now. 'She says we may stay for as long as we need to. In a short time, we will come into our money, and we will set up a little house. Just you and me, Irene.'

Irene nodded and got up and looked out of the window. She felt a sense of loss so profound, she had to hold onto the edge of the window sill. She remembered their first day – the taste of the pineapple, the peace and beauty of what she had thought they were being offered. It could, it could perhaps have been the paradise they had been promised. She had felt herself to be part of it. Had this been a weakness in her? She had come to believe that her infirmity, which until then had hung on her like a curse, might have a positive use here amongst the dreamers. That her takings could provide direction, even offer solace. She knew now that much of this feeling had been induced by the tincture which had taken her too deep and too far, and yet there was still a part of her that wondered about where she had gone and what she had seen. The dream and the paradise still lingered in her. How could it not when she rested halfway between two worlds? So much had happened in the short time they had been there. The terrible things that Peters and Martin and Angela had done, each in their own way, each according to the darkness that drove them. She thought of Angela's death at her own hands in the chapel, lying next to The Beloved on the floor, as if even then she could not bear to be parted from him. All that blood that the maids had cleaned away on their hands and knees. She thought of the babies that had lost their lives in that dark place. She shivered.

'Do not think about it, Irene,' Ruby said. 'We will leave it all behind us.'

'Such things do not remain behind, they travel with us,' Irene said.

They were all lined up at the gate. As their luggage was put on the carriage, the sisters said their farewells. Edith gave Ruby an orchid, its stem wrapped with yellow ribbon. Norah cried big, childlike tears. Miriam touched their faces in turn, and then briskly told them to behave properly at all times. 'Even you, Ruby,' she said, softening her words with a smile. Hester stood with the others. Their mother had decided to stay even though the sisters had both tried to persuade her otherwise.

'I am settled here,' was all she would say, and on her face was no sign of loss, only what she still believed she had.

'Goodbye, Mother,' Ruby said now. 'You know where we are if you should ever change your mind.' She kissed Hester's absent face.

Just as the carriage was about to leave, there was a shout, and Philip Hodge appeared at the door.

'I thought I would be too late,' he said.

He was still pale from the effects of his injury which he had been lucky to survive. It had not just been the physical impact of what had happened that he had struggled to recover from. The memory of Angela's death haunted him. Again and again, he saw her in the chapel – the blankness in her eyes, the thrust of the knife as it bit into her skin, the way her body had fallen. He felt that he should somehow have been able to prevent her death, although Ruby had told him that there was nothing else he could have done and that he had shown uncommon bravery. Although he loved her thinking so, he did not feel that the little he had done justified her admiration.

Following all that had happened, and without ever accepting culpability in his own involvement, or indeed being expected to do so, Jowler had retired, and was no doubt eking out what remained of his life in his usual comfort. He was probably just this minute sitting somewhere with his fingers in a jar of honey. Philip had been promoted as a result of his endeavours. Learning this news, his first feeling was sadness that his mother would not know of his elevation. She might have been even more content if she had been privy to another, far more important development. Beyond his wildest imagining, it seemed that Ruby had some regard for him. There was a softness in the way she looked at him that gave him a kind of wondering hope. She had been to visit him at his cottage several times while he was recovering, and had put flowers in the jug on the kitchen table and washed the pots and hung them up where his mother used to hang them. They had talked for hours about small, important things.

'Look who has come to see you off!' he exclaimed.

Strapped across the front of him, in a complicated papoose of linen and leather was a baby.

'I have adopted Pearl' he said, smiling widely. 'We shall be some kind of a family.'

Pearl opened her eyes and stared through the window at them. Her gaze was intent and blue. Something in the cast of Ruby's hat, or the shape of Irene's face, or something else entirely, made her smile and then laugh as if she could not stop, and the chortling sound was so infectious, that everyone else began to laugh, too, even Miriam.

'And it is all right if we come, Pearl and I, to visit you in Bridgwater?' Philip asked, looking at Ruby.

'I will not turn you away,' Ruby answered. 'I would like to see the child again,' and then seeing the downward turn of his head, 'and you, too, of course, Inspector Hodge.'

It seemed that all that needed to be said, had been said, and the carriage driver flicked his whip, and then, right at the last minute, Hester's face appeared at the carriage window. Just for a moment she looked as she used to do in the days when Arthur sat in the chair next to hers in their old house.

'Be sure to put flowers on your father's grave. *Promise me* you will not forget,' she said, and held for a moment onto Irene's hand, and then let it go.

On the way back to Bridgwater, the pink fields they had driven past before were now black and hard looking. It seemed unlikely they would ever bloom and soften again. In the sky, the crows wheeled, looking for somewhere to land.

'I feel so different to when we made this journey the first time!' Ruby exclaimed.

'A great deal has changed in us both,' Irene replied.

Ruby looked out of the window and thought of the man she had just left behind and of the tender way he had stroked Pearl's head as he was saying goodbye.

'I think Philip is a good man,' she said, flushing a little, and looking at her sister as if for confirmation.

'Philip, eh?' Irene teased. 'When he is around, I think you barely see anything or anyone else!'

'It may not always have been true,' Ruby said, taking her sister's hand and placing it against her cheek in a gesture of love and as a plea for forgiveness, 'but no man, even one with a handsome face and an even handsomer heart, will ever blind me again. Although I will admit, but only to you my dear Irene, that I very much want to see him again.'

'I doubt that our mother would have countenanced such an association even before she had determined we were to be saints.'

'The things that were significant to me before, to *us* before, do not seem to be so now,' Ruby replied. 'Now I only want to do the things that will make me happy. I never want to listen again to what others say about what I should do or how I should feel.'

'And how do you mean to fill your days?'

'I have a notion to become an inventor,' Ruby said grandly. 'I am going to devise a clock that people can wear. A dainty one for slender wrists. It will be powered by a weight, balanced on some kind of a pivot. The movement of the arm will translate into motion through gears in its winding mechanism. I am not sure of the details yet, although I have drawn parts of it out. When it is finished, I will give it to you so that when you are taken, you will always know how long you have been away.'

'That would be very useful,' Irene said, smiling.

'What do you wish for?' Ruby asked.

'I wish for my sister always to be near me and to wear a time piece on my arm, showing me all the perfect hours,' Irene replied.

Goldie has gone. I watched her from my attic window. I did not want her last sighting of me to be a bumbling, stuttering one, so I sent my farewell through the air. She felt it because she lifted her head to me and waved. Her face was like the sun. That I helped her ... me, Trench. It will always be my best pride and my best happiness. Now I can say, if anyone should ask, that something cleaved to me, and I to it. I will go from the community soon. Maybe I will find a place with a door that I can leave open or shut, just as I choose. A place circled by thick hedgerows and with airy fields beyond. Until that time comes, I will walk, and look at what has been given to me, and feel the light, wherever it falls.

Acknowledgments

The Taking of Irene Hart was inspired by a true story. There was a cult in rural Somerset at the time my novel is set, and a leader of that cult who did not live by the dogma he expounded. Although some of the details of the community and the man at the helm are factual, the story I have written is almost totally reimagined, and none of the characters really existed. The focus for the book is my interest in how there is nothing that is so outlandish, irrational, and unfair, that there will be people who accept it, and people who justify it.

I would like to thank my agent Luigi Bonomi for his continuing support, and Kate Bradley at Harper Collins for her solidarity and friendship. Thanks also to my friends and family who have borne the stops and starts of my writing career with encouragement and faith.

ONE MORE CHAPTER

YOUR NUMBER ONE STOP FOR PAGETURNING BOOKS

The author and One More Chapter would like to thank everyone who contributed to the publication of this story...

Analytics
James Brackin
Abigail Fryer

Audio
Fionnuala Barrett
Ciara Briggs

Contracts
Laura Amos
Laura Evans

Design
Lucy Bennett
Fiona Greenway
Liane Payne
Dean Russell

Digital Sales
Lydia Grainge
Hannah Lismore
Emily Scorer

Editorial
Janet Marie Adkins
Kara Daniel
Arsalan Isa
Charlotte Ledger
Ajebowale Roberts
Jennie Rothwell
Emily Thomas

Harper360
Emily Gerbner
Jean Marie Kelly
emma sullivan
Sophia Wilhelm

International Sales
Peter Borcsok
Ruth Burrow
Colleen Simpson

Marketing & Publicity
Chloe Cummings
Emma Petfield

Operations
Melissa Okusanya
Hannah Stamp

Production
Denis Manson
Simon Moore
Francesca Tuzzeo

Rights
Helena Font Brillas
Ashton Mucha
Zoe Shine
Aisling Smythe

Trade Marketing
Ben Hurd
Eleanor Slater

The HarperCollins Distribution Team

The HarperCollins Finance & Royalties Team

The HarperCollins Legal Team

The HarperCollins Technology Team

UK Sales
Isabel Coburn
Jay Cochrane
Sabina Lewis
Holly Martin
Harriet Williams
Leah Woods

eCommerce
Laura Carpenter
Madeline ODonovan
Charlotte Stevens
Christina Storey
Jo Surman
Rachel Ward

And every other essential link in the chain from delivery drivers to booksellers to librarians and beyond!

ONE MORE CHAPTER

YOUR NUMBER ONE STOP FOR PAGETURNING BOOKS

One More Chapter is an award-winning global division of HarperCollins.

Sign up to our newsletter to get our latest eBook deals and stay up to date with our weekly Book Club!
[Subscribe here.](#)

Meet the team at
[www.onemorechapter.com](#)

Follow us!
🐦 @OneMoreChapter_
📘 @OneMoreChapter
📷 @onemorechapterhc

Do you write unputdownable fiction? We love to hear from new voices. Find out how to submit your novel at
[www.onemorechapter.com/submissions](#)